THE SECRET OF THE HUNT

After supper, but before sunset made reading impractical, the shaman Madyu settled down with two of the books he'd brought back from the Old Time. One of them was about the diseases of cats. He put it down in disgust; this book was crammed full of words he not only didn't know but couldn't define from context.

He picked up the other volume, convinced it would be even worse. Even the title looked like a nonsense word: *Taxonomy*. He opened the book. Then his eye lit on a sentence. "The so-called scientific name attached to any organism remains constant throughout the world."

He stared at those words until darkness made them illegible. If they meant what he thought they did, he'd just stumbled across the biggest Old Time treasure ever, bigger than gold, bigger than jewels . . .

By Harry Turtledove
Published by Ballantine Books:

The Videssos Cycle:
    THE MISPLACED LEGION
    AN EMPEROR FOR THE LEGION
    THE LEGION OF VIDESSOS
    SWORDS OF THE LEGION

The Tale of Krispos:
    Book One: KRISPOS RISING
    Book Two: KRISPOS OF VIDESSOS
    Book Three: KRISPOS THE EMPEROR

NONINTERFERENCE

A WORLD OF DIFFERENCE

KALEIDOSCOPE

EARTHGRIP

DEPARTURES

THE GUNS OF THE SOUTH

WORLDWAR: IN THE BALANCE
WORLDWAR: TILTING THE BALANCE
WORLDWAR: UPSETTING THE BALANCE*

*Forthcoming

DEPARTURES

Harry Turtledove

A Del Rey® Book
BALLANTINE BOOKS • NEW YORK

A Del Rey® Book
Published by Ballantine Books

Library of Congress Catalog Card Number: 93-90071

ISBN 0-345-38011-8

Printed in Canada

First Edition: June 1993

10 9 8 7 6 5 4

TABLE OF CONTENTS

Author's Note	ix
COUNTING POTSHERDS	1
DEATH IN VESUNNA (with Elaine O'Byrne)	29
DEPARTURES	51
ISLANDS IN THE SEA	63
NOT ALL WOLVES	88
CLASH OF ARMS	96
PILLAR OF CLOUD, PILLAR OF FIRE	103
REPORT OF THE SPECIAL COMMITTEE ON THE QUALITY OF LIFE	141
BATBOY	146
THE LAST REUNION	156
DESIGNATED HITTER	174
GLADLY WOLDE HE LERNE	184
THE BARBECUE, THE MOVIE, AND OTHER UNFORTUNATELY NOT SO RELEVANT MATERIAL	188
IN THE PRESENCE OF MINE ENEMIES	200
THE R STRAIN	218
LURE	233

viii   Contents

SECRET NAMES   237

LES MORTES D'ARTHUR   256

LAST FAVOR   290

NASTY, BRUTISH, AND . . .   321

AUTHOR'S NOTE

The stories in this book appear in chronological order, starting in the early second century B.C. and ending about a thousand years from now. Rather more are science fiction than fantasy; it's hard to tell into which genre a couple of them fall. They are intended to amuse and, with a little luck, to provoke thought. Some of the notes talk about how they came to be written, others about the ideas they examine. One of the things that make science fiction and fantasy the exciting fields they are is that they let a writer look at ideas from angles impossible to achieve in other genres. I hope you enjoy these unusual angles.

Our own civilization owes Greece in the fifth century B.C. so much: democracy, the drama, the liberation both of the examination of the natural world and of historical inquiry from the straitjacket of theology. But before these things could flower, Greece had to succeed in repelling the invasion of the Persian Empire, the mightiest state of the day. This she did, by a narrow margin. But suppose Greece had failed . . .

COUNTING POTSHERDS

THE SHIP CLUNG CLOSE TO LAND, LIKE A ROACH scuttling along a wall. When at last the coast veered north and west, the ship conformed, steering oars squealing in their sockets and henna-dyed wool sail billowing as it filled with wind to push the vessel onto its new course.

When the ship changed direction, the eunuch Mithredath summoned the captain to the starboard rail with a slight nod. "We draw near, then, Agbaal?" Mithredath asked. His voice, a nameless tone between tenor and contralto, was cool, precise, and intelligent.

The Phoenician captain bowed low. The sun sparked off a silver hoop in his left ear. "My master, we do." Agbaal pointed to the headland the ship had just rounded. "That is the Cape of Sounion. If the wind holds, we should be in Peiraieus by evening—a day early," he added slyly.

"You will be rewarded if we are," Mithredath promised. Agbaal, satisfied, bowed again and, after glancing at his important passenger for permission, went back to overseeing his crew.

Mithredath would have paid gold darics from his own purse to shorten the time he spent away from the royal court, but there was no need for that: he had come to this western backwater at the royal command and so could draw upon the treasury of Khsrish, King of Kings, as he required. Not for the first time, he vowed that he would not stint.

The day was brilliantly clear. Mithredath could see a long way. The only other ships visible were a couple of tiny fishing

1

boats and a slow, wallowing vessel probably full of wheat from Egypt. Gulls mewed and squawked overhead.

Mithredath tried to imagine what the narrow, island-flecked sea had looked like during those great days four centuries before, when the first Khsrish, the Conqueror, had led his huge fleet to the triumph that had subjected the western Yauna to Persia once and for all. He could not; he was not used enough to ships to picture hordes of them all moving together like so many sheep in a herd on its way to the marketplace of Babylon.

That thought, he realized with a wry nod, showed him what he was most familiar with: the baking but oh so fertile plain between the Tigris and Euphrates. He also knew Ektabana well, the summer capital of the Kings of Kings, nestled in the shade of Mount Aurvant, though he had never suffered through a winter there. But until this journey he had never thought to travel on the sea.

Yet to his surprise Mithredath was finding a strange sort of beauty here. The water over which he sailed was a blue deep enough almost to be wine-purple, the sky another blue so different as to make him wonder how the same word could apply to both. The land rising steeply from sea to sky was by turns rocky and bare and shaggy with green-gray olive trees. The combination was peculiar but somehow, in its own way, harmonious.

True to his promise, Agbaal brought Mithredath to his destination with the sun still in the sky. True to his, the eunuch pressed a pair of goldpieces into the captain's palm. Agbaal bowed almost double; his swarthy face glowed with pride when Mithredath offered him a cheek to kiss, as if the two of them were near in rank.

The docks swarmed with the merchant folk of the Western Sea: There were Phoenicians like Agbaal, in turbans, tunics, and mantles; Italians wearing long white robes draped over one shoulder; and, of course, there were many native Yauna or, as they called themselves, Hellenes, milling about. Their slightly singsong speech was heard more than Aramaic, the empire's common tongue, understood everywhere from India to the edges of the Gallic lands.

Mithredath's rich brocaded robes, the gold bracelets on his wrists, and the piles of baggage his servants brought onto the docks drew touts—as a honey pot draws flies, he thought sourly. He picked a fellow whose Aramaic had less of a Hellenic hiss to it than most, then said, "Be so good as to lead me to the satrap's palace."

"Of course, my master," the man said, but his face fell. He would still get his fee from Mithredath, but had just had his hopes dashed of collecting another from the innkeeper upon whom he would have foisted Mithredath. *Too bad,* Mithredath thought.

He was used to Babylon's sensible grid of streets; these small western towns had their narrow, stinking lanes running every which way and sometimes abruptly petering out. He was glad he had hired a guide; anyone unfamiliar with these alleys could not have found his way through them.

Though larger than its neighbors, the satrap's residence—palace, Mithredath discovered, was far too grand a word—looked like any other house hereabouts. It presented a plain, whitewashed front to the world. Mithredath sniffed. To his way of thinking, anyone who *was* someone should let the world know it.

He paid the guide—well enough to keep him from sneering but not extravagantly—and rapped on the door with his pomegranate-headed walking stick. A moment later a guard opened the little eye-level observation window to peer out at him. "Who comes?" the fellow demanded fiercely.

Mithredath stood where the man could see him clearly and answered not with the accented Aramaic in which he had been challenged but in pure, clear Persian:

"I am Mithredath, *saris*"—somehow, in his own tongue, "eunuch" became almost a word of pride—"and servant to Khsrish, King of Kings, king of lands containing many men, king in this great earth far and wide, son of Marduniya the king, an Achaemenid, a Persian, son of a Persian, of Aryan seed. May Ahura Mazda smile upon him and make long his reign. I am come to the satrapy of the Yauna of the western mainland upon a mission given me from his own royal lips. I would discuss this with your master, the satrap Vahauka."

He folded his arms across his chest and waited.

He did not wait long. He heard a thump on the other side of the door and guessed the guard had dropped his spear in surprise. Mithredath did not smile. Years at the court of the King of Kings had schooled him against revealing his thoughts to a dangerous world. His face was perfectly composed when the guard flung the door wide and shouted, "Enter, servant of the King of Kings!"

The guard bowed low. Mithredath walked past him, returning

the courtesy with a bow barely more than a nod. Some people, he thought, deserved to be reminded from time to time of their station.

As he had intended, more people in the satrap's residence than the door guard heard his announcement. A majordomo came rushing to greet him in the outer hall. He wore the rectangular mantle of a Hellene over Persian trousers. His bow Mithredath returned in full; he would be a power in this miniature court.

The majordomo said, "Excellent *saris*"—he was a cautious one, too, Mithredath thought, again not smiling—"his Highness Vahauka, great satrap of the Yauna of the western mainland, now dines with the secretary, with the *ganzabara* of the satrapy, and with the general of the garrison. He bids you join them if your long journey from the court of the King of Kings, may Ahura Mazda smile upon him and make long his reign, has not left you too tired."

"The gracious invitation honors me," Mithredath said. "I accept with pleasure." He was glad to get the chance to meet the *ganzabara* so soon; the financial official was the one who would have to meet his tablet of credit from the court.

"Come this way, then." The majordomo led Mithredath out to the central courtyard where the satrap and his officers were dining. Here at last the eunuch felt himself among Persians again, for most of the courtyard was given over to a proper paradise, a formal garden of roses, tulips, and other bright blooms. Their fragrance, mingled with the odors of cookery, made Mithredath's nostrils twitch.

"Lord Vahauka, I present the *saris* Mithredath, servant of the King of Kings," the majordomo said loudly. Mithredath began to prostrate himself, as he would have before Khsrish, but Vahauka, a lean, gray-bearded Persian of about fifty, stopped him with a wave. The satrap turned his head, presenting his cheek to the eunuch.

"My lord is gracious," Mithredath said as he stepped up to Vahauka and let his lips brush the satrap's beard.

"We are both the King of Kings' servants; how can our ranks greatly differ?" Vahauka said. His fellow diners nodded and murmured in agreement. He went on, "Mithredath, I present you to my secretary Rishi-kidin"—a perfumed, sweating Babylonian in linen undertunic, wool overtunic, and short white cloak—"the *ganzabara* Hermippos"—a clean-shaven Hellene who, like the majordomo, wore trousers—"and the general of this satrapy, Tadanmu''—a Persian with a no-nonsense look in his eyes, dressed rather more plainly than suited his station.

Mithredath kissed more cheeks. After the satrap's example, his aides could hardly show the eunuch less favor. The feel of Hermippos' face was strange; only among his own kind was Mithredath used to smooth skin against his lips. Not being the only beardless person present made him feel extraordinarily masculine. He laughed at himself for the conceit.

"Here, sit by me," Vahauka said when the introductions were done. He shouted for his servants to bring Mithredath food and wine. "Refresh yourself; when you have finished, perhaps you will favor us by telling what business of the King of Kings, may Ahura Mazda smile upon him and make long his reign, brings you to this far western land."

"With pleasure, my lord," Mithredath said. Then for some time he was busy with food and drink. The wines were excellent; the satrapy of the Yauna of the western mainland was known for its grapes, though grapes were one of the few things it was known for, even in Babylon. The food pleased Mithredath less. Vahauka might be used to salted olives, but one was enough to last Mithredath a lifetime.

Servants lit torches as twilight gave way to darkness. Insects fluttered around the lights, whose smoke was sweet with frankincense. Every so often a nightjar or bat would dive into view, snatch a bug, and vanish again.

The majordomo led in three flute girls wearing only wisps of filmy cloth. Vahauka sent them away, saying, "Our distinguished guest's news will prove more interesting than their songs and dances, which we have all seen and heard before, and surely he will not miss them in any way."

Mithredath glanced at the satrap from under lowered brows. Was that a sly dig at his condition? If so, Vahauka was a fool, which might account for his governing only this undistinguished satrapy. Eunuchs' memories for slights were notoriously long, and Mithredath soon would be far closer to the ear of the King of Kings again than Vahauka could dream of coming.

For the moment, of course, Mithredath remained the soul of courtesy. "As my lord wishes. Know, then, that I am come at the command of the King of Kings, may Ahura Mazda smile upon him and make long his reign, to learn more of the deeds of his splendid forefather the first Khsrish, called the Conqueror, that those deeds may be celebrated once again and redound to the further glory of the present King of Kings, who proudly bears the same name."

A brief silence followed as the officials thought over what he had said. Vahauka asked, "This is your sole commission, excellent *saris*?"

"It is, my lord."

"Then we will be pleased to render you such assistance as we may be capable of," the satrap said fulsomely. His aides were quick to echo him. Mithredath heard the relief in their voices. He knew why it was there: no misdeed of theirs had come to the notice of the King of Kings.

"You want to learn how the first Khsrish took Hellas, eh?" Hermippos said. Mithredath almost failed to recognize the King of Kings' name in his mouth; flavored by his native speech, it came out sounding like "Xerxes." The *ganzabara* went on. "The ruins of Athens, I suppose, would be the best place for that."

"Aye!" "Indeed!" "Well said!" Vahauka, Rishi-kidin, and Tadanmu all spoke at once. Mithredath smiled, but only to himself. How eager they were to get him out of their hair! Perhaps they, or some of them, *were* up to something about which Khsrish should know.

Still, Hermippos had a point. As Mithredath had learned in Babylon preparing for this mission, Athens had led the western Yauna in their fight against the Conqueror. The eunuch sighed. Having come so far already, he supposed poking through rubble could not make things much worse.

Hermippos said, "If you like, excellent *saris*, I will provide you with a secretary who reads and writes not only Aramaic but also the Hellenic tongue. It is still often used here and in the ancient days of which you spoke would have been the only written language, I suppose."

"I accept with thanks," Mithredath said sincerely, dipping his head. He'd picked up a few words of the tongue of the Hellenes on his westward journey, but it had never occurred to him that he might also need to learn the strange, angular script the locals used. He sighed again, wishing he were home.

Vahauka might have been peering into his thoughts. "Tell us of the news of the court, Mithredath. Here in this distant land we learn of it but slowly and imperfectly."

Nodding, Mithredath gave such gossip as he thought safe to give; he had no intention of setting out all of Khsrish's business—or his scandals—before these men he did not know. He was, though, so circumspect that he blundered, for after he was through, Tadanmu observed, "You have said nothing, excellent *saris*, of the King of Kings' cousin, the great lord Kurash."

"I pray your pardon, my lord. I did not mention him because he has been seeing to his estates these past few months and hence is not currently in attendance upon the King of Kings, may Ahura Mazda smile upon him and make long his reign. Lord Kurash is well, though, so far as I know, and I have heard he has new sons by two of his younger wives."

"And likely hiked up the midwife's skirts after she came away from each one of them, to celebrate the news." Tadanmu chuckled. Kurash's prowess and his zeal in exercising it were notorious.

The general asked more of Kurash. Mithredath declined to be drawn out, and Tadanmu subsided. Mithredath made a mental note all the same. Kurash's ambitions, or rather the forestalling of them, were the main reason the eunuch had come to the satrapy of the Yauna of the western mainland. New glory accruing to Khsrish the Conqueror would also reflect onto his namesake, the present occupant—under Ahura Mazda—of the throne of the Kings of Kings.

Mithredath drained his cup and held it out for more. A servant hurried up to fill it. The eunuch sipped, rolled the wine around in his mouth so he could appreciate it fully, and nodded in slow pleasure. Here was one reason, anyhow, to approve of this western venture.

He cherished such reasons. He had not found many of them.

"My lord?"

Mithredath looked around to see who the young Hellene was addressing, then realized with a start that the fellow was talking to him. The ignorance of these provincials! "No lord I," he said. "I am but a *saris* in the service of the King of Kings."

He watched a flush rise under the young man's clear skin. "My apologies, my—excellent *saris*," the Hellene said, correcting himself. "You are called Mithredath, though, are you not?"

"That is my name," the eunuch admitted, adding icily, "You have the advantage of me, I believe."

The fellow's flush grew deeper. "Apologies again. My name is Polydoros; I thought Hermippos would have mentioned me. If it please you, I am to be your guide to the ruins of Athens."

"Ah!" Mithredath studied this Polydoros with fresh interest.

But no, his first impression had been accurate: the fellow was well on the brash side of thirty. Wondering if the *ganzabara* was trying to palm some worthless relative off on him, he said cautiously, "I had looked for an older man."

"To be fluent in Aramaic and the Hellenic tongue both, you mean?" Polydoros said, and Mithredath found himself nodding. The Hellene explained, "It's coming from a banking family that does it, excellent *saris*. Most of the inland towns in this satrapy still cling to the old language for doing business, so naturally I've had to learn to read and write it as well as speak it."

"Ah," Mithredath said again. That made a certain amount of sense. "We'll see how things go, then."

"Very good," Polydoros said. "What are your plans? Will you travel up to the ruins each day or had you planned actually to stay in Athens?"

"Just how far inland is it?" Mithredath asked.

"A parasang and a half, maybe."

"Close to two hours walk each way? In the little time I'd have in the ruins, how could I hope to accomplish anything? I'd sooner pitch a tent there and spend a much shorter while in a bit more discomfort. That will let me return to the east all the sooner."

"As you wish, excellent *saris*. After tomorrow, I shall be at your service."

"Why not go tomorrow?" Mithredath asked rather grumpily. "I can send my servants out at once to buy tent cloth and other necessities."

"You pardon, sir, but as I said, I am of a banking family. Tomorrow the monthly silver shipment from the Laurion mines south of here will arrive, and I'll need to be present to help with weighing and assaying the metal. The mines don't produce as they did when the great lode was found not long after Hellas came under Persia, but there will still be close to a talent of silver: forty or fifty pounds of it, certainly."

"Do what you must, of course," Mithredath said, yielding to necessity. "I'll look forward to seeing you morning after next, then." He bowed, indicating that Polydoros could go.

But the Hellene did not depart immediately. Instead he stood with a faraway expression on his face, looking through Mithredath rather than at him. The eunuch was growing annoyed when at last Polydoros said dreamily, "I wonder how the conquest would have gone, had the Athenians stumbled onto that silver before Khsrish's"—he pronounced it *Xerxes'*, too—"campaign. Money buys the sinews of war."

A banker indeed, Mithredath thought scornfully. "Money does not buy bravery," he said.

"Perhaps not, excellent *saris*, but even the bravest man, were he naked, would fare badly against an armored warrior with a spear. Had Athens been able to build ships to match the Persian fleet, the Hellenes might not have fallen under the empire's control."

Mithredath snorted. "All the subject peoples have their reasons why they should have held off Persia. None did."

"Of course you are right, excellent *saris*," Polydoros said politely, wise enough to hide his true feelings, whatever they were. "It was but a fancy of the moment." He bowed. "Till the day after tomorrow." He hurried off.

"I came to the proper decision." Mithredath lifted his soft felt cap from his head and used it to wipe sweat from his face. "I shouldn't care to have to make this journey coming and going each day."

"As you say, excellent *saris*." With a broad-brimmed straw hat and thin, short Hellenic mantle, Polydoros was more comfortably dressed than Mithredath, but he was sweating, too. Behind them the eunuch's servants and a donkey bore their burdens in stolid silence. One of the servants led a sheep that kept trying to stop and nibble grass and shrubs.

Something crunched under Mithredath's shoe. He looked down and saw a broken piece of pottery and, close by it, half-buried in weeds, a chunk of brick. "A house stood here once," he said. He heard the surprise in his voice and felt foolish. But knowing this wilderness had been a city was not the same as stumbling over its remains.

Polydoros was more familiar with the site. He pointed. "You can see a fragment of the old wall there among the olive trees."

Had he noticed it, Mithredath would have taken it for a pile of rocks. Now that he looked closely, though, he saw they had been worked to fit together.

"Most of what used to be here, I suppose, has been carried off over the years," Polydoros said. Mithredath nodded. Stealing already worked stone would be easier for a peasant than working it himself. Polydoros pointed again, to the top of one of the hillocks ahead. "More of the wall around the akropolis—

the citadel, you would say in Aramaic—is left because it's harder to get the rock down."

"Aye," Mithredath said, pleased to find the Hellene thinking along with him. It was his turn to point. "That is the way up to the—the citadel?" At the last moment he decided against trying to echo the local word Polydoros had used.

The Hellene dipped his head, a gesture Mithredath had learned to equate with a nod. "Of course, it would have been an easier ramp to climb when it was kept clear of brush," Polydoros said dryly.

"So it would." The eunuch's heart was already beating fast; he had endured more exertion on this western journey than ever before in his life. Still, he had a job to do. "Let us go up. If that is the citadel, the ruins there will be important ones and may tell me what I need to learn of Athens."

"As you say, excellent *saris*."

On reaching the top of the akropolis, Mithredath felt a bit like a conqueror himself. Not only was the ancient ramp overgrown, it was also gullied. One of the eunuch's servants limped with a twisted ankle; had the donkey stumbled into that hole, it probably would have broken a leg. Mithredath was winded, and even Polydoros, who seemed ready for anything, was breathing hard.

Rank grass and weeds also grew on the flat ground on top of the citadel, between the stones of the wrecked wall, and over the lower parts of the destroyed buildings the Persians had sacked so long ago. One of those buildings, a large one, had been unfinished when Athens fell. Marble column drums thrust up from the undergrowth. Mithredath could still see scorch marks on them.

In front of those half columns stood a marble stele whose shape was familiar to the eunuch—there were many like it in Babylon—but which did not belong with the ruins around it. Nor was the inscription carved onto that stele written in the local language, but in Aramaic and in the wedge-shaped characters the Persians had once used and the native Babylonians still sometimes employed.

A thrill ran through Mithredath as he read the Aramaic text: " 'Khsrish, King of Kings, declares: You who may king hereafter, of lies beware. I, Khsrish, King of Kings, having pulled down this city, center of the rebel Yauna, decree that it shall remain wilderness forevermore. You who may be king hereafter and obey these words, may Ahura Mazda be your friend and may your seed be made numerous; may Ahura Mazda make your days long; may whatever you do be successful. You who may be king hereafter, if you see this stele and its words and follow them not, may Ahura Mazda curse you, and of your seed more may there not be, and may Ahura Mazda pull down all you make as I, Khsrish, King of Kings, have pulled down this city, center of the rebel Yauna.'

"A mighty lord, Khsrish the Conqueror, to have his decree obeyed down across the years," Mithredath said, proud to be of the same Persian race as the long-ago King of Kings, though of his own seed, of course, more there would never be.

"Mighty indeed," Polydoros said tonelessly.

Mithredath looked at him sharply, then relaxed. Polydoros was, after all, a Hellene. Expecting him to be overjoyed before an inscription celebrating the defeat of his forefathers was too much to ask.

The eunuch rummaged in one of the packs on the donkey's back until he found a sheet of papyrus, a reed pen, and a bottle of ink. He copied the Aramaic portion of Khsrish's inscription. He presumed the Persian text said the same thing, but could not read it. Perhaps some magus with antiquarian leanings might still be able to, perhaps not. The present Khsrish would care only about the Aramaic. Of that the eunuch was certain.

He looked at what he had written. He frowned and compared the papyrus to the text carved into the stele. He had copied everything written there. Still, something seemed to be missing.

Perhaps Polydoros could supply it; he was a native of these parts. Mithredath turned to him. "Tell me, please, good Polydoros, do you know the name of the king of Athens whom Khsrish the Conqueror overcame?"

The Hellene frowned. "Excellent *saris*, I do not. The last king of Athens whose name I know is Kodros, and he is a man of legend, from long before the time of Xerxes."

"I might have known this was going too smoothly." Mithredath sighed. Then he brightened. "It was to learn such things, after all, that I came here." He scratched his head; he did not approve of loose ends. "But how is it you know of this—Kodros, you said?—and not of the man who must have been Athens's last king?"

"Excellent *saris*," Polydoros said hesitantly, "in the legends of my people Kodros *is* the last king of Athens."

"Ridiculous," Mithredath snorted. "*Someone* must rule, is it not so? This Athens must have been an enemy worthy of

Khsrish's hatred for him to destroy it utterly and afterward curse it. Such an enemy will have had rulers, and able ones, to oppose the King of Kings. How can it have lacked them for all the time since the death of Kodros? Did not one lead it all those years? I cannot believe that.''

''Nor I,'' Polydoros admitted.

''Very strange.'' Mithredath glanced over to the unhappy sheep his servants had urged—and dragged—up the overgrown ramp. ''Here, before Khsrish's victory stele, seems as good a spot as any to offer up the beast.'' He drew the dagger that hung from his belt and cut a spray of leaves from a nearby bush. He put the leaves in his cap. ''They should be myrtle, but any will do in a pinch.''

Polydoros watched Mithredath lead the sheep over to the marble pillar and set the dagger against its neck. ''Just like that?'' the Hellene asked. ''No altar? No ritual fire? No libation? No flute players? No grain sprinkled before you sacrifice?''

''The good god Ahura Mazda does not need them to hear my prayer.''

Polydoros shrugged. ''Our rites are different.''

Mithredath cut the sheep's throat. As the beast kicked toward death, he beseeched Ahura Mazda to help him succeed in his quest for knowledge with which to glorify the King of Kings. He was forbidden to pray for any more personal or private good, but with this sacrifice had no need to do so in any case.

''Does your god require any of the flesh of you?'' Polydoros asked as the eunuch began the gory job of butchering the carcass and setting the disjointed pieces on a heap of soft greenery.

''No, it is mine to do with as I will. A magus should pray over it, but as none is here, we shall have to make do.''

''Is that garlic growing over there? It will flavor the meat once it's cooked.'' Polydoros licked his chops.

Mithredath felt saliva flow into his own mouth. He turned to a servant. ''You can get a fire going now, Tishtrya.''

''What are you doing?'' Polydoros asked the next morning.

''Looking through the notes I made before I left Babylon,'' Mithredath said. ''Here, I knew there was something that would tell me who ruled here when the first Khsrish came. An old tablet says he led Dēmos of Athens into captivity. Who is this Dēmos, if Kodros was the last king here?''

'' 'Dēmos' isn't a who, I'm afraid, excellent *saris*, but rather a what,'' Polydoros said. ''Whoever wrote your tablet wanted to celebrate the King of Kings, as you do, but did not know the Hellenic tongue well. 'Dēmos of Athens' simply means 'the people of Athens.' ''

"Oh." Mithredath sighed. "If you knew the trouble I had finding that—'' He shuffled scraps of papyrus, briefly looked happy, then grew cautious again. "I also found something about 'Boulē of Athens.' Someone told me ē was the feminine ending in your language, so I took Boulē to be Dēmos' wife. You're going to tell me that's wrong, too, though, aren't you?''

Polydoros dipped his head. "I'm sorry, but I must, excellent *saris*. 'Boulē' means 'council.' ''

"Oh." The eunuch's sigh was longer this time. "The people of Athens, the council of Athens—where is the king of Athens?'' He glared at Polydoros as if the young banker were responsible for making that elusive monarch disappear. Then he sighed once more. "That's what I came here to find out, I suppose. Where are we most likely to find whatever records or decrees this town kept before it came under the rule of the King of Kings?''

"There are two likely places," Polydoros said after a visible pause for thought that made Mithredath very much approve of him. "One is up here, in the citadel. The other would be down there''— He pointed north and west —"in the agora, the city's marketplace. Anyone who came into the city from the countryside to do business would be able to read them there.''

"Sensible," Mithredath said. "We'll cast about here for a while, then, and go down again later. The fewer trips up and down that ramp I take, the happier I shall be." When Polydoros agreed, the eunuch turned to his servants. "Tishtrya, Raga, you will be able to help in this enterprise, too. All you need do is look for anything with writing on it and let me or Polydoros know if you actually find something.''

The servants' nods were gloomy; they had looked forward to relaxing while their master worked. Mithredath expected little from them but did not feel like having them sit idle. He was surprised when, a few minutes later, one of them came trotting through the rubble and undergrowth, waving excitedly to show he had found something.

"What is it, Raga?'' the eunuch asked.

"Words, master, carved on an old wall," Raga replied. "Come see!''

"I shall," Mithredath said. He and Polydoros followed the servant back to where his companion was waiting. Tishtrya proudly pointed at the inscription. The eunuch's hopes fell at once: it was too short to be the kind of thing he was seeking. He turned to Polydoros. "What does it say?"

"*Kalos Arkhias*," the Hellene replied. " 'Arkhias is beautiful.' It's praise of a pretty boy, excellent *saris*, nothing more; you could see the like chalked or scratched on half the walls in Peiraieus."

"Nasty buggers," Tishtrya muttered under his breath in Persian. Polydoros' eyes went hard for a moment, but he said nothing. Mithredath upbraided his servant; at the same time he made a mental note that the Hellene understood some Persian.

The search resumed. The citadel of Athens was not a large place; a man could easily walk the length of it in a quarter of an hour. But how many such trips would he have to take across it, Mithredath wondered, to make sure he missed nothing? Assuming, of course, he added to himself a moment later, anything was there to be missed.

Polydoros sat down in the narrow shade of an overthrown chunk of masonry and fanned himself with his straw hat. He might have been thinking with Mithredath's mind, for he said, "This could take forever, you know, excellent *saris*."

"Yes," was all Mithredath cared to reply to that obvious truth.

"We need to plan what to do, then, rather than simply wandering about up here," the Hellene went on. Mithredath nodded; Polydoros seemed to have a talent for straightforward thinking. After more consideration Polydoros said, "Let's make a circuit of the wall first. Decrees often go up on the side of a wall so people can see them. It is not the same in Babylon?"

"It is," Mithredath agreed. He and Polydoros made their way back to the ramp up which they had come.

They walked north and east along the wall. Mithredath's heart beat faster when he saw letters scratched onto a stone, but it was only another graffito extolling a youth's beauty. Then, when they were about halfway along the northern reach of the wall, opposite the ruins of some many-columned building, Polydoros suddenly pointed and exclaimed, "There, by Zeus; that's what we're after!"

Mithredath's eyes followed the Hellene's finger. The slab Polydoros had spied was flatter and paler than the surrounding stones. As they hurried toward it, Mithredath saw the slab was covered with letters in the angular script the Hellenes used for their own language. If this was someone praising a pretty boy, he'd been very long-winded.

"What does it say?" the eunuch asked. He fought against excitement; for all he knew, the inscription had been ancient when Khsrish took Athens.

"Let me see." Polydoros studied the letters. So, in his more ignorant way, did Mithredath. He could see that the stone carving here was more regular than the scratchings his servants and he and Polydoros had come upon before. That in itself, he suspected, marked an official document.

"Well?" he asked impatiently. He took out pen and ink and papyrus and got ready to transcribe the words Polydoros was presumably rendering into Aramaic.

"This is part of what you seek, I think," the Hellene said at last.

"Tell me, then!" Had he been a whole man, Mithredath's voice would have cracked; as he was what he was, it merely rose a little.

"I'm about to. Here: 'It seemed good to the council and to the people' . . . *boulē* and *dēmos* again, you see?"

"A plague on the council and people!" Mithredath broke in. "Who in Ahura Mazda's name was the king?"

"I'm coming to that, I think. Let me go on: 'With the tribe of Antiokhis presiding, Leostratos serving as chairman, Hypsikhides as secretary—' "

"The king!" Mithredath shouted. "Where is the name of the king?"

"It is not on the stone," Polydoros admitted. He sounded puzzled. Mithredath, for his part, was about ready to grind his teeth. Polydoros continued. "This may be it: 'Aristeides proposed these things concerning the words of the prophetess of Delphi and the Persians:

" 'Let the Athenians fortify the citadel with beams of wood as well as stone to meet the Persians, just as was bade by the prophetess. Let the council choose woodsmen and carpenters to do this, and let them be paid from the public treasury. Let all this be done as quickly as possible, Xerxes already having come to Asian Sardis. Let there be good fortune to the people of Athens.' "

"Read it over again," Mithredath said. "Read it slowly so that I can be sure I have your Yauna names correct."

"Not all Hellenes are Ionians," Polydoros said. Mithredath shrugged. How these westerners chose to divide themselves was their business, and he did not care one way or the other. But

Khsrish, back in Babylon, would think of them all as Yauna. And so, in his report, Yauna they would be.

Polydoros finished reading. Mithredath's pen stopped its scratching race across the sheet of papyrus. The eunuch read what he had written. He read it again. "Is, ah, Leostratos the ruler of Athens, then? And this Aristeides his minister? Or is Aristeides the king? The measure is his, I gather."

"So it would seem, excellent *saris*," Polydoros said. "But our words for 'king' are *anax* and, more usually, *basileus*. Neither of those is here."

"No," Mithredath said morosely. He mentally damned all the ancient Athenians to Ahriman and the House of the Lie for confusing him so. Khsrish and his courtiers would *not* be pleased if Mithredath had traveled so far, had spent so much gold from the King of Kings' treasury, without finding what he had set out to find. Nothing was more dreadful for a eunuch—for anyone, but for a eunuch especially—than losing the favor of the King of Kings.

Mithredath read the translated inscription once more. "You have rendered this accurately into Aramaic?"

"As best I could, excellent *saris*," Polydoros said stiffly.

"I pray your pardon, good Polydoros," the eunuch said. "I meant no disrespect, I assure you. It's only that there is much here I do not understand."

"Nor I," Polydoros said, but some of the ice was gone from his voice.

Mithredath bowed. "Thank you. Help me, then, if you will, to put together the pieces of this broken pot. What does this phrase mean: 'it seemed good to the council and to the people'? Why does the stone carver set that down? Why should anyone care what the people think? Theirs is only to obey, after all."

"True, excellent *saris*," Polydoros said. "Your questions are all to the point. The only difficulty"—he spread his hands and smiled wryly—"is that I have no answers to them."

Mithredath sat down on a chunk of limestone that, from its fluted side, might once have been part of a column. Weeds scratched his ankles through the straps of his sandals. A spider ran across his instep and was gone before he could swat it. In the distance he heard his servants crunching through brush. A hoopoe called its strange, trilling call. Otherwise silence ruled the dead citadel.

The eunuch rubbed his smooth chin. "How is Peiraieus

ruled? Maybe that will tell me something of Athens's ways before the Conqueror came.''

"I beg leave to doubt it, excellent *saris*. The city is no different from any other in the empire. The King of Kings, may Zeus and the other gods smile on him, appoints the town governor, who is responsible to the satrap. In the smaller towns the satrap makes the appointment.''

"You're right. That doesn't help.'' Mithredath read the inscription again. By now he was getting sick of it and put the papyrus back in his lap with a petulant grunt. '' 'The *people*,' '' he repeated. "It almost sounds as if they and the council are sovereign and these men merely ministers, so to speak.''

"I can imagine a council conducting affairs, I suppose,'' Polydoros said slowly, "though I doubt one could decide matters as well or as fast as a single man. But how could anyone know about what all the people of a city thought on a question? And even if for some reason the people were asked about one matter, surely no one could expect to reckon up what they thought about each of the many concerns a city has every day.''

"I was hoping you would give me a different slant on the question. Unfortunately, I think just as you do.'' Mithredath sighed and heaved himself up off his makeshift seat. "I suppose all we can do now is search further and hope we find more words to help us pierce this mystery.''

The eunuch, the Hellene, and the two servants prowled the citadel for the next two days. Tishtrya almost stepped on a viper, but killed it with his stick before it could strike. Mithredath came to admire the broken statuary he kept stumbling over. It was far more restrained than the ebullient, emotional sculpture he was used to, but had a spare elegance of its own.

The searchers came across a good number of inscriptions, but none that helped unravel the riddle the first long one had posed. Most were broken or worn almost to illegibility. Twice Polydoros found the formula "it seemed good to the council and to the people.'' Each time Mithredath swore in frustration because the rest of the stone was, in one case, buried beneath masonry and therefore would have taken twenty men to move, and in the other case missing altogether.

"Enough of this place,'' Mithredath said on the evening of that second day. "I don't care any longer if the answer is right under my feet. I think it would run away from me like a rabbit from a fox if I dug for it. Tomorrow we will search down below, in the marketplace. Maybe our luck will be better there.''

No one argued with him, although they all knew they had not thoroughly explored the citadel—that would be a job for months or years, not days. They rolled themselves in their blankets—no matter how hot the days were, the nights stayed chilly—and slept.

The marketplace had fewer ruins than the citadel. "How do I know this still *is* part of the marketplace?" Mithredath asked pointedly as he, Polydoros, and the servants picked their way along through grass, bushes, and brush. Before Polydoros could answer, the eunuch added, "Aii!" He had just kicked a large stone, with painful results.

He pushed away the brush that hid it. It was a very large stone; he felt like a idiot for not having seen it. In his anger, he bent down to push the stone over. "Wait!" Polydoros said. "It has letters on it." He read them and began to laugh.

"What, if I may ask, strikes you funny?" Glacial dignity, Mithredath thought, was preferable to hopping up and down on one foot.

"It says, 'I am the boundary stone of the agora,' " Polydoros told him.

"Oh," the eunuch said, feeling foolish all over again.

The most prominent wrecked building was a couple of minutes' walk north of them; its wrecked facade had eight columns, two of them still standing at their full height and supporting fragments of an architrave. "Shall we examine that first?" Polydoros asked, pointing.

Mithredath's throbbing toes made him contrary. "No, let's save it for last and wander about for a while. After all, it isn't going anywhere."

"As you wish," Polydoros said politely. Behind them, Mithredath's servants sighed. The eunuch pretended he had not heard.

"What's that?" Mithredath asked a minute or so later, seeing another piece of stone poking up from out of the weeds—seeing it, thankfully, before he had a closer encounter with it.

"By the shape, it's the base a statue once stood on," Polydoros said. He walked over to it. "Two statues," he amended. "I see insets carved for four feet. Ah, there's writing on it here." He pulled weeds aside and read, " 'Harmodios and Aristogeiton, those who slew the tyrant Hipparkhos.' "

"What's a tyrant?" Mithredath frowned at the unfamiliar word. "Some sort of legendary monster?"

"No, merely a man who ruled a city but was not of any kingly line. Many towns among the Hellenes used to have them."

"Ah. Thank you." Mithredath thought about that for a moment, then said incredulously, "There was in the marketplace of Athens a statue celebrating men who killed the city's ruler?"

"So it would seem, excellent *saris*," Polydoros said. "Put that way, it is surprising, is it not?"

"It's madness," the eunuch said, shuddering at the idea. "As well for all that Persia conquered you Yauna. Who knows what lunacy you might otherwise have loosed on the world?"

"Hmm," was all Polydoros said to that. The Hellene jerked his chin toward the ruined building, which was now quite close. "Shall we go over to it now?"

But Mithredath reacted to the Hellenic perversity exemplified by the ruined statue base with perversity of his own: "No, we'll go around it, see what else is here." He knew he was being difficult, and reveled in it. What could Polydoros do about it?

Nothing, obviously. "As you wish," the Hellene repeated. He then proceeded to skirt the ruins by an even larger margin than Mithredath would have chosen. *Take that*, the eunuch thought. Smiling behind Polydoros' back, he followed him north and west.

Still, enough was enough. "I'm certain *this* isn't the marketplace any more," Mithredath said when the Hellene had led him almost all the way to Athens' overthrown gates.

"No, I suppose not," Polydoros admitted. "Are you ready to head back now?"

"More than ready." Mithredath caught Polydoros' eye. They grinned at each other, both of them a little sheepish. Mithredath glanced at his servants. They did not seem amused, and knew better than to seem annoyed.

Something crunched under the eunuch's foot. Curious, he bent down. Then, more curious, he showed Polydoros what he had found. "What's this?"

"An *ostrakon*—a potsherd," Polydoros amended, remembering to put the Yauna word into Aramaic.

"I knew *that*," Mithredath said impatiently. "I've stepped on enough of them these past few days. But what's this written on it?"

"Hmm?" Polydoros took a closer look. "A name—Themistokles, son of Neokles."

"Why write on a potsherd?"

"Cheaper than papyrus." Polydoros shrugged. "People are always breaking pots and always have sherds around."

"Why just a name, then? Why not some message to go with it?"

"Excellent *saris*, I have no idea."

"Hrmp," Mithredath said. He took another step and heard another crunch. He was not especially surprised to find another potsherd under his foot; as Polydoros had said, people were always breaking pots. He was surprised, though, to find he had stepped on two sherds in a row with writing on them. He handed the second piece of broken pottery to Polydoros and pointed at the letters.

"Themistokles, Neokles' son, again," the Hellene said.

"That's all?" Mithredath asked. Polydoros dipped his head to show it was. The eunuch gave him a quizzical look. "Good Polydoros, why write just a man's name—just his name, mind you, nothing else—on two different pieces of broken pottery? If one makes no sense, does twice somehow?"

"Not to me, excellent *saris*." Polydoros shifted his feet like a schoolboy caught in some mischief by his master. This time his sandal crunched on something. Mithredath felt a certain sense of inevitability as Polydoros looked at the sherd, found writing on it, and read, "Themistokles, son of Neokles."

The eunuch put hands on hips. "Just how many of these things are there?" He turned to his servants. "Tear out some brush here. My curiosity has the better of me. Let's see how many sherds we can turn up."

The look Raga and Tishtrya exchanged was eloquent. Like any master with good sense, Mithredath pretended not to see it. The servants bent and began uprooting shrubs and weeds. They moved at first with the resigned slowness servants always used on unwelcome tasks, but then even they began to show some interest as sherd followed sherd in quick succession.

"Themistokles, Neokles' son," Polydoros read again and again, and then once, to vary the monotony, "Themistokles of the district Phrearrios." He turned to Mithredath and raised an eyebrow. "I think we may assume this to be the same man referred to by the rest of the sherds."

"Er, yes." Mithredath watched the pile of potsherds grow by Polydoros' feet. He began to feel like a sorcerer whose spell had proved stronger than he had expected.

His servants had speculations of their own. "Who d'you

suppose this Themis-whatever was?'' Tishtrya asked Raga as they worked together to uproot a particularly stubborn plant.

"Probably a he-whore putting his name about so he'd have plenty of trade," Raga panted. Mithredath, listening, did not dismiss the idea out of hand. It made more sense than anything he'd been able to think of.

"Themistokles, son of Neokles," Polydoros said almost an hour later. He put down another sherd. "That makes, ah, ninety-two."

"Enough." Mithredath threw his hands in the air. "At this rate we could go on all summer. I think there are more important things to do."

"Like the ruin, for example?" Polydoros asked slyly.

"Well, now that you mention it, yes," Mithredath said with such grace as he could muster. He kicked a foot toward the pile of potsherds. "We'll leave this rubbish here. I see no use for it but to prove how strange the men of Athens were, and it would glorify neither Khsrish the Conqueror nor through him our Khsrish IV, may Ahura Mazda make long his reign, to say he overcame a race of madmen."

The eunuch's servants laughed at that: they were Persians, too. Polydoros managed a lopsided smile. He was on the quiet side as the four men made their way back to the ruined building in the marketplace.

Once they were there, the Hellene quickly regained his good spirits, for he found he had a chance to gloat. "This building is called the *Stoa Basileios*," he said, pointing to letters carved on an overthrown piece of frieze. "The Royal Portico. If we wanted to learn of kings, we should have come here first."

Chagrin and excitement warred in Mithredath. Excitement won. "Good Polydoros, you were right. Find me here, if you can, a list of the kings of Athens. The last one, surely, will be the man Khsrish overcame." Which will mean, he added to himself, *that I can get out of these ruins and this whole backward satrapy.*

Seized perhaps by some of that same hope, Raga and Tishtrya searched the ruins with three times the energy they had shown hunting for potsherds. Stones untouched since the Persian sack save by wind, rain, and scurrying mice went crashing over as the servants scoured the area for more bits of writing.

Mithredath found the first new inscription himself, but already had learned not to be overwhelmed by an idle wall scratching.

All the same, he called Polydoros over. " 'Phrynikhos thinks Aiskhylos is beautiful,' " the Hellene read dutifully.

"About what I expected, but one never knows." Mithredath nodded and went on looking. He had been gelded just before puberty; feeling desire was as alien to him as Athens's battered rocky landscape. He knew he would never understand what drove this Phrynikhos to declare his lust for the pretty boy. Lust—other men's lust—was just something he had used to advance himself, back when he was young enough to trade on it. Once in a while, abstractly, he wondered what it was like.

Raga let out a shout that drove all such useless fancies from his mind. "Here's a big flat stone covered with letters!" Everyone came rushing over to see. The servant went on. "I saw this wasn't one stone here but two, the white one covering the gray. So I used my staff to lever the white one off, and look!" He was as proud as if he'd done the writing himself.

Mithredath plunged pen into ink and readied his papyrus. "What does it say?" he asked Polydoros.

The Hellene plucked nervously at his beard and looked from the inscription to Mithredath and back again. The eunuch's impatient glare finally made him start to talk: " 'It seemed good to the council and to the people—' "

"What!" Mithredath jumped as if a wasp had stung him. "More nonsense about council and people? Where is the list of kings? In Ahura Mazda's name, where if not by the Royal Portico?"

"I would not know that, excellent *saris*," Polydoros said stiffly. "If I may, though, I suggest you hear me out as I read. This stone bears on your quest, I assure you."

"Very well." It wasn't very well, but there was nothing Mithredath could do about it. Grouchily, he composed himself to listen.

" 'It seemed good to the council and to the people,' " Polydoros resumed, " 'with the tribe of Oineïs presiding, Phainippos serving as chairman, Aristomenes as secretary, Kleisthenes proposed these things concerning *ostrakismos*—' "

"What in Ahriman's name is *ostrakismos*?" Mithredath asked.

"Something pertaining to *ostraka*—potsherds. I don't know how to put it into Aramaic any more precisely than that, excellent *saris*; I'm sorry. But the words on the stone explain it better than I could in any case, if you'll let me go on."

Mithredath nodded. "Thank you, excellent *saris*," Polydoros said. "Where was I? Oh, yes: 'Concerning *ostrakismos*: Each year, when the sixth tribe presides, let the people decide if they wish to hold an *ostrakophoria*.' " Seeing Mithredath roll his eyes, Polydoros explained, "That means a meeting to which potsherds are carried."

"I presume this is leading somewhere," the eunuch said heavily.

"I believe so, yes." Polydoros gave his attention back to the inscribed stone. " 'Let the *ostrakophoria* be held if more of the people are counted to favor it than to oppose. If at the *ostrakophoria* more than six thousand potsherds are counted, let him whose name appears on the largest number of *ostraka* leave Athens within ten days for ten years, suffering no loss of property in the interim. May there be good fortune to the people of Athens from this.' "

"Exiled by potsherds?" Mithredath said as his pen scratched across the sheet of papyrus. "Even for Yauna, that strikes me as preposterous." Then he and Polydoros looked first at each other, then back the way they had come. "Raga! Tishtrya! Go gather up the sherds we were looking at. I think we may have a need for them, after all." The servants trotted off.

"I also think we may," Polydoros said. "Let me read on: 'Those who have been ordained to leave the city: in the year when Ankises was *arkhon*—' "

"*Arkhon?*" Mithredath asked.

"Some officer or other." Polydoros shrugged. "It means 'leader' or 'ruler,' but if a man only held the post a year, it can hardly have been important, can it?"

"I suppose not. Go on."

" 'In the year when Ankises was *arkhon*, Hipparkhos, son of Kharmos; in the year when Telesinos was *arkhon*, Megakles, son of Hippokrates; in the year when Kritias was *arkhon*—' " The Hellene broke off. "No one was exiled that year, it seems. In the next, when Philokrates was *arkhon*, Xanthippos, son of Ariphron, was exiled, then no one again, and then—" He paused for effect. "—Themistokles, son of Neokles."

"Well, well." Mithredath scribbled furiously, pausing only to shake his head in wonder. "The people really did make these choices, then, without a king to guide them."

"So it would seem, excellent *saris*."

"How strange. Did the *ostrakismos*"—Mithredath stumbled over the Yauna word, but neither Aramaic nor Persian had an equivalent—"fall upon anyone else?"

"Not in the next two years, excellent *saris*," Polydoros said, "but in the year when Hypsikhides was *arkhon*, the Athenian people chose exile for Xerxes, son of Dareios, who can only be the King of Kings, the Conqueror. I would guess that to be a last gesture of defiance; the list of *arkhontes* ends abruptly with Hypsikhides."

"Very likely you are right. So they tried to exile Khsrish, did they? Much good it did them." Mithredath finished writing. The servants were coming back, carrying in a leather sack the sherds that had helped exile a man. Their shadows were long before them; Mithredath saw with surprise that the sun had almost touched the rocky western horizon. He turned to Polydoros. "It would be dark by the time we got back to Peiraieus. Falling into a pothole I never saw holds no appeal. Shall we spend one more night here and return with the light of morning?"

The Hellene dipped his head. "That strikes me as a good plan, if you are satisfied you have found what you came to learn."

"I think I have," Mithredath said. Hearing that, Tishtrya and Raga began to make camp close by the ruins of the Royal Portico. Bread and goat cheese and onions, washed down with river water, seemed as fine a feast as any of the elaborate banquets Mithredath had enjoyed in Babylon. Triumph, he thought, was an even better sauce than pickled fish.

His servants dove into their bedrolls as soon as they finished eating; their snores all but drowned out the little night noises that came from beyond the circle of light around the camp fire. Mithredath and Polydoros did not go to sleep right away. The eunuch was glad to have company. He felt like talking about the strange way the Athenians had run their affairs, and the Hellene had shown himself bright enough to have ideas of his own.

"No sign of a king anywhere," Mithredath said, still bemused at that. "I wonder if they settled everything they needed to decide on by counting potsherds."

"I would guess they probably must have, excellent *saris*," Polydoros said. "All the inscriptions read, 'It seemed good to the council and to the people.' How would they know that— why would they write that?—if they had not counted potsherds to know what seemed good to the people?"

"There you have me, good Polydoros. But what if something that 'seemed good to the people' was in fact bad for them?"

"Then they suffered the consequences, I suppose. They certainly did when they decided to oppose Xerxes.'' Polydoros waved at the dark ruins all around.

"But they were the leading Yauna power at the time, were they not? They must have been, or Khsrish would not have obliterated their city as a lesson to the others. Until they chose to fight him, they must have done well."

"A king can also make an error," Polydoros said.

"Oh, indeed." Being a courtier, Mithredath knew better than the Hellene how gruesomely true that could be. "But," he pointed out, "a king knows the problems that face his land. And if by some mischance he should not, why, then he has his ministers to point them out to him so that he may decide what needs to be done. How could the people—farmers, most of them, and cobblers and potters and dyers—how could they even have hoped to learn the issues that affected Athens, let alone what to do about them?"

"There you have me," Polydoros confessed. "They would be too busy, I'd think, working just to stay alive to be able to act, as you say, more or less as ministers in their own behalf."

Mithredath nodded. "Exactly. The king decides, the ministers and courtiers advise, and the people obey. So it is, so it has always been, so it always will be."

"No doubt you are right." An enormous yawn blurred Polydoros' words. "Your pardon, excellent *saris*. I think I will imitate your servants." He unrolled his blanket and wrapped it around himself. "Will you join us?"

"Soon."

Polydoros did not snore, but before long was breathing with the slow regularity of sleep. Mithredath remained some time awake. Every so often his eyes went to the bag of potsherds, which lay close by Raga's head. He kept trying to imagine what being an Athenian before Khsrish the Conqueror had come had been like. If the farmers and potters and such ruled themselves by counting sherds, would they have made an effort to learn about all the things Athens was doing so they could make sensible choices when the time came to put the sherds in a basket for counting or whatever it was they did? What would it have been like to be a tavern keeper, say, with the same concerns as a great noble?

The eunuch tried to imagine it, felt himself failing. It was as alien to him as lust. He knew whole men felt that, even if he could not. He supposed the Athenians might have had this other sense, but he was sure he did not.

He gave it up and rolled himself in his blanket to get some rest. As he grew drowsy, his mind began to roam. He had a sudden mental picture of the whole vast Persian Empire being run by people writing on potsherds. He had visions of armies of clerks trying to transport and count them and of mountains of broken pottery climbing to the sky. He fell asleep laughing at his own silliness.

Third-rate town though it was, Peiraieus looked good to Mithredath after some days pawing through the ruins of dead Athens. He paid Polydoros five gold darics for his help there. The Hellene bowed low. "You are most generous, excellent *saris*."

Mithredath presented his cheek for a kiss, then said, "Your assistance has but earned its fitting reward, good Polydoros."

"If you will excuse me, then, I'm off to see how much work has fallen on my table while I was away." At Mithredath's nod, Polydoros bowed again and trotted away. He turned back once to wave, then quickly vanished among the people crowding the port's streets.

"And now we are off to the satrap's residence," the eunuch told his servants. "I shall inform Vahauka of the success of my mission and draw from the *ganzabara*"— Mithredath snapped his fingers— "What was the fellow's name?"

"Hermippos, wasn't it, sir?" Tishtrya said.

"Yes; thank you. I shall draw from Hermippos the funds we need for our return journey to Babylon. After giving Polydoros his due, we are for the moment poor, but only for the moment."

"Yes, sir. I like the sound of going home fine, sir," Tishtrya said. Raga nodded.

"I wouldn't be sorry never to see this satrapy again myself," Mithredath admitted, smiling.

The satrap's residence was busier in the early morning than it had been at nightfall. A couple of guards stood outside the entrance to make sure the line of people waiting to see Vahauka and his officials stayed orderly.

Mithredath recognized one of the guards as the man who had been at the door the evening he'd arrived. He went up to the fellow. "Be so good as to convey me to his Excellency the satrap," he said. "I don't care to waste an hour of my time standing here."

The guard made no move to do as Mithredath had asked.

Instead, he looked down his long, straight nose at the eunuch and said, "You can just wait your turn like anybody else."

Mithredath stared. "Why, you insolent—" He started to push past, but the guard swung up his spear. "What do you think you're playing at?" the eunuch said angrily.

"I told you, no-stones—wait your turn." The spear head pointed straight at Mithredath's belly. It did not waver. The guard looked as though he would enjoy thrusting it home.

Mithredath glanced at his servants. Like any travelers with a shekel's weight of sense, he, Tishtrya, and Raga all carried long daggers as protection against robbers. Neither servant, though, seemed eager to take on a spear-carrying soldier, especially when the man served the local satrap. Seething, Mithredath took his place in line. "I shall remember your face," he promised the guard.

"And I'll forget yours." The lout laughed loudly at his own wit.

The line crawled ahead, but Mithredath was too furious to become bored. The revenges he invented grew more and more chilling as he got hotter and hotter. A soldier who thwarted one of the royal eunuchs—even a soldier so far from Babylon as this guard—was asking to have his corpse given to ravens and kites.

The eunuch had thought Vahauka would signal him forward as soon as he saw him, but the satrap went right on with his business. At last Mithredath stood before him. Mithredath started to prostrate himself and waited for Vahauka to stop him and offer his cheek. Vahauka did not. Feeling his stomach knot within him, the eunuch finished the prostration.

When he rose, he had his face under control. "My lord," he said, and gestured toward the bag of potsherds Raga held, "I am pleased to report my success in the mission personally set me by Khsrish, King of Kings"—he stressed the ruler's name and title—"may Ahura Mazda make long his reign."

Vahauka yawned. Of all the responses Mithredath might have expected, that was the last.

Having to work now to keep his voice from stumbling, the eunuch went on. "As I have succeeded, I plan to draw funds from the *ganzabara* Hipparkhos for my return voyage to Babylon."

"No." Vahauka yawned again.

"My lord, must I remind you of my closeness to the King of Kings?" Only alarm made Mithredath's threat come out so baldly.

"No-balls, I doubt very much if you ever have been—or ever will be—close to Kurash, Kings of Kings, may Ahura Mazda smile upon him and make long his reign."

"Ku—" The rest of the name could not get through the lump of ice that suddenly filled Mithredath's throat.

"Aye, Kurash. A ship came in with the word he'd overthrown and slain your worthless Khsrish the day you left for the old ruined inland town. Good riddance, says I. Now we have a real King of Kings again, and now I don't have to toady to a half-man anymore, either. And I won't. Get out of my sight, wretch, and thank the good gods I don't stripe your back to send you on your way."

The satrap's mocking laughter pursued Mithredath as he left the hall. His servants followed, as stunned as he.

Even the vestiges of dignity deserted him as soon as he was out of sight of the satrap's residence. He sat down heavily and buried his face in his hands so he would not have to see the passersby staring at him.

Tishtrya and Raga were muttering back and forth. "Poor," he heard one of them say. "He can't pay us any more."

"Well, to Ahriman with him, then. What else is he good for?" the other replied. It was Raga. He dropped the leather sack. The potsherds inside clinked. The sack came open. Some sherds spilled out.

Mithredath did not look up. He did not look up at the sound of his servants—no, his ex-servants, he thought dully—walking away, either.

They were some time gone when at last the eunuch began to emerge from his shock and despair. He picked up a sherd. Because one man had died, his own life, abruptly, was as shattered as the pot from which the broken piece had come, as shattered as long-ago Athens.

He climbed slowly to his feet. Perhaps he could beg one of his darics back from Polydoros. It would feed and lodge him for a couple of weeks. Then he could—what? At the moment he had no idea. For that matter, he did not even know if the Hellene would give him the gold.

One thing at a time, he thought. He stopped a man and asked the way to the bankers' street. The man told him. Nodding his thanks, he tossed the potsherd on the leather sack and started off.

This story was my first professional sale. It was not, however, my first professional appearance. The magazine that bought it, *Cosmos*, folded after four issues—and before the story saw print. It later ran in *Isaac Asimov's*. The idea from which it sprang came from my ex-wife, who was not then ex-, whose name appears in the table of contents as coauthor. The research and almost all the writing are mine. The marriage ended up failing, as sometimes happens. The story, I think, still works.

DEATH IN VESUNNA

"MORE WINE, GENTLEMEN?" CLODIUS EPRIUS asked, eyeing his two guests with faint distaste. He had wanted to leave for his country estate to supervise the harvest, but this dinner meeting was keeping him stranded in Vesunna like some vulgar lampseller. When both men nodded, he sighed and rose from his couch. Picking up the red earthenware jug, he filled their cups and poured himself a hefty dollop, as well.

All drank; the two strangers murmured appreciatively. That warmed Eprius a little. He said, "It's not Falernian, but this is a fine vintage. It was laid down the year Hadrian died, eight—no, nine years ago now. A fine vintage," he repeated. "Do you know, they're even shipping our Aquitanian wine to Britain these days."

"Really?" One of his visitors, a short blondish fellow who called himself Lucius, looked interested. His comrade kept his nose in his cup. A tall, solidly built man with hard, dark eyes, he had not said three words all through dinner. Lucius had introduced him as Marcus.

For no reason he could name, Eprius' guests disturbed him. It was not their accent, though Lucius, who did most of the talking, flavored his Latin in a curious fashion. No, the way they looked at their surroundings nettled their host more. Itinerant booksellers like these men would have seen many splendid villas in their travels, to be sure. Eprius knew his house would not have seemed imposing to anyone newly come from Rome or Antioch. But a fountain laughed in the courtyard, and the statues

29

around it were good work. So was the hunting scene picked out in mosaic on the dining room floor; craftsmen from Rome had created it. His home was no hovel. It did not deserve Lucius' patronizing stare or the contempt Marcus scarcely bothered to conceal.

He drained his wine. "Well, good sirs," he said, "you told me you had a proposition I might find interesting, could it be kept in sufficient privacy. I have met your request. My servants are already at my other home, and I've given my valet the evening off. I am at your disposal, gentlemen. How do you wish to entice me?"

"We thank you, my friend," Lucius replied, "for a fine meal and for the kindness you have shown two men you do not know. We will think your courtesy limitless indeed if you answer one question for us."

"Ask, sir, ask."

"I am sure you know Vesunna is not a town to which we usually travel, fine though it may be. But while we were in Massilia we heard a rumor so astounding, if true, that we hurried north to investigate."

"You have not asked your question," Eprius pointed out. There was a tinge of smugness in his voice, and Lucius did not miss it.

"It's true, then. You do have a copy of Sophokles' *Aleadai*?"

"And if I should?"

"May we see it?" For the first time Lucius displayed real eagerness. Even Marcus' dour features almost smiled.

"I keep it in my private suite. Wait here a moment, if you will." Taking a lamp to light his way, Eprius bustled out of the dining room, down the hall, and into his sanctum. The first thing he spied there was a stout walking stick. He seized it gratefully, for he had been a trifle lame since falling from a horse a couple of years before.

He shuffled rolls of papyrus, finding Book Three of the *Aeneid*, Book One of the *Iliad*, a bill from the sheep doctor Valerius Bassus, Book Seven of the *Aeneid*, and, at last, the work he sought. A copy of the *Aleadai* had been in his family for almost three hundred years. One of his ancestors had been a centurion in Lucius Mummius' army when that general had sacked Corinth, and had taken the original document as part of his loot. Finding that the ravages of time had made it almost illegible, Eprius' grandfather had had it recopied. It had been rare then. Eprius still recalled the old man chuckling as he described the surprise of the copyist who redid it. He could well understand booksellers coming a long way in search of such a work.

Lucius took the roll like a lover caressing his beloved. Yet he handled its spindles clumsily, almost, thought Eprius, as if he were not used to unrolling a book to read it. Don't be a fool, he told himself: A book dealer sees more books in a month than you will in ten years. The wine has simply made his fingers awkward. He certainly reads well enough—he isn't even moving his lips, which is more than you can claim for your reading.

A passage seemed to please the stranger, who began to read aloud. His accent was, if anything, stronger in Greek than in Latin, but he paid scrupulous heed to the complex meter of the tragedian's verse. Despite himself, Eprius was impressed.

Lucius read silently once more, faster and still faster, whipping through the scroll now with a speed that left Eprius blinking. A lamp went out, but Lucius never noticed. He read aloud again:

" 'Stop! It is enough to have been called father,
If indeed I begot you. But if not, the harm is less,
For what one believes carries more weight than the truth.' "

He turned in triumph to Marcus. "That clinches it!" he said. "This is one of the sections Stobaeus quotes, and this is the genuine *Aleadai*!"

"Of course it's genuine," Eprius said in aggrieved tones. These fellows had approached him. Did they now think he was trying to cheat them? And who was Stobaeus? The name was not familiar.

Neither of his guests was listening to him. They sprang from their couches, Lucius carefully put the *Aleadai* down first, and capered about in ridiculous fashion. They slapped each other's backs, swatted each other's palms, and clasped each other's wrists, all the while making interlocking rings of thumbs and forefingers. Barbarians after all, Eprius thought.

Little by little they calmed down. Marcus' glee subsided into wariness, but Lucius' face was lit by that special joy felt when something long sought was at last found. "This is indeed a treasure," he said. "What price would you put on it?"

Eprius smiled. "A curious sort of merchant you are, to let a prospective seller know how much you esteem his goods."

Marcus looked alarmed, but Lucius said smoothly, "Under

any other circumstances you would be right, but not today. You see, I have a standing offer for this work from a gentleman at Rome whose name I am sure you would recognize were I at liberty to disclose it. Quite a sizable offer, in fact.''

That made sense. Many senators and other officials were zealots in the pursuit of culture. Eprius nodded, and as he did, Marcus' watchful mask settled back over his face. ''How sizable an offer?'' Eprius asked.

''Large enough so that I can afford to offer you—hmm—seventy-five aurei and still turn a handsome profit.''

''Seventy-five aurei?'' Eprius tried hard not to show how startled he was. That was many, many times the going rate, even for a rare book. ''A princely sum! Why is your unnamed patron so anxious to acquire the *Aleadai*?''

''It is the only play of Sophokles he lacks.''

''Come now, do you take me for an utter idiot? I doubt if even the library of Alexandria could make that claim. My friend, I do not know what your game is, but find someone else to play the dupe.''

''Do you think we are trying to defraud you? This will persuade you otherwise.'' Lucius drew out a leather purse and tossed it to Eprius. He opened it. Ruddy in the lamplight, gold-pieces spilled into his palms. They clinked sweetly.

''Well, well,'' he said at last. ''I owe you an apology, good sirs, both for what I said and for what I thought. Let me take the roll to our local copyist, and you may have either the original or the copy within a week, just as you please. Aemilius Ruso is a friend of mine; I assure you he has a fine hand, and he is careful, too.''

''I am afraid that won't quite do, friend Eprius. A condition of the sale is absolute privacy, and it is a condition on which I have no discretion whatever. We must have this work now. Is the price inadequate? I can sweeten it a bit, I think.''

'' 'Money buys men friends and honors, too.' So says the poet in this very play. But money will not buy the only copy of the *Aleadai*, for it has been an heirloom in my family for eleven generations. I see no reason not to share it, but I will not give it up.''

''A hundred aurei?''

Eprius' face froze. He refilled the purse and threw it at Lucius' feet. ''You insult me, sir. I must bid you a good evening.'' He held out his hand for the play.

Reluctantly, Lucius began to give it back to him, but Marcus reached out and held him back. His smile and his heavily accented voice were deliberately offensive. "I think we keep this," he said.

"What? Get out, you rogues, you lashworthy rascals!" Despite graying hair and growing paunch, Eprius was still fairly quick on his feet. His walking stick thudded down on Marcus' shoulder. The *Aleadai* fell to the floor. "Get out, robbers, get out!" Eprius shouted.

"Bastard!" Marcus snarled. He ducked the next swing of the stick. Stars exploded inside Eprius' head as a solid right sent him spinning back over his couch to the floor. Somehow he held on to his stick. Too angry to fear facing two younger men, he surged forward, crying "Thieves! Thieves!" at the top of his lungs.

Marcus' hand snaked under his tunic. Eprius saw it emerge with a curiously shaped metal object. One of Marcus' fingers twitched on it, and Eprius heard the beginning of a barking roar. Something sledged him in the forehead, and he never saw or heard anything again.

Lou Muller, who in Vesunna called himself Lucius the book dealer, stared in horror at the crumpled corpse that had been Clodius Eprius. The gun shot still seemed to echo in the room. "Jesus H. Christ, Mark!" he said, and he was not speaking Latin at all. "The patrol—"

"Lou, you can take the patrol and stuff it right on up—" Mark Alvarez tucked away the pistol and rubbed his shoulder. "The old son of a bitch damn near broke my collarbone. What was I supposed to do, let him yell until all the neighbors came? Speaking of which—" He scooped up the *Aleadai* and trotted into the street. His partner followed, still expostulating.

"Oh, shut up and listen to me, will you, please?" Alvarez growled. "Why do we make a good team, anyway? It's not just because you're the fellow who knows his way around the second-century empire and I'm the one with the pull to get a timer. I've got the brains to get you out of trouble when you screw up, which you did. For one thing, even I know—you've told me often enough—Stobaeus isn't going to be born for a couple of hundred years yet. For another, and worse, that geezer was never going to sell us the play after you got his back up."

"But I offered him seventy-five aurei!"

"That didn't impress him, now did it? And it doesn't impress me, either. What're seventy-five aurei to us? Thirty credits for the gold (always thanking God for fusion-powered transmutation), the same for some authentic molds, and voilà! Aurei! Whereas we can—and we will—get easily fifty thousand credits for a lost play of Euripides."

"Sophokles," Muller corrected absently.

"Whatever. And as for the Time Patrol, why are we here in the boondocks instead of at the library of Alexandria? Why do we insist on so much privacy when we make our deals? Just so they won't run across us. And they won't. Erasing this fellow won't leave any clues downtime. We don't change anyone's ancestry, because his wife's been dead for years. We *did* check him out, you know." He glanced over his shoulder. "Did anyone see us leave?"

"I don't think so. But my God, Mark, a bullet—"

"What about it? Nobody here will ever figure out how he died. The local yokels'll call it the wrath of the gods or something, and then they'll forget it. All we have to do is sit tight for three weeks until the timer recharges, and then it's back to 2059 and lots of lovely money."

"I suppose so," Muller agreed slowly. "I kind of liked old Eprius, though."

"Liked him? Lou, he was just a stupid savage, like all the other stupid savages here and now. Look around. Is there anything here but filth and disease and superstition? You couldn't pay me to time if it weren't for xanthomycin. Come on, let's get back to the inn. Like the fellow said, my man, the play's the thing, and we've got it."

"What about the gold?"

"You want to go back and get it? Relax; it'll confuse the issue, anyway." They walked on in silence until they came to the inn. "What a dump," Alvarez sighed. "Oh, well, at least it has a bed, and I need sleep right now. We've had a busy night."

The sound of a fist crashing against his door hauled Gaius Tero from the depths of slumber. Stifling a curse, he climbed out of bed and threw on a mantle. His wife stirred and muttered drowsily. "It sounds like business, Calvina," he said. "Go back to sleep." A forlorn hope indeed, with his door being battered down. "I'm coming, I'm coming!" he shouted, and the pounding stopped. As tesserarius of Vesunna's seven-man detachment of vigiles, he wondered what had gone wrong now. Had someone knocked over Porcius' wine shop again, or had Herennius

Fundanus' firetrap of a stable finally decided to go up in smoke? Either way, the responsibility fell on him, for the vigiles were constabulary and fire brigade both.

He threw open the door. Just as he had expected, there stood the panting figure of Larcius Afer, who had the watch that night. "Well, what is it?" Tero demanded, adding hopefully, "I don't smell smoke." The siphon, which was the city's chief fire-fighting implement, was a pain in the fundament to deploy and use.

"No, sir," Afer agreed. He paused to wipe sweat from his face. The night was warm, and he had plainly run some distance. Tero, who was not the most patient of men, glared at him until he continued. "Clodius Eprius has been killed."

"What do you mean, killed? Has he been murdered?"

"Killed, sir," Afer repeated stolidly. "Kleandros is with the body now. He'll be able to tell you more than I can, I'm sure."

"Obviously," Tero snapped. Still, he was glad the Greek doctor would be there. They were old friends, though they argued constantly.

The tesserarius ducked back into his house for sandals, then accompanied his fellow vigil to the dead man's home. It was a couple of hours before dawn, and a waning crescent moon shed a wan light over the town. Nevertheless, it was dark enough to make Tero glad his companion carried a torch.

Eprius lived (or rather, had lived) at the opposite end of town from Tero's home. He and Afer tramped through Vesunna's central forum, silent save for the sound of their footsteps. At its very heart was the temple dedicated to the city's tutelary gods. Its huge circular cella made it currently the biggest structure in Vesunna, but the amphitheater being built not far away promised to dwarf it and everything else in the town.

Tero wondered idly what the old Petrocorii, the Celtic tribe that had founded Vesunna, would have thought of such an incredibly huge edifice. Magic, without a doubt: Anything was magical to someone who did not know how to do it.

His thoughts turned back to Eprius. Why would anyone want to kill the old fool? Tero knew him fairly well, and also knew he had not a single enemy in town. Had some footpad done away with him? Tero tried to pump Larcius Afer, but Afer shook his head, saying, "You'll have to see for yourself." With a small shock, the tesserarius realized his subordinate was frightened. That was very strange. Before settling in Vesunna, the two of them had served together on the Rhine, and Tero knew full well that the skirmishes there had thoroughly inured Afer to the sight of gore.

It seemed as if most of Eprius' neighbors were gathered outside his front door. Well, Tero thought, that's scarcely surprising. They all started talking at once when they saw him, raining questions down on his unprepared head. "I don't know a damned thing yet," he said, pushing his way through the crowd. "If you'll let me by, maybe I'll find out something."

Kleandros met him at the entrance. Tero liked the sharp-tongued physician. They had worked together before, and once or twice a month they would meet for wine, a friendly game of draughts, and much good talk. Still, the doctor's elegant slimness always made the squarely built Tero feel like a poorly trained dancing bear. Just by standing before him, Kleandros made him suddenly and acutely aware of his own uncombed hair, the patches and stains on his cloak, and the ragged bit of leather hanging from one sandal. As usual, he disguised his feelings with raillery. "Hello, quack," he said. "What do you have for me today?"

An opening like that would normally make Kleandros sputter and fume, but today he did not rise to the bait. Under the curling black ringlets he combed low on his forehead, his face was grim as he answered, "Hello, Tero. I'm glad to see you. You'd best come look for yourself." He was speaking Greek instead of Latin, something he did only when very upset. Tero began to worry in earnest.

The physician led him down the dark entry hall to the dining room. Someone had refilled and lit all the lamps there; the flames cast multiple dancing shadows. Three couches had been grouped together in one corner of the room. One was overturned, and the wall behind it bore a sinister stain. The vigil looked a question at Kleandros, who nodded. "Poor Eprius is behind the couch," Kleandros said. "Tell me what you make of him."

"Why me? You're the doctor," Tero said, but he walked around the couch.

Both on the Rhine and as a vigil in Vesunna, Gaius Tero had seen the results of more violent deaths than he liked to remember. Yet the corpse in this quiet room shook him in a way none of the others, however grisly, ever had. He was in the presence of the unknown, and little fingers of ice crawled up his back as he viewed its handiwork.

Eprius' body lay on its right side; its right hand still clutched a stick. Tero barely noticed, for his gaze was fixed in horrified fascination at the ruin that had been its head. There was a neat hole about the width of Tero's little finger over the left eye. A small stream of blood ran down over Eprius' face to join the pool beneath his head. Already flies were beginning to buzz about it.

Bad as that was, it was far from the worst. Whatever had drilled through Eprius' forehead had smashed out through the back of his head, tearing his skull open from the inside out. Much of the left rear quadrant of his head was a sickening soup of brain, pulverized bone, scalp, and hair. It was that which had stained the wall; blood cemented the gory fragments to the plaster.

The hobnails of Larcius Afer's sandals clicked on mosaic tiles as he came up. Dread was on his face; his fingers writhed in a sign to avert evil. "It was Jupiter's thunderbolt slew him," Afer said. "Two or three of the neighbors heard him cry out, and then the terrible roar of the thunderbolt itself—and not a cloud in the sky. His man Titus had the evening free, and when he got home, he found this."

Tero had never been one to fear the gods unduly, but he felt the little hairs on the back of his neck trying to rise as he listened to Afer. Surely nothing in his experience could have produced the ghastly wound he saw. To have Kleandros throw back his head and laugh was unbelievable. Tero wondered if the doctor had taken leave of his senses, and Afer stared at him indignantly.

"How many men has either of you known to be killed by the gods?" Kleandros demanded. "I've been a doctor for twenty years now, and I've never seen one yet."

"There's always a first time," Afer said.

"I suppose so," Kleandros conceded. "But Clodius Eprius? Good heavens, man, use your head for something more than a place to hang your hair. The worst thing Clodius Eprius ever did in his whole life was to drink so much wine that a couple of his friends had to carry him home. If the gods started killing everybody who did that, why, there wouldn't be five men left alive in the empire by this time tomorrow. No, I'm afraid that if the gods left it to Nero to kill himself and soldiers to do away with Caligula, they wouldn't have much interest in Clodius Eprius."

Afer was still far from convinced. "What did kill him, then?" he demanded.

"I haven't the slightest idea right now, but I intend to try to find out instead of moaning about Jupiter."

The physician's healthy skepticism gave Tero the heartening

he needed to shake off his superstitious fear and begin thinking like a vigil once more. He quizzed Eprius' neighbors, but learned nothing Afer had not already told him. There had been shouts and then a crash, but nobody had seen anyone fleeing Eprius' home. Titus proved even less informative than the neighbors. He was grief-stricken and more than a little hung over. When Eprius had given him the night off, he had not questioned his master, but headed straight for the wine and girls of Aspasia's lupanar, where he had roistered the night away. When he came back and found Eprius' body, he rushed out to get Kleandros, and that was all he knew. Tero left him sitting with his head in his hands and went back to the dining room.

"Learn anything?" Kleandros asked.

"Nothing. Maybe Jupiter did kill him."

Kleandros' one-word reply was rude in the extreme. Tero managed an answering grin, but it was strained. His eyes kept going back to the blood-spattered wall. In the middle of the spatters was a ragged hole. "What's this?" he said.

"How should I know?" Kleandros said. "Maybe Eprius used to keep a tapestry nailed there and was clumsy taking it down."

"I don't think so. I've been here more than once, and I don't remember any wall hangings." Tero took a knife from his belt and chipped away at the plaster, enlarging the hole. At its bottom was a little button of metal. No, not a button, a flower, for as Tero dug it out he saw that little petals of lead had peeled back from a brass base. Never in all his years had he seen anything like it. He tossed it up and down, up and down, whistling tunelessly.

"Give me that!" Kleandros said, grabbing it out of the air. He examined it curiously. "What is it, anyway?"

"I was hoping you could tell me."

"I couldn't begin to, any more than I could begin to tell you what killed Eprius."

Something almost clicked in Tero's mind, but the thought would not come clear. "Say that again!" he demanded.

Kleandros repeated.

He had it. "Look," he said, "where did we find this strange thing?"

"Is this your day to do Sokrates? Very well, best one, I'll play along. We found this strange thing in a hole in the wall."

"And what was all around the hole in the wall?"

"Clodius Eprius' brains."

"Very good. Bear with me one more time. How did Clodius Eprius' brains get there?"

"If I knew that, I wouldn't be standing here pretending to be Euthyphron," Kleandros snapped. "I've seen a fair number of dead men, but never one like this." He looked at the piece of metal in his hand, and his voice grew musing. "And I've never seen anything like this, either. You think the one had something to do with the other, don't you?"

Tero nodded. "If you could somehow make that thing go fast enough, it would make a respectable hole—it didn't make a bad hole in the wall, you know."

"So it didn't. It probably used to have a tip shaped more like an arrowhead, too; that lead is soft, and it would get smashed down when it hit. See what a brilliant pair we are. We only have one problem left: how in Zeus' holy name does the little hunk of metal get moving so fast?"

"Two problems," Tero corrected. "Once you get the little piece of metal moving, why do you use it to blow out Clodius Eprius' brains?"

"Robbery, perhaps."

"Maybe. Titus should know if anything is missing. Until he can figure that out, I think I'm going home and back to bed. Wait a moment; what's this?" Almost out of sight under one of the couches was a small leather bag. Tero stooped to pick it up and exclaimed in surprise. It was far heavier than he'd expected. He knew of only two things combining so much weight with so little bulk, lead and— He opened the bag, and aurei flooded into his hand.

"So much for robbery," Kleandros said, looking over his shoulder. The images of Trajan, Hadrian, and Antoninus Pius looked mutely back, answering none of the questions the two men would have put to them. The only time Tero had ever held so much gold at once was when he'd gotten his mustering-out bonus on leaving his legion.

He looked up to find Kleandros still studying the coins, a puzzled expression on his face. "What now?" Tero asked.

It was the doctor's turn to have trouble putting what he saw into words. "Does anything strike you as odd about this money?" he said at last.

"Only that no robber in his right mind would leave it lying under a couch."

"Apart from that, I mean. Is there anything wrong about the money itself?"

"An aureus is an aureus," Tero shrugged. "The only thing wrong with them is that I see them too seldom."

Kleandros grunted in exasperation. He plucked an aureus of Trajan from the pile in Tero's hand and held it under the vigil's nose, so close that Tero's eyes started to cross as he looked at it. Tero shrugged again; to him it seemed like any fresh-minted goldpiece. He said so.

"To me, too," Kleandros said. "And that is more than a little out of the ordinary, since Trajan has been dead—what is it? Thirty years now, I think. I was somewhere in my teens when he died, and I'm far from a youth now, worse luck. Yet here is one of his coins, bright and unworn. More than one, in fact," he said, picking out three or four more. They lay in his hand, alike as peas in a pod.

And that was wrong, too. No coin had the right to be identical to its fellows; they were stamped out by hand, one at a time. There were always differences, sometimes not small ones, in shape and thickness. Not here, though. Both men noticed it at the same time, but neither was as disturbed as he would have been a few hours before. "Everything we've found here is impossible," Tero said, "and this is just one little impossibility among the big ones."

It was growing light outside. Tero swore disgustedly. "I might as well stay up now. Care to join me for an early cup of wine?"

"Thank you, no. But if you don't mind, I'll cadge a meal from you and Calvina this evening. We can talk more then, and maybe squeeze some sense from all this."

"I doubt it, truth to tell. But I'll expect you a little past sunset."

"Fine."

Tero swallowed his last morsel of ham, wiped his fingers, and sighed loudly. "Why did I ever quit the legions?" he said. "I'd twenty times rather fight the German lurking in his gloomy forest than face another day like this one."

"That bad?" Kleandros asked between bites of apple.

"You should know—you started me on it." The vigil did not feel right about dropping all his troubles on his friend, but he had had a bellyful. The story of Clodius Eprius' death had raced through Vesunna, gaining fresh embellishments with each teller. It did not take long for people to be saying that all the Twelve Immortals had visited the town, destroying not only Eprius but his house and those of his neighbors, too. More than one panicky citizen hastily packed up his belongings and headed for the country.

None of that sat well with Vesunna's two duumvirs, and both of those worthies came down heavily on Tero, demanding that he find the murderer at once. "What will this do to the name of our city?" one said, though Tero knew that what he meant was: "I do not want my year in office recalled only for a gruesome killing." He promised to do his best, though he had few illusions about how good that was going to be.

Late in the afternoon Eprius' servant Titus came in with two more bits of depressing news: first, the gold the vigil had found was definitely not Eprius'; and, second, as far as he could tell after a quick search, nothing was missing from his late master's home. Larcius Afer was there to hear that, and his superior smile made Tero want to kick him in the teeth.

That he did tell Kleandros; it galled him too much for silence. The doctor pursed his lips and said judiciously, "If a fool laughed at me, I'd take it for a compliment."

"So would I, were I sure he was wrong. But what do we have here? A murder committed for no reason with an impossible weapon that produces an incredible wound. I think I'd rather believe in an angry god."

"Who leaves behind a purse full of counterfeit aurei? No god would do that."

"No person would, either," Tero pointed out. "And they aren't counterfeits, either; they're pure gold. Rusticius the jeweler checked them for me this afternoon."

"Did he? How interesting. Yes." Kleandros said nothing more, but a look of satisfaction spread across his face.

"You know something!" Tero accused.

"I have some ideas, at any rate. Did I ever tell you that I studied medicine under Diodoros of Alexandria?"

There were times when Tero found his friend's evasiveness maddening. This, it seemed, was going to be one of them. "No," he said, "you never did. Why do you see fit to impart this bit of information to me now?"

"I am coming to that, never fear. You see, Diodoros himself was learning his skill in Alexandria when Heron son of Ktesibios was at the height of his fame."

Tero had to admit he did not know the name.

"Do you not? A pity; he was a remarkable man, probably one of the finest machine makers the world has ever seen. Diodoros was fascinated by his contraptions, and he never tired of talking about them. Really amazing things: a device for dispensing sacramental water that worked only when a copper was inserted, a trumpet made to sound by opening a nearby door, bronze animals that moved like live ones, and many other things.''

"He sounds like a sorcerer."

"No, he was an artificer and nothing more. One of the things he made, not really more than a toy, was what he called an aeolipile."

"All of this must lead somewhere, I suppose. What might an aeolipile be?"

Kleandros explained: a water-filled cauldron was fitted atop with a hollow ball mounted on a hollow tube. Directly opposite the tube's entrance into the ball was a pivot, which was attached to the cauldron's lid. The ball itself was fitted with bent nozzles; when a fire was lit beneath the cauldron, steam traveled up the hollow tube and out through the nozzles, making the ball spin merrily. "Do you see what I'm getting at?" the doctor asked. "In this device the force of the steam escaped continuously, but if some way were found to block it up for a time and then release it all at once, it could give a little metal pellet a very strong push indeed."

Tero took another pull at his wine while he thought. The idea had more than a little appeal, for it gave a rational picture of how the killing might have taken place. Still . . . "A cauldron, you say. How big a cauldron?"

"I have no idea. I've never seen the machine in action myself, only heard Diodoros talk about it."

"Somehow I find it hard to imagine Clodius Eprius letting anyone set up a cauldron in the middle of the room and then aim a little ball at him. And whoever would be using it would have to wait for his water to boil before it would go off, wouldn't he?"

"I suppose so," Kleandros said sulkily.

"Not only that, anyone hauling a cauldron through the middle of Vesunna would get himself noticed. Even if I don't know what killed Eprius, I can tell you a couple of things about it: you can use it right away, and you can carry it around without having it seen. I'm afraid your whatever-you-call-it misses the mark both ways." Seeing his friend's hurt expression, Tero went on. "If you could make one big enough, it might make a good ballista, though." I wonder why our generals never thought of anything like that, he thought, a little surprised at himself.

"Your logic is convincing," Kleandros said, adding, "Damn it!" a moment later.

"Let's give up on the weapon for now," Tero suggested. "It matters less than the person who used it. If we had some way of knowing who he was, we might catch him, thunderbolt thrower or no."

"A good point," Kleandros said. "Whoever he was, we can be fairly sure he was from outside the empire."

"Why do you say that?"

"We know of no weapons to fit the bill within our land, do we? Also, why would a citizen need to carry coins that weren't genuine but would pass one by one? If they are true gold, that only makes the argument stronger."

"A spy!"

"You may have something there. But who would want to spy on Vesunna, and why?"

Tero opened his mouth for a reply, then realized he did not have a good one. No one had ever seen a German in the town, and Parthia was at the other end of the world. Besides, he was sure neither the Germans nor the Parthians had weapons that could blow large holes in men's heads. If they did, they would have used them on Roman soldiers long before. In fact, anyone who had such a weapon could master the world, and surely would have done so by now. It made no sense at all.

What other foreigners were there? There were nomads south of Roman Africa, and others east of the Germans. There was an island off the coast of Britain, but it was full of savages, too. There was— "Men from Atlantis, perhaps?"

"My dear Tero, I would be the last to deny Platon was a man of godlike intellect, and the *Timaios* has always been one of my favorite dialogues. Still, as far as I can see, in it he invents Atlantis in order to portray an idealized way of life. And, as Aristoteles said, 'He who invented it destroyed it,' for, if you'll remember, Platon says it sank beneath the waves thousands of years ago."

"That's a pity, because I don't see how a spy could come from any country we know well." He explained his reasoning to the doctor, who nodded.

"Where does that leave us?" Kleandros asked.

"Right where we started—ramming our heads into a stone wall. A plague on it for now. Did you bring your *Iliad* with you? I'd sooner bend my brain around that for a while." Slowly but surely, over the course of years, Kleandros was teaching the vigil to read Greek; most cultured citizens of the empire were bilingual. Tero spoke Greek fairly well: though more elastic, its basic structure was much like that of Latin, and there were more than a few similarities of vocabulary as well. But Homer was something else. His hexameters were splendid and his picture of the heroes of the Trojan War supremely human, but his antique vocabulary and archaic grammatical forms often made Tero want to tear his hair.

Line by line they fought their way through the opening of Book Sixteen, where Patroklos begs Akhilleus to let him borrow his armor and drive the Trojans from the ships of the Akhaians, which they had begun to burn. Akhilleus, hesitant at first, assented when he saw the fire going up, and

"Patroklos armed himself with shining bronze."

"I hate these funny-looking datives," Tero said, but went on:

"First he put well-made greaves on his calves;
They had guards of silver on them.
Then on his breast he put the cleverly made shining
Corselet of Aiakos' swift-footed scion.
He slung his silver-nailed bronze sword from his shoulder,
And after it a great stout shield as well."

"Bronze, bronze, bronze!" Tero said. "Bronze this, bronze that. One cohort of my legion could have gone through all the heroes of the Trojan War, Akhaians and Trojans both, in about an hour and a half. Ten years? No wonder it took them ten years with tactics like theirs. They run at each other, throw their spears, and then start looking for rocks to fling. And nobody cares about the fellow next to him until the poor sod gets a spear in the groin. Then they fight over his armor, not him."

"You have the soul of a turnip," Kleandros said; he had heard Tero's complaints many times. "That we are better at killing people than they were in Akhilleus' day is no cause for celebrating."

"Nevertheless, I wonder what shining-helmed Hektor would have thought if one morning he woke up and found my old legion around his walls instead of those Akhaian cattle thieves. Can you imagine it? Earthworks, siege towers, catapults, rams. He couldn't have held that town three days against us. I think I'd have paid money to see his face."

"He probably would have been like Afer, convinced all the gods were angry at him."

"And yet we would just have been men with skills he didn't have, not demigods or heroes. It's very strange." Tero returned to his home and plowed on doggedly even after his attention began to wander. The truth was that he did not want to think about Eprius' corpse, though he suspected he would see it in his dreams for years to come. Crimes were hard enough to solve at any time; but this one had an impossible wound, an unknown but highly potent weapon, a good many cleverly counterfeited aurei, and, to make matters worse, no visible motive. "What verb does *lelalesthô* come from?" he asked Kleandros.

The knock on Tero's door a few days later was so tentative, he was only half-sure he'd heard it. Nonetheless, he went to the door and opened it to find Eprius' valet Titus waiting for him.

"Come in, come in," the vigil said. "What can I do for you?"

"Thank you very much," the servant replied. His Latin, though grammatically perfect, still carried a faint guttural touch of his native Syriac. When comfortably seated, he went on, "I've had the time now to go through my late master's effects more thoroughly, and I've found something I think you ought to know."

"Ah?" Tero leaned forward. "Tell me more . . ."

The two time travelers walked through the center of Vesunna. The tune Alvarez was whistling would not be written for another nineteen centuries, but he couldn't have cared less. In less than a day the timer would recharge itself and he'd return to the era where he belonged, a richer man. He looked about. He'd had enough of painted marble statues littering the city square, enough of the stink of ordure and the slimy feel of it under his feet, enough of drafty clothes, bad syrupy wine, and a language he barely understood! And he'd had enough of bedbugs, too; he scratched under his mantle. His fingers brushed the leather of his shoulder holster, and he smiled a little. The weight of the revolver was a comfort, like a paid-up insurance policy.

Lou was silent beside him, watching the tide of humanity ebb and flow. Today was market day, and the square was packed. To Alvarez the merchants and their customers were so many gabbling barbarians, but for some incomprehensible reason Lou chose to regard them as people. Most of the time this inspired nothing but disdain in Alvarez, but now his all-encompassing good humor even included his partner. Lou might be a weakling, but he knew his stuff. He had tracked that play of Sophokles from nothing but the vaguest rumor, and now it looked as if there would be an unexpected bonus in this squalid town. Who would have thought a copy of Hieronymos of Kardia's lost history would have ended up here? It would be worth plenty: not as much as the Sophokles, perhaps, but still a nice piece of change.

Whoever this fellow was, this Kleandros Harmodios' son who owned the Hieronymos, he wanted enough for it. Aemilius Ruso, the local scribe, had offered what was a good price by here-and-now standards, and Kleandros had turned him down flat. Alvarez chuckled. He and Lou would have no trouble on that score.

Despite directions, they got lost more than once searching out Kleandros' house. The streets of Vesunna were winding alleyways, and one blank house front looked very much like another; to the locals, display belonged to the interior of a house, not the outside. Alvarez was beginning to mutter to himself when Lou stopped at a door no different from half a dozen others nearby and said, "This is it, I think."

"How can you tell?" Alvarez asked, but Lou was already knocking. The door swung open, revealing a spare but handsome man wearing a white chlamys and sandals with leather lacings reaching almost to his knees. It was Greek dress, Alvarez realized: this must be Kleandros himself. Good. If Kleandros was answering the door himself, that must mean he was taking seriously the privacy instructions he'd gotten. Alvarez looked him over. In his own time he would have guessed Kleandros to be in his mid-fifties, but the wear and tear was harder here, so he was probably younger. Still, if he was a doctor, he might take better care of himself than most of the locals. Maybe not, though—some of the things the second century judged medicinal were amazing.

"Come in, come in," Kleandros was saying. "You must be the gentlemen who inquired about my history." Lou admitted it. "Very good. Will you join me in the courtyard? The day is far too fine to be cooped up inside without need."

Kleandros was not as rich a man as Clodius Eprius, who had used the income of his country estate to beautify his home in Vesunna. Fewer rooms opened onto this courtyard, and it was bare of the elegant statuary that had been Eprius' delight. There was a fountain at the center of the courtyard, though, and flowers of many kinds and colors grew in neatly trimmed rows, bright against drab plaster and pale stone.

The doctor seated his guests on a limestone bench and offered them wine. When they accepted, he served it to them in cups of the same red-glazed ware Eprius had used. It was decorated with embossed reliefs and called terra sigillata, or sealing-wax ware, after the color of the glaze. The stuff was everywhere in Gaul; it was made locally and had nearly driven the more expensive Italian pottery from the market.

Putting down his cup, Kleandros said, "Now to business. I am not eager to sell the history of Hieronymos, but I have a need for ready cash. What will you give me for it?"

A long haggle ensued. Lou had learned from his mistake with Eprius not to show too much eagerness, and as for Kleandros, he might have been arguing with some farmer over the price of a sack of beans. Alvarez was stifling yawns when they finally agreed that twenty-eight aurei did not seem too unreasonable. Lou was not yawning; he was sweating.

"Whew!" Kleandros said. "You drive a hard bargain, my friend. I suppose you would like to inspect the work now?"

"I would," Lou agreed.

"Wait a moment, then, and I will fetch it." Kleandros disappeared into the house. While he was gone, Lou counted out the requisite number of gold coins and made a little pile of them.

Kleandros' face lit up when he returned with the scrolls and saw the money. "Splendid!" he said, scooping up the aurei. "I'm glad you brought what money you needed with you; waiting is hard on the nerves." He studied the coins intently, so much so that Alvarez began to worry. Perhaps noticing the time traveler watching him, the doctor grinned and said, "It's amazing how much more handsome an emperor's face is when you see it on gold."

"True," Mark said, and he grinned back. For the first time he got a hint of his partner's point of view; Kleandros didn't seem like a bad fellow, for a savage. The doctor idly flipped a goldpiece in the air once, twice, three times.

Lou had been reading the work Kleandros had given him. At first his grin had been as wide as the Greek's, but little by little it fell from his face, replaced first by puzzlement and then by anger. "What are you trying to palm off on us?" he demanded of Kleandros. "This is not Hieronymos of Kardia's history; it's the work of Diodoros of Sicily, who borrowed from him."

Alvarez's newfound liking for Kleandros flickered and blew out. Muscles bunched in his arms as he rose. If this downtime dimbulb was trying to cheat them, he was going to remember it for the rest of his life.

A crash behind him made him whirl, hand darting for his gun. Half a dozen fully armored Romans had burst from their concealment within Kleandros' house and were rushing him, swords drawn, faces grim over their shields. Lou screamed in terror and started to run. Barking an oath, Alvarez snapped off a quick shot. It went wild. Before he could fire again, Kleandros seized his arm and dragged it down. Desperate now, Alvarez smashed at the doctor with his left fist. Kleandros fell with a groan, but by then the soldiers were on the time traveler. A sword knocked the gun from his hand. It flew spinning into the flowers. Punching and kicking to the last, he was borne to the ground and trussed like a hog on the way to the slaughterhouse. Lou Muller got the same treatment; a magnificent flying tackle had brought him down just inside Kleandros' front door.

One of Alvarez's captors, a broad-shouldered, grizzled fellow of about fifty, knelt over him, saying, "I arrest you for the murder of Clodius Eprius." Alvarez spat at him; in return he got a buffet that loosened his teeth. "Eprius was a friend of mine," the Roman said.

"You were right, Tero," another trooper said. "They are human, after all."

"I told you so, Afer. You owe me two aurei." Tero turned to Kleandros and helped him to his feet. A dark bruise was forming under the doctor's left eye, but he did not seem badly hurt.

The byplay went on without much attention from Alvarez. He was in pain and sunk deep in despair; the timer would automatically return to 2059 twenty-four hours after it recharged unless someone reset it, and it did not look as if he or Lou would have the chance. He was stuck here and now forever. No, revise that—his future here looked limited, too.

He realized Tero was saying something to him, but did not take the trouble to understand. Tero kicked him in the ribs, not unkindly, and repeated: "Tell me, barbarian, how many years lie between our time and yours?"

Alvarez felt his world coming apart. Somehow these savages had managed to seize him, and now they knew his secret as well. He strained wildly at his bonds, trying to break free, but one thing the Romans plainly knew was how to tie firm knots. "You are the barbarians!" he shouted.

Tero and Kleandros bent over him, faces intent. "It's true, then?" the Greek whispered. "You do come from the future?"

Utterly beaten, Alvarez said, "Yes."

"I thought so," Tero breathed. "Quite by accident, it occurred to me how much more we know now than the heroes of the Trojan Wars. That set me thinking—how much more still would the men who come after us learn? Surely they would have powers we do not: terrible weapons, who knows what? Simpler things, too: the ability to make one coin just like another, for instance. How do you do that, anyway?"

"Molds," Alvarez said dully.

"Ah? Interesting. It's neither here nor there, though. Even after I got my notion, I still had to figure out why the men of the future would want anything from *us* in the first place. That stymied me for a long, long time. By my own logic, you had to have everything we do, and more besides. And then Eprius' body servant found that one of his master's books was missing, a rare one."

"Rare?" Kleandros interjected. "If I had known Eprius had a copy of the *Aleadai*, I might have killed him myself."

"You see?" Tero said. "It's so easy for a book to be lost forever if few copies are made of it. Works like the *Aleadai* are valuable now—how much more would they be worth in some future time if between now and then they'd been lost altogether? A great deal, I have no doubt. Enough to steal for, enough to kill for? Once we knew the sort of thing you were after, it was easy enough to set a trap, and you walked right into it."

Kleandros added, "My apologies for not using an authentic copy of Hieronymos of Kardia, but, you see, no one in town owns one."

This was all a bad dream, Alvarez though. It could not be happening. To be caught was bad enough, but then to be lectured by these stupid barbarians . . .

He must have said that aloud, for Tero's lips tightened. He realized the English phrase was close enough to the Latin from which it had come to let the Romans understand him.

"Us, barbarians?" Tero said. "On the contrary. What are the marks of the barbarian? Surely one is acting without thinking ahead to see what results might come of what you do. Did you do that when you used your thunder weapon? Hardly. And because we were ignorant of your device, did you think us dolts?

You were stupid to reveal it to us at all. No, man from another time, if either of us deserves to be called a barbarian, it is you.''

He stood and turned to his men. ''Take them away,'' he said.

One of the most enjoyable games in science fiction is to imagine how history would have changed if one of its great figures had taken a different path: if Alexander the Great hadn't died young, if Napoleon had; if Julius Caesar hadn't been assassinated, if Franklin D. Roosevelt had. But secular leaders are not the only people who shape history. Here is an example of another sort of figure not performing as he did in the world we know.

DEPARTURES

THE MONKS AT IR-RUHAIYEH DID NOT TALK CA-sually among themselves. They were not hermits; those who wanted to be pillar sitters like the two Saints Simeon went off into the Syrian desert by themselves and did not join monastic communities. Still, the Rule of Saint Basil enjoined silence through much of the day.

Despite the Cappadocian Father's Rule, though, a whispered word ran through the monastery regardless of the canonical hour: "The Persians. The Persians are marching toward Ir-Ruhaiyeh."

The abbot, Isaac, heard the whispers, though the monks had to shout when they spoke to him. Isaac was past seventy, with a white beard that nearly reached his waist. But he had been abbot here for more than twenty years and had been a simple monk for thirty years before that. He knew what his charges thought almost before they thought it.

Isaac turned to the man he hoped would one day succeed him. "It will be very bad this time, John. I feel it."

The prior shrugged. "It will be as God wills, Father Abbot." He was half the abbot's age, round-faced, and always smiling. What from other men might have seemed prophecy of doom came from his lips as a prediction of good fortune.

Isaac was not cheered, not this time. "I wonder if God does not mean this to be the end for us Christians."

"The Persians have come to Ir-Ruhaiyeh before," John said stoutly. "They raided, they moved on. When their campaigns were through, they went back to their homeland once more, and life resumed."

51

"I was here," Isaac agreed. "They came in the younger Justin's reign, and Tiberius', and Maurice's. As you say, they left again soon enough or were driven off. But since this beast of a Phokas murdered his way to the throne of the Roman Empire—"

"Shh." John looked around. Only one monk was nearby, on his hands and knees in the herb garden. "One never knows who may be listening."

"I am too old to fear spies overmuch, John," the abbot said, chuckling. At that moment the monk in the herb garden sat back on his haunches so he could wipe sweat from his strong, swarthy face with the sleeve of his robe. Isaac chuckled again. "And can you seriously imagine *him* betraying us?"

John laughed, too. "That one? No, you have me there. Ever since he came to us, he's thought of nothing but his hymns."

"Nor can I blame him, for they are a gift from God," Isaac said. "Truly he must be inspired to sing the Lord's praises so sweetly when he knew not a word of Greek before he fled his horrid paganism to become a Christian and a monk. Romanos the Melodist was a convert, too, they say—born a Jew."

"Some of our brother's hymns are a match for his, I think," John said. "Perhaps they love Christ the more for first discovering Him with the full faculties of grown men."

"It could be so," Isaac said thoughtfully. Then, as the monk in the garden resumed his work, the abbot came back to his worries. "When I was younger, we all knew the Persians were harriers, not conquerors. Sooner or later our soldiers would drive them back. This time I think they are come to stay."

John's sunny face was not well adapted to showing concern, but it did now. "You may be right, Father Abbot. Since the general Narses rebelled against Phokas, since Germanos attacked Narses, since the Persians beat Germanos and Leontios—"

"Since Phokas broke his own brother's pledge of safe conduct for Narses and burned him alive, since Germanos was forced to become a monk for losing to the Persians—" Isaac took up the melancholy tale of Roman troubles. "Our armies now are a rabble, those which have not fled. Who will, who can, make King Khosroes' soldiers leave the empire now?"

John looked this way and that again and lowered his voice so that Isaac had to lean close to hear him at all. "Perhaps it would be as well if they did stay. I wonder," he went on wistfully, "if the young man with them truly is Maurice's son Theodosios. Even with Persian backing, he would be better than Phokas.''

"No, John.'' The abbot shook his head in grim certainty. "I am sure Theodosios is dead; he was with his father when Phokas overthrew them. And while the new emperor has many failings, no one can doubt his talent as a butcher.''

"True enough.'' John sighed. "Well, then, Father Abbot, why *not* welcome the Persians as liberators from the tyrant?''

"Because of what I heard from a traveler out of the east who took shelter with us last night. He was from a village near Daras, where the Persians have now decided how they will govern the lands they have taken from the empire. He told me they were beginning to make the Christians thereabouts become Nestorians.''

"I had not heard that, Father Abbot,'' John said, adding a moment later, "Filthy heresy!''

"Not to the Persians. They exalt Nestorians above all other Christians, trusting their loyalty because we who hold to the right belief have persecuted them so they may no longer live within the empire.'' Isaac sadly shook his head. "All too often, that trust has proved justified.''

"What shall we do, then?'' John asked. "I will not abandon the faith, but in truth I would sooner serve the Lord as a living monk than as a martyr, though His will be done, of course.'' He crossed himself.

So did Isaac. His eyes twinkled. "I do not blame you, my son. I have lived most of my life, so I am ready to see God and His Son face to face whenever He desires, but I understand how younger men might hesitate. Some, to save their lives, might even bow to heresy and forfeit their souls. I think, therefore, that we should abandon Ir-Ruhaiyeh so no one will have to face this bitter choice.''

John whistled softly. "As bad as that?'' His glance slid to the monk in the garden, who had looked up but went back to his weeding when the prior's eye fell on him.

"As bad as that,'' Isaac echoed. "I need you to begin drawing up plans for our withdrawal. I want us to leave no later than a week from today.''

"So soon, Father Abbot? As you wish, of course; you know you have my obedience. Shall I arrange for our travel west to Antioch or south to Damascus? I presume you will want us safe behind a city's walls.''

"Yes, but neither of those,'' the abbot said. John stared at him in surprise. Isaac went on. "I doubt Damascus is strong enough to stand against the storm that is rising. And Antioch—Antioch is all in commotion since the Jews rose and murdered the patriarch, may God smile upon him. Besides, the Persians are sure to make for it, and it can fall. I was a tiny boy the last time it did; the sack, I have heard, was ghastly. I would not want us caught up in another such."

"What then, Father Abbot?" John asked, puzzled now.

"Ready us to travel to Constantinople, John. If Constantinople falls to the Persians, surely it could only portend the coming of the Antichrist and the last days of the world. Even that may come. I find it an evil time to be old."

"Constantinople. The city." John's voice held awe and longing. From the Pillars of Herakles to Mesopotamia, from the Danube to Nubia, all through the Roman Empire, Constantinople was *the* city. Every man dreamed of seeing it before he died. The prior ran fingers through his beard. His eyes went distant as he began to think of what the monks would need to do to get there. He never noticed Isaac walking away.

What did call him back to his surroundings was the monk leaving the herb garden a few minutes later. Had the fellow simply passed by, John would have paid him no mind. But he was humming as he walked, which disturbed the prior's thoughts.

"Silence, Brother," John said reprovingly.

The monk dipped his head in apology. Before he had gone a dozen paces, he was humming again. John rolled his eyes in rueful despair. Taking the music from that one was the next thing to impossible, for it came upon him so strongly that it possessed him without his even realizing it.

Had he not produced such lovely hymns, the prior thought, people might have used the word "possessed" in a different sense. But no demon, surely, could bring forth glowing praise of the Trinity and the Archangel Gabriel.

John dismissed the monk from his mind. He had many more important things to worry about.

"A nomisma for that donkey, that piece of crow bait?" The monk clapped a hand to his tonsured pate in theatrical disbelief. "A goldpiece? You bandit, may Satan lash you with sheets of fire and molten brass for your effrontery! Better you should ask for thirty pieces of silver. That would only be six more, and would show you for the Judas you are!"

After fierce haggling the monk ended up buying the donkey for ten silver pieces, less than half the first asking price. As the trader put the jingling miliaresia into his pouch, he nodded respectfully to his recent opponent. "Holy sir, you are the finest bargainer I ever met at a monastery."

"I thank you." Suddenly the monk was shy, not the fierce dickerer he had seemed a moment before. Looking down to the ground, he went on. "I was a merchant once myself, years ago, before I found the truth of Christ."

The trader laughed. "I might have known." He gave the monk a shrewd once-over. "From out of the south, I'd guess, by your accent."

"Just so." The monk's eyes were distant, remembering. "I was making my first run up to Damascus. I heard a monk preaching in the marketplace. I was not even a Christian at the time, but it seemed to me that I heard within me the voice of the Archangel Gabriel saying, 'Follow!' And follow I did, and follow I have, all these years since. My caravan went back without me."

"A strong call to the faith indeed, holy sir," the trader said, crossing himself. "But if you ever wish to return to the world, seek me out. For a reasonable share of the profits I know you will bring in, I would be happy to stake you as a merchant once again."

The monk smiled, teeth white against tanned, dark skin and gray-streaked black beard. "Thank you, but I am content and more than content with my life as it is. *Inshallah*—" He laughed at himself. "Here I've been working all these years to use only Greek, and recalling what I once was makes me forget myself so easily. *Theou thelontos*, I should have said—God willing—I would have spent all my days here at Ir-Ruhaiyeh. But that is not to be."

"No." The trader looked east. No smoke darkened the horizon there, not yet, but both men could see it in their mind's eyes. "I may find a new home for myself, as well."

"God grant you good fortune," the monk said.

"And you, holy sir. If I have more beasts to sell, be sure I shall look for a time when you are busy elsewhere."

"Spoken like a true thief," the monk said. They both laughed. The monk led the donkey away toward the stables. They were more crowded now than at any other time he could recall, with horses, camels, and donkeys. Some the monks would ride; others would carry supplies and the monastery's books and other holy gear.

Words and music filled the monk's mind as he walked toward the refectory. By now the words came more often in Greek than in his native tongue, but this time, perhaps because his haggle with the merchant had cast his memory back to the distant pagan days he did not often think of anymore, the idea washed over him in the full guttural splendor of his birth speech.

Sometimes he crafted a hymn line by line, word by word, fighting against stubborn ink and papyrus until the song had the shape he wanted. He was proud of the songs he shaped that way. They were truly his.

Sometimes, though, it was as if he saw the entire shape of a hymn complete at once. Then the praises to the Lord seemed almost to write themselves, his pen racing over the page not as an instrument of his own intelligence but rather as a channel through which God spoke for Himself. Those hymns were the ones for which the monk had gained a reputation that reached beyond Syria. He often wondered if he had earned it. God deserved more credit than he did. But then, he would remind himself, that was true in all things.

This idea he had now was of the second sort, a flash of inspiration so blinding that he staggered and almost fell, unable to bear up under its impact. For a moment he did not even know—or care—where he was. The words, the glorious words reverberating in his mind, were all that mattered.

And yet, because the inspiration came to him in his native language, his intelligence was also engaged. How could he put his thoughts into words his fellows here and folk all through the empire would understand? He knew he had to; God would never forgive him, nor he forgive himself, if he failed here.

The refectory was dark but, since it was filled with summer air and sweating monks, not cool. The monk took a loaf and a cup of wine. He ate without tasting what he had eaten. His comrades spoke to him; he did not answer. His gaze was inward, fixed on something he alone could see.

Suddenly he rose and burst out, "There is no God but the Lord, and Christ is His Son!" That said what he wanted to say, and said it in good Greek, though without the almost hypnotic intensity the phrase had in his native tongue. Still, he saw, it served his purpose: several monks glanced his way, and a couple, having heard only the bare beginning of the song, made the sacred sign of the cross.

He noticed the others in the refectory only peripherally. Only later would he realize he had heard John say in awe to the abbot Isaac, "The holy fit has taken him again."

For the prior was right. The fit had taken him, and more strongly than ever before. Words poured from somewhere deep within him: "He is the Kindly, the Merciful, Who gave His only-begotten Son that man might live. The Lord will abide forever in glory, Father, Son, and Holy Spirit. Which of the Lord's blessings would you deny?"

On and on he sang. The tiny part of him not engaged in singing thanked God for granting him what almost amounted to the gift of tongues. His spoken Greek, especially when dealing with things of the world, was sometimes halting. Yet again and again now he found the words he needed. That had happened before, but never like this.

"There is no God but the Lord, and Christ is His Son!" Ending as he had begun, the monk paused, looking around for a moment as he slowly came back to himself. His knees failed him; he sank back to his bench. He felt drained but triumphant. The only comparison he knew was most unmonastic: he felt as he had just after a woman.

He rarely thought these days of the wife he had left with all else when he had given over the world for the monastery. He wondered if she still lived; she was a good deal older than he. With very human vanity, he wondered if she ever thought of him. With his own characteristic honesty, he doubted it. The marriage had been arranged. It was not her first. Probably it would not have been her last, either.

The touch of the prior's hand on his arm brought him fully back to the confines he had chosen as his own. "That was most marvelous," John said. "I count myself fortunate to have heard it."

The monk dipped his head in humility. "You are too kind, reverend sir."

"I do not think so." John hesitated, and went on anxiously, "I trust—I pray—you will be able to write down your words so those not lucky enough to have been here on this day will yet be able to hear the truth and grandeur of which you sang."

The monk laughed—again, he thought, as he might have at any small thing after going in unto his wife. "Have no fear there, reverend sir. The words I recited are inscribed upon my heart. They shall not flee me."

"May it be as you have said," the prior told him.

John did not, however, sound as if he believed him. To set his mind at ease, the monk sang the new hymn again, this time not in the hot flush of creation but as one who brought out an old and long-familiar song. "You see, reverend sir," he said when he was done. "What the Lord, the Most Bountiful One, has granted me shall not be lost."

"Now I have been present at two miracles," John said, crossing himself. "Hearing your song the first time and then, a moment later, again with not one single change, not a different word, that I noticed."

With his mind the monk felt of the texture of his creation, comparing his first and second renditions of the hymn. "There were none," he said confidently. "I would take oath to it before Christ the Judge of all."

"No need on my account. I believe you," John said. "Still, even miracles, I suppose, may be stretched too far. Therefore I charge you, go at once to the writing chamber and do not leave it until you have written out three copies of your hymn. Keep one yourself, give me one, and give the third to any other one of the brethren you choose."

For the first time in his life, the monk dared protest his prior's command. "But reverend sir, I should not waste so much time away from the work of preparing for our journey to the city."

"One monk's absence will not matter so much there," John said firmly. "Do as I tell you, and we will bring to Constantinople not only our humble selves but also a treasure for all time in your words of wisdom and prayer. That is why I bade you write out three copies: if the worst befall and the Persians overrun us, which God prevent, then one might still reach the city. And one must, I think. These words are too important to be lost."

The monk yielded. "It shall be as you say, then. I had not thought on why you wanted me to write out the hymn three times—I thought it was only for the sake of Father, Son, and Holy Spirit."

To his amazement, John bowed to him. "You are most saintly, thinking only of the world of the spirit. As prior, though, I have also to reckon with this world's concerns."

"You give me too much credit," the monk protested. Under his swarthy skin he felt himself grow hot, remembering how moments ago he had been thinking, not of the world to come, but of his wife.

"Your modesty becomes you," was all John said to that. The

prior bowed again, discomfiting the monk even more. "Now I hope you will excuse me, for I have my work to see to. Three fair copies, mind, I expect from you. In that matter I will accept no excuses."

The monk made one last try. "Please, reverend sir, let me labor, too, and write later, when our safety is assured. Surely I will earn the hatred of my brethren for being idle while they put all their strength into readying us to go."

"You are not idle," John said sternly. "You are in the service of the Lord, as are they. You are acting under my orders, as are they. Only vicious fools could resent that, and vicious fools will have to deal with *me*." The prior set his jaw.

"They will do as you say, reverend sir," the monk said—who could dare disobey John? "But they will do it from obedience alone, not from conviction, if you take my meaning."

"I know what you mean," the prior said, chuckling. "How could I be who I am and not know it? Here, though, you are wrong. Not a man who was in the refectory and heard your hymn will bear you any but the kindest of wills. All will be as eager as I am to have it preserved."

"I hope you are right," the monk said.

John laughed again. "How could I be wrong? After all, I am the prior." He thumped the monk on the back. "Now go on and prove it for yourself."

With more than a little trepidation, the monk did as he had been ordered. He was surprised to find John right. Though he sat alone in the writing chamber, from time to time monks bustling past paused a moment to lean their burdens against the wall, stick their heads in the doorway, and encourage him to get his song down on papyrus.

The words flowed effortlessly from his pen—as he'd told the prior, they truly were inscribed upon his heart. He took that to be another sign of God's speaking directly through him with this hymn. He sometimes found writing a barrier; the words that sang in his mind seemed much less fine when written out. And other times his pen could not find the right words at all, and what came from it was not the fine thing he had conceived but only a clumsy makeshift.

Not today. When he finished the first copy, the crucial one, he compared it to what he had sung. It was as if he had seen the words of the hymn before him as he wrote. Here they were again, as pure and perfect as when the Lord had given them to him. He bent his head in thanksgiving.

He took more papyrus and began the second and third copies. Usually when he was copying, his eyes went back to the original every few words. Now he hardly glanced at it. He had no need, not today.

He was no fine calligrapher, but his hand was clear enough. After so long at Ir-Ruhaiyeh, writing from left to right had even begun to seem natural to him.

The bell rang for evening prayer. The monk noticed, startled, that the light streaming in through the window was ruddy with sunset. Had his task taken any longer, he would have had to light a lamp to finish it. He rubbed his eyes, felt for the first time how tired they were. Maybe he should have lit a lamp. He did not worry about it. Even if the light of the world was failing, the light of the Holy Spirit had sustained him while he wrote.

He took the three copies of the hymn with him as he headed for the chapel. John, he knew, would be pleased that he had finished writing in a single afternoon. So much still remained to be done before the monks left Ir-Ruhaiyeh.

Donkeys brayed. Horses snorted. Camels groaned, as if in torment. Isaac knew they would have done the same had their loads been a single straw rather than the bales and panniers lashed to their backs. The abbot stood outside the monastery gates, watching monks and beasts of burden file past.

The leave-taking made him feel the full weight of his years. He rarely felt them, but Ir-Ruhaiyeh had been his home all his adult life. One does not abandon half a century and more of roots without second thoughts.

Isaac turned to John, who stood, as he so often did, at the abbot's right hand. "May it come to pass one day," Isaac said, "that the Persians be driven back to their homeland so our brethren may return here in peace."

"And may you lead that return, Father Abbot, singing songs of rejoicing in the Lord," John said. The prior's eyes never wandered from the gateway. As each animal and man came by, he made another check mark on the long roll of papyrus he held.

Isaac shook his head. "I am too old a tree to transplant. All other soil will seem alien to me; I shall not flourish elsewhere."

"Foolishness," John said. For all his effort, though, his voice lacked conviction. Not only was he uneasy about reproving the abbot in any way, he also feared that Isaac knew whereof he spoke. He prayed both he and his superior were wrong.

"As you will." The abbot sounded reassuring—deliberately

so, John thought. Isaac knew John had enough to worry about right now.

The procession continued. At last it came to an end: almost three hundred monks were trudging west in hope and fear. "Is everyone safely gone?" Isaac asked.

John consulted his list, now black with checks. He frowned. "Have I missed someone?" He shouted to the nearest monk in the column. The monk shook his head. The question ran quickly up the line, and was met everywhere with the same negative response.

John glowered down at the unchecked name and muttered under his breath. "He's off somewhere devising another hymn," the prior growled to Isaac. "Well and good—on any day but this. By your leave—" He started back into the now-abandoned monastery.

"Yes, go fetch him," Isaac said. "Be kind, John. When the divine gift takes him, he forgets all else."

"I've seen." John nodded. "But even for that we have no time today, not if we hope to stay in this world so God may visit us with His gifts."

Entering Ir-Ruhaiyeh after the monks had gone out of it was like seeing the corpse of a friend—no, John thought, like the corpse of his mother, for the monastery had nurtured and sheltered him as much as his fleshly parents had. Hearing only the wind whistle through the courtyard, seeing doors flung carelessly open and left so forever made John want to weep.

His head came up. The wind was not quite all he heard. Somewhere among the deserted buildings a monk was singing quietly to himself, as if trying the flavor of words on his tongue.

John found him just outside the empty stables. His back was turned, so even as the prior drew near he caught only snatches of the new hymn. He was not sure he was sorry. This song seemed to be the complement of the one the monk had created in the refectory; instead of praise for the Lord, it told of the pangs of hell in terms so graphic that ice walked John's back.

"For the unbelievers, for the misbelievers, the scourge. Their hearts shall leap up and choke them. Demons shall seize them by feet and forelocks. Seething water shall be theirs to drink, and—" The monk broke off abruptly, jumping in surprise as John's hand fell on his shoulder.

"Come, Brother Mouamet," the prior said gently. "Not even for your songs will the Persians delay. Everyone else has gone now; we wait only on you."

For a moment, he did not think the monk saw him. Then Mouamet's face cleared. "Thank you, reverend sir," he said. "With the Lord giving me this hymn, I'd forgotten the hour." The abstracted expression that had raised awe in John briefly returned. "I think I shall be able to recover the thread."

"Good," the prior said, and meant it. "But now—"

"—I'll come with you," Mouamet finished for him. Sandals scuffing in the dust, they walked together out of the monastery and set out on the long road to Constantinople.

I've written a series of stories set in a world where Muhammad, instead of founding Islam, converted to Christianity on a trading mission into Syria and ended his days a monk (the previous tale in this book, "Departures," shows his monastic life; a later one here will look at that world several hundred years after his conversion). The world of "Islands in the Sea" looks at the other side of the coin and considers what things might have been like had the Byzantine Empire, instead of shielding southeastern Europe from Islam for hundreds of years, collapsed under the weight of an early Arab onslaught.

ISLANDS IN THE SEA

A.H. 152 (A.D. 769)

The Bulgar border guards had arrows nocked and ready as the Arab horsemen rode up from the south. Jalal ad-Din as-Stambuli, the leader of the Arab delegation, raised his right hand to show it was empty. "In the name of Allah, the Compassionate, the Merciful, I and my men come in peace," he called in Arabic. To be sure the guards understood, he repeated himself in Greek.

The precaution paid off. The guards lowered their bows. In Greek much worse than Jalal ad-Din's, one of them asked, "Why for you come in peace, whitebeard?"

Jalal ad-Din stroked his whiskers. Even without the Bulgar's mockery, he knew they were white. Not many men who had the right to style themselves *as-Stambuli*, the Constantinopolitan, still lived. More than fifty years had passed since the army of Suleiman and Maslama had taken Constantinople and put an end to the Roman Empire. Then Jalal ad-Din's beard had not been white. Then he could hardly raise a beard at all.

He spoke in Greek again: "My master the Caliph Abd ar-Rahman asked last year if your Khan Telerikh would care to learn more of Islam, of submission to the one God. This past spring Telerikh sent word that he would. We are the embassy sent to instruct him."

The Bulgar who had talked with him now used his own

hissing language, Jalal ad-Din supposed to translate for his comrades. They answered back, some of them anything but happily. They were content in their paganism, Jalal ad-Din guessed—content to burn in hell forever. He did not wish that fate on anyone, even a Bulgar.

The guard who knew Greek confirmed his thought, saying, "Why for we want your god? Gods, spirits, ghosts good to us now."

Jalal ad-Din shrugged. "Your khan asked to hear more of Allah and Islam. That is why we are here." He could have said much more, but deliberately spoke in terms a soldier would understand.

"Telerikh want, Telerikh get," the guard agreed. He spoke again with his countrymen, at length pointed at two of them. "This Iskur. This Omurtag. They take you to Pliska, to where Telerikh is. Iskur, him know Greek a little, not so good like me."

"Know little your tongue, too," Iskur said in halting Arabic, which surprised Jalal ad-Din and, evidently, the Bulgar who had been doing all the talking till now. The prospective guide glanced at the sun, which was a couple of hours from setting. "We ride," he declared, and started off with no more fanfare than that. The Bulgar called Omurtag followed.

So, more slowly, did Jalal ad-Din and his companions. By the time Iskur called a halt in deepening twilight, the mountains that made the northern horizon jagged were visibly closer.

"Those little ponies the Bulgars ride are ugly as mules, but they go and go and go," Da'ud ibn Zubayr said; he was a veteran of many skirmishes on the border between the caliph's land and Bulgaria. He stroked the mane of his elegant Arab-bred mare.

"Sadly, my old bones do not." Jalal ad-Din groaned with relief as he slid off his own horse, a soft-gaited gelding. Once he had delighted in fiery stallions, but he knew that if he took a fall now he would shatter like glass.

The Bulgars stalked into the brush to hunt. Da'ud bent to the laborious business of getting a fire going. The other two Arabs, Malik ibn Anas and Salman al-Tabari, stood guard, one with a bow, the other with a spear. Iskur and Omurtag emerged into firelight carrying partridges and rabbits. Jalal ad-Din took hard unleavened bread from a saddlebag: no feast tonight, he thought, but not the worst of fare, either.

Iskur also had a skin of wine. He offered it to the Arabs and grinned when they declined. "More for me, Omurtag," he said.

The two Bulgars drank the skin dry and soon lay snoring by the fire.

Da'ud ibn Zubayr scowled at them. "The only use they have for wits is losing them," he sneered. "How can such folk ever come to acknowledge Allah and his Prophet?"

"We Arabs were wine-bibbers, too, before Muhammad forbade it to us," Jalal ad-Din said. "My worry is that the Bulgars' passion for such drink will make Khan Telerikh less inclined to accept our faith."

Da'ud dipped his head to the older man. "Truly it is just that you lead us, sir. Like a falcon, you keep your eye ever on our quarry."

"Like a falcon, I sleep in the evening," Jalal ad-Din said, yawning. "And like an old falcon, I need more sleep than I once did."

"Your years have brought you wisdom." Da'ud ibn Zubayr hesitated, as if wondering whether to go on. Finally he plunged: "Is it true, sir, that you once met a man who had known the Prophet?"

"It is true," Jalal ad-Din said proudly. "It was at Antioch, when Suleiman's army was marching to fight the Greeks at Constantinople. The grandfather of the innkeeper with whom I was quartered lived with him still: he was a Medinan, far older then than I am now, for he had soldiered with Khalid ibn al-Walid when the city fell to us. And before that, as a youth, he accompanied Muhammad when the Prophet returned in triumph from Medina to Mecca."

"*Allahu akbar,*" Da'ud breathed: "God is great. I am further honored to be in your presence. Tell me, did—did the old man grant you any *hadith*, any tradition, of the Prophet that you might pass on to me for the sake of my enlightenment?"

"Yes," Jalal ad-Din said. "I recall it as if it were yesterday, just as the old man did when speaking of the journey to the Holy City. Abu Bakr, who was not yet caliph, of course, for Muhammad was still alive, started beating a man for letting a camel get loose. The Prophet began to smile and said, 'See what this pilgrim is doing.' Abu Bakr was abashed, though the Prophet did not actually tell him to stop."

Da'ud bowed low. "I am in your debt." He repeated the story several times; Jalal ad-Din nodded to show him he had learned it perfectly. In the time-honored way, Da'ud went on, "I have this *hadith* from Jalal ad-Din as-Stambuli, who had it from—what was the old man's name, sir?"

"He was called Abd al-Qadir."

"Who had it from Abd al-Qadir, who had it from the Prophet. Think of it—only two men between Muhammad and me." Da'ud bowed again.

Jalal ad-Din returned the bow, then embarrassed himself by yawning once more. "Your pardon, I pray. Truly I must sleep."

"Sleep, then, and Allah keep you safe till the morning comes."

Jalal ad-Din rolled himself in his blanket. "And you, son of Zubayr."

"Those are no mean works," Da'ud said a week later, pointing ahead to the earthen rampart, tall as six men, that ringed Pliska, Telerikh's capital.

"That is a child's toy next to the walls of Constantinople," Jalal ad-Din said. "A double wall, each one twice that height, all steep stone, well ditched in front and between, with all the Greeks in the world, it seemed, battling from atop them." Across half a century, recalling the terror of the day of the assault, he wondered still how he had survived.

"I was born in Constantinople," Da'ud reminded him gently.

"Of course you were." Jalal ad-Din shook his head, angry at himself for letting past obscure present that way. It was something old men did, but who cares to remember he is old?

Da'ud glanced around to make sure Iskur was out of earshot, lowered his voice. "For pagan savages, those are no mean works. And see how much land they enclose—Pliska must be a city of greater size than I had supposed."

"No." Jalal ad-Din remembered a talk with a previous envoy to Telerikh. "The town itself is tiny. This earthwork serves chiefly to mark off the grazing lands of the khan's flocks."

"His flocks? Is that all?" Da'ud threw back his head and laughed. "I feel as if I am transported to some strange new world, where nothing is as it seems."

"I have had that feeling ever since we came through the mountain passes," Jalal ad-Din said seriously. Da'ud gave him a curious look. He tried to explain: "You are from Constantinople. I was born not far from Damascus, where I dwell yet. A long journey from one to the other, much longer than from Constantinople to Pliska."

Da'ud nodded.

"And yet it is a journey through sameness," Jalal ad-Din

went on. "Not much difference in weather, in crops, in people. Aye, more Greeks, more Christians in Constantinople still, for we have ruled there so much less time than in Damascus, but the difference is of degree, not of kind."

"That is all true," Da'ud said, nodding again. "Whereas here—"

"Aye, here," Jalal ad-Din said with heavy irony. "The olive will not grow here, the sun fights its way through mists that swaddle it as if it were a newborn babe, and even a Greek would be welcome, for the sake of having someone civilized to talk to. This is a different world from ours, and not one much to my liking."

"Still, we hope to wed it to ours through Islam," Da'ud said.

"So we do, so we do. Submission to the will of God makes all men one." Now Jalal ad-Din made sure Iskur was paying no attention. The nomad had ridden ahead. Jalal ad-Din went on, "Even Bulgars." Da'ud chuckled.

Iskur yelled something at the guards lounging in front of a wooden gate in Pliska's earthen outwall. The guards yelled back. Iskur shouted again, louder this time. With poor grace, the guards got up and opened the gate. They stared as they saw what sort of companions Iskur led.

Jalal ad-Din gave them a grave salute as he passed through the gate, as much to discomfit them as for any other reason. He pointed ahead to the stone wall of Pliska proper. "You see?"

"I see," Da'ud said. The rectangular wall was less than half a mile on a side. "In our lands, that would be a fortress, not a capital."

The gates of the stone wall were open. Jalal ad-Din coughed as he followed Iskur and Omurtag into the town: Pliska stank like—stank worse than—a big city. Jalal ad-Din shrugged. Sooner or later, he knew, he would stop noticing the stench.

Not far inside the gates stood a large building of intricately carved wood. "This Telerikh's palace," Iskur announced.

Tethered in front of the palace were any number of steppe ponies like the ones Iskur and Omurtag rode and also, Jalal ad-Din saw with interest, several real horses and a mule whose trappings did not look like Arab gear. "To whom do those belong?" he asked, pointing.

"Not know," Iskur said. He cupped his hands and yelled toward the palace. Yelling, Jalal ad-Din thought wryly, seemed the usual Bulgar approach toward any problem. After a little while, a door opened. The Arab had not even noticed it until then, so lost was its outline among carvings.

As soon as they saw someone come out of the palace, Iskur and Omurtag wheeled their horses and rode away without a backward glance at the ambassadors they had guided to Pliska. The man who had emerged took a moment to study the new arrivals. He bowed. "How may I help you, my masters?" he asked in Arabic fluent enough to make Jalal ad-Din sit up and take notice.

"We are envoys of the Caliph Abd ar-Rahman, come to your fine city"—Jalal ad-Din knew when to stretch a point—"at the bidding of your khan to explain to him the glories of Islam. I have the honor of addressing . . . ?" He let the words hang.

"I am Dragomir, steward to the mighty Khan Telerikh. Dismount; be welcome here." Dragomir bowed again. He was, Jalal ad-Din guessed, in his late thirties, stocky and well made, with fair skin, a full brown beard framing a rather wide face, and gray eyes that revealed nothing whatever—a useful attribute in a steward.

Jalal ad-Din and his companions slid gratefully from their horses. As if by magic, boys appeared to hitch the Arabs' beasts to the rails in front of the palace and carry their saddlebags into it. Jalal ad-Din nodded at the other full-sized horses and the mule. "To whom do those belong, pray?" he asked Dragomir.

The steward's pale but hooded eyes swung toward the hitching rail and returned to Jalal ad-Din. "Those," he explained, "are the animals of the delegation of priests from the Pope of Rome at the bidding of my khan to expound to him the glories of Christianity. They arrived earlier today."

Late that night, Da'ud slammed a fist against a wall of the chamber the four Arabs shared. "Better they should stay pagan than turn Christian!" he shouted. Not only was he angry that Telerikh had also invited Christians to Pliska as if intending to auction his land to the faith that bid highest, he was also short-tempered from hunger. The evening's banquet had featured pork. Furthermore, Telerikh had not attended; some heathen Bulgar law required the khan always to eat alone.

"That is not so," Jalal ad-Din said mildly.

"And why not?" Da'ud glared at the older man.

"As Christians they would be *dhimmis*—people of the book— and thus granted a hope of heaven. Should they cling to their pagan practices, their souls will surely belong to Satan till the end of time.''

"Satan is welcome to their souls, whether pagan or Christian,'' Da'ud said. "But a Christian Bulgaria, allied to Rome, maybe even allied to the Franks, would block the true faith's progress northward and could be the spearpoint of a thrust back toward Constantinople.''

Jalal ad-Din sighed. "What you say is true. Still, the true faith is also true, and the truth surely will prevail against Christian falsehoods.''

"May it be so,'' Da'ud said heavily. "But was this land not once a Christian country, back in the days before the Bulgars seized it from Constantinople? All the lands the Greeks held followed their usages. Some folk hereabouts must be Christian still, I'd wager, which might incline Telerikh toward their beliefs.''

A knock on the door interrupted the argument. Da'ud kept one hand on his knife as he opened the door with the other. But no enemies stood outside, only four girls. Two were colored like Dragomir—to Jalal ad-Din's eyes, exotically fair. The other two were dark, darker than Arabs, in fact; one had eyes that seemed set at a slant. All four were pretty. They smiled and swayed their way in.

"Telerikh is no Christian,'' Jalal ad-Din said as he smiled back at one of the light-skinned girls. "Christians are not allowed concubines.''

"The more fools they,'' Da'ud said. "Shall I blow out the lamps, or leave them burning?''

"Leave them,'' Jalal ad-Din answered. "I want to see what I am doing . . .''

Jalal ad-Din bowed low to Khan Telerikh. A pace behind him, Da'ud did the same. Another pace back, Malik ibn Anas and Salman al-Tabari went to one knee, as suited their lower rank.

"Rise, all of you,'' Telerikh said in passable Arabic. The khan of the Bulgars was about fifty, swarthy, broad-faced, wide-nosed, with a thin beard going from black to gray. His eyes were narrow, hard, and shrewd. He looked like a man well able to rule a nation whose strength came entirely from the ferocity of its soldiers.

"Most magnificent khan, we bring the greetings of our master the caliph Abd ar-Rahman ibn Marwan, his prayers for your health and prosperity, and gifts to show that you stand high in his esteem," Jalal ad-Din said.

He waved Salman and Malik forward to present the gifts: silver plates from Persia, Damascus-work swords, fine enamelware from Constantinople, a robe of glistening Chinese silk, and, last but not least, a *Qu'ran* bound in leather and gold, its calligraphy the finest the scribes of Alexandria could provide.

Telerikh, though, seemed most interested in the robe. He rose from his wooden throne, undid the broad bronze belt he wore, and shrugged out of his knee-length fur caftan. Under it he had on a linen tunic and trousers and low boots. Dragomir came up to help him put on the robe. He smiled with pleasure as he ran a hand over the watery-smooth fabric.

"Very pretty," he crooned. For a moment Jalal ad-Din hoped he was so taken by the presents as to be easily swayed. But Telerikh, as the Arab had guessed from his appearance, was not so simple. He went on, "The caliph gives lovely gifts. With his riches, he can afford to. Now please take your places while the envoys of the Pope of Rome present themselves."

Dragomir waved the Arab delegation off to the right of the throne, close by the turbaned boyars—the great nobles—who made up Telerikh's court. Most were of the same stock as their khan; a few looked more like Dragomir and the fair girl Jalal ad-Din had so enjoyed the night before. Fair or dark, they smelled of hard-run horses and ancient sweat.

As he had with the caliph's embassy, Dragomir announced the papal legates in the throaty Bulgarian tongue. There were three of them, as Jalal ad-Din had seen at the banquet. Two were gorgeous in robes that reminded him of the ones the Constantinopolitan grandees had worn so long ago as they vainly tried to rally their troops against the Arabs. The third wore a simple brown woolen habit. Amid the Bulgar chatter, meaningless to him, Jalal ad-Din picked out three names: Niketas, Theodore, and Paul.

The Christians scowled at the Arabs as they walked past them to approach Telerikh. They bowed as Jalal ad-Din had. "Stand," Telerikh said in Greek. Jalal ad-Din was not surprised he knew that language; the Bulgars had dealt with Constantinople before the Arabs took it, and many refugees had fled to Pliska. Others had escaped to Italy, which no doubt explained why two of the papal legates bore Greek names.

"Excellent khan," one of the envoys said, also in Greek, "we are saddened to see you decked in raiment given you by our foes as you greet us. Does this mean you hold us in contempt and will give us no fair hearing? Surely you did not invite us to travel so far merely for that?''

Telerikh blinked, glanced down at the silk robe he had just put on. ''No,'' he said. ''It only means I like this present. What presents have you for me?''

Da'ud leaned forward and whispered into Jalal ad-Din's ear: ''More avarice in that one than fear of hell.'' Jalal ad-Din nodded. That made his task harder, not easier. He would have to play politics along with expounding the truth of Islam. He sighed. Ever since he learned Telerikh had also bid the men from Rome hither, he'd expected no less.

The Christians were presenting their gifts, and making a great show of it to try to disguise their not being so fine as the ones their rivals had given—Jalal ad-Din's offerings still lay in a glittering heap beside Telerikh's throne. ''Here,'' Theodore intoned, ''is a copy of the Holy Scriptures, with a personal prayer for you inscribed therein by his holiness the Pope Constantine.''

Jalal ad-Din let out a quiet but scornful snort. ''The words of Allah are the ones that count,'' he whispered to Da'ud ibn Zubayr, ''not those of any man.'' It was Da'ud's turn to nod.

As he had with the *Qu'ran*, Telerikh idly paged through the Bible. Perhaps halfway through, he paused and glanced up at the Christians. ''You have pictures in your book.'' It sounded almost like an accusation; had Jalal ad-Din said it, it would have been.

But the Christian in the plain brown robe, the one called Paul, answered calmly. ''Yes, excellent khan, we do, the better to instruct the many who cannot read the words beside them.'' He was no longer young—he might have been close to Jalal ad-Din's age—but his voice was light and clear and strong, the voice of a man sure in the path he had chosen.

''Beware of that one,'' Da'ud murmured. ''He has more holiness in him than the other two put together.'' Jalal ad-Din had already reached the same conclusion, and did not like it. Enemies, he thought, ought by rights to be rogues.

He got only a moment to mull on that, for Telerikh suddenly shifted to Arabic and called to him, ''Why are there no pictures in your book to show me what you believe?''

''Because Allah the one God is infinite, far too mighty for our tiny senses to comprehend, and so cannot be depicted,'' he said, ''and man must not be depicted, for Allah created him in his image from a clot of blood. The Christians' own scriptures say as much, but they ignore any law which does not suit them.''

"Liar! Misbeliever!" Theodore shouted. Torchlight gleamed off his tonsured pate as he whirled to confront Jalal ad-Din.

"No liar I," Jalal ad-Din said; not for nothing had he studied with men once Christian before they saw the truth of Muhammad's teaching. "The verse you deny is in the book called Exodus.''

"Is this true?" Telerikh rumbled, scowling at the Christians.

Theodore started to reply; Paul cut him off. "Excellent khan, the verse is as the Arab states. My colleague did not wish to deny it.'' Theodore looked ready to argue. Paul did not let him, continuing, "But that law was given to Moses long ago. Since then, Christ the Son of God has appeared on earth; belief in him assures one of heaven regardless of the observance of the outdated rules of the Jews.''

Telerikh grunted. "A new law may replace an old if circumstances change. What say you to that, envoy of the caliph?''

"I will quote two verses from the *Qu'ran*, from the *sura* called The Cow," Jalal ad-Din said, smiling at the opening Paul had left him. "Allah says, 'The Jews say the Christians are astray, and the Christians say it is the Jews who are astray. Yet they both read the Scriptures.' Which is to say, magnificent khan, that they have both corrupted God's word. And again, 'They say: "Allah has begotten a son." Allah forbid!' ''

When reciting from the *Qu'ran*, he had naturally fallen into Arabic. He was not surprised to see the Christians following his words without difficulty. They too would have prepared for any eventuality on this mission.

One of Telerikh's boyars called something to the khan in his own language. Malik ibn Anas, who was with Jalal ad-Din precisely because he knew a little of the Bulgar speech, translated for him: "He says that the sacred stones of their forefathers, even the pagan gods of the Slavs they rule, have served them well enough for years upon years, and calls on Telerikh not to change their usages now.''

Looking around, Jalal ad-Din saw more than a few boyars nodding. "Great khan, may I speak?" he called. Telerikh nodded. Jalal ad-Din went on, "Great khan, you need but look about you to see proof of Allah's might. Is it not true that my lord the caliph Abd ar-Rahman, peace be unto him, rules from the Western Sea to India, from your borders to beyond the deserts of Egypt? Even the Christians, who know the one God imperfectly, still control many lands. Yet only you here in this small country follow your idols. Does this not show you their strength is a paltry thing?''

"There is more, excellent khan." Niketas, who had been quiet until then, unexpectedly spoke up. "Your false gods isolate Bulgaria. How, in dealing with Christians or even Muslims, can your folk swear an oath that will be trusted? How can you put the power of God behind a treaty, to ensure it will be enforced? In what way can one of you lawfully marry a Christian? Other questions like these will surely have occurred to you, else you would not have bid us come."

"He speaks the truth, Khan Telerikh," Jalal ad-Din said. He had not thought a priest would have so good a grasp of matters largely secular, but Niketas did. Since his words could not be denied, supporting them seemed better than ignoring them.

Telerikh gnawed on his mustaches. He looked from one delegation to the other, then back again. "Tell me," he said slowly, "is it the same god both groups of you worship, or do you follow different ones?''

"That is an excellent question," Jalal ad-Din said. No, Telerikh was no fool. "It is the same god: there is no God but God. But the Christians worship him incorrectly, saying he is Three, not One."

"It is the same God," Paul agreed, once more apparently overriding Theodore. "Muhammad is not a true prophet and many of his preachings are lies, but it is the same God, who gave his only begotten Son to save mankind."

"Stop!" Telerikh held up a hand. "If it is the same God, what difference does it make how I and my people worship him? No matter what the prayers we send up to him, surely he will know what we mean."

Jalal ad-Din glanced toward Paul. The Christian was also looking at him. Paul smiled. Jalal ad-Din found himself smiling back. He too felt the irony of the situation: He and Paul had more in common with each other than either of them did with the naive Bulgar khan. Paul raised an eyebrow. Jalal ad-Din dipped his head, granting the Christian permission to answer Telerikh's question.

"Sadly, excellent khan, it is not so simple," Paul said. "Just as there is only one true God, so there can be only one true way to worship him, for while he is merciful, he is also just and will not tolerate errors in the reverence paid him. To use a homely example, sir, would it please you if we called you 'khan of the Avars'?''

"It would please me right well, were it true," Telerikh said with a grim chuckle. "Worse luck for me, though, the Avars have a khan of their own. Very well, priest, I see what you are saying.''

The Bulgar ruler rubbed his chin. "This needs more thought. We will all gather here again in three days' time to speak of it further. Go now in peace, and remember"—he looked sternly from Christians to Muslims—"you are all my guests here. No fighting between you, or you will regret it.''

Thus warned, the rival embassies bowed their way out.

Jalal ad-Din spent more time before his next encounter with the priests exploring Pliska than he had hoped to. No matter how delightful he found his fair-skinned pleasure girl, he was not a young man: for him, between rounds meant between days.

After the barbarous richness of Telerikh's wooden palace, the Arab found the rest of the town surprisingly familiar. He wondered why until he realized that Pliska, like Damascus, like Constantinople, like countless other settlements through which he had passed at one time or another, had been a Roman town once. Layout and architecture lingered long after overlords changed.

Jalal ad-Din felt like shouting when he found a bath house not only still standing but still in use; from what his nose had told him in the palace, he'd doubted the Bulgars even suspected cleanliness existed. When he went in, he found most of the bathers were of the lighter-colored folk from whom Dragomir and his mistress had sprung. They were, he'd gathered, peasant Slavs over whom the Bulgars proper ruled.

He also found that, being mostly unacquainted with either Christianity or Islam, they let in women along with the men. It was scandalous; it was shocking; in Damascus it would have raised riots. Jalal ad-Din wished his eyes were as sharp as they'd been when he was forty, or even fifty.

He was happily soaking in a warm pool when the three Christian envoys came in. Theodore hissed in horror when he saw the naked women, spun on his heel, and stalked out. Niketas started to follow, but Paul took hold of his arm and stopped him. The older man shrugged out of his brown robe and sank with a sigh of pleasure into the same pool Jalal ad-Din was using.

Sergios, by his expression still dubious, joined him a moment later.

"Flesh is flesh," Paul said calmly. "By pledging yourself to Christ, you have acknowledged that its pleasures are not for you. No point in fleeing, then."

Jalal ad-Din nodded to the Christians. "You have better sense, sir, than I would have looked for in a priest," he told Paul.

"I thank you." If Paul heard the undercurrent of irony in the Arab's voice, he did not let it affect his own tone, which briefly shamed Jalal ad-Din. Paul went on, "I am no priest in any case, only a humble monk, here to advise my superiors if they care to listen to me."

" 'Only!' " Jalal ad-Din scoffed. But, he had to admit to himself that the monk sounded completely sincere. He sighed; hating his opponents would have been much easier were they evil. "They would be wise to listen to you," he said. "I think you are a holy man."

"You give me too much credit," Paul said.

"No, he does not," Niketas told his older colleague. "Not just by words do you instruct the barbarians hereabouts but also through the life you live, which by its virtues illuminates your teachings."

Paul bowed. From a man squatting naked in waist-deep water, the gesture should have seemed ludicrous. Somehow it did not.

Niketas turned to Jalal ad-Din. "Did I hear correctly that you are styled as-Stambuli?"

"You did," the Arab answered proudly.

"How strange," Niketas murmured. "Perhaps here God grants me the chance to avenge the fall of the Queen of Cities."

He spoke as if the caliph's armies had taken Constantinople only yesterday, not long before he was born. Seeing Jalal ad-Din's confusion, Paul said, "Niketas' mother is Anna, the daughter of Leo."

"Yes?" Jalal ad-Din was polite, but that meant nothing to him. "And my mother was Zinawb, the daughter of Mu'in ibn Abd al-Wahhab. What of it?"

"Ah, but your grandfather, however illustrious he may have been (I do not slight him, I assure you), was never *Basileus ton Rhomaion*—emperor of the Romans."

"*That* Leo!" Jalal ad-Din thumped his forehead with the heel of his hand. He nodded to Niketas. "Your grandfather, sir, was a very devil. He fought us with all he had, and sent too many brave lads to paradise before their time.''

Niketas raised a dark eyebrow. His tonsured skull went oddly with those bushy brows and the thick beard that covered his cheeks almost to the eyes. "Too many, you say. I would say, not enough.''

"So you would,'' Jalal ad-Din agreed. "Had Leo beaten us, you might be Roman Emperor yourself now. But Abd ar-Rahman, the commander of the faithful, rules Constantinople, and you are a priest in a foreign land. It is as Allah wills.''

"So I must believe,'' Niketas said. "But just as Leo fought you with every weapon he had, I shall oppose you with all my means. The Bulgars must not fall victim to your false belief. It would be too great a blow for Christendom to suffer, removing from us all hope of greater growth.''

Niketas' mind worked like an emperor's, Jalal ad-Din thought. Unlike many of his Christian colleagues, he understood the long view. He'd shown that in debate, too, when he pointed out the problems attendant on the Bulgars' staying pagan. A dangerous foe—Pope Constantine had sent to Pliska the best the Christians had.

Whether that would be enough . . . Jalal ad-Din shrugged. "It is as Allah wills,'' he repeated.

"And Telerikh,'' Paul said. When Jalal ad-Din looked at him in surprise, the monk went on. "Of course, Telerikh is in God's hands, too. But God will not be influenced by what we do. Telerikh may.''

"There is that,'' Jalal ad-Din admitted.

"No telling how long all this arguing will go on,'' Telerikh said when the Christian and Muslim embassies appeared before him once more. He spoke to Dragomir in his own language. The steward nodded and hurried away. A moment later, lesser servants brought in benches, which they set before Telerikh's throne. "Sit,'' the khan urged. "You may as well be comfortable.''

"How would you have us argue?'' Jalal ad-Din asked, wishing the bench had a back but too proud to ask for a chair to ease his old bones.

"Tell me of your one god,'' Telerikh said. "You say you and the Christians follow him. Tell me what you believe differently about him, so I may choose between your beliefs.''

Jalal ad-Din carefully did not smile. He had asked his question to seize the chance to speak first. Let the Christians respond to him. He began where any Muslim would, with the *shahada*, the profession of faith: " '*La illaha ill'Allah: Muhammadun rasulu'llah*; There is no God but Allah; Muhammad is the prophet of Allah.' " Believe that, magnificent khan, and you are a Muslim. There is more, of course, but that is of the essence."

"It is also a lie," Theodore broke in harshly. "Excellent khan, the books of the Old Testament, written hundreds of years before God's Son became flesh, foretold his coming. Neither Old nor New Testament speaks one word of the Arab charlatan who invented this false creed because he had failed as a camel driver."

"There is no prophecy pertaining to Muhammad in the Christians' holy books because it was deliberately suppressed," Jalal ad-Din shot back. "That is why God gave the Prophet his gifts, as the seal of prophecy."

"The seal of trickery is nearer the truth," Theodore said. "God's only begotten Son, Jesus Christ, said that prophecy ended with John the Baptist, but that false prophets would continue to come. Muhammad lived centuries after John and Jesus, so he must be false, a trick of the devil to send men to hell."

"Jesus is no son of God. God is one, not three, as the Christians would have it," Jalal ad-Din said. "Hear God's own words in the *Qu'ran*: 'Say, God is one.' The Christians give the one God partners in the so-called Son and Holy Spirit. If he has two partners, why not three, or four, or more? Foolishness! And how could God fit into a woman's womb and be born like a man? More foolishness!"

Again it was Theodore who took up the challenge; he was a bad-tempered man, but capable all the same. "God is omnipotent. To deny the possibility of the Incarnation is to deny that omnipotence."

"That priest is twisty as a serpent," Da'ud ibn Zubayr whispered to Jalal ad-Din. The older man nodded, frowning. He was not quite sure how to respond to Theodore's latest sally. Who was he to say what Allah could or could not do?

Telerikh roused him from his unprofitable reverie by asking, "So you Arabs deny Jesus is the son of your one god, eh?"

"We do," Jalal ad-Din said firmly.

"What do you make of him, then?" the khan said.

"Allah commands us to worship none but himself, so how can he have a son? Jesus was a holy man and a prophet, but nothing more. Since the Christians corrupted his words, Allah inspired Muhammad to recite the truth once more.''

"Could a prophet rise from the dead on the third day, as God's Son did?" Theodore snorted, clapping a dramatic hand to his forehead. "Christ's miracles are witnessed and attested in writing. What miracles did Muhammad work? None, the reason being that he could not."

"He flew to Jerusalem in the course of a night," Jalal ad-Din returned, "as the *Qu'ran* records—in writing," he added pointedly. "And the crucifixion and resurrection are fables. No man can rise from the dead, and another was set on the cross in place of Jesus."

"Satan waits for you in hell, blasphemer," Theodore warned. "Christ healed the sick, raised the dead, stopped wind and rain in their tracks. Anyone who denies him loses all hope of heaven, and may garner for his sin only eternal torment."

"No, that is the fate reserved for those who make one into three," Jalal ad-Din said. "You—"

"Wait, both of you." Telerikh held up a hand. The Bulgar khan, Jalal ad-Din thought, seemed more stunned than edified by the arguments he had heard. The Arab realized he had been quarreling with Theodore rather than instructing the khan. Telerikh went on. "I cannot find the truth in what you are saying, for each of you and each of your books makes the other a liar. That helps me not at all. Tell me instead what I and my people must do if we follow one faith or the other."

"If you choose the Arabs' false creed, you will have to abandon both drinking wine and eating pork," Theodore said before Jalal ad-Din could reply. "Let him deny it if he may." The priest shot the Arab a triumphant look.

"It is true," Jalal ad-Din said stoutly. "Allah has ordained it."

He tried to put a bold face on it, but knew Theodore had landed a telling blow. The mutter that went up from Telerikh's boyars confirmed it. A passion for wine inflamed most nonbelievers, Jalal ad-Din thought; sadly, despite the good counsel of the *Qu'ran*, it could capture Muslims as well. And as for pork—judging from the meals they served at Pliska, the Bulgars found it their favorite flesh.

"That is not good," Telerikh said, and the Arab's heart sank.

A passion for wine . . . passion! "Magnificent khan, may I ask without offense how many wives you enjoy?"

Telerikh frowned. "I am not quite sure. How many is it now, Dragomir?"

"Forty-seven, mighty khan," the steward replied at once, competent as usual.

"And your boyars?" Jalal ad-Din went on. "Surely they also have more than one apiece."

"Well, what of it?" the khan said, sounding puzzled.

Now Jalal ad-Din grinned an unpleasant grin at Theodore. "If you become a Christian, magnificent khan, you will have to give up all your wives save one. You will not even be able to keep the others as concubines, for the Christians also forbid that practice."

"What?" If Telerikh had frowned before, the scowl he turned on the Christians now was thunderous. "Can this be true?"

"Of course it is true," Theodore said, scowling back. "Bigamy is a monstrous sin."

"Gently, my brother in Christ, gently," Paul said. "We do not wish to press too hard upon our Bulgar friends, who, after all, will be newly come to our observances."

"That one is truly a nuisance," Da'ud whispered.

"You are too right," Jalal ad-Din whispered back.

"Still, excellent khan," Paul went on, "you must not doubt that Theodore is correct. When you and your people accept Christianity, all those with more than one wife—or women with more than one husband, if any there be—will be required to repudiate all but their first marriages and to undergo penance under the supervision of a priest."

His easy, matter-of-fact manner seemed to calm Telerikh. "I see you believe this to be necessary," the khan said. "It is so strange, though, that I do not see why. Explain further, if you will."

Jalal ad-Din made a fist. He had expected Christian ideas of marriage to appall Telerikh, not to intrigue him with their very alienness. Was a potential monk lurking under those fur robes, under that turban?

Paul said, "Celibacy, excellent khan, is the highest ideal. For those who cannot achieve it, marriage to a single partner is an acceptable alternative. Surely you must know, excellent khan, how lust can inflame men. And no sin is so intolerable to prophets and other holy men as depravity and sexual license, for the Holy Spirit will not touch the heart of a prophet while he is engaged in an erotic act. The life of the mind is nobler than that of the body; on this, Holy Scripture and the wise ancient Aristotle agree.''

"I never heard of this, ah, Aristotle. Was he a shaman?'' Telerikh asked.

"You might say so,'' Paul replied, which impressed Jalal ad-Din. The Arab knew little of Aristotle, hardly more than that he had been a sage before even Roman times. He was certain, however, that Aristotle had been a civilized man, not a barbarous pagan priest. But that was surely the closest equivalent to sage within Telerikh's mental horizon, and Paul deserved credit for recognizing it.

The Bulgar khan turned to Jalal ad-Din. "What have you to say about this?''

"The *Qu'ran* permits a man four lawful wives, for those able to treat them equally well,'' Jalal ad-Din said. "For those who cannot, it enjoins only one. But it does not prohibit concubines.''

"That is better,'' the khan said. "A man would get bored bedding the same woman night after night. But this business of no pork and no wine is almost as gloomy.'' He gave his attention back to the priests. "You Christians allow these things?''

"Yes, excellent khan, we do,'' Paul said.

"Hmm.'' Telerikh rubbed his chin. Jalal ad-Din did his best to hide his worry. The matter still stood balanced, and he had used his strongest weapon to incline the khan to Islam. If the Christians had any good arguments left, he and the fate of the true faith in Bulgaria were in trouble.

Paul said, "Excellent khan, these matters of practice may seem important to you, but in fact they are superficial. Here is the key difference between the Arabs' faith and ours: the religion Muhammad preached is one that loves violence, not peace. Such teaching can only come from Satan, I fear.''

"That is a foul, stinking lie!'' Da'ud ibn Zubayr cried. The other two Arabs behind Jalal ad-Din also shouted angrily.

"Silence!'' Telerikh said, glaring at them. "Do not interrupt. I shall give you a chance to answer in due course.''

"Yes, let the Christian go on,'' Jalal ad-Din agreed. "I am sure the khan will be fascinated by what he has to say.''

Glancing back, he thought Da'ud about to burst with fury. The younger man finally forced out a strangled whisper: "Have you gone mad, to stand by while this infidel slanders the Prophet, may blessings be upon his head?''

"I think not. Now be still, as Telerikh said. My ears are not what they once were; I cannot listen to you and Paul at once."

The monk was saying, "Muhammad's creed urges conversion by the sword, not by reason. Does not his holy book, if one may dignify it by that title, preach the holy war, the *jihad*"—he dropped the Arabic word into his polished Greek— "against all those who do not share his faith? And those who are slain in their murderous work, says the false prophet, attain to heaven straightaway." He turned to Jalal ad-Din. "Do you deny this?"

"I do not," Jalal ad-Din replied. "You paraphrase the third *sura* of the *Qu'ran*."

"There, you see?" Paul said to Telerikh. "Even the Arab himself admits the ferocity of his faith. Think also on the nature of the paradise Muhammad in his ignorance promises his followers."

"Why do you not speak?" Da'ud ibn Zubayr demanded. "You let this man slander and distort everything in which we believe."

"Hush," Jalal ad-Din said again.

"Rivers of water and milk, honey and wine, and men reclining on silken couches and being served—served in all ways, including pandering to their fleshly lusts, as if souls could have such concerns—by females created especially for the purpose." Paul paused, needing a moment to draw in another indignant breath. "Such carnal indulgences—nay, excesses—have no place in heaven, excellent khan."

"No? What does, then?" Telerikh asked.

Awe transfigured the monk's thin, ascetic face as he looked within himself at the afterlife he envisioned. "Heaven, excellent khan, does not consist of banquets and wenches; those are for gluttons and sinners in this life and lead to hell in the next. No, paradise is spiritual in nature, with the soul knowing the eternal joy of closeness and unity with God, peace of spirit, and absence of all care. That is the true meaning of heaven."

"Amen," Theodore intoned piously. All three Christians made the sign of the cross over their breasts.

"That is the true meaning of heaven, you say?" Telerikh's blunt-featured face was impassive as his gaze swung toward Jalal ad-Din. "Now you may speak as you will, man of the caliph. Has this Christian told accurately of the world to come in his faith and in yours?"

"He has, magnificent khan." Jalal ad-Din spread his hands

and smiled at the Bulgar lord. "I leave it to you, sir, to pick the paradise you would sooner inhabit."

Telerikh looked thoughtful. The Christian clerics' expressions went from confident to concerned to horrified as they gradually began to wonder, as Jalal ad-Din had already, just what sort of heaven a barbarian prince might enjoy.

Da'ud ibn Zubayr gently thumped Jalal ad-Din on the back. "I abase myself before you, sir," he said, flowery in apology as Arabs so often were. "You saw farther than I." Jalal ad-Din bowed on his bench, warmed by the praise.

His voice urgent, the priest Niketas spoke up: "Excellent khan, you need to consider one thing more before you make your choice."

"Eh? And what might that be?" Telerikh sounded distracted. Jalal ad-Din hoped he was; the delights of the Muslim paradise were worth being distracted about. Paul's version, on the other hand, struck him as a boring way to spend eternity. But the khan, worse luck, was not altogether ready to abandon Christianity on account of that. Jalal ad-Din saw him focus his attention on Niketas. "Go on, priest."

"Thank you, excellent khan." Niketas bowed low. "Think on this, then: in Christendom the most holy Pope is the leader of all things spiritual, true, but there are many secular rulers, each to his own state: the Lombard dukes, the king of the Franks, the Saxon Angle kings in Britain, the various Irish princes, every one a free man. But Islam knows only one prince, the caliph, who reigns over all Muslims. If you decide to worship Muhammad, where is there room for you as ruler of your own Bulgaria?"

"No one worships Muhammad," Jalal ad-Din said tartly. "He is a prophet, not a god. Worship Allah, who alone deserves it."

His correction of the minor point did not distract Telerikh from the major one. "Is what the Christian says true?" the khan demanded. "Do you expect me to bend the knee to your khan as well as your god? Why should I freely give Abd ar-Rahman what he has never won in battle?"

Jalal ad-Din thought furiously, all the while damning Niketas. Priest, celibate the man might be, but he still thought like a Greek, like a Roman Emperor of Constantinople, sowing distrust among his foes so they defeated themselves when his own strength did not suffice to beat them.

"Well, Arab, what have you to say?" Telerikh asked again.

Jalal ad-Din felt sweat trickle into his beard. He knew he had let silence stretch too long. At last, picking his words carefully, he answered. "Magnificent khan, what Niketas says is not true. Aye, the caliph Abd ar-Rahman, peace be unto him, rules all the land of Islam. But he does so by right of conquest and right of descent, just as you rule the Bulgars. Were you, were your people, to become Muslim without warfare, he would have no more claim on you than any brother in Islam has on another."

He hoped he was right and that the jurists would not make a liar of him once he got back to Damascus. All the ground here was uncharted: no nation had ever accepted Islam without first coming under the control of the caliphate. Well, he thought, if Telerikh and the Bulgars did convert, that success in itself would ratify anything he did to accomplish it.

If . . . Telerikh showed no signs of having made up his mind. "I will meet with all of you in four days," the khan said. He rose signifying the end of the audience. The rival embassies rose too, and bowed deeply as he stamped between them out of the hall of audience.

"If only it were easy," Jalal ad-Din sighed.

The leather purse was small but heavy. It hardly clinked as Jalal ad-Din pressed it into Dragomir's hand. The steward made it disappear. "Tell me, if you would," Jalal ad-Din said, as casually as if the purse had never existed at all, "how your master is inclined toward the two faiths about which he has been learning."

"You are not the first person to ask me that question," Dragomir remarked. He sounded the tiniest bit smug: *I've been bribed twice*, Jalal ad-Din translated mentally.

"Was the other person who inquired by any chance Niketas?" the Arab asked.

Telerikh's steward dipped his head. "Why, yes, now that you mention it." His ice-blue eyes gave Jalal ad-Din a careful once-over. Men who could see past their noses deserved watching.

Smiling, Jalal ad-Din said, "And did you give him the same answer you will give me?"

"Why, certainly, noble sir." Dragomir sounded as if the idea of doing anything else had never entered his mind. Perhaps it had not. "I told him, as I tell you now, that the mighty khan keeps his own counsel well, and has not revealed to me which faith—if either—he will choose."

"You are an honest man." Jalal ad-Din sighed. "Not as helpful as I would have hoped, but honest nonetheless."

Dragomir bowed. "And you, noble sir, are most generous. Be assured that if I knew more, I would pass it on to you." Jalal ad-Din nodded, thinking it would be a sorry spectacle indeed if one who served the caliph, the richest, mightiest lord in the world, could not afford a more lavish bribe than a miserable Christian priest.

However lavish the payment, though, it had not bought him what he wanted. He bowed his way out of Telerikh's palace and spent the morning wandering through Pliska in search of trinkets for his fair-skinned bedmate. Here too he was spending Abd ar-Rahman's money, so only the finest goldwork interested him.

He went from shop to shop, sometimes pausing to dicker, sometimes not. The rings and necklaces the Bulgar craftsmen displayed were less intricate, less ornate than those which would have fetched the highest prices in Damascus but had a rough vigor of their own. Jalal ad-Din finally chose a thick chain studded with fat garnets and pieces of polished jet.

He tucked the necklace into his robe and sat down to rest outside the jeweler's shop. The sun blazed down. It was not as high in the sky, not as hot, really, as it would have been in Damascus at the same season, but this was muggy heat, not dry, and seemed worse. Jalal ad-Din felt like boiled fish. He started to doze.

"*Assalamu aleykum*—peace to you," someone said. Jalal ad-Din jerked awake and looked up. Niketas stood in front of him. Well, he'd long since gathered that the priest spoke Arabic, though they'd only used Greek between themselves till now.

"*Aleykum assalamu*—and to you, peace," he replied. He yawned and stretched and started to get to his feet. Niketas took him by the elbow and helped him rise. "Ah, thank you. You are generous to an old man, and one who is no friend of yours."

"Christ teaches us to love our enemies." Niketas shrugged. "I try to obey his teachings as best I can."

Jalal ad-Din thought that teaching a stupid one— the thing to do with an enemy was to get rid of him. The Christians did not really believe what they said, either; he remembered how they'd fought at Constantinople, even after the walls breached. But the priest had just been kind—no point in churlishly arguing with him.

Instead, the Arab said, "Allah be praised, day after tomorrow the khan will make his choice known." He cocked an eyebrow at Niketas. "Dragomir tells me you tried to learn his answer in advance."

"Which can only mean you did the same." Niketas laughed dryly. "I suspect you learned no more than I did."

"Only that Dragomir is fond of gold," Jalal ad-Din admitted.

Niketas laughed again, then grew serious. "How strange, is it not, that the souls of a nation ride on the whim of a man both ignorant and barbarous. God grant that he choose wisely."

"From God come all things," Jalal ad-Din said. The Christian nodded; that much they believed in common. Jalal ad-Din went on, "That shows, I believe, why Telerikh will decide for Islam."

"No, you are wrong there," Niketas answered. "He must choose Christ. Surely God will not allow those who worship him correctly to be penned up in one far corner of the world and bar them forever from access to whatever folk may lie north and east of Bulgaria."

Jalal ad-Din started to answer, then stopped and gave his rival a respectful look. As he had already noticed, Niketas' thought had formidable depth to it. However clever he was, though, the priest who might have been Emperor had to deal with his weakness in the real world. Jalal ad-Din drove that weakness home: "If God loves you so well, why has he permitted us Muslims dominion over so many of you, and why has he let us drive you back and back, even giving over Constantinople, your imperial city, into our hands?"

"Not for your own sake, I'm certain," Niketas snapped.

"No? Why, then?" Jalal ad-Din refused to be nettled by the priest's tone.

"Because of the multitude of our own sins, I'm certain. Not only was—is—Christendom sadly riddled with heresies and false beliefs, even those who believe what is true all too often lead sinful lives. Thus your eruption from the desert, to serve as God's flail and as punishment for our errors."

"You have answers to everything—everything but God's true will. He will show that day after tomorrow through Telerikh."

"That he will." With a stiff little bow, Niketas took his leave. Jalal ad-Din watched him go, wondering if hiring a knifeman would be worthwhile in spite of Telerikh's warnings. Reluctantly, he decided against it; not here in Pliska, he thought. In Damascus he could have arranged it and never been traced, but he lacked that sort of connection. Too bad.

Only when he was almost back to the khan's palace to give

the pleasure girl the trinket did he stop to wonder whether Niketas was thinking about sticking a knife in *him*. Christian priests were supposed to be above such things, but Niketas himself had pointed out what sinners Christians were these days.

Telerikh's servants summoned Jalal ad-Din and the other Arabs to the audience chamber just before the time for midafternoon prayers. Jalal ad-Din did not like having to put off the ritual; it struck him as a bad omen. He tried to stay serene. Voicing the inauspicious thought aloud would only give it power.

The Christians were already in the chamber when the Arabs entered. Jalal ad-Din did not like that, either. Catching his eye, Niketas sent him a chilly nod. Theodore only scowled, as he did whenever he had anything to do with Muslims. The monk Paul, though, smiled at Jalal ad-Din as if at a dear friend. That only made him worry more.

Telerikh waited until both delegations stood before him. "I have decided," he said abruptly. Jalal ad-Din drew in a sudden, sharp breath. From the number of boyars who echoed him, he guessed that not even the khan's nobles knew his will. Dragomir had not lied, then.

The khan rose from his carved throne and stepped down between the rival embassies. The boyars muttered among themselves; this was not common procedure. Jalal ad-Din's nails bit into his palms. His heart pounded in his chest till he wondered how long it could endure.

Telerikh turned to face southeast. For a moment Jalal ad-Din was too keyed up to notice or care. Then the khan sank to his knees, his face turned toward Mecca, toward the Holy City. Again Jalal ad-Din's heart threatened to burst, this time with joy.

"La illaha illa'llah: Muhammadun rasulu'llah," Telerikh said in a loud, firm voice. "There is no God but Allah; Muhammad is the prophet of Allah." He repeated the *shahada* twice more, then rose to his feet and bowed to Jalal ad-Din.

"It is accomplished," the Arab said, fighting back tears. "You are a Muslim now, a fellow in submission to the will of God."

"Not I alone. We shall all worship the one God and his prophet." Telerikh turned to his boyars and shouted in the Bulgar tongue. A couple of nobles shouted back. Telerikh jerked his arm toward the doorway, a peremptory gesture of dismissal. The stubborn boyars glumly tramped out. The rest turned toward Mecca and knelt. Telerikh led them in the *shahada* once, twice, three times. The khan faced Jalal ad-Din once more. "Now we are all Muslims here."

"God is most great," the Arab breathed. "Soon, magnificent khan, I vow, many teachers will come from Damascus to instruct you and your people fully in all details of the faith, though what you and your nobles have proclaimed will suffice for your souls until such time as the *ulama*—those learned in religion—may arrive."

"It is very well," Telerikh said. Then he seemed to remember that Theodore, Niketas, and Paul were still standing close by him, suddenly alone in a chamber full of the enemies of their faith. He turned to them. "Go back to your Pope in peace, Christian priests. I could not choose your religion, not with heaven as you say it is—and not with the caliph's armies all along my southern border. Perhaps if Constantinople had not fallen so long ago, my folk would in the end have become Christian. Who can say? But in this world, as it is now, Muslims we must be, and Muslims we shall be."

"I will pray for you, excellent khan, and for God's forgiveness of the mistake you make this day," Paul said gently. Theodore, on the other hand, looked as if he were consigning Telerikh to the hottest pits of hell.

Niketas caught Jalal ad-Din's eye. The Arab nodded slightly to his defeated foe. More than anyone else in the chamber, the two of them understood how much bigger than Bulgaria was the issue decided here today. Islam would grow and grow, Christendom continue to shrink. Jalal ad-Din had heard that Ethiopia, far to the south of Egypt, had Christian rulers yet. What of it? Ethiopia was so far from the center of affairs as hardly to matter. And the same fate would now befall the isolated Christian countries in the far northwest of the world.

Let them be islands in the Muslim sea, he thought, if that was what their stubbornness dictated. One day, *inshallah*, that sea would wash over every island, and they would read the *Qu'ran* in Rome itself.

He had done his share and more to make that dream real, as a youth by helping to capture Constantinople and now in his old age by bringing Bulgaria the true faith. He could return once more to his peaceful retirement in Damascus.

He wondered if Telerikh would let him take along that fair-skinned pleasure girl. He turned to the khan. It couldn't hurt to ask.

I got the idea for this one looking out the kitchen window while I was doing the dishes. It's far from the only story notion that's come to me in an unexpected place while I was doing something that wasn't even remotely connected to writing. The trick is to get the idea down on paper before you lose it again. "Not All Wolves" is a story of man's inhumanity to man, among other things.

NOT ALL WOLVES

Archbishopric of Cologne: 1176

A full moon hung in the clear dark sky. Dieter ran through the streets of Cologne. Mud splashed under the pads of his feet. It flew up to stick in lumps in the matted fur of his tail. He turned sharply and dashed down a narrow, stinking alley.

Much too close behind him, someone cried, "There he goes! That way!" A score of men or more were hunting him. Their high, excited shouts reminded him of the baying of wolves.

Had he been in his own familiar body, he might have laughed, or cried, or both at once. In the wolf's shape he wore, he could only whimper. He tried to run faster.

Torches appeared at the mouth of the alley, casting a flickering light down its length. Dieter's eyes saw that only as brighter grayness. A wisp of breeze brought him the smell of torch-smoke, and of his pursuers. He could smell their fear, and their resolve.

The men knew nothing of the wondrous things his nose told him, any more than a deaf man could follow a minnesinger's song. But their eyes, now, were keener than his; they were many; and they could plan. More shouts rang out:

"There he is!" "Which way did he turn?" "To the left!" "No, to the right, you idiot!" "Yes, to the right! I saw him too!" "Klaus, Joachim, and Hans, up to the street of the tailors, and quickly! Don't let the cursed beast get through that way!"

And one more cry over and over again: "Kill the werewolf!"

It's not my fault, Dieter wanted to explain. *I do no harm.* But when he opened his wolf's jaws, only a wolf's growl came out.

And those wolf's jaws, he could not deny, held a full set of wolf's teeth. He could feel them, jagged against his tongue, which hung from the side of his mouth as he panted in the air he needed to run and run and run.

Inside the body of a wolf, though, he kept the wits he had had as a boy. If the street of the tailors was still unblocked, he might yet break away from the pack yes, that was the proper word, he thought at his heels.

Too late, too late! He heard Klaus, Joachim, and Hans beat him to the corner. They all carried torches; two had clubs, and the other a woodcutter's ax. They looked this way and that. Good, Dieter thought. They did not know he was close by. They were only three, after all, not twenty. He sprang at them.

Two screamed like lost souls and fled. The third had more courage in him. His club thudded against Dieter's ribs. Pain flared, then died. Dieter's flesh mended with unnatural speed. Had the fellow thought to swing the torch, though, he might have done true harm.

Dieter gave him no chance to think of that. He snarled horribly and ran by. He was ahead of his pursuers again. But he was not free of them, as he had hoped. The brave man pounded after him, yelling. His cries, and the shrieks the other two were letting out, were sure to draw the rest of the mob.

All Dieter wanted was a place to be left alone to wait out the night. Come morning, he knew, he would be himself again: thirteen, an orphan, making his living as best he could, doing odd jobs for weavers and tanners, enamelers and smiths.

Was it four months ago the change first came on him? Other changes had started not long before then. His voice had begun to crack and to deepen. Fine, fuzzy down appeared on his cheeks. The second- and third-hand tunics and breeches he wore seemed suddenly to bind, and to leave him bare at the wrists and ankles.

Every lad he knew went through those changes. But not every lad he knew turned into a wolf when the moon was full.

The first time it happened, by luck Dieter had been alone. Even after he struggled out of the clothes that no longer fit his new shape, he did not realize fully what he was. It was not until he changed back at sunrise and saw the wolf's prints in the dirt of the empty stable where he'd spent the night did he begin to understand. And with understanding came fear.

The next night of the full moon, and the one after that, he had sought out deserted places to wait through the change. When he was a wolf, he had no urge to tear the throat out of every man and beast he saw; past stealing a flitch of bacon, he had gone hungry on nights the change struck him. He also had no illusions about the townsfolk believing that.

He had been on his way to hide this time, too. But that fat fool of a swordsmith had kept him working late, and the moon rose while he was still on the street.

A woman screamed. He could not really blame her. Had he seen someone turn from boy to wolf before his eyes, he thought he would have screamed himself. The hunt had been on ever since.

"Kill the werewolf!"

He was growing heartily tired of that cry. But the one that came after it made the hair along his spine stand up: "Aye, burn it in the old market square in front of Saint Martin's church, as we did the wizard last year!"

The crowd, people said, had jammed the square. Dieter had not gone himself. He had no stomach for such spectacles. He had not escaped it altogether, though; the stench of burnt flesh lingered for days in front of the church. Even then, he had taken more notice of smells than most folk. No wonder, he thought.

He imagined himself—in wolf's shape or boy's, it would not matter—tied to a stake, with little yellow flames licking through the fagots toward his tender flesh. He threw back his head and howled, a long cry of fear and desolation.

The shouts behind him redoubled. Dogs yelped frantically. Lights appeared in windows as people fetched lamps or candles from beside their beds to try to see what was going on.

Some of them, Dieter knew, would join the chase. He should have kept quiet. But the mere idea of burning had ripped the wail from him. By God, they would *not* burn him!

By God! Hope ran through him. It was dizzying, so much so that he almost stumbled into a pile of garbage at the edge of the street. Surely a priest could lift this curse from him!

He seldom went to church. He had to worry about keeping his belly, if not full, then at least with something in it—on Sunday no less than any other day. But he knew where every church in the town was. They were likely places for work—and handouts.

Even had he been next door to Saint Martin's, he would not have gone there, not after the shouts of burning him in front of it. But Saint Martin's lay close by the Rhine, far away from the ancient maze of streets through which he was running. This central part of Cologne, he had heard, went back to the legendary days of Rome.

Of Rome he knew nothing save the name. He did know he

was near the church of Saint Cäcilien. If none of the men who hunted him was waiting down this street—

None was. He turned right, then left. There stood Saint Cäcilien's church, its doors open to the needy. No one, Dieter thought, had ever been more needy than he. He climbed awkwardly up the stairs—stairs were made for creatures with two legs, not four—and into the church.

It looked different from the way he remembered, and not just because he was seeing it only in shades of gray. Now his eyes were also lower to the ground. The pews seemed a forest around him.

In boy's shape, too, he hardly noticed the incense in the air. It was just part of how churches smelled. As a wolf, though, the bitterness of myrrh and frankincense's sharp spicy scent made his nose twitch and tingle. He gasped, then sneezed once, twice, three times.

A priest was walking up the aisle to the altar. He carried a long staff with a crucifix on the end. At the sneezes, he whirled around in surprise. "Good health to—" he began, then stopped in horror when he saw who—or, rather, what—had sneezed.

Dieter trotted toward him. He opened his mouth to ask the priest's blessing. That showed him the one flaw in his plan. As a wolf, he could not tell the man what he needed.

The priest saw only a great hairy beast rushing at him with gaping jaws. *"Lieber Gott!"* he gasped. With no other weapon he could reach, he swung his staff at the wolf.

The crucifix was silver. The blow hurt Dieter as much as if he had been human. Howling in pain and dismay, he whirled about and fled from the church, tail between his legs. "A wolf! A wolf!" the priest shouted behind him.

Some of the hunters were just drawing near Saint Cäcilien's. They yelled and pointed when they saw Dieter streak out. They ran after him. His savage growl, though, made them think twice about coming close. Having been hurt already, he now acted and sounded fiercer than before.

But the men did cut him off from the new market square. He growled, deep in his throat. So many streets led off the square, he would have had his choice of escape routes. Instead, his pursuers were forcing him away—and the priest's hue and cry would only bring more people out after him. Already he could hear new voices, smell new scents among those who chased him.

He was halfway down a street before it jogged to show him it had only the exit down which he had come. A tall, barred gate of stout timbers blocked the other end. He yelped and whimpered. He was trapped here. Too late to double back now; his pursuers had plugged the way out.

They knew it, too. "We have him now!" one shouted. "He can't get into the Jews' quarter at night. Come on!"

Dieter snarled, this time at himself. He should have remembered that the Jews were closed off from the rest of the city between sunrise and sunset. The men were coming closer fast. He could not go back through them. He stood there, panting. Part of him, the exhausted part, wanted to lie down and give up.

Then he thought of the flames again. No, he could not let the hunters take him. He ran for the gate and flung himself upward.

He had imagined himself easily clearing the timbers, landing lightly on the far side. His head and forelegs cleared, sure enough, but his belly slammed against the gate hard enough to drive half the wind from him. He hung there a moment, stunned. His hind feet scrabbled for purchase. The wood was rough; his claws bit. Leaving skin and hair behind, he dragged himself over, fell like a stone to the ground.

His undignified scramble had let him be seen. "There he went!" a man yelled from the other side of the gate. The fellow pounded on it with his fist. "Here, you damned Jews, open up!"

Dieter raced away. Now he had time to find a hiding place without any of his pursuers liable to spot him diving for cover. He would not keep that chance for long. Several men were battering at the gate, one, by the sound of it, with an axe. "Open up!" they shouted at the top of their lungs. "You damned stupid Jews, there's a werewolf loose among you!"

That would make the gates open if anything did, Dieter thought. He knew he never hurried to do anything for people who cursed him and called him names. He suspected the Jews were no different from him in that, no matter that they had their own strange faith. But he would run if someone screamed, "Fire, you fool!" The Jews might swallow insults for the sake of hunting him down.

He rounded a corner, and almost ran into an old man crossing the street. They both stopped, staring at each other. The old Jew did not run shrieking, as so many had.

Behind Dieter, clamor grew. Either someone would come open the gate or soon the men who hunted him soon would break it down.

The frozen tableau that gripped Dieter and the man could not last, not with shouts of "Werewolf!" flying thick and fast. Dieter was about to run when the old Jew spoke: "Come with me, and quickly!" He opened a door, gestured urgently.

Dieter hesitated. All the wild, wolfly instincts in him rebelled at trusting any man. The boy he still was had trouble believing anyone would want to help him in his present state. But the old man had not known he was coming. No trap could be waiting for him inside that house. And even if one somehow was, what could a frail graybeard do against any wolf, let alone a werebeast?

The sound of the gate creaking open decided him. His hunters were in the Jewish quarter, and the Jews likely would be after him, too. Everyone was against him save, this one old man. He grabbed at that like a drowning man grabbing for a log. He darted inside.

The old man shut the door behind them. "Get under the table there," he said. When Dieter had, he draped a cloth over it that hung down to the floor on all sides. Then he lit a couple of candles at a little brazier and set them on the table. Dieter's world, the little square of it he could see, went from black to gray. The old man rustled about for another couple of minutes, then sat down. His knees pushed at the tablecloth.

"Now we wait," he said. Dieter whined softly to show he had heard.

They did not wait long. A knock came at the door. "Avram, are you there?" a man asked.

"Where else would I be, with the candles lit?" the old Jew said. "It's late, David. Why do you come around asking foolish questions?"

"Avram, will you please open up?" the other man, David, asked. "Some of the good folk from outside the gate are with me. They are searching, they say, for a—a wolf."

The stool creaked as Avram rose. Dieter heard him open the door. "A wolf? In Cologne?"

"So they say," David told him. "They seemed most urgent. We thought it wiser to let them come in, no matter the hour."

"Is that the commotion I heard?" Avram sounded grumpy and disapproving. "It was loud enough to disturb my studies."

"Too bad, old Jew." Dieter shivered at the sound of the new voice—it belonged to the man who had dared swing a club at him. "When a werewolf is loose in the city, we don't care what we disturb to find it." Others shouted agreement.

"Well, I have seen no wolves, were or otherwise, gentlemen. I've been at my books since sundown. May I go back to them?"

"Since sundown, you say? Why are your candles so long?"

Dieter had to clamp his jaws shut to keep from whimpering in terror. Not only was this hunter a brave man, he also was no one's fool.

Avram just shrugged; Dieter heard his robe rustle. "Because the last pair guttered out not long ago, and I lit these from them. Why else?"

"Hrmmp. You've seen or heard nothing out of the ordinary, you say?"

"Not till you came," Avram replied sharply.

"You watch your mouth, Jew, or you'll watch the few teeth you have left go flying into the mud." But after that the man turned back to his comrades. "If this old bugger's been here all night, the cursed beast can't have sneaked in. On to the next house." Dieter heard them tramping away.

Avram shut the door and walked back over to the table. He did not lift the cloth. Very softly, he said, "I'll stay down here reading until these candles fail. Don't come out till then. I'll leave a dish of water for you. You'd be wiser to stay the night here, I think. In the morning, in your proper shape, you'll have an easier time getting back to your own affairs."

Dieter wished he could answer in words. He thumped his tail against the floor. Avram grunted. The old Jew sat down, began turning pages and, every so often, muttering to himself.

When one candle went out, he got up. As he had promised, he poured water from a jug and set it by the table. He blew out the other candle. "Sleep well, wolf," he said. He went up the stairs in the dark.

Even though no one could see him now, Dieter did not come out for a long time. When at last he did, he bent his head over the bowl and lapped it dry, then slurped drops of water from his chin and whiskers with his tongue. Fleeing was thirsty work.

He went back under the table to sleep. If it grew light before he changed back to himself, he wanted the concealment the cloth would bring.

He woke to find one of his feet poking a table leg. One of his feet . . . It was hairless, clawless, with five toes all in a row. It was dirty but pink under the dirt. He could see it was pink. "I'm Dieter," he whispered. His mouth formed words. He was a boy again.

He crawled out from under the table, stood up. He realized he was naked, and saw he had a small scar on his belly that had not been there before: a souvenir, he supposed, of his scramble over the gate. He made a cloak of the tablecloth.

He had just wrapped it around himself when old Avram came downstairs. "So that's what you look like, eh?" the old Jew said. He handed Dieter a bundle of clothes. "Here. Put these on. You're apt to look out of place, wearing table linen in the street."

The clothes were not new, but were better than what Dieter was used to wearing. They fit well enough. As he dressed, Avram cut him cheese and bread for breakfast. He had not known how hungry he was until he saw he had finished before Avram was even half done with his smaller portion.

"Want more?" Avram asked.

"No, thank you." Dieter paused. "Thank you," he said again, in a different tone of voice.

The old Jew gave a gruff nod. "It should be safe now to go back to your part of the city, boy."

"Yes." Dieter started for the door, then stopped. He turned back to Avram. "May I ask you something?"

"Ask," Avram said around a mouthful of bread and cheese.

"Why did you save me?" Dieter blurted. "I mean—everyone else who saw me wanted to kill me on sight. What made you so different from the rest of them?"

Avram sat silent so long on his stool that Dieter wondered if he had somehow offended him. At last the old Jew said slowly, "One thing you should remember always—you are not the only one ever hunted down Cologne's streets."

Dieter thought about that. He never really had before. Jews falling victim to mobs were just part of life in the city to him, like chamber pots being hurled into the street from second-floor windows or famine one year in four. The Jews, though, he realized, might not see it like that.

Indeed, Avram was going on, as much to himself as to Dieter, "No, lad, and not all wolves run on four legs, either. You ask me, the ones with two are worse. Keep clear of them, and you'll do all right." He opened the door.

Yesterday, Dieter thought as he stepped into the cool damp air of early morning, he would have had no idea what the old Jew was talking about. Now he knew. With a last nod to Avram, he started down the street. He would have to find some work to do if he expected to eat lunch.

Medieval heralds were endlessly ingenious. This story springs from their habit of granting arms to *all* sorts of individuals. Every example of heraldry cited herein is genuine. Hmm. If heraldry really is a science, does that make "Clash of Arms" science fiction?

CLASH OF ARMS

THE TOURNAMENT HELD EVERY OTHER YEAR at the castle of Thunder-ten-tronckh in Westphalia always produced splendid jousting, luring as it did great knights from all over Europe. Indeed, one tourney year the lure proved too much even for Magister Stephen de Windesore, who left his comfortable home outside London to travel to the wilds of Germany.

You must understand at once that Magister Stephen did not arrive at the castle of Thunder-ten-tronckh to break a lance himself. Far from it. He was fat and well past fifty. While that was also true of several of the knights there, no more need be said than that Magister Stephen habitually rode a mule.

His sharpest weapon was his tongue, and at the castle of Thunder-ten-tronckh or, to be more accurate, in a tavern just outside the castle he was having trouble with that. The Westphalians used a dialect even more barbarous than his own English, and his French, I fear, was more of the variety learned at Stratford-atte-Bowe than around Paris. On the other hand, he spoke very loudly.

"Me? I don't care a fig for cart horses and arrogant swaggerers in plate," he declared to anyone who would listen. To emphasize the point, he gestured with a mug of beer. Some slopped over the edge and splashed the table. He did not miss it; it was thin, bitter stuff next to the smooth English ale he liked.

"You don't like jousts, why did you come?" asked an Italian merchant whose French that was hardly better than Magister Stephen's. The Italian was chiefly interested in getting the best price for a load of pepper, cinnamon, and spikenard, but he had an amateur's passion for deeds of dought.

Magister Stephen fixed him with a cold gray eye. "The arms, man, the arms!"

"Well, of course the arms! *Arma virumque cano*," the merchant said, proving that he owned some smattering of a classical education. He made cut-and-thrust motions.

"Dear God, if You are truly all-wise, why did You make so many dullards?" Magister Stephen murmured, but in English. Returning to French, he explained, "Not weaponry. What I mean is coats of arms, heraldry, blazonry—d' you understand me?"

The Italian smote his forehead with the heel of his hand. "Ai, the stupidity of me! Truly, I am seventeen different kinds of the hindquarters of a she-donkey! Heraldry your honor meant! And I myself an armigerous man!"

"You, sir?" Magister Stephen eyed his chance-met comrade with fresh interest. He certainly did not look as if he came from any knightly or noble line, being small, skinny, excitable, and dressed in mantle, tunic, and tights shabbier than Stephen's own. Still, it could be. The Italians were freer with grants of arms to burgesses than were the northern countries.

"Indeed yes, sir," the merchant replied, paying no attention to Magister Stephen's scrutiny. "I am Niccolo dello Bosco—of the woods, you would say. When I am at home, you see, I am to be found in the forest outside Firenze. It is a truly lovely town, Firenze. Do you know it?"

"Unfortunately, no," Magister Stephen said. He was thinking that it was not unfortunate at all. He had been to Milan once, to watch a tourney and came away with a low opinion of Italian manners and cookery. That, however, was neither here nor there. "And your arms, sir, if I may ask?"

"But of course. A proud shield, you will agree: Gules a fess or between three frogs proper."

Magister Stephen whipped out quill and ink and a small sketchbook. Rather than carrying a variety of colors around for rough sketches, he used different hatchings to show the tinctures: vertical stripes for the red ground of the shield, with dots for the broad gold horizontal band crossing the center of the escutcheon. His frogs were lumpy-looking creatures. He glanced up at dello Bosco, who was watching him in fascination. "Why 'three frogs proper'?" he asked. "Why not simply 'vert'?"

"They are to be shown as spotted."

"Ah." Magister Stephen made the necessary correction. "Most interesting, Master dello Bosco. In England I know of but one family whose arms bear the frog or rather the toad:

that of Botreaux, whose arms are Argent, three toads erect sable.''

The Italian smiled. "From *batracien*, no doubt. A pleasant pun, yes?''

"Hmm?'' Magister Stephen owned a remorselessly literal mind. "Why, so it is.'' His chuckle was a little forced.

The approaching jingle of harness and clop of heavy hooves in the street told of another party of knights on its way to the castle of Thunder-ten-tronckh. Anxious to see their arms, Magister Stephen tossed a coin down on the tabletop and waited impatiently for his change. He pocketed the sixth of a copper and hurried out of the tavern.

To his annoyance, he was familiar with all but one of the newcomers' shields. He was just finishing his sketch of that one when dello Bosco appeared at his elbow and nudged him. "There's something you won't find often,'' the Italian said, nodding toward one of the stalls across the road. "A trader who can't give his stock away.''

"Oh, yes, him.'' Magister Stephen had noticed the bushy-bearded merchant in a caftan the day before. He was a Greek from Thessalonike, come to the castle of Thunder-ton-tronckh with a cartload of fermented fish sauce. To northern noses, though, the stuff smelled long dead. Now the Greek was reduced to smearing it on heels of bread and offering them as free samples to people on the street, most of whom took one good whiff and fled.

"Timeo Danaos et donas ferentis," dello Bosco laughed, watching yet another passerby beat a hasty retreat from the stall.

"You know Vergil well,'' Magister Stephen said.

"Yes, very well,'' dello Bosco agreed, and Magister Stephen sniffed at the ready vanity of an Italian.

Another party of knights came clattering up the road toward the castle. "It seems our day for surprises,'' dello Bosco said, pointing at one horseman's arms. "Or have you seen pantheons before?''

Magister Stephen did not answer; he was drawing furiously. He knew of the pantheon from his study of heraldic lore, but he had *not* seen the mythical beast actually depicted on a shield. It had the head of a doe, a body that might have come from the same creature, a fox's tail, and cloven hooves. It was shown in its proper colors: the hooves sable, body gules powdered with golden stars.

"Quite unusual,'' Magister Stephen said at last, tucking his sketchbook back inside his tunic. Then he turned to dello Bosco, who had been waiting for him to finish. "Sir, you astonish me. Not one in a thousand would have recognized a pantheon at sight."

The merchant drew himself up stiffly; even so, the crown of his head was below the level of Magister Stephen's chin. "I am not one in a thousand—I am myself. And being armigerous, is it not proper for me to know heraldry?"

"Oh, certainly. Only—"

Dello Bosco might have been reading his thoughts, for he divined the exact reason for the hesitation. "You think I am stupid for because I am not noble born, eh? Why do I not thrash you for this?" He was hopping up and down in fury, his cheeks crimson beneath their Mediterranean swarthiness.

Magister Stephen cocked a massive fist. "I promise you, you would regret the attempt."

"Do I care a fig for your promises, you larded tun?"

"Have a care with your saucy tongue, knave, or I will be the one to thrash you."

"Not only fat but a fool. In my little finger I know more of heraldry than is in all your empty head."

Magister Stephen's rage ripped free. "Damn me to hell if you do, sir!" he roared loudly enough to make heads turn half a block away.

"Big-talking pile of suet. Go home to mama; I do not waste my time on you." Dello Bosco gave a theatrical Italian gesture of contempt, spun on his heel, and began to stalk away.

Magister Stephen seized him by the shoulder and hauled him back. White around the lips, the Englishman grated, "Dare to prove your boasts, little man, or I will kill you on the spot. Contest with me, and we shall see which of us can put a question the other cannot answer."

"What stake will you put up for this, ah, contest of yours?" dello Bosco said, wriggling free of the other's grip.

Magister Stephen laughed harshly. "Ask what you will if you win. You shall not. As for me, all I intend is flinging you into a dung heap to serve you as you deserve for insolence to your betters."

"Wind, wind, wind," dello Bosco jeered. "As challenged, I shall ask first. Is it agreed?"

"Ask away. The last question counts for all, not the first."

"Very well, then. Tell me, if you will, the difference between a mermaid and a melusine."

"You have a fondness for monsters, it seems," Magister Stephen remarked. "No doubt it suits your character. To your answer: these German heralds have a fondness for melusines, and draw them with two tails to the mermaid's one." Dello Bosco shrugged and spread his hands. Magister Stephen said, "My turn now. Why is the bar sinister termed a mark of bastardy?"

"Because all English speak French as poorly as you," his opponent retorted. "*Barre* is French for 'bend,' and the bend sinister does show illegitimacy. Any child knows that bars, like the fess run straight across the shield, and so cannot be called dexter or sinister." Magister Stephen did his best to hide his chagrin.

They threw questions there at each other in the street, and gave back answers as swiftly. Magister Stephen's wrath soon faded, to be replaced by the spirit of competition. All his wit focused on finding challenges for dello Bosco and on meeting the Italian's. Some of those left him sweating. Wherever he had learned his heraldry, dello Bosco was a master.

Magister Stephen looked up, amazed, to realize it was twilight. "A pause for a roast capon and a bottle of wine?" he suggested. "Then to my chamber and we'll have this out to the end."

"Still the belly first, is it?" dello Bosco said, but he followed the Englishman back into the inn from which they had come several hours before.

Refreshed, Magister Stephen climbed the stairs to the cubicles over the taproom. He carried a burning taper in one hand and a fresh bottle in the other. After lighting a lamp, he stretched out his straw palliasse and waved dello Bosco to the rickety footstool that was the little rented room's only other furniture.

"My turn, is it not?" Magister Stephen asked. At the Italian's nod, he said, "Give me the one British coat of arms that has no charge upon the shield."

"A plague on you and all the British with you," dello Bosco said. He screwed up his mobile face in thought, and sat a long time silent. Just as a grinning Magister Stephen was about to rise, he said, "I have it, I think. Did not John of Brittany—the earl of Richmond, that is—bear simply 'ermine'?"

"Damnation!" Magister Stephen exploded, and dello Bosco slumped in relief.

Then he came back with a sticker of his own: "What beast is it that has both three bodies and three ears?"

Magister Stephen winced. He frantically began reviewing the

monsters of blazonry. The lion tricorporate had but one head, with the usual number of ears. The chimaera had—no, it had three heads and only one body. The hydra was drawn in various ways, with seven heads, or three, but again a single body.

"Having trouble?" dello Bosco asked. In the lamplight his eyes were enormous; they seemed almost a deep crimson rather than black, something that Magister Stephen had not noticed, and that only added to his unease.

The hot, eager gaze made him want to run like a rabbit—like a rabbit! He let out a great chortle of joy. "The cony trijunct on the arms of Harry Well!" he exclaimed. "The bodies are disposed in the dexter and sinister chief points and in base, each joined to the others by a single ear around the fess point."

Dello Bosco sighed and relaxed once more. Still shuddering at his narrow escape, Magister Stephen cudgeled his brain for the fitting revenge. Suddenly he smiled. "Tell me the formal name of the steps to be depicted under the Cross Calvary."

But dello Bosco answered at once: "Grieces." He came back with a complicated point of blazonry.

Magister Stephen made him repeat it, then waded through. "Two and three, Or a cross gules," he finished, panting a bit.

"Had you blazoned the first and fourth 'a barry of six' instead of 'azure, three bars or,' I would have had you," dello Bosco said.

"Yes, I know." Yet even though Magister Stephen had given the correct response, the feel of the contest changed. He was rattled, and asked the first thing that popped into his head; dello Bosco answered easily. Then he asked a question so convoluted as to make the one before elementary by comparison.

Magister Stephen barely survived it, and took a long pull at the wine jar when he had finished. Again, his opponent brushed aside his answering sally; again, he came back with a question of hideous difficulty. The cycle repeated several times; at every query Magister Stephen's answers came more slowly and with less certainty. Dello Bosco never faltered.

The lamp in the little room was running low on oil. Its dying flickers made dello Bosco seem somehow bigger, as if he were gathering strength from Magister Stephen's distress. Every time he hurled a question now, he leaned forward, hands on his knees, waiting for the Englishman's stumbling replies like a hound that has scented blood.

He handled Magister Stephen's next question, on the difference between the English and Continental systems for showing cadency, with such a dazzling display of erudition that the Englishman, desperate as he was, wanted to jot down notes. But there was no time for that. Stretching lazily, dello Bosco said, "I grow weary of the game, I fear. So, then, a last one for you: tell me what arms the devil bears."

"What? Only the devil knows that!" Magister Stephen blurted.

At that moment the lamp went out, yet the chamber was not dark, for Niccolo dello Bosco's eyes still glowed red, like burning coals. When he spoke again, his voice was deeper, richer, and altogether without Italian accent. "I see that you do not know, in any case, which is a great pity for you. Nor is it wise to bet with strangers—but then, I told you you were a fool."

Dello Bosco chuckled. "And now to settle up the wager. What was that you said? 'Damn me to hell if you do, sir'? Well, that can be arranged." He strode forward and laid hold of Magister Stephen. His grip had claws.

Dello Bosco had not mentioned the Mountain by the Dark Wood outside Firenze, or the Gateway there, or the writing above it. *"Lasciate ogni speranza, voi ch'entrate,"* Magister Stephen read as he was dragged through. Even in such straits he was observant, and cried, "No wonder you said you knew Vergil well!"

"Indeed. After all, he lives with me."

Then the lesser demons took control of their new charge from their master. To show their service, they bore his arms: Gules, a fess or between three frogs proper. Magister Stephen found that very funny—but not for long.

I've written seven stories that feature the exploits of Basil Argyros, a fourteenth-century Byzantine official in a world where Muhammad was monk rather than prophet (see also "Departures" and "Islands in the Sea" in this volume). Six of those stories appear together in the collection *Agent of Byzantium* (New York: Congdon & Weed, 1987). This is the seventh. Chronologically, it fits between the second and third chapters of *Agent of Byzantium*. Like the others in the series, however, it is intended to stand by itself as well.

PILLAR OF CLOUD,
PILLAR OF FIRE

BASIL ARGYROS' SHADOW WAS ONLY A SMALL black puddle on the deck timbers under his feet. The sun stood almost at the zenith, higher in the sky than he had ever known it. He used the palm of his hand to shield his eyes from its fierce glare as he peered southward past the ship's bowsprit. The blue waters of the Middle Sea stretched unbroken before him.

He turned to a sailor hurrying past. "Did the captain not say we'd likely spot land today?"

The sailor, a lean, sun-toasted man who wore only loincloth and sandals, gave a wry chuckle. "Likely's not certain, sir, and today's not done." His Greek had a strong, hissing Egyptian accent. He was heading home.

Argyros wanted to ask another question, but the fellow had not paused to wait for it. He had work to keep him busy; aboard ship, passengers had little better to do than stand around, talk, and gamble—Argyros was up a couple of gold nomismata for the trip. Even so, he had been bored more often than not.

He remembered a time when he would have relished the chance to spend a week or so just thinking. Those were the days before his wife and infant son had died in the smallpox epidemic at Constantinople two years ago. Now when his mind was idle, it kept drifting back to them. He peered south again, hoping the pretense of purpose would hold memory at bay. Sometimes it worked, sometimes it didn't. Today it didn't, not very well.

103

Still, getting away from the imperial capital helped give distance to his sorrow. That was why he had volunteered to go to Alexandria. His fellow magistrianoi looked at him as if they thought he was mad. Likely they did. Anything that had to do with Egypt meant trouble.

Right now, though, Argyros relished trouble, the more, the better. A troubled present would keep him too occupied to think back to his anguished past. He could—

A shout from the port rail snapped him out of his reverie. "The pharos!" cried a passenger, obviously another man with time on his hands. "I see the stub of the pharos!" His arm stabbed out.

Argyros hurried to join him, looking in the direction he was pointing. Sure enough, he saw a white tower thrusting itself up past the smooth sea horizon. The magistrianos shook his head in chagrin. "I would have spied it before if I'd looked southeast instead of due south," he said.

The man beside him laughed. "This must be your first trip across the open ocean, if you think we can sail straight to where we're going. I count us lucky to have come so close. We won't have to put in at some village to ask where we are, and risk being pirated."

"If the pharos were fully rebuilt, its beacon fire and the smoke from it could be spied a day's sail away," Argyros said. " 'And the Lord went before them by day in a pillar of cloud to lead them the way; and by night in a pillar of fire, to give them light; to go by day and night.' "

He and the other man both crossed themselves at the Biblical quotation. So did the sailor with whom Argyros had spoken before. He said, "Sirs, captains have been petitioning emperors to get the pharos rebuilt since the earthquake knocked it down a lifetime ago. They're only now getting around to it." He spat over the rail to show what he thought of the workings of the Roman Empire's bureaucracy.

Argyros, who was part of that bureaucracy, understood and sympathized with the sailor's feelings. Magistrianoi—secret investigators, agents, sometimes spies—could not grow hidebound, not if they wanted to live to grow old. But officials with lawbooks had governed the empire from Constantinople for almost a thousand years. No wonder they often moved slow as flowing pitch. The wonder, sometimes, was that they moved at all.

The man who had first seen the pharos said, "Seems to me

the blasted Egyptians are more to blame for all the delays than his Majesty Nikephoros.'' He turned to Argyros for support. "Don't you think so, sir?''

"I know little of such things," the magistrianos said mildly. He shifted to Latin, a tongue still used in the empire's western provinces but hardly ever heard in Egypt. "Do you understand this speech?''

"A little. Why?'' the passenger asked. The sailor, not following, shook his head.

"Because I can use it to remind you it might not be wise to revile Egyptians when the crew of this ship is nothing else but.''

The man blinked, then gave a startled nod. If the sailor had been offended, he got no chance to do anything about it. Just then, the captain shouted for him to help shift the lines to the foresail as the ship swung toward Alexandria. "As well we're west of the city" Argyros observed. "The run into the merchantmen's harbor will be easier than if we had to sail around the island of Pharos.''

"So it will.'' The other passenger nodded. Then he paused, took a long look at the magistrianos. "For someone who says he knows little of Alexandria, you're well informed.''

Argyros shrugged, annoyed with himself for slipping. It might not matter now, but could prove disastrous if he did it at the wrong time. He did know more of Alexandria than he had let on—he knew as much as anyone could who had never come there before. Research seemed a more profitable way to spend his time than mourning.

He even knew why the pharos was being restored so slowly despite Nikephoros' interest in having it shine once more. That was why he had come. Knowing what to do about the problem was something else again. No one in Alexandria seemed to. That, too, was why he'd been sent.

The ship glided into the harbor of Eunostos—Happy Return. The island of Pharos (from which the famous lighthouse drew its name) shielded the harbor from storms out of the north, while the Heptastadion, the seven-furlong causeway from the mainland to Pharos, divided it from the Great Harbor to the east. The Great Harbor was reserved for warships.

The Heptastadion was not quite what Argyros had expected. He'd not thought to ask much about it, and the ancient authors who had written of it termed it an embankment. So it had been, in their time. But centuries of accumulating silt had made it into an isthmus almost a quarter mile wide. Houses and shops and manufactories stood alongside the elevated roadway to the island. The magistrianos' frown drew his heavy eyebrows—eyebrow, really, for the hair grew together above his nose—down over his deep-set eyes. He wondered what else he would find that was not in the books.

Ships and boats of all types and sizes filled the harbor of Eunostos: tubby square-rigged merchantmen like the one on which Argyros traveled, fishing boats with short-luffed lugsails that let them sail closer to the wind, many-oared tugs. Two of those strode spiderlike across the water to Argyros' vessel as it neared the harbor's granite quays.

"Brail up your sail, there!" a man called from one of them. The sailors rushed to obey. The tugs, their bows padded with great coils of rope, chivied the ship into place against one of the quays. Sailors threw lines to waiting dockmen, who made the merchantman fast to the dock. Argyros slung his duffel over his shoulder, belted on his sword, and climbed the gangplank. As he stepped onto the quay, one of the line handlers pointed to the blade and said, "You want to be careful whipping that out, friend. This here's a big city—you get caught using a sword in a brawl and the prefect's men'll chop off your thumbs to make sure you don't do it twice."

The magistrianos looked down his long, thin nose. "I live in Constantinople—not just a city but *the* city."

Only in Alexandria would anyone have disagreed with that. But the dockman just grunted and said, "Newcomer." He gave the word a feminine ending, so Argyros knew it meant Constantinople and not himself. Before Constantine had turned sleepy Byzantium into the New Rome, Alexandria had been the premier city of the Roman east. Its citizens, plainly, still remembered . . . and resented.

The magistrianos carried his gear down the quay and into the city. He thought about walking along the Heptastadion to take a close look at the troubled pharos right away, but decided to settle in first. The weight of the duffel bag, which seemed to grow heavier at every step he took, played a large part in his decision.

He found a room not far from where the Heptastadion joined the mainland; the cross-topped domes of the nearby church of St. Athanasios gave him a landmark that would be visible from a good part of Alexandria. Though the town's streets made an orderly grid, Argyros was glad for any extra help he could get in finding his way around.

By the time he had unpacked, the sun was setting in crimson

splendor above the Gate of the Moon to the west. Making headway with Alexandrian officials, he had been warned, was an all-day undertaking; no point in trying to start just as night was falling. He bought a loaf of bread, some onions, and a cup of wine at the tavern next to his lodgings, then went back, hung the gauzy mosquito-netting he had rented over his bed, and went to sleep.

He dreamed of Helen, Helen as she was before the smallpox had robbed her of first her beauty and then her life. He dreamed of her laughing blue eyes, of the way her lips felt on his, of her sliding a robe from her white shoulders, of her intimate caress—

He woke then. He always woke then. The sweat that bathed him did not spring from the weather; the north wind kept Alexandria pleasant in summer. He stared into the darkness, wishing the dream would either leave him or, just once, go on a few seconds more.

He had not touched a woman since Helen died. In the first months of mourning, he thought long and hard about abandoning the secular world for the peace of the monastery. The thought went through him still, now and again. But what sort of monk would he make when, as the dreams so clearly showed, fleshly pleasures yet held such power in his mind?

Slowly, slowly, he drifted back toward sleep. Maybe he would be lucky—or unlucky—enough to find the dream again.

In Constantinople, a letter with the seal and signature of George Lakhanodrakon would instantly have opened doors and loosened tongues for Argyros: the Master of Offices was one of the chief ministers of the *Basileus* of the Romans. Argyros was too junior a magistrianos to know the leader of the corps at all well, but who could tell that—who would risk angering George Lakhanodrakon?—from the letter?

It worked in Alexandria, too, but only after a fashion and only in conjunction with some out-and-out bribery. Two weeks, everything Argyros had won on board ship, and three nomismata more disappeared before a secretary showed him into the office of Mouamet Dekanos, deputy to the Augustal prefect who governed Egypt for the *Basileus*.

Dekanos, a slight, dark man with large circles under his eyes, read quickly through the letter Argyros presented to him: " 'Render this my trusted servant the same assistance you would me, for he has my full confidence,' " the administrator finished. He shoved the pile of papyri on his desk to one side, making a clear space in which he set the document from the capital. "I'll be glad to help you, uh, Argyros. Your business I can hope to finish one day, which is more than I can say for this mess here." He scowled at the papyri he had just moved.

"Illustrious sir?" Argyros said. Dekanos was important enough for him to make sure he sounded polite.

"This mess here," the prefect's deputy repeated with a sour sort of pride, "goes all the way back to the days of my name saint."

"Of Saint Mouamet?" Argyros felt his jaw drop. "But it's—what?—seven hundred years now since he converted to Christianity."

"So it is," Dekanos agreed. "So it is. If you know that, I suppose you know of the Persian invasion that sent him fleeing from his monastery to Constantinople."

The magistrianos nodded. Born a pagan Arab, Mouamet had found Christ on a trading run into Syria, and ended his life as an archbishop in distant Ispania. He had also found a gift for hymnography; his canticles in praise of God and Christ were still sung all through the Empire. After such a remarkable and holy life, no wonder he had quickly been recognized as a saint.

Dekanos resumed, "That was the worst the Persians have ever hit the empire. They even ruled here in Alexandria for fifteen years, and ruled by their own laws. A good many bequests were granted whose validity was open to challenge when Roman rule returned. This mess here"—he liked to repeat himself, Argyros noticed—"is *Pcheris vs. Sarapion*. It's one of those challenges."

"But it's—what?—seven hundred years!" Now it was Argyros' turn to say the same thing over again, this time in astonished protest.

"So?" Dekanos rolled his eyes. "Egyptian families are usually enormous; they don't die out, worse luck. And they love to go to law—it's more fun than the hippodrome, and with better odds, too. *And* any judgment can be endlessly appealed: The scribe misspelled this word, they'll say, or used an accusative instead of a genitive, which obviously changes the meaning of the latest decree. Obviously." Argyros had never heard it used as a swearword before. "And so—"

Living in an empire that had endured thirteen centuries since the Incarnation, and was mighty long before that, the magistrianos had always thought of continuity as something to be striven for. Now, for the first time, he saw its dark side; some timely chaos should long since have swept *Pcheris vs. Sarapion* into oblivion. No wonder Mouamet Dekanos had pouches under his eyes.

With an effort Argyros dragged his thoughts back to the matter at hand. "As you have read, sir, the Emperor, may Christ preserve him, would be pleased if the rebuilding of your great pharos here proceeded at a more rapid pace. Through the Master of Offices, he has sent me from Constantinople to try to move the process along in any way I can."

The Augustal prefect governed Alexandria and Egypt from what had been the palace of the Ptolemies before Rome acquired the province. The promontory stood on Lokhias Point, which jutted into the sea from the eastern part of the city. By luck, the window in Dekanos' chamber faced northwest, toward the half-finished tower of stone that would—or might—one day become the restored lighthouse. At more than half a mile, the workers there would have seemed tiny as ants from the office, but there were none to see. Argyros' nod and wave said that more plainly than words.

Dekanos frowned. "My dear sir, we have been petitioning Constantinople for leave to rebuild the pharos since the earthquake toppled it, only to be ignored by several emperors in succession. Only eight years have gone by since at last we were granted permission to go to work." Argyros would not have said *only*, but Argyros did not have *Pcheris vs. Sarapion* and its ilk to deal with, either. "We've not done badly since."

"No indeed, not on the whole," Argyros said with what seemed to be agreement. "Still, his Imperial Majesty is disappointed that progress has been so slow these past two years. Surely in a land so populous as this, he feels, adequate supplies of labor are available for the completion of any such task."

"Oh, aye, we have any number of convicted felons to grub rock in the quarries, and any number of strong-backed brainless oafs to haul it to the pharos." Dekanos kept his voice under tight control—he was as wary of Argyros as the other way round—but his choice of words showed his anger. "Skilled workers, though, stone-carvers and concrete-spreaders and carpenters for scaffolding and all the rest, are not so easy to come by. We've had trouble with them." He looked as if the admission pained him.

It puzzled the magistrianos. "But why? Surely they must obey an imperial order to provide their services."

"My dear sir, I can see you do not know Alexandria." Dekanos' chuckle held scant amusement. "The guilds—"

"Constantinople also has guilds," Argyros interrupted. He still felt confused. "Every city in the empire has its craftsmen's associations."

"No doubt, no doubt. But does Constantinople have *anakhoresis*?"

" 'Withdrawal'?" the magistrianos echoed. Now he was frankly floundering. "I'm sorry, but I don't follow you."

"The word means more than just 'withdrawal' in Egypt, I fear. The peasants in the farming villages along the Nile have always had the custom of simply running away—withdrawing—from their homes when taxes get too heavy or the flood fails. Usually they come back as things improve, though they may turn to banditry if the hard times last."

"Peasants do that all over the empire, all over the world." Argyros shrugged. "How is Egypt any different?"

"Because here, *anakhoresis* goes a good deal further than that. If, say, a man is executed and the locals feel the sentence was unjust, whole villagefuls of them may withdraw in protest. And if"—Dekanos was ahead of the magistrianos' objection—"we try to punish the ringleaders or force the villagers back to their places, we're apt to just incite an even bigger *anakhoresis*. A couple of times the whole Nile valley has been paralyzed, from the Delta all the way down to the First Cataract."

Argyros understood the horror that came into the Alexandrian's voice at the prospect. In Constantinople, officials feared riots the same way, because one once had grown till it had almost cast Justinian the Great from his throne. Every province, the magistrianos supposed, had special problems to give its rulers sleepless nights.

All the same, something did not add up here. "The peasants are not restless now, though, or you would not have said you had plenty of unskilled labor available," Argyros said slowly.

"Very good," Dekanos said, plainly pleased the magistrianos had stayed with him. "You are right, sir. Very good. But here in Alexandria, you see, the guilds have also learned to play the game of *anakhoresis*. Let something not go to their liking, and they walk away from their jobs."

"And that—"

"—is what has happened with the pharos, yes."

"May the Virgin preserve us all." Argyros felt his head begin to ache.

"There's more." Mouamet Dekanos seemed to take morbid pleasure in going on with his bad news. "As I say, this is Alexandria; we've dealt with guild *anakhoreseis* before—or with one guild's withdrawing, anyway. But *all* the guilds pulled out of working on the pharos at the same time, and none will go back till they *all* agree they're happy. And this is Alexandria, where no one wants to agree with anyone about anything."

"Well," the magistrianos said, doing his best to hold on to reason, "they must all have been happy once upon a time or no work ever would have been done. What made them want to, uh, withdraw in the first place?"

"Good question," Dekanos said. "I wish I had a good answer for you."

"So do I."

Most of the letters on the signs above shops in Alexandria's western district looked Greek, but most of the words they spelled out were nonsense to Argyros. He knew no Coptic; as well as confusing his eyes, the purring, hissing speech filled his ears, for the quarter known as Rhakotis had for centuries been the haunt of native Egyptians.

The locals eyed him suspiciously. His inches and relatively light skin said he was not one of them. But those same inches and the sword on his belt warned he was no one to trifle with. Hard looks were as far as the natives went.

He stopped into a cobbler's shop that advertised itself not only in Coptic but in intelligible if badly spelled Greek. As he'd hoped, the man inside had a smattering of that language. "Can you tell me how to find the street where the carpenters work?" the magistrianos asked. He jingled coins in his hand.

The cobbler did not hold out an open palm, though. "Why you want to know?" he growled.

"The leaders of their guild will have shops there, surely. I need to speak with them," Argyros said. The fellow, he noticed, had not denied knowing; he did not want to get his wind up. When the cobbler still said nothing, Argyros gave a mild prod. "If I intended anything more, would I not come with a squadron of soldiers who know *exactly* where the guildsmen work?"

The cobbler grinned at that. His teeth were very white against his dark brown skin. "Suppose you might," he admitted. He gave directions, so quickly that Argyros made him slow down

and repeat them several times. Alexandria's grid of streets helped
strangers find their way around, but only so much.

The magistrianos had a good ear for instructions. After only
a couple of wrong turns, he found himself on a street loud with
the pounding of hammers and fragrant from sawdust. Again he
looked for a shop with a bilingual sign. When he found one, he
stepped in and waited for the carpenter to look up from the chair
he was repairing. The carpenter said something in Coptic, and
then, after a second look at Argyros, tried Greek: "What can I
do for you today, sir?"

"You can start by telling me why the carpenters' guild has
withdrawn from work on the pharos."

The carpenter's face, which had been open and interested a
moment before, froze. "That's not for me to say, sir," he answered slowly. "You need to talk to one of the chiefs."

"Excellent," Argyros said, making the man blink. "Suppose
you take me to one."

Outmaneuvered, the carpenter set down his mallet. He turned
his head and shouted. After a few seconds a stripling who looked
just like him came out of a back room. A rapid colloquy in
Coptic followed. The carpenter turned back to Argyros. "My
son will watch the shop while we are gone. Come."

He sounded resentful, and kept looking back at the mallet on
the floor. Then he saw the magistrianos' hand resting on the hilt
of his sword. Shaking his head, he led Argyros out into the
street.

Argyros glanced up at the sign again. "Your name is Teus?"
he asked. The carpenter nodded. "And who is the man to whom
you're taking me?"

"He is called Khesphmois," Teus said. He kept his mouth
shut the rest of the way to Khesphmois' shop.

KHESPHMOIS—MASTER CARPENTER, the sign above the estab-
lishment declared in Greek and, Argyros supposed, Coptic. The
look of the place did not contradict the sign's claim. It was three
times the size of Teus' shop, and on a busier corner to boot.
People bustled in and out, and the racket of several men working
carried out to the street.

Teus led Argyros through the beaded entrance curtain that
did something, at least, to keep flies outside. A carpenter looked
up from the dowel he was filing, smiled and nodded at Teus.
The fellow did not seem to be Khesphmois himself, for Teus'
sentence had the master carpenter's name in it and sounded like
a question.

The other man's reply had to mean something like "I'll bring him." He got up and hurried off. When he came back from behind a pile of boards a moment later, he had with him another man, one with only a few more years than Argyros' thirty or so. The magistrianos was expecting a graybeard, but this vigorous fellow had to be Khesphmois.

So he was. Teus bowed to him, at the same time dropping a hand to his own knee, an Egyptian greeting Argyros had already seen a dozen times in the streets of Rhakotis. When Khesphmois had returned the salute, Teus spoke for a couple of minutes in Coptic, pointing at the magistrianos as he did so.

Khesphmois' round, clean-shaven face went surprisingly stern as Teus drew to a close. Like Teus—like all the carpenters in the shop—he wore only sandals and a white linen skirt that reached from his waist to just above his knees, but he also clothed himself in dignity. In good Greek, he asked Argyros, "Who are you, a stranger, to question the long-established right of our guild to withdraw from a labor we have found onerous past any hope of toleration?"

"I am Basil Argyros, magistrianos in the service of his imperial majesty, the *Basileus* Nikephoros III, from Constantinople," Argyros replied. Khesphmois' shop went suddenly quiet as everyone within earshot stopped work to stare. Into that sudden silence, the magistrianos went on. "I might add that in Constantinople guilds have no right of *anakhoresis*, long-established or otherwise. Seeking as he does to restore what is an ornament to your city and its commerce, the Emperor does not look with favor on your refusal to cooperate in that work. He has sent me here"—a slight exaggerration but, one that would not be wasted on the carpenters—"to do what I can to move it forward once more."

The carpenters spoke to—before long, yelled at—one another in Coptic. Argyros wished he could follow what they were saying. Whatever it was, it got hotter by the second. Finally Khesphmois, who had been less noisy than most, raised his hand in an almost imperial gesture of command. Quiet slowly returned.

The master carpenter told Argyros, "This is *not* Constantinople, sir, and you would do well to remember it. So would the Emperor. You may tell him so, if you have his ear." Khesphmois spoke in dry tones, seemingly used to officials who boasted of their lofty connections. Argyros felt his ears grow hot. Khesphmois continued. "Perhaps you should pick another guild to try to frighten. The carpenters stand firm.'' Teus and those of Khesphmois' men who knew Greek snarled agreement.

"You misunderstand me—" Argyros began to protest.

"And you misunderstand us," Khesphmois broke in. "Now go, or it will be the worst for you. Get out!" Just because he hadn't shouted before, Argyros had judged that he did not care to. That was a mistake.

The magistrianos kept his hand away from his sword this time. Too many men had too many potential weapons close by. "The prefect will hear of your intransigence," he warned. "He may try to root it out by force."

"He has known of it for a long time," Khesphmois retorted. "And if he uses force, there will be *anakhoresis* by every guild in Alexandria. We will stop the city. He knows that, too. So—" He jerked a thumb toward the curtain of beads.

Furious and frustrated, Argyros turned to go. He was reaching out to shove the beads aside when someone behind him called, "Wait!" He spun around, startled. It was a woman's voice.

"Zois," Khesphmois said, naming her and at the same time letting the magistrianos know from the mixture of patience and annoyance in his voice that she was his wife. He had used that same tone with Helen, and she with him, many times. As always, sorrow stabbed him when he thought of her.

"Don't 'Zois' me," the woman snapped; her Greek was as good as her husband's. "You are making a mistake if you turn this man from Constantinople into an enemy."

"I don't think so," Khesphmois said, also in Greek. Maybe only a couple of his men spoke it, Argyros thought, and he wanted to keep the family spat as private as he could. He was sure that was a forlorn hope, but grateful because it let him follow the talk.

"I know you don't. That's why I came out," Zois said. She was a few years younger than her husband, slim where he would soon be portly, and quite short. Her high cheekbones were the best feature of her swarthy face, those and her eyes, which were very large and dark. Her chin was delicate, but the wide mouth above it was at the moment thin and firmly set.

The magistrianos waited for Khesphmois to send his wife away for interfering in men's business. As he would learn, though, Egyptians were easier about such things than was usual at Constantinople. And even in the capital, men who exercised all the control over wives legally theirs were most of them unhappily wed.

"Can you afford to be wrong?" Zois demanded. Her hand went to the silk collar of her blue linen tunic. Only someone well off could have afforded the ornament. "If you are wrong, we will lose everything, and not just us but all the carpenters and all the other guilds. If someone comes all the way from Constantinople to see to this business, he will not just up and leave."

"Your lady wife"— Argyros gave her his best bow— "is right. I am not especially wise, but I am especially stubborn. I should also tell you I am not a good man to sink in a canal, in case the thought crossed your mind. Magistrianoi look after their own."

"No," Khesphmois said absently; that he was still more intent on arguing with Zois made Argyros believe him. To her, his hands on hips in irritation, the master carpenter went on, "What would you have me do, then? Call off the *anakhoresis* now?"

"Of course not," she answered at once. "But why not show him the reasons for it? He *is* from far away; what can he know of how things are here in Alexandria? When he sees, when he hears, maybe he will have the influence in the capital to make the prefect and his henchmen easier on us. What have you to lose by trying?"

"Maybe, maybe, maybe," Khesphmois mocked. "Maybe I will turn into a crocodile and spend the next hundred years basking on a sandbank, too, but I don't lose any sleep over it." Still, for his wife's last question he had no good answer, and so, scowling, he growled to Argyros, "Come along, then, if you must. I'll take you to the pharos, and we'll find out if you have eyes in your head to see with."

Teus and a couple of other carpenters started to protest, but Khesphmois shouted them down in a Coptic that sounded pungent. "Thank you," the magistrianos said to him, and got only another scowl for an answer. The magistrianos turned to Zois and bowed again. "And thank you, my lady." He spoke as formally as if to a Constantinopolitan noblewoman, as much in the hope of vexing Khesphmois as for any other reason.

He was surprised when Zois dipped her head in the same elegant acknowledgment one of those noblewomen might have used. He had a moment to notice how gracefully her neck curved. Then Khesphmois repeated, "Come along, you." Without waiting to see whether Argyros would follow, the master carpenter stamped out into the street.

The magistrianos hurried after him. "Good-bye," Zois called. "Good-bye, the both of you." That nearly brought Argyros up short, not so much because she was polite enough to include him but because she had used the dual number, the special—and most archaic—grammatical form reserved for pairs.

Even coming from his imagined noblewoman, the dual would have sounded pretentious. Hearing it from an Egyptian carpenter's wife was strange indeed. Argyros wondered where she could have learned it. Thinking back, he decided that was the first time she became an individual for him.

At the time, though, the thought was gone in an eyeblink, because he had to hustle along to catch up with Khesphmois. The master carpenter was short and stocky but moved with a grim determination that Argyros, even with his longer legs, was hard-pressed to match.

He tried several times to make small talk. Khesphmois answered only in grunts. The one thing Argyros really wanted to say—"Your wife is an interesting woman"—he could not, not to a man he had known less than an hour and one who was no friend of his. He soon walked on in silence, which seemed to suit Khesphmois well enough.

The master carpenter might also have been impervious to heat, no mean asset in Alexandria. He tramped along the raised road that still marked the path of the original, narrow Heptastadion, then east on the southern coast of the island of Pharos to the base of the lighthouse there.

The pharos, even in its present half-rebuilt state, grew more awe-inspiring with every step Argyros took toward it. He had long thought no building could be grander than Constantinople's great church of Hagia Sophia, but the sheer vertical upthrust of the pharos had a brusque magnificence of its own. Already it was taller than the top of Hagia Sophia's central dome, and would reach twice that height if it ever was finished.

Khesphmois craned his neck at the towering pillar, too. "It only goes to show," he said, "that Alexandria breeds real men."

Argyros snorted, suspecting locals had been using that

joke on newcomers for all the sixteen centuries since Sostratos first erected (coming up with that word made the magistrianos short all over again) the phallos. *Pharos*, he corrected himself sternly, ordering his mind to stop playing tricks with words. Suddenly he felt every day of his two years of celibacy.

His mental order proved easier to carry out than he had expected. As he and Khesphmois approached the lighthouse, he began to take more notice of the line of men marching in front of it. Some of them carried placards. Argyros frowned, puzzled. "Are they mendicant monks?" he asked the master carpenter. "They are not in monastic garb."

Khesphmois threw back his head and laughed. "Hardly. Come with me yet a little farther, and you will see."

Shrugging, the magistrianos obeyed. He saw that not all the men by the pharos were marching, after all. The ones who were just standing around looked like a squad of light infantry—they had no body armor, but wore helmets and carried shields and spears. They also looked monumentally bored. One trooper, in fact, was fast asleep, leaning back against the lighthouse's lowest course of stonework.

The marchers seemed hardly more excited than the soldiers; Argyros was certain they were doing something they had done many times before. Then he drew close enough to read their placards, and doubted in rapid succession his conclusions and his eyesight.

THIS LABOR IS TOO DANGEROUS FOR ANY MAN TO CARRY OUT, one sign said. PALTRY PAY FOR DEADLY WORK, another shrieked. CARPENTERS AND CONCRETE-SPREADERS WITHDRAW TOGETHER, shouted a third. Others were in Coptic, but the magistrianos had no doubt they were equally inflammatory.

"Why don't the soldiers drive them away?" he demanded of Khesphmois. "Why are they here, if not for that? Have the guilds bribed the commander of the watch to let this sedition go on?" He was shocked to the core. Such an insolent display at Constantinople—or any other town he knew— would instantly have landed the marchers in prison.

"At least your questions are to the point," the master carpenter said. "A good thing, since you have so many of them."

"May your answers match my questions, then." Argyros

felt brief pride at his sardonic response; he did not want Khesphmois to know just how disturbed he was.

"Very well," Khesphmois said. "The soldiers are here mostly to see that the marchers do no pilfering. And no, we have not bribed the watch commander, though I must say we tried. But Cyril is an honest man, worse luck for us."

By then, the magistrianos suspected that trying to hide his shock was a losing battle. Anywhere else in the Empire, if artisans refused to work—in itself unlikely—soldiers would simply force them to return. But Mouamet Dekanos struck Argyros as being bright enough to try that if he thought it would work. That meant, Argyros concluded unhappily, that Khesphmois and the other guild leaders really could immobilize Alexandria if these weird privileges of theirs were tampered with.

"Egypt," Argyros muttered. Nowhere else in the Empire would such nonsense as *Pcheris vs. Sarapion* have dragged on for seven hundred years, either. The magistrianos gathered himself and turned back to Khesphmois. "Why," he asked carefully, "have all you workers chosen to withdraw?"

The master carpenter looked at him with something like respect. "Do you know, you are the first official who ever bothered to ask that. The prefect and his staff just told us to go back to work, the way they do during a usual *anakhoresis*. Any other time we would, eventually. But not now. Not here. So they have waited, not daring to set soldiers on us and not knowing what else to do, and we have stayed away and nothing has got done."

That sounded appallingly likely to Argyros. If a contested inheritance could stay contested for seven centuries, what were a couple of years here or there in putting a pharos back together? Delay would be a way of life for the local bureaucrats, here even more than in most of the Empire. Well, one of the things magistrianoi were for was shaking up officials too set in their ways.

"I'm asking," the magistrianos said. "Why haven't you gone back to work?"

"By Saint Cyril, I'll show you," Khesphmois exclaimed. "Follow me, if you've the stomach—and the head—for it."

He walked past the sign-carriers, waving to a couple from the carpenters' guild. The watchmen only nodded at him; by now, Argyros supposed, they must know him as well as their own officers. The magistrianos, who was on their side, got more hard looks than the master carpenter.

Khesphmois walked into the pharos. Argyros followed

still. Their footsteps echoed in the gloom within. Khesph-mois hurried over to the spiral stair just inside the doorway and started up.

The stairway was almost as dark as the chamber that led to it, though window openings set at intervals into the thick wall gave enough light for the magistrianos to see where he was putting his feet. The idea of stumbling and rolling down so long a stairway made his sweat turn cold.

By the time he reached the top even of the truncated pharos, Argyros had sweat in plenty. Ahead of him, Khesphmois still seemed fresh. The magistrianos muttered to himself as he panted up the last few steps. His time behind a desk in Constantinople was making him soft.

Alexandria's usual northerly breeze helped cool him while he got his breath back. He turned his back to the breeze and peered across the Great Harbor at the city. The view was superb. He even towered high above the ancient obelisks—"Cleopatra's Needles," the locals called them, but they were older than that—not far from the Heptastadion's southern root.

He had no idea how long he might have stood there staring, but Khesphmois' dry cough recalled him to himself. "I didn't bring you up here to sightsee," the master carpenter said. "Look straight down."

A long stride and a short one brought the magistrianos to the edge of the stone block on which he stood. No fence or rail separated him from a couple of hundred feet of empty space. He cautiously peered over the edge; only the discipline he had acquired in the Roman army kept him from going to his knees or belly first. Far, far below, the marchers and watchmen looked as tiny as insects. Argyros was anything but sorry to step back. "A long way down," he observed, stating the obvious.

Khesphmois had been watching him closely. "You're a cool one," he said, not sounding happy to admit it. "But how would *you* like to be working up here instead of just standing?"

"I wouldn't," the magistrianos admitted at once. "But then, it's not my proper trade."

"Working this high is no one's proper trade," Khesphmois said. "If you take a wrong step, if someone bumps you by accident, if a piece of scaffolding breaks while you're on it, even if you make a bad stroke with your hammer, over you go and nothing's left of you but a red smear on the rocks. There are plenty of them down below, and there would have been many more if we hadn't staged the *anakhoresis*.''

''Some, certainly,'' Argyros nodded. ''Some trades are dangerous: the mines, the army, and, plainly, working at heights like this. But why do you say many?''

''The pharos is square in section thus far, yes?'' Khesphmois said.

The magistrianos nodded again.

''Well, the next part is to be octagonal and narrower—a tiny bit narrower,'' the master carpenter went on. ''What would you expect to happen to the carpenters who will have to face inward with almost no room at all to put their feet while they try to set up scaffolds, or to the stonecutters who try to climb onto the scaffolding to trim and polish the outsides of the blocks, or to the concrete-spreaders who take away the excess that squeezes out from between the courses of blocks?''

''The risks are worse now, you're telling me,'' Argyros said slowly.

''That's just what I'm telling you.''

''How do we make them less, then?'' the magistrianos asked. ''Enough less, I mean, to get the various guilds to come back to work? Alexandria and the whole Empire need this pharos restored.''

''And Alexandria and the whole empire care not a moldy fig how many workers die restoring it,'' Khesphmois said bitterly. ''Now you've seen the problem, man from Constantinople. What do you aim to do about it?''

''Right now, I don't know,'' Argyros said. ''I truly do not. I work no miracles, though this is a column any pillar-sitting saint might envy.''

Khesphmois grunted. ''You're honest, at any rate. You—'' He stopped; the magistrianos had raised a hand.

''I wasn't finished. One way or another I will find you an answer. I swear it by God, the Virgin, and St. Mouamet, who as patron of changes will be apt to hear my oath.''

''So he will.'' Khesphmois crossed himself; Argyros copied the gesture. The master carpenter went on, ''Whether the Augustal prefect and his staff pay you any heed, though, is something else again.'' Without waiting for an answer, he started down the stairway. After a final long look at the panorama of the city, Argyros followed.

That afternoon, back on the mainland once more, he peered out toward the half-erected pharos. Thinking of it like that reminded him of the bawdy pun he had unwittingly made earlier in the day. And thinking of that pun made *him* come half-erect.

He scowled and clenched his fists, trying to force his body back under the control of his will. His body, as bodies do, resisted. Oh, you'd make a fine monk, he told himself angrily, a wonderful monk; they'd canonize you after you died, under the name St. Basil Priapos. This was a fine way to remember Helen.

But he remembered her all too vividly, remembered the touch of her lips and the surge of her body against his. He caught himself wondering how Zois would be. That thought made him angrier than ever. Not only was it shameful lust, it betrayed the memory of his dead wife. He still wondered, though.

When he dreamed that night, as always he woke too soon.

"My dear sir, surely you are joking!" Mouamet Dekanos' eyebrows climbed toward his hairline. "You want me to sit down and dicker with these, these laborers? Think of the ghastly precedent it would set! Ghastly!"

"I've thought of it," Argyros admitted. "I don't like it. I don't like seeing the pharos still half-built, either. Nor does the Emperor. That problem is immediate. The precedent will just have to take care of itself."

Dekanos stared at him as if he had just proposed converting the whole population of the Roman Empire to Persian sun worship by force. "Precedent, my dear sir, is part of the glue that holds the Empire together," he said stiffly.

"So it is," the magistrianos said. "The grain shipments from Alexandria to Constantinople are another part, and the Emperor has lost patience with having ships on their way back here go astray without need. In this case, he reckons that of greater importance than precedent."

"So *you* say," Dekanos retorted. "So you say."

"Would you like me to meet with the Augustal prefect and ask his opinion of your attitude?"

The Alexandrian functionary's face went dark with anger. "You're bluffing."

"Try me." As a matter of fact, Argyros was. In an argument with someone from the distant, resented capital, he was sure the prefect would back his own aide. Had he been an intimate of the Master of Offices instead of merely one of his magistrianoi, though, not even the Augustal prefect could have afforded to ignore him. And George Lakhanodrakon's letter made him seem to be one. He rose, took out the parchment and unrolled it, and flourished it in Dekanos' face. "You *do* recall this, I hope."

"Well, what if I do?" Dekanos was still scowling. "For that matter," he went on angrily, "how will you be able to gather all these fractious guild leaders together and make them and their guild members abide by anything they might agree to? For all you know, they will say one thing to ease the pressure on them and then turn around and do just the opposite."

When the official shifted the basis of the argument, Argyros knew he had his man. "If they did that, would they not have gone beyond the bounds even of what you Alexandrians tolerate in an *anakhoresis*?" he asked. "You could then use whatever force you had to with less fear of bringing the whole city to the point of insurrection."

"Perhaps." Dekanos pursed his lips. "Perhaps."

"As for gathering the leaders of the guilds," the magistrianos said persuasively, "leave that to me. I wouldn't think of formally involving you with speaking to them until everything on the other side was in readiness."

"Certainly not," Dekanos said, mollified by Argyros' apparent concern for proper procedure. "Hmm. Yes, I suppose you can go forward, then, provided you do it on those terms and provided you stress our unique clemency in treating with the artisans in this one special case."

"Of course," the magistrianos said, although he had no intention of stressing anything of the sort. He bowed his way out of Dekanos' office and did not grin until his back was to the Alexandrian. Grinning still, he headed for Khesphmois' shop in the district of Rhakotis.

He did not see the master carpenter when he walked through the beaded curtain. Only one of the journeymen was there, luckily one who spoke some Greek. The fellow said, "He not back till tomorrow. He helping build—how you say?—grandstand for parade. Busy all night, he say." The man chuckled. "He terrible mad about that. I there, too, but have this cabinet to repair for rich man. He want it now, no matter what. Rich men like that."

"Yes," Argyros said, though he knew nothing of being rich from personal experience. He hesitated, then asked, "What does the parade celebrate?"

"Feast day for St. Arsenios."

"Oh." Argyros wondered what the saint, a man who had withdrawn from the world to live out his life as a monk in the Egyptian desert, would think of having his memory celebrated with a large, noisy parade. He shrugged. That was the Alexandrians' problem. Khesphmois was his. "I'll come back tomorrow afternoon, then. I do need to see your master." He turned to go, thinking that as long as he was in this part of the city, Teus might direct him to some other master carpenters.

"Can I do anything to help you, man from Constantinople?"

Argyros had just put his hand in the entranceway to thrust aside the strings of beads. Now he jerked it back. Small spheres of glass and painted clay clicked off one another. "Truly I don't know, my lady," he said. His unspoken thought was, That depends on how much influence you have on your husband.

Zois might have picked it out of the air. "I know you did not come all this way simply to see *me*," she said, her eyebrows and the corners of her mouth lifting slightly in a cynical smile. Eve might have worn that smile, Argyros thought, when God came to talk business with Adam, and later given Adam his comeuppance for the visit. He put aside his blasphemous maunderings; Zois was going on, "Still, perhaps we could discuss it over a cup of wine."

The magistrianos' eyes flicked to the journeyman carpenter, but the fellow did not look up from the work he had resumed. And no wonder: with her husband absent, Zois had not presumed to come out alone to speak with Argyros. A servant girl stood behind him, a pretty little thing who could not have been more than fifteen and who was, the magistrianos saw, about eight months pregnant.

He considered. "Thank you," he said at last. "Maybe we could."

"This way," Zois said, then spoke in Coptic to the servant girl, who dipped her head and hurried off. "Don't let fear of Lukra's spying on us worry you," Zois told the magistrianos as she led him back toward the rooms where she and Khesphmois lived. "She has no Greek. My husband

did not take her on for that.'' She smiled her ancient smile
again.

Like the shop, the home behind it was of mud brick. The
rooms were small and rather dark. The furniture was splendid, though, which surprised Argyros until he remembered
Khesphmois' trade.

Lukra came back a few minutes later with wine, dates
candied in honey, and sheets of flat, chewy unleavened
bread. Zois waited for the girl to pour the wine, then spoke
again in Coptic. Lukra disappeared. ''She will not be back,''
Zois said, nodding to herself. She raised her cup to the
magistrianos. ''Health to you.''

''Health to you,'' he echoed, drinking. The vintage was
not one he knew, which meant it was most likely a local
one not reckoned fine enough to export. It was not bad,
though, and had a tartness that cut through the cloyingly
sweet taste of the dates.

Zois ate, then wiped her hands and patted at her mouth
with a square of embroidered linen. ''Now,'' she said when
she was through, ''what do you need from Khesphmois?''

''His cooperation in getting the other leaders of the carpenters' guild and the men who head the rest of the guilds
that have withdrawn from work on the pharos to talk with
the Augustal prefect's deputy so they can agree on a way to
get construction started again.''

Her eyes, already large, seemed to grow further as she
widened them in surprise. ''You can arrange this?''

''If the guildsmen will play their part, yes. I already have
agreement from the prefect's deputy. The pharos is too important not only to Alexandria but to all the Empire to be
delayed by this *anakhoresis*.''

''I agree,'' Zois said at once. ''I warned Khesphmois
from the outset that the guilds were facing too dangerous a
foe in the city government, because it could crush them if
their stubbornness pushed it to the point of wanting to. I
will help with anything that has a hope of ending the *anakhoresis* peacefully.''

''Thank you.'' Argyros did not tell her the Augustal prefect and his staff were as frightened of the guilds' power as
she was of the government's. Having both sides wary was
probably a good idea. He went on, ''Do you think you can
sway your husband to your point of view?''

''I suspect so. Khesphmois is more likely to insist on

having his own way on matters where there is no risk to him.'' The magistrianos thought that was only sensible, and true of anyone. Then Zois went on. ''Take Lukra, for instance. Khesphmois did.'' Bitterness welled forth in her voice.

''*Did* he?'' Argyros' interest, among other things, rose. So *that* was why she was seeing him alone, he thought: for the sake of revenge on her husband. That was sinful. So was the act of adultery itself. At the moment, the magistrianos did not care. Relief would have been easy to buy at any time since Helen died. Despite his body's urgings, he had held back.

This, though . . . Zois was attractive in an exotic way, clever enough for him to hope to enjoy her mind as well as her body. And she might be his for as long as he was in Alexandria, long enough, perhaps, for something more than desire—or her anger at Khesphmois—to bind them together. It would not be what he had known with his wife, but it could be better than the emptiness that had ruled his life these past years.

He got up and took a step toward Zois' chair. Then he noticed she had not stopped talking while lust had filled his head. She was saying, ''But for all his faults, he is not a bad man at bottom, you know. I would not see him hurt in any way, and he would be, he and many others, if the *anakhoresis* were put down by force.''

''Yes, that's likely so,'' the magistrianos agreed woodenly. He sat back down.

Zois sighed. ''If God had not willed that I be barren, I am sure Khesphmois would have left Lukra alone. And when the child is born, he and I will rear it as if it were our own.'' Her laugh was shaky. ''Here I am going on about my own life, when you came to talk of weighty affairs. I do apologize.''

''Think nothing of it, my lady.'' Now the magistrianos' voice sounded as it should. So *that* was why she was seeing him alone, he thought again, but this time with a different reason behind the *that*: Unburdening herself to a sympathetic stranger had to be easier than talking with a neighbor or friend here. A stranger would not be likely to gossip.

Argyros laughed at himself. Before he married Helen, he had never imagined himself irresistible to women. Thinking Zois had found him so was bracing. It made him proud. He knew what pride went before. Even as he had that thought, he felt himself falling.

"You are a kind man," Zois said. "As I told you, I will do my best to make sure my husband lends his influence to meeting with the prefect's men and trying to end the *anakhoresis*. And now, would you care for another date?" She held out the platter to him.

"No, thank you." When the magistrianos got up this time, he did not approach the master carpenter's wife. "I'm glad I can count on you, but now I do have other business to attend to." He let her show him out.

As the beads clicked behind him, he wondered what the other business was. For the life of him, he could not think of any. Maybe escaping his own embarrassment counted.

He walked north to the street of Kanopos, Alexandria's main east-west thoroughfare, the one on which Saint Athanasios' church fronted. With nothing better to do, he thought he would imitate many of the locals and lie down in his room during the midday heat.

Someone plucked at the sleeve of his tunic. He whirled, one hand dropping to the hilt of his sword—like any large city, Alexandria was full of light-fingered rogues. But this was no rogue—it was a girl two or three years older than Zois' maidservant. Under the paint on her face, she might have been pretty were she less thin. "Go to bed with me?" she said. Argyros would bet it was most of the Greek she knew. No, she had a bit more, a price: "Twenty folleis."

A big copper coin for an embrace . . . The magistrianos had rejected such advances before without having to think twice. Now, his blood already heated from what he had thought—no, hoped, he admitted to himself—he heard himself say, "Where?"

The girl's face lit up. She *was* pretty, he saw, at least when she smiled. She led him to a tiny chamber that opened onto an alley a couple of blocks from the street of Kanopos. With the door shut, the cubicle was hot, stuffy, and nearly night-dark. Argyros knew the much-used straw pallet would have bugs, but the girl was pulling her shift off over her head, lying down and waiting for him to join her. He did.

Afterward, he saw her scorn even in the gloom. After so long without a woman, he had spent himself almost at once. But that long denial was not to be relieved with a single round. "You pay twice," she warned, but then she was moving with him, urging him on. Harlots had their wiles, he knew, but he thought he pleased her the second time. He knew he pleased himself.

He knew he pleased her when he gave her a silver miliaresion, much more than she had asked of him. Maybe, for a while, she would be a little less scrawny.

His conscience troubled him as he finished the interrupted walk to his room. Such a sordid way to end his mourning for his wife: a skinny whore in a squalid crib. But he had not stopped mourning Helen, nor would he ever. He had only proved what he already knew—that wish as he might, he was not fit by nature for the single life.

And knowing that, would it have been better, he asked himself, to have returned to the sensual world with an act of adultery as well as one of fornication? He thought of Zois, of how attractive he had found her, and was not sure of the answer.

With an expression of barely concealed dislike, Mouamet Dekanos watched the guildsmen file into the meeting chamber. Argyros, who was sitting at one side of the table (he had left Dekanos the head) gave him credit for trying to conceal it.

The guildsmen were not even trying. They glowered impartially at both men waiting for them. They also frankly gaped at the magnificence of the hall in which they were received. Even in their finest clothes, they looked out of place, or rather looked like what they were—workmen in a palace.

"Illustrious sirs," Khesphmois said, nervously dipping his head to Argyros and Dekanos. As he slid into a chair, he went on. "These men with me are Hergeus son of Thotsytmis of the concrete spreaders' guild, and Miysis son of Seias of the guild of stonecutters."

"Yes, thank you, Khesphmois," Dekanos said. "Of course, I have had dealings with all you gentlemen"—he spit out the word as if it tasted bad—"before, but your comrades will be new to Argyros. He is here all the way from Constantinople itself to help us settle our differences."

"Illustrious sir," Hergeus and Miysis murmured as they took their seats. Like the other Alexandrians Argyros had met, they made a good show of looking unimpressed at the mention of the capital.

Miysis, the magistrianos thought, carried it off better. The stonecutters' leader was a squat, powerful man in his mid-fifties. His nose had been broken and a scar seamed one weathered cheek, but the eyes in that bruiser's face were disconcertingly keen. After sizing Argyros up, he turned to Dekanos and demanded, "How's he going to do that, illustrious sir, when we already know what's going on and can't see any way out?" Though his voice was a raspy growl, he did not speak bad Greek.

"I will leave that to the magistrianos to explain for himself," Dekanos answered.

"Thank you," Argyros said, ignoring the tone that made Dekanos' reply mean, *I haven't the slightest idea.* "Sometimes, gentlemen, ignorance is an advantage. Both sides in this *anakhoresis*, I would say, have clung so long and stubbornly to their own views that they have forgotten others are possible. Perhaps I will be able to show you all something new yet acceptable to everyone."

"Pah," was all Miysis said to that. Hergeus added, "Perhaps I'll swim the length of the Nile tomorrow, too, but I wouldn't bet on it."

His grin made the words sting less than they would have otherwise. Like Khesphmois, he was young to be a guild leader, but there the resemblance between them ended. Hergeus was tall for an Egyptian, and as skinny as the trollop Argyros had bedded a few days before.

"We are here talking together," Khesphmois pointed out. "That is something new."

The master carpenter, Argyros knew, was to some degree an ally, if only because this meeting set his prestige on the line. The magistrianos had trouble caring. Memories of the way he had abandoned his self-imposed celibacy kept crowding in on him. The act itself shamed him less than the thoughtless way he had yielded to his animal urges.

Hergeus had said something to him while he was woolgathering. Frowning, he pulled himself back to the matter at hand. "I'm sorry, sir, I missed that."

"Seeing things we can't again, eh?" But the concrete-pourer was smiling still, in a way that invited everyone to share his amusement. "Well, I just want to know how you can make the risk of death and maiming worth the niggardly wages we got for work on the pharos."

"We pay as well as anyone else," Dekanos snapped, nettled.

"But I can make chairs and cabinets without the fear of turning into a red splash on the ground if I sneeze at the wrong time," Khesphmois said.

"Would higher pay bring you back to the pharos?" Argyros asked.

The three guild representatives looked at one another. Then they all looked at Mouamet Dekanos. "Out of the question," he said. "The precedent that would set is pernicious."

"It's not just the silver, anyhow," Miysis said. "My lads would sooner do other work, and that's all there is to it. We're tired of using guild fees to pay for funerals. We had as many in the work on the pharos as in a couple of generations before."

"Enough silver might tempt some concrete-spreaders back," Hergeus said. "The young ones, the bolder ones, the ones with families to worry over. The ones up to their chins in debt, too, I suppose."

"Aye, some of us, too, I would say," Khesphmois agreed. "*Enough* silver."

"Yes, and let us grant your first demand here and what would come of it?" Dekanos said. "You'd make another and another till you'd hold out for a nomisma every hour on the hour. Who could afford to pay you then?"

Hergeus chuckled. "It's a problem I'd like to have."

"It's not one the powerful men of the city would like to have," Dekanos retorted. That brought things down to basics, Argyros thought. Naturally Dekanos worried first about Alexandria's upper classes; they were the men he had to keep happy. Even the Augustal prefect needed to worry about what they thought, though his responsibility was to the Emperor. If they turned against him, what could he accomplish?

That was also true of the guilds, however, at least this time, although Dekanos seemed unwilling to recognize it. Argyros did not care one way or the other. All he wanted to see was the pharos getting taller again. He said, "I think we can keep the problem of precedent from getting out of hand if we establish a special rate of pay for the specific task of rebuilding the lighthouse. Then we will not have to worry about it again unless the earth trembles again, which God prevent.''

''I don't care what we get paid,'' Miysis said. ''So long as we have any other work at all, we won't go near the cursed pharos. Money's no good to a dead man. And I'd like to see you make it go up without us stonecutters.''

Argyros felt like kicking the stubborn guildsman under the table. ''Purely for the sake of discussion,'' he said to Khesphmois and Hergeus, ''how much of a boost in pay would it take to bring your comrades out once more?''

The two locals spoke together in rapid Coptic. Khesphmois switched to Greek: ''Twice as much, and not a single copper follis less.''

Dekanos clapped a hand to his forehead, cried, ''You made a mistake, Argyros! You summoned men from the thieves' guild to meet with me.'' To the guildsmen he said, ''If you hope to gain anything from this meeting, you must show reason. I might, perhaps, under the special circumstances the magistrianos described, seek authorization for a raise of, ah, say, one part in twelve, but surely could not gain approval for any more than that.''

''One part in twelve is no raise at all. Look at the wealth around you!'' Khesphmois exclaimed, waving his hand at the chamber in which they sat. Far from being overawed, the master carpenter was clever enough to use that splendor as a weapon for his cause. Argyros was impressed; Dekanos was plainly discomfited.

''You are willing, then, illustrious sir, to raise our pay?'' Hergeus asked.

''As I said, under these special circumstances—'' Dekanos began.

The concrete-spreaders' leader cut him off with a wave of the hand. ''You said before that you wouldn't give us any raise at all. If a woman says she won't and then does after you give her ten nomismata, she's just as much a whore as if she did it for a follis. The only difference is her price, and that you can dicker over. That's what we're down to now, illustrious sir: dickering over the price. And I stand with Khesphmois—one part in twelve is no raise at all.''

Mouamet Dekanos glowered at Hergeus. ''Your tongue is altogether too free.'' The official glowered at Argyros, too, presumably for putting him in a position where he had to listen to blunt talk from a social inferior. Argyros hardly noticed. Every mention of whores brought his mind back to the girl he had bedded, and seemed calculated only to lacerate his conscience.

Reality returned when Dekanos began drumming his fingers on the table. "Who's best to declare what a fair raise would be?" the magistrianos said quickly to cover his lapse. "Neither side here trusts the other. Why not let, hmm, the patriarch of Alexandria arbitrate the dispute."

He had been thinking out loud, nothing more, but the words seemed a happy inspiration the moment they were out of his mouth. He smiled, waiting for Dekanos and the guildsmen to acclaim his Solomonic wisdom.

Instead, they all stared at him. "Er, which patriarch of Alexandria?" Dekanos and Khesphmois asked at the same time, the first time they had been more than physically together since they had sat down at the same table.

"*Which* patriarch?" The magistrianos scratched his head.

"For politeness' sake I will assume all three of these gentlemen are of orthodox faith," Dekanos said, "and also because assuming otherwise would bring down on me one more trouble than I need right now. Surely, however, many of their followers adhere to the dogmas"—he did not, Argyros noticed, say "heresy—"of the Monophysites, and thus would not trust the Orthodox patriarch to be disinterested. And I certainly cannot grant official recognition to the monophysites', ah, leader." Dekanos did not say patriarch, either, not in the same breath with monophysites.

Argyros felt his face grow hot. He gave an embarrassed nod. The monophysites—those who believed Christ to have had only one nature, the divine, after the Incarnation—had been strong in Egypt for nine hundred years, ecumenical councils to the contrary notwithstanding. Of course they would have a shadow ecclesiastical organization of their own, and of course Dekanos could not formally treat with it. Doing so would imply that orthodoxy was not the only possible truth. No official of the Roman Empire could ever admit that; Argyros was reluctant to think it even as a condition contrary to fact.

"This is all so much moonshine," Miysis rumbled. The stonecutter got to his feet and stomped toward the door, adding over his shoulder, "I already said once it's not the money, and I meant it. My lads'll find other things to do, thank you very much, illustrious sir." He walked out.

"Damnation." Mouamet Dekanos glared after him, then slowly turned back to the other two guild leaders. "Do you gentlemen feel the same way? If you do, you're welcome to leave now, and we'll let the city garrison try to return you to obedience."

"You'd not do that," Khesphmois exclaimed. "Calling out the soldiers would—"

"—Set all Alexandria aflame," Dekanos finished for him. "I know. But what good are soldiers if they cannot be used? The Emperor wants this pharos built. If I have to choose between offending the Alexandrian guilds and offending the *Basileus* of the Romans, I know what my choice will be."

If he was bluffing, he was a dab hand at hiding it. Argyros would not have cared to find out, and he had far more experience with officials' ploys than did either Khesphmois or Hergeus. The two guildsmen exchanged appalled glances. They had been confident Dekanos would not try to coerce them back to work. If they were wrong . . .

"I think we might talk further," Hergeus said quickly, "especially since your Illustriousness has shown himself willing to move on the matter of wages."

"Not any too willing." Having gained an advantage, Dekanos looked ready to hold on to it.

Khesphmois saw that clearly. "If it pleases the illustrious sir," he suggested, "we would agree to leaving the matter of how large our raise should be in the hands of the magistrianos here. He represents the Emperor, who as you say is eager to have the lighthouse restored. If it weren't for him, we wouldn't be talking at all. I expect he'd be fairer than any local man I can think of."

Argyros wondered if Khesphmois would have said that if he knew how badly the magistrianos had wanted to go to bed with his wife. Still, the master carpenter had a point. "I will make this settlement," Argyros said, "if all of you swear by Father, Son, and Holy Spirit, by the Virgin, and by your great Alexandrian saints Athanasios, Cyril, and Pyrrhos to abide by the terms I set down." He was pleased with himself for thinking to add the Alexandrian saints to the oath; monophysites revered them along with the orthodox.

"I will swear that oath for myself and on behalf of my guild," Khesphmois said at once, and did so. When he was through, Hergeus echoed him.

Their eyes swung to Dekanos. He let them stew for a while, then said gruffly, "Oh, very well. Time to have this cursed *anakhoresis* settled." He swore the oath.

"Thank you, gentlemen, for your trust in me. I hope I can deserve it," Argyros said. He was stalling; events had piled up faster than he was quite ready for. After some thought, he went on. "As for the matter of pay, justice, I am sure, lies between the demands of the two sides. Therefore, let pay for work on the pharos henceforth be half again the usual rate, for all guilds."

"Let it be so," Dekanos said promptly. The nods from Hergeus and Khesphmois were reluctant; the master carpenter's expression showed him unhappy with the choice he'd made.

Argyros raised a hand. "I am not finished. As we have all agreed, work on the pharos is uncommonly dangerous. Therefore, if a guildsman should die of an accident while doing that work, let the city government of Alexandria rather than his guild pay for his funeral."

This time Khesphmois and Hergeus quickly agreed, while Mouamet Dekanos sent the magistrianos a sour stare. Argyros bore up under it. Unlike Dekanos, he had looked down from the top of the pharos; he could imagine with gut-wrenching clarity what the results of even the smallest slip would be.

And if a worker did slip, he would bring disaster not just upon himself but also on his family. Argyros thought of the troubles Helen would have had bringing up Sergios as a widow had he rather than his wife and son perished in the smallpox epidemic. He said, "Finally, if a married worker should die of an accident while working on the pharos, let the city government of Alexandria settle on his widow and children, if any, a sum equal to, ah, six months' pay, for he will have died in service to the city and it is unjust to leave his family destitute on account of that service."

"No!" Dekanos said. "You go too far, much too far."

"Remember the oath you swore!" Khesphmois shouted at him, while Hergeus added, "Will you turn a profit on dead men's blood?"

Argyros sat silent, waiting Dekanos out. Finally the official said, "As I have sworn an oath, I must abide by it. But, sir, I shall also send a letter to the Master of Offices setting forth in detail the manner in which you have over-stepped your authority. In detail.''

"My authority, illustrious sir, is to get work started on the pharos once more. When you write to George Lakhan-odrakon, do please remember to mention that I have done so." The magistrianos turned to Khesphmois and Hergeus. "Your guilds will end the *anakhoresis* on the terms I have set forth?"

"Yes," they said together. Khesphmois muttered some-thing in Coptic to Hergeus. Then, catching Argyros' eye, he translated: "I said I'd told him you could be trusted." The magistrianos dipped his head. Pleased by the compli-ment, he even forgot for a moment what he'd wanted to do with Zois.

Two weeks later, not another stone had gone into place on the pharos. Argyros stood in front of a half-built church. Miysis, mallet and chisel in hand, stared down at him from the top of a large limestone block. "I told you no before, and I still mean no," the stonecutter said.

"But why?" Argyros said, craning his neck. "The car-penters and cement-spreaders have agreed to end the *an-akhoresis*, and agreed gladly. Half again regular pay and compensation to widows and orphans is nothing to sneeze at."

Miysis spat, though not, the magistrianos had to admit, in his direction. "The carpenters and cement-spreaders are fools, if you ask me. What good does pay and a half do a dead man, or even blood money for his family? Me, I'm plenty happy to work a safer job for less money, and my lads think the same. We stay withdrawn."

As if to show that was his last word on the subject, he started chiseling away at the limestone block again. Chips flew. One landed in Argyros' hair. He stepped back, think-ing dark thoughts. When he walked off, Miysis lifted the mallet in an ironic farewell salute.

The magistrianos, head down, walked north between the Museion's three exedra and the Sema of Alexander the Great without glancing at either the lecture halls to the left or the marble tomb to the right. Only when he almost bumped into one of the men lined up to see Alexander's remains in their coffin of glass did he take a couple of grudging steps to one side.

"Miserable muttonhead," he mumbled, "happy to work his cursed safer job while the pharos goes to perdition." He stopped dead in his tracks, smacked fist into palm. "Happy, is he? Let's just see how happy he'll be!"

Then, instead of glumly walking, Argyros was trotting, sometimes running, toward the Augustal prefect's palace. He arrived panting and drenched in sweat but triumphant. Mouamet Dekanos raised an eyebrow when the magistrianos burst past lesser functionaries into his office. "What's all this in aid of?" he asked.

"I know how to end the *anakhoresis*. At last I know."

"This I will believe when I see it, and not before I see it," Dekanos said. "You came close, I grant you that, but how do you propose to move the stonecutters to the pharos if they are content with lesser pay for other work?"

Argyros grinned a carnivore grin. "How content will they be with no pay for no work?"

"I don't follow," Dekanos said.

"Suppose an edict were to go out in the Augustal prefect's name, suspending all construction in stone in Alexandria for, say, the next three months? Don't you think the stonecutters would start to get a trifle hungry by then? Hungry enough, even, to think about going back to work on the pharos?"

Dekanos' eyes went wide. "They might. They just might. And since they weren't party to the agreements with the other guilds, we wouldn't even have to pay them extra."

The magistrianos had thought about that, too, in the third of an hour it had taken him to get to the prefect's palace. He would enjoy revenge for Miysis' insolence. Still, he said, "No, I think not. The contrast between those who do work on the pharos and have extra silver to jingle in their pouches and those who do not and have none—"

"A distinct point," Dekanos said. "Very well, let it be as you say. Some wealthy men will scream when their houses stand a while half-built—"

"The Emperor of the Romans is screaming now because his pharos has stood too long half-built."

"A distinct point," Dekanos repeated. He shouted for scribes.

Not even a journeyman carpenter was working at Khesphmois' shop when Argyros pushed his way through the curtain of beads. Only a servant lounged in the open courtyard. As far as the magistrianos could see, the fellow's main job was to make sure no one came in and made off with the partly made or partly repaired furniture there.

The servant scrambled to his feet when Argyros came in. He bowed and said something in Coptic. The magistrianos spread his hands. "What you want?" the servant asked in broken Greek.

"Is your master at home?" Argyros asked, speaking slowly and clearly—and also loudly. "I wish to pay my respects to him."

"Him not here," the servant said after Argyros had repeated himself a couple of times. "Him, everyone at—how you say?—pharos. Work there all time. You want, you come sabbath day after prayers. Maybe here then."

"I won't be here then," Argyros said. "My ship sails for Constantinople day after tomorrow."

He saw the servant had not understood him and, sighing, began casting about in his mind for simpler words. He was just starting over when he heard a familiar voice from the living quarters behind the shop: "Is that you, Basil Argyros of Constantinople?"

"Yes, Zois, it is."

She came out a moment later. "It's good to see you again. Would you care for some wine and fruit?" Nodding, the magistrianos stepped toward her. The servant started to come, too. Zois stopped him with a couple of sentences of crackling Coptic. To Argyros, she explained, "I told Nekhebu that Khesphmois wants him out here keeping an eye on the furniture, not inside keeping an eye on me. I can take care of myself; the furniture can't."

"I'm sure you can, my lady." Argyros let her lead him into the chamber where they had talked before.

This time she brought out the wine and dates herself. "Lukra had her brat last week, and she's still down with a touch of fever," she said. "I expect she will get over it." Her voice was enigmatic; Argyros could not tell whether she wanted the serving girl to recover.

He said, "I came to thank Khesphmois for all he did to help end the *anakhoresis*. Since I'm lucky enough to see you, let me thank you also for helping to turn him in that direction. I'm grateful."

She sipped her wine, nibbled daintily on a candied date,

the pink tip of her tongue flicking out for a moment as it toyed with the fruit. "Did I hear you say you were leaving Alexandria day after tomorrow?"

"Yes. It's time for me to go. The pharos is a-building again, and so I have no need to stay any longer."

"Ah," she said, which might have meant anything or nothing. After a pause that stretched, she went on, "In that case, you can thank me properly."

"Properly?" Somehow, Argyros thought, Zois' eyes suddenly seemed twice as large as they had just before. She leaned back in her chair. He admired the fine curve of her neck. Then he was kneeling beside that chair, bending to kiss the smooth, warm flesh of her throat. Even if he was wrong, said the calculating part of him that never quite slept, Khesphmois had already returned to the pharos.

But he was not wrong. Zois' breath sighed out; her hands clasped the back of his head. "The bedroom?" Argyros whispered sometime later.

"No. Lukra's chamber is next to it, and she might overhear." For all her sighs, Zois still seemed very much in control of herself. "We will have to manage here."

The room had neither couch nor, of course, bed, but not all postures required them. Manage they did, with Zois on her knees and using her chair to support the upper part of her body. She was almost as exciting as Argyros had imagined; in this imperfect world, he thought before all thought fled, one could hardly hope for more.

She gasped with him at the end, but he was still coming back to himself when she turned to look over her shoulder at him and say, "Pull up your breeches." As he did so, she swiftly repaired her own dishevelment. Then she waved him back to his own chair, remarking, "Khesphmois must not know what we've done. *I* do, which is what matters."

"So you were only using me to pay back Khesphmois?" he asked, more than a trifle nettled. Here he had thought he was desired for his sake, but instead found himself merely an instrument to Zois. This, he realized uncomfortably, had to be how a seduced woman felt.

Zois' reply reinforced his discomfort. "We all use one another, do we not?" She softened that a moment later, adding with a smile, "I will say I enjoyed this use more than some—more than most, even."

Something, that, but not enough. How many was most?

Argyros did not want to know. He got to his feet. "I'd best head back to my lodging," he said. "I still have some packing to do."

"For a ship that sails in two days?" Zois' smile was knowing. "Go, then, if you think you must. As I said, though, I did enjoy it. And I *will* give Khesphmois your thanks. I'd not be so rude as to forget that."

"I'm so glad," Argyros muttered. Zois giggled at his ostentatiously held aplomb, which only made him cling to it more tightly. The bow he gave her was as punctilious as if he'd offered it to the Master of Offices' wife. She giggled again. He left, hastily.

On the way back to his room—he really had no better place to go—he reflected on the changes he had made since coming to Alexandria. From celibate to fornicator to adulterer, all in the space of a few weeks, he thought, filled with self-reproach. Then he remembered that he would eagerly have become an adulterer before, had he thought Zois willing. Now he knew just how willing she was, and found something other than delight in the knowledge.

Yet he also knew how sweet her body was, and the whore's as well. Having fallen from celibacy, he doubted he would ever be able to return to it. As well, then, that he had not let grief drive him into a monastery. His instinct there had been right: he was much too involved with the things of this world to renounce it for the next until he drew his last breath. Best to acknowledge that fully, and live with the consequences as best he could.

Thinking that, he let himself take some pride in his success here. One day, before too many more years had passed, Alexandria's beacon would shine again, saving countless sailors as time went by. Had he not come to help set things right, that might have been long delayed or accomplished only through bloodshed. And preventing such strife might earn him credit in heaven to set in the balance against the weight of his sins.

He could hope, anyway.

"Argyros! Wait!"

The magistrianos set his duffel on the planking of the dock, turned to find out who was shouting at him. He was surprised to see Mouamet Dekanos hurrying up the quay toward him. "I thought you'd be just as glad to have me go far away," he said as the Alexandrian bureaucrat came near.

Dekanos smiled thinly: "I understand what you mean. Still, the pharos *is* going up, and I did have *something* to do with that. Besides which, I stay here, while you *are* going far away. My contribution will be remembered." He checked to make sure no one was listening and lowered his voice. "I will make sure it is remembered."

"I daresay you will." Argyros chuckled. He understood Dekanos' logic perfectly well. What he did not understand was why the official was carrying a duffel bag larger and fuller than his own. He pointed to it. "What have you there?"

"I was most impressed with your ability to bring together two sides, neither of which was truly interested in finding a solution to their dispute until you intervened," Dekanos said obliquely.

Argyros gave a polite bow. "You're very kind, illustrious sir. Still—"

"You don't think I answered you," Dekanos finished for him.

"No."

"Ah, but I did, for, you see, I've brought you another long-standing dispute which neither side seems interested in solving. What I have here, illustrious sir, is *Pcheris vs. Sarapion*—all of it." With a sigh of relief, he set his burden down. It *was* heavier than Argyros' sack; through his sandals, the magistrianos felt the dock timbers briefly quiver at its weight.

"You're sure that's all?" he asked, intending irony.

The attempt failed. "I do think so," Dekanos answered seriously. "If not, the documents you have should refer back to any that happen to be missing."

"Oh, very well," Argyros said, laughing, "I'll take it on. As you say, after the pharos, something this small should be easy. The winds won't favor my ship as much on the way back to Constantinople; God willing, I should be to the bottom of your case by the time I'm there. It will make the voyage less boring."

"Thank you." Dekanos wrung the magistrianos' hand. "Thank you." The Alexandrian official bowed several times before taking his leave.

Argyros shrugged quizzically as he watched him go. In

his days in the imperial army, he'd sometimes received less effusive thanks for saving a man's life. He shrugged again as he carried the two sacks onto the ship. He opened the one full of legal documents.

Long before the pharos of Alexandria slipped below the southern horizon, he suspected Mouamet Dekanos had done him no favor. Long before he reached Constantinople again, he was sure of it.

Ancient and medieval societies struggled along without most of the benefits we moderns take for granted: anesthesia, plumbing, refrigeration, and the telephone and television. Our ancestors were far more racist, sexist, violent, and fanatical than we are today. (I don't care who you are—go back enough generations and you'll prove me right. "Enough," in most cases, is a number smaller than five.) But our ancestors also did not burden themselves with certain other things we take for granted nowadays. Their world would have been rather more complicated if they had.

REPORT OF THE SPECIAL COMMITTEE ON THE QUALITY OF LIFE

30 November 1491
To: Their Hispanic Majesties Fernando II and Isabella
From: The Special Committee on the Quality of Life
Re: The environmental impact upon Spain of the proposed expedition of the Genoese navigator Cristóbal Colón, styled in his native Italian Cristoforo Colombo

The commission of learned men and mariners, established by your Majesties under the chairmanship of Fr. Hernando de Talavera, during the period 1486–90 studied exhaustively the proposals set forth by the Genoese captain Colón and rejected them as being extravagant and impractical. In the present year a second commission, headed by the grand cardinal, Pedro González de Mendoza, has also seen fit to decline the services of Colón. The present Special Committee on the Quality of Life finds itself in complete accord with the actions of the previous two bodies of inquiry. It is our unanimous conclusion that the rash scheme advocated by this visionary would, if adopted, do serious damage to the finances and ecology of Spain; that this damage, if permitted, would set a precedent for future, more severe, outrages of our environment; that even if successful it

141

would unacceptably alter the life-style of the citizens of Spain; and, most important, that the proposed voyage would expose any sailors engaged thereon to unacceptable risks of permanent bodily illness and injury and even death.

Certain people may perhaps suggest that the sea program of this kingdom is essential to its future growth. To this uninformed view we may only offer our wholehearted opposition. The Atlantic sea program offers extremely high expenses and hazards in both men and matériel for gains at best speculative but most likely nonexistent. Now more than ever, resources need to be concentrated at home to bring the long war against the heathen Moors of Granada to a successful conclusion. At such a crucial time the state should waste no money on a program whose returns, if any, will not be manifest for some decades.

If funding must be committed to the sea program, it should be earmarked for national defense goals in the Mediterranean Sea, not spent on wild-eyed jaunts into the trackless and turbulent Atlantic. Unless and until we succeed in overcoming the corsair gap now existing, our southern coast will remain vulnerable to attacks from Algeria and Morocco even after the Moors of Granada are brought under our control. Moreover, if we fail to move against the heathen states of Africa, they shall surely fall under the aegis of the expansionist Ottoman Sultanate, with potential profound consequences to the balance of power in the area, as strong infidel forces will then be able to strike at our routes to our Italian possessions.

It may be argued that shipbuilding will aid the economy of those areas near ports. This view is superficial and shortsighted. True, jobs may be provided for lumberjacks, carpenters, sailmakers, etc., but at what cost to the world in which they live? Barring reforestation projects, for which funding does not appear to be forthcoming, any extensive shipbuilding venture will inevitably result in the deforestation of significant areas of the kingdom and the deformation of the long-established ecological patterns of the wildlife therein. In any case, it is questionable if shipbuilding represents the ideal utilization of our limited timber resources. The quantity of wood required to construct an ocean-going vessel could better be used to provide low-income housing for whole villages of peasants or could furnish many underprivileged citizens with firewood sufficient for an entire year. Further, especially for long voyages such as that urged by Colón, ships must carry extensive stores (this point will again be alluded to later in the report). The question must be posed as to whether our agricultural industry is even adequate to care for the needs of the populace of Spain itself. Surely an affirmative answer to this question, such as cannot with assurance be made at present, is necessary before expansion can be contemplated and resources diverted for it. We must put a halt to these environmentally disadvantageous programs before they become so ingrained in our life-style that their removal presents difficulties.

There is yet another factor to be considered, one closely related to that referred to in the previous sentence. Even if Colón precisely fulfills his expectations, what will the consequences of this success be for Spain? Many substances about which we know little, and which may well be hazardous, will begin to enter the kingdom in large quantities, and control over their sale and distribution will be difficult to achieve. We run a substantial risk of seeing our nation filled with addicts to toxins now unknown. Nor is it possible to discount the dangers of ideological contamination, which is as much to be feared as is physical. It is doubtful if the inhabitants of the distant lands the Genoan plans to visit share our religious and cultural benefits. Yet it is probable that some of their number may settle on our soil and attempt to disseminate their inadequate but perhaps seductive doctrines among our populace. As we are now on the point of expelling the Jews from our state and have nearly overcome the Muslim Moors, why should we hazard the homogeneity we have at last achieved after almost eight centuries of sustained effort?

The sudden influx of new goods will also disturb our traditional economic organization. There can be no doubt that there will be an increase in the monetary supply because of the profit made by reselling eastern goods throughout Europe, but can a corresponding increase in the volume of goods and services be predicted? If the answer to this question is in the negative, as all current economic indicators would imply, then the "success" of Colón would seem to bring with it a concomitant inflationary pressure which would tend to eat into the profits of that "success" and would make life more difficult and expensive for the average Spaniard. Also, any substantial increase in the sea program would entail the diversion of labor from its traditional concerns to maritime activity. Such a shift could not help but further disjoint our economy and cannot be anticipated with anything other than trepidation. The dislocation could even be so severe as to cause emigration to the eastern lands, which would of course entail a drain of the best of the kingdom's populace from its shores.

Finally, if the government of Spain is to approve, fund, and provide manpower for the Colón expedition, it must have some assurance that it is not dangerously imperiling the health and future well-being of the members of that expedition. Such assurance is not at all easy to come by. The dangers of a seaman's trade are well known, and he performs his duties on what can only be described as a diet of "junk food": hardtack, salt meat, and dried peas, with perhaps a bit of cheese. This regimen is manifestly unhealthful, and Colón and the men under his charge would be unable to supplement it except by fishing. They would not enjoy the advantage, as do sailors of the Mediterranean Sea and also the Portuguese in their journeys down the coast of Africa, of replenishing their supplies at relatively brief intervals, but would be compelled to make do once having departed the Canary Islands. Nor is the situation in regard to potables much better, these being restricted to casked water and wine. The probability is extremely high that at least some of the former will go bad; the latter not only faces this danger but, if drunk to excess, has the potential of severely compromising the efficiency of ship's operations and thereby reducing an already low safety margin. Sleeping arrangements are equally substandard; indeed, for almost everyone they are nonexistent. Ships are so designed that only the captain has a cabin with a bunk, and even this private space is scarcely more than that to be found in a closet ashore. Sailors and underofficers sleep where they are able to find room, in the same clothing they have worn during the day. Thus the life-support systems of any expeditionary force at the current level of technology must be deemed inadequate.

Navigational instruments are also crude in the extreme. Quadrant and astrolabe are so cumbersome, and so likely to be grossly affected by ship's motion, as to be little more useful than dead reckoning in the determination of latitude; dead reckoning alone serves in estimating longitude. For a voyage of the length anticipated by Colón, these factors, in combination with the stormy nature of the Atlantic and the likelihood of meeting unanticipated hazards with no support facilities upon which to fall back, give the Genoan's proposals a degree of risk so high no merciful sovereign could in good conscience allow his subjects to endanger themselves in the pursuit thereof.

Therefore, it is the determination of the Special Committee on the Quality of Life, appointed by your Hispanic Majesties as per the environmental protection ordinances of the realm, that the proposals of Colón do in the several ways outlined above comprise a clear and present danger to the quality and security of life within the kingdom, and that they should for that reason be rejected. Respectfully in triplicate submitted by

Jaime Nosénada
Chairman of the Special Committee
on the Quality of Life

I've loved baseball since I was a kid—not just playing and watching it, but its lore, its history. It is, I suppose, the game for someone who, like me, trained as a historian: It has more respect for its past and more detailed records of that past, than any other major American sport. This story is a Ring Lardner pastiche, save that its hero encounters problems on and off the field that none of Lardner's southern boys ever had to deal with.

BATBOY

Boston
September 3, 191–

Dear Willie,

Youll see by the address and the picture that was took of me the other day what has happened. Sure enough the Browns has bought my contract and I am in the BIGS at last! The way I found out was like this. I had just finished shutting out Knoxville when old Charlie told me the owner wanted to tell me somethin. I thot I was in dutch again especially when he ups & says Rip we're gonna have to get rid o you this time. But he had a grin and a train ticket & so here I am.

They is all dam yankees up here excepting some of the ballplayers. The country is pretty but its full of rocks. They do feed you good. I have had scrod which is almost as good as catfish.

I have a roommate for the hotel. His name is Laszlo Kovacs or some bohunk thing like that. Hes a rook too up from Syracuse. He plays second mostly. Not a bad fellow I guess. Dont say much tho. Well I can talk enuf for two as you has told me before this.

Got to stop now. They is yelling for me to go down to this Fenway Park where the Red Sox are at. It is a nice place to play. Pass my love on to Ma & say Hello to Sally for me. I wouldnt ask you to do that if you wasnt married, & my Brother. Show her the picture of me in my uniform if you get the chance.

Your loving brother,
Rip (a big leaguer even if it is the Browns)

Boston
September 4, 191–

Dear Willie,

Well I must say they surely do things backards in this American League. I got me the chance to pitch yesterday on account of the Red Sox was hitting line drives off everybody what stuck his head out the dugout. So the mgr says Come on kid get loose lets see what you can do. I did & he stuck me in figuring since they had us down 10–3 I couldnt make things no worse.

So in I come and just to keep me interested its 2nd & 3rd & no outs. I popped up the 1st fellow I pitched to & the next one hits right back to me. This is easy Im thinking cause the next spot is the pitcher. Big lefty name of George Somethin—a girl's name I think. Well he hit my curve like he knew it was comin & winds up on 3rd with a big grin on his ugly mug. Then I get the leadoff man. Which is why I say this is a backards league. The pitchers hit and the hitters dont.

Come to that the Browns is backards, too. They do not do too poor at first & then get weaker & weaker as the season goes along. Lazlo or however you spell it was talkin about that with a newspaper fellow in the hotel last night. Fellow's name is Gyula Nagy so I guess he is a bohunk too. In fact I know he is. Part of the time they was using bohunk lingo which sounds like nothin I have heard before I can tell you.

This Gyula has a son called Zoltan which is a heathen sounding name if ever I heared one. Because his Pa travels with the team & all they let him wear a little uniform & fetch balls & bats around & the like. An all right little tyke I think tho my roomie didnt rightly take to him. I will say he is funny looking with just the one eyebrow growing acrost his forehead like that

We go to New York next. I will rite you from there.

Your Brother,
Rip

P.S.—Remember none of the runs what scored counted against me on account of they was on base already when I come in.

New York
September 7, 191–

Dear Willie,

I thot the towns in the Southern Assn was big this year till I seen Boston but I can tell you this New York makes Boston look like Opelousas back home beside it. Every kind of furriner lives here & I think a few yankees, too. No I dont mean the baseball team tho they been giving us fits since we got in town.

Well they might cause we is into our September Swoon which is what that Gyula fellow calls it but you got to remember he is a riter. This Polo Grounds where the Yankees I mean the base-ball ones this time play has fences even shorter down the line than Sulphur Dell in Nashville. But could we reach em? Not a prayer of it. Never did you see so many little squibs & pops in all your born days.

We is dead on the field, too. Balls that should ought to be caut or picked up easy go thru which makes the pitchers cuss. But they aint throwin hard either it looks like to me. Maybe Ill get some work on account of it.

About the bounciest thing on the whole team is that Zoltan which I told you about in my last letter. He was kind of sollem-like in Boston but has perked up remarkable on the train ride south. Its a caution to see him jumpin & carryin on in the dug-out. His little cheeks is just as red as a couple of boiled craw-dads. Funny I didnt spy that before.

Will close now as Laszloo which as you can see I still dont ritely know how to spell is taking me to a bohunk restaurant he found out about some ways. I would sooner have grits but cant find em up here.

Again pass on my love to Ma & affecktion to Sally. For you too now as I think of it.

Your brother,
Rip

New York
September 8, 191–

Dear Willie,

Now that I have ate bohunk food I see why they was so eager to cross the ocean & come over here to get away from it is why. The stuffed cabbage was not too bad & there was beer to wash it down but what is done to pork chops is a caution I tell you. You could smell em coming before they was out of the kitchen they had that much garlic on em. I was a blame fool to let Laslo order for me.

Well even he made heavy going. My eyes was watering fit to kill as I made shift to eat em. If Ma hadnt always taut me to clean my plate I would of gived up after the 1st bite. Ma never tried eating these tho which is lucky for her. I like to died.

When we got back to the hotel we stunk up the lobby good.

Two of our ballplayers who was in there lit up cheroots & I mean big ones the second we walked in. Between the smoke & us a sweet young thing which had been makin eyes at Doc our short-stop passed out altogether. It was what they call a sensation.

Just then Gyoola & his boy Zoltan come out of the elevator. I went over to say Hello thinking as how bein bohunks their own selves they wouldnt mind what I smell like. & Gyoola does say Hello nice as you please. But Zoltan his eyes rolled up in his head & for a second I thot he was going to faint like the lady if thats what she was. Then he kind of run away from me. I dont think his Pa knew what to make of it & I surely didnt. Laslo his eyes got very big but he didn't say nothin.

Here is another funny thing. A good half a dozen of the fellows on the team say they seen a bat flapping round their winders in the middle of the night. Me I call that right peculiar on account of bats not much favoring towns & especially not one the size of New York.

I didnt see no bats. This morning I turned to Laslo & said Probably we scared em away the way we stunk last nite. & without batting an eye which is a joke I guess he says Probably. These furriners & almost furriners is peculiar people.

Love to you and Ma,
Rip

P.S.—I will be home in time to help with the harvest so dont you worry about that none.

New York
September 9, 191–

Dear Willie,

Well it was a big day for this here hotel room yesterday. Lazlo got to start when Del our reglar 2nd baseman turned up sick. I dont know what was rong with him but he was pale as a fishbelly. You could see the spot where he must of cut hisself shaving under his chin just like a coal on a snowbank. I hope it aint catchin.

But about Lazlo. He sure dont seem tired. He got 2 hits & stole a base & was robbed another time & played good in the field. We lost again 2–1 but it was not his fault.

Nor mine neither. The mgr throwed me in in the 5th when we was down 2–0 already but had 2 men on so he batted for Grover who had started. Not that it helped on account of the pinch batter hit into a double play. But I pitched 4 innings & did not give up a run & would have got a win if our hitters had been good for anything.

Which reminds me of somethin that right ticked me off. Remember how I said the other day how Zoltan would hop around & cheer for us in his little Brownie suit? Well he didnt do no cheerin for Lazlo even tho they is both bohunks. Means he was quiet all day seein as how the rest of them didnt do nothin like I said.

After the game I says somewhat to Lazlo about it but he dont seem the least bit fazed. He says His rootin I can do without. You make heads or tails of it for I cannot.

Your Brother,
Rip

Detroit
September 11, 191–

Dear Willie,

Seems as how Lazlo & Gyoola & Zoltan is filling up all my letters but there has been another dustup among em since I rote you last. The latest hoorah commenced on the train between New York & here. It might not of happened if Lazlo had not got hisself likkered up. He is fond of whiskey but not much for holding it.

I had a few myself but having started on corn squeezins no store-bought whiskey can shift me which I know you will understand. I was takin Lazlo back to our Pullman when who shd we run into but Gyoola. My roomie like to spit in his eye. He rears back and comes out with Do you know what kind of unnatural monster your son is?

Your drunk says Gyoola which was true & Your crazy which I did not think too far off either. But Lazlo goes Crazy am I & shouts something in that furrin tongue o theirs. Gyoola gapes at him like a new-caut fish & says You are crazy sharper this time. But Lazlo comes back in that old country lingo & pretty soon they was slangin each other for all they was worth if the noise ment anything. I wish I knew what they was sayin cause it sounded lively.

Then Lazlo ups & swings on him which proves Gyoola was rite on account of Gyoola would make 3 of him. I give him credit Gyoola didnt swing back he is a gentleman. I got my arms round my roomie at last & hauled him to bed.

By the time he was in the bunk he got the upper this trip he had went from fightin drunk to cryin drunk carryin on about how Gyoola is a fine fellow but deseeved & changelings & I dont know what all. His yarns what I could make out of em is wilder than anything I ever heered old Jacob tell who was a slave before the States War.

Well when I climed into the lower they was somethin in the bed with me. I thot it was roaches but it was cloves of garlic I found when I pulled one out. I says How did this get here and Lazlo answers back I put em there & you leave em. I want no truck with your heathen superstishun I says & do you know what he does next? He hands me down a crucifix like the Papists use & says Take this then. Thank you I will keep the garlic I tell him & he shuts up.

More of the team is down with whatever it is Del has. If it hadnt come on so sudden Id call it hookworm. They are all washed out & listless like people with the worm suckin on em. But I heered somewheres the yankee parts o the country dont have hookworm so it cant be that.

It is a terrible thing to happen to us because with Ty and Wahoo Sam and the rest the Tigers whale the ball against the best of teams & how are we supposed to stay with em with half the players sick & the rest draggin? If we lose they will blame the pitchers they always do.

Love to you and Ma and your Kate,
Your brother Rip

P.S.—Got your telegram in New York. I am glad to hear Sally says she is proud of me.

Detroit
September 12, 191–

Dear Willie,

I am commencing to wonder if maybe I am the crazy one & not Laszlo after all. It is on account of what I seen or rather didnt see in the hotel this morning. It is a fine place much fancier than the ones we stayed at in Boston or New York. One wall of the lobby is a mirror I suppose to make it seem bigger then it is not that it needs to because it dont.

We come in erly in the morning draggin our tails some because tho you can sleep in a Pullman its not near as good as a bed. Players & reporters & such was mingled with porters totin our bags & a few o what the Reverend would call scarlet wimmin. You neednt mention them last to Ma or Sally either.

Anyways to make a long story short while we was all checkin in & the clerks was yellin for bellhops & the like I happen to look round in the mirror to see if my new Panama which you must see was strait on my head. It was but what should I spy in the glass but a little boys suit without a little boy in it if you take my meaning. There was nothin like that in our crowd only Zoltan smiling at me. His teeth is uncommon white & long & sharp. Like I say he was smilin but not real frendly like I didnt think.

I says If that dont beat all & point out what I seen to Laslo who was standing by me cause were roomies as you recollect. And he looks too & dam me if his eyes dont near roll back in his head. But when he catches Zoltan lookin our way he makes out like everything is alrite. Hes good. Remember me not to play poker against him.

Nobody else seemed to notice nothin amiss.

When we was up in our room Laslo rounds on me & says this is the last proof now do you see what sort of feind it is? It is a vampire. What on earth is that I ask & he tells me more then I bargined for. Seems this vampire crechur is a kind o bloodsuckin hant the bohunks has which ifn you fail to kill itll leech a man to death.

We got to kill it Laslo says all rile up. I says Well that may be a good idear but how do you aim to go about it? It dont sound easy from what he says & I know from old Jacob as how hants is never easy to be rid of. But bein a bohunk hisself Laslo has a skeme which may work.

I hope so. The Browns is ragged enuf with all the blood in em & purely hopeless without. The Tigers done trounced us today & look like doin it again tomorrow. We had 3 reglars out o the lineup. This has got to stop so I am with Laslo all the way tho there is likely to be some risk. But no hant is a match for a good Southern man. I will tell you how we done in my next letter.

Love to you from yr Brother
Rip

P.S.—If it goes rong give the picture of me in uniform to Sally to remember me by. Dont read this part to Ma. The more I think the scareder I get.

Detroit
September 14, 191–

Dear Willie,

The Lord be praised the deed is like they say done. Laszlo and I is well tho the thing turned out much more tighter than either one of us reckoned it wld. What we done was take down all the garlic & other heathen charms Laszlo been usin to keep the hant away & the crucifix too & wait for it or rather Zoltan I mean to pay us a call. Nite before last he didnt either on account of he suspected a snare or because he was eatin somewheres else. The whole team is so peaked these days I couldnt cipher out which ones was fed on last.

Well we left the hoodoos down again last nite & sat up waiting for whatever was going to happen. We did not want to be caut napping for sure! As we had done this the nite before too & slept a little of the day, I confess I was yawnin.

Then lookin out the winder I seen the bat what had been seen round before. I reckon thats what it was anyways for it seen me too & flied closer. I just had time to give Laszlo the sign & let him get out of sight longside the winder afore it come up.

I dont quite know how to tell what happened next. I was lookin into its eyes & its like I heered a voice in my head saying Let me in let me in. And I couldnt of said No even if I wanted to which at the time I didnt. That vampire hant charmed me with them red opticks of it's just like a snake charmin a bird down out of a tree for it to swaller.

Laszlo said after I was like a machine when I up and opened the winder. I dont hardly recollect one way or the other. All I remember is them eyes. In my head I heered that voice again Give me your neck it was sayin. & I twisted my chin to one side like a shote which dont know its about to be slaughtered.

Then its like there was a scream only it werent a noise at all only in between my ears. Laszlo had sprang out from where he was hidin & landed the hant a smart one with his crucifix. We didnt know what that would do neither him or me but we found out right quick. They was a thump a real one this time & insted of the bat at my neck there was Zoltan on the floor naked as the day he was born only I reckon he werent born at all when you think about it.

He was still part hant tho. I had thunk his teeth was long before well now he had a set the bobcat we ketched last winter would of been proud of. He was smilin like a wild crechur & I got to tell you them eyes still dragged at me somethin fierce.

Not at Laszlo. I reckon the cross saved him. Maybe them Catholics is not as rong as we think. Anyways he hauls out a railroad spike & slams it into Zoltan's chest. I heard that shreek again in my mind & I reckon in Laszlo's too on account of his hands was shakin but he did not let go. He shoved that spike in harder & deeper.

Zoltan's mouth was open so wide I thot itd go clean round to the back of his head. I was moving like a man in a dream still but when Laszlo cussed at me I done the last thing we planned out which was fling a whole garlic down his I mean Zoltan's trap. I dont know if that shifted him or the spike but then he give a last riggle & his eyes well if they was lamps youd say they was blowed out. All a sudden I was alrite again.

Laszlo and me the both of us yelled then on account of it wasnt no little boy on the spike any more but a bat the same size Zoltan had been & just as dead too. & then the bat melted away like snow in a thaw & there was nothin on the rug excepting the spike which Laszlo had dropped and the garlic.

So its done I reckon. I wish I cld sleep for a week but we got a game tomorrow. I bet we whup em too.

> Your Brother safe & sound,
> Rip

> Detroit
> September 15, 191–

Dear Willie,

Well whup em we didnt I am afraid. The Tigers they is a good team & that Ty runs & hits like a madman & you cant pitch around him either or Sam or Bobby will kill you if he dont. So we lost again.

But the boys which was most bloodsucked are looking better & so I have no douts things will get better soon. & heres a funny thing. Nobody remembers nothin about Zoltan & what he was doing to em but for me and Lazslo.

Come to that nobody remember nothin about Zoltan at all. Laszlo & me we run into Gyula at breakfast & was not sure what to say or nothin. Finally Lazslo asks him Hows your son & he looks at my roomie like he was off his head & says I aint got no son nor never did. Lazslo & me look at each other & press it no farther I can tell you.

& you remember how Zoltan was in the dugout with us and all? Well his little uniform is plumb disappeared & nobody knows where it has gone nor misses it neither. When I asks the mgr What become o the batboy he gives me the same look Gyula done gave Lazslo & says This team aint never had no batboy.

Thats what you think I says But dont worry he done flied out for the last time. & I laughs & laughs even tho hes reamin me

up one side & down the other. Sometimes there aint no point in
tellin people things anyhow is all I can say.

Your loving Brother,
Rip

This story sprang from the research that produced the novel *The Guns of the South*. Indeed, Captain Thorpe briefly appears in the novel. He truly was captain of Company A of the Forty-seventh North Carolina and did write its regimental history. He was, in fact, still alive in the 1920s, when he did more historical work on the regiment. He may even have attended the Confederate reunion at Richmond in 1932.

THE LAST REUNION

THE TRAIN PULLED TO A STOP. "RICHMOND!" the conductor shouted. "All out for Richmond!" The man in the long gray coat with the brass buttons slowly got to his feet, made his way down the aisle. A porter walked behind him with his bags. People waited respectfully until he had passed, then began filing out after him.

The conductor touched a finger to the brim of his cap in salute. "Watch your step as you get out, General. Let me give you a hand, suh."

John Houston Thorpe waved away the offered assistance. "If I can't manage a couple of steps, young fellow, you may as well bury me. And I'm no general. I'm proud I was a captain, and I've never claimed anything more."

Taking some of his weight on his stick, he descended from the passenger car without difficulty. Richmond in June was warm and muggy, but so was Rocky Mount, North Carolina, from which he'd come. The weather was not what made his shoulders sag for a moment; it was the weight of the past.

He'd come through Richmond in 1863 with the rest of the Forty-seventh North Carolina, hot and eager to join Lee's Army of Northern Virginia in the great invasion of the North that would set the Confederacy free forever. He'd been dapper and handsome, with slicked-down black hair and a thin little mustache of which he'd been inordinately proud.

Now—how had sixty-nine years slid by? Inside, he felt like a dashing youth still. The body that moved only slowly, the thick spectacles, the gnarled hand he often cupped behind one ear—

were they truly his? Surely it was the world that had changed, not himself.

A flashbulb exploded in front of his face, filling his vision with purple spots. No flashbulbs when he'd been here before; in those days, having a photograph taken meant standing solemn and statue-still until the long exposure ended. He nodded. Yes, it was the world that had changed.

"Welcome to Richmond, General!" the fellow behind the flash camera shouted. "Have you come here other times since the end of the war?"

"Never once," Thorpe answered with a sort of pride. "But now, I thought, if I don't come now—when shall I have another chance?"

"What do you think of the city, General?" the man asked.

As his eyes cleared, Thorpe saw the fellow had a PRESS tag tucked into his hatband—a reporter, then. "I'm no general," he repeated, a bit testily: a reporter was supposed to know such things. "What do I think of Richmond? I've not seen much yet, but it strikes me as a big city. Of course, it did that a while ago, too."

The laugh that once rang musically was now a rusty croak, but he loosed it all the same. When he'd first come north to Richmond, not a town in North Carolina had held as many as five thousand inhabitants; no wonder the Confederate capital, then near forty thousand, seemed to him a metropolis swollen past belief. These days Rocky Mount was on its way to being a city of the size Richmond had been then. He wondered why he failed to find it large. Perhaps because he and Rocky Mount had grown together. But his town had grown up, while he . . . somehow he had just grown old.

From behind him, the porter said, "You come on with me, suh. I'll take you to the cab stand." The colored man picked up his suitcases again and raised his voice: "Make way fo' the general here! Make way, folks!"

And people *did* clear a path. Following in the porter's wake, Thorpe reflected that the illegitimate promotion people insisted on foisting on him was worth something, at any rate, if it got him through the crowded train station so easily. He laughed again.

"What's funny, suh?" the porter asked.

"When I was a soldier here, I doubt the people would have moved aside so readily for any *real* general, save maybe Robert E.

Lee, as they do now for me. I led no great armies, only a ragtag company. My only claim to notice is my span of years."

"There's worse ones than that, suh," the porter observed. Thorpe slowly nodded; judging by what he'd seen in the second half of his long life, there were many such worse claims, most of them trumpeted uncommonly loud.

The Negro dropped Thorpe's bags for a moment to stick his fingers in his mouth and give forth with a piercing whistle. A taxi driver waved to show he'd heard. The porter grabbed the suitcases again and headed for the boxy Chevrolet. Behind him, Thorpe made the best speed he could.

Pretty girls paused to stare wide-eyed at him as he went by. He remembered that from his soldier days, too. Then he wouldn't have minded getting some of those girls alone. He fondly remembered a couple of leaves spent in the city's seamier districts. The most respectable girls nowadays showed more rounded flesh than any shameless woman had in his youth, but desire was only a memory, too.

Between them, the porter and the taxi driver tossed his bags into the back seat of the cab. Thorpe dug in his pocket, and pulled out a quarter. The porter beamed; a quarter was worth far more in these hard times in 1932 than it had been in the inflation-raddled Richmond of the War between the States: "God bless you, suh!"

"God bless you, too," Thorpe said. Back in the old days, he would have tipped a slave who served as well as this porter had. Negroes had been free now long enough for a man to go from birth to old age in that span of years—not old age like his own, of course, but age old enough. It hadn't worked out as dreadfully as long-ago fire-eaters feared it would, so perhaps Abe Lincoln was right all along. Right or not, Lincoln prevailed. The proof of it was that Thorpe couldn't even recall the last time he'd wondered about the justice of emancipation.

"Where to, General?" the taxi driver asked.

"Camp De Saussure, wherever that may be," Thorpe answered. He didn't bother correcting the man. Apparently he was to be a general for the duration, whether he liked it or not. If that was so, he decided he might as well like it. He'd grown used to far worse things over the years.

"That's what they're calling the Lee Camp Soldiers' Home for the reunion," the driver said as he held the car door open for Thorpe. "In honor of General De Saussure of the United Confederate Veterans, isn't it?"

"Yes, I think so." Thorpe slowly, carefully bent to sit down in the taxi. C.A. De Saussure actually called himself a general because he headed the veterans' organization. Thorpe did not think much of that. All the real generals who'd worn gray (and those who'd worn blue as well) were dead.

The taxi pulled away from the curb. Soon it was tooling along at an effortless thirty-five miles an hour. The John Houston Thorpe who had visited Richmond not far past the midpoint of a vanished century would never have believed such a thing. His great-grandchildren took it utterly for granted: to them, a horseback ride was an hour's amusement at a fair, not the only way to go from one place to another. Thorpe himself rarely thought about automobiles these days. This afternoon, though, he was seeing new things in an old mirror.

The driver had his window open to bring in the breeze. Thorpe was half-dozing until a loud roar overhead jerked him back to full awareness. "Damned airplanes," the taxi man said. "They fly so low sometimes, one of 'em'll come right down in the middle of traffic one fine day, mark my words."

Thorpe didn't answer. The taxi driver was young; men had probably been flying his whole life. To Thorpe, cars were wonderful and useful-but easy enough to take in stride. At airplanes he would never cease to marvel if he lived another ninety-odd years. He knew quiet pride that the very first one had left the ground less than a hundred miles from where he lived.

As the reporter had, the driver asked him whether he'd been in Richmond since the States War. When he answered no, the fellow said, "Bet it's changed a fair bit since then."

"That it has," Thorpe said. "In those days there wasn't a paved road in Richmond, the town was either full of mud or full of dust, the flies swarmed fit to drive a man mad, and everything smelled of horse manure." He chuckled to watch the taxi driver's jaw drop. "Every town, South and North, was like that then, though I don't suppose it gets into the history books. They didn't have flush toilets in those days, either. You're lucky to be a young man in such a marvelous time."

The Chevrolet was far from a new automobile; its springs had seen better days. Nevertheless, on the asphalted highway it rode smoother than any carriage over dirt. Thorpe tried to imagine what a carriage would have felt like had he whipped a two-horse team up anywhere close to the speed he was making now. Pointless effort—a carriage at full tilt would have overturned the second it hit a stone or a pothole.

"But the glory then—" the driver began.

Thorpe broke in: "No glory to dying in camp of smallpox or measles or scarlet fever. No glory to typhoid, either, or to perishing of fever after your wound went bad—and it would, for we had no medicines. No glory to having your arm cut off and tossed on a pile outside a tent or under a tree while the surgeon shouted 'Next!' No, sir, don't speak to me of glory."

The taxi driver chewed on that for the next couple of minutes, as if it were a piece of meat stuck between his teeth. At last he said, hesitantly now, "General, if that's how you feel, why did you come?"

"To see the men who went through it with me one last time before I die," Thorpe said. "No one who didn't can possibly imagine what it was like." It was true enough, as far as it went, but Thorpe wondered if it went far enough. Take away the remembered dirt and pain and hunger and terror and something remained behind, something that had drawn him from Rocky Mount after all these years. He scorned the idea of glory, as most men did who had seen war face to face. But something was there, even if he didn't care to try to name it for a taxi driver.

The taxi stopped in front of the Soldiers' Home: low cottages on greensward, with a few bigger buildings among them: a hospital, a dining hall, a chapel. The driver got out, opened Thorpe's door for him, and hauled his bags off the back seat.

"What is the fare?" Thorpe asked.

"Thirty-five cents, General, anywhere inside Richmond city limits."

"When I was here last, young man, this was far to the west of the city limits." The first coin that came into Thorpe's hands was a half dollar. "Here you are. I have no need for change."

"Thank you, General!" Smiling, the taxi driver carried the suitcases toward a cottage with a large sign in front of it: WELCOME, CONFEDERATE VETERANS.

A colored man standing by the door hurried forward. "Here, I'll take charge of those, suh," he told the driver, who relinquished the bags, nodded to Thorpe, and hurried back toward his automobile. The colored man held the cottage door open. "You go right on in, General, so as they can get your name and figure out which cottage you belong in. We'll make you right comfortable here, I promise you that."

"I'm certain of it," Thorpe said. Through the door, he saw several old men (several *other* old men, he reminded himself) in gray suits talking with some younger folks who sat behind tables and shuffled through file boxes. He got in line behind one of the veterans.

The fellow turned around. His beard was bushy and white, but his eyebrows had somehow stayed black as coal. He chuckled rheumily. "Might as well be waitin' my turn at mess call. Makes me think I really am back in the army, after all."

"Yes, I remember that," Thorpe said. The four words were plenty to push him back in time, to make him smell the cook fires, hear the chatter of men around him, even to taste the hot corn-bread that had been so much of what he ate for so long.

He got to the head of this line sooner than he usually had at mess call—but then, so many fewer men were here now. One of the young men asked his name, went through a box marked T–Z, and pulled out a badge. "You'll be in Cottage C, General Thorpe. Pick any vacant bed there. I hope you enjoy your stay. Do you need help pinning that on, sir?"

"No, thank you," Thorpe proceeded to prove it. "The rheumatism doesn't have hold of me too badly. Cottage C, you said?"

"That's right, General. It's also on your badge below your name, in case—" The young fellow thought twice. "Well, just in case."

In case you forget, he'd started to say. Thorpe declined to take offense. So many men his age had wits that began to wander. His, though, so far as he knew, were still sound. He'd written the history of his regiment back around the turn of the century, and only a handful of years had passed since he'd compiled a roster of men from Nash and Edgecombe counties who'd served in the Forty-seventh North Carolina. Now he thought he was the only soldier of his regiment left alive.

The colored man—one of the helpers at the Soldiers' Home, no doubt—was still waiting when Thorpe came back outside. "Cottage C, is it?" he said, reading the badge. "You just follow me, General. It's not far."

Thorpe followed. In the old days, teaching a Negro to read had been against the law. Some had thought blacks too stupid to learn, anyhow. Obviously, they hadn't known everything there was to know.

The beds in the cottage proved to be steel-framed army cots with scratchy woolen blankets and stiffly starched sheets and pillowcases. Thorpe chose one by the window, to get the benefit of whatever breeze there might be. "Sorry we can't put you folks up in higher style, General," the attendant said as he set down the suitcases. "Most of the time, though, there's just a dozen or so old soldiers in the home, and we got seven, eight hundred of you all comin' to visit."

"Don't worry," Thorpe said. "Every man of us here will have known worse accommodations than these, I promise you." He looked at his army cot. In his army days no such creature existed. He'd slept on pine boughs piled in a frame, rolled in his blanket (a far more ragged and threadbare specimen than the one on the cot), or just on bare ground. And even a pillow! Back then, such had been undreamed-of luxury.

The colored man declined a tip—"This here's my job, suh"— and hurried away to help some other newly arrived veteran settle in. Thorpe left the clapboard cottage, too, and walked slowly over to the dining hall. It wasn't yet supper time, but several veterans were in there passing time with a deck of cards. A couple of them paused between hands to squirt jets of tobacco juice at a spattered spittoon.

Looking at the white beards, the bald heads, the gnarled fingers, Thorpe wondered why he'd come. Wasn't it better to remember the men who'd fought under the Stars and Bars as young and dashing and brave rather than seeing what time had done to them—and to him? Then someone tapped him on the shoulder. "Hello, stranger. You look like you could do with a nip of something better'n water."

Thorpe turned. Of course the man behind him was wrinkled and old. Everyone here was wrinkled and old. But the fellow looked alert and cheerful; in fact, behind gold-rimmed spectacles, his eyes held a gleam that said he'd probably been a prime forager when he wore the gray in earnest.

"A nip, eh?" Thorpe said. "I have been wondering where I might find one, not being from these parts." Prohibition didn't stop drinking, but made it harder to get started in a town where you didn't know somebody.

The other veteran set a finger alongside his nose, then produced a silver flask from a waistcoat pocket. "Help yourself, but leave enough for me, too."

The whisky wasn't very good, but Thorpe had drunk whisky that wasn't very good for a great many years. He squinted at the other man's badge. "I am in your debt, Mr., uh, Ledbetter. What unit, if I may ask?"

"Army of Northern Virginia, Eighth Alabama. Call me Jed."

"I'm John, then. You fought in Hill's corps, too? I was Forty-seven North Carolina, Henry Heth's corps. You were in Mahone's, am I right?''

"So I was, by God. Your memory still works, John. So does mine, even if my pecker don't. Yeah, I was there for all of it . . . ah, hell, not quite; the Yankees caught me two days before Appomattox.''

"I stayed with it till the end,'' Thorpe said. Then he fell silent. Even after a span of years close to the biblical threescore and ten, some memories remained sharp enough to wound.

Ledbetter let him be, as any of the veterans would have. After a while he said, "Well, it ain't what we wanted it to be back then, but it ain't too bad, neither.'' Thorpe nodded gratefully; that much was true. Ledbetter changed the subject a little: "I got in here last night, and they feed you royal, that they do. If we'd had rations like these when we were in the field, we'd've *won* that goddamn war, no doubt about it.''

"I was thinking the same thing about the beds,'' Thorpe said.

Ledbetter's laughter was not a croak, but the hearty cackle of a laying hen. "John, you have that one dead on, and I'm not jokin'. Why, I remember the time I had to sleep in a tree four nights runnin'. That weren't the worst of it, neither. I—'' The story went on for some time. Thorpe believed not a word of it.

He suspected most of the old men here had stories like that. Several of the poker players wore coats studded with badges from so many past reunions that they looked like field marshals from some Balkan army better at bragging than fighting. Their yarns would have grown in the telling every time they were trotted out, too. By now few would resemble anything that had actually happened.

Jed Ledbetter shuffled off toward the bathroom. Thorpe stood around for a while, watching the men playing cards. Sure enough, they had stories by the trainful. As the shadows lengthened, one of them got up and turned on the electric lights. In the old days, Thorpe thought, it would have been an oil lamp or a candle, and endless eyestrain. No one else seemed to notice the change from then to now.

Again he'd wondered why he'd come, what he had in common with these garrulous oldsters. The only answer he could find was that the war had defined their lives, as it had his. He'd been with them at their beginnings; seeing them at the end of things seemed fitting, too.

"Generals, please,'' a woman in nurse's whites called over

and over till she had the veterans' attention. "We need you to go out for a little while so we can set the room up for supper."

Thorpe left without complaint. The poker players followed more slowly, grumbling all the way. He smiled. That took him back across the years. Some of the men in his company had left their cards back in camp when they went into battle, so as not to have to explain the devil's pasteboards to St. Peter if they got killed. But others, like these old fellows, would sooner have played than eaten.

As six o'clock drew near, more and more veterans gathered on the grass outside the dining hall. Quite a few of them had flasks, which they weren't shy in sharing. After three or four had gone by, Thorpe began to feel merry. He joined in the cheer—not quite a real Rebel yell, but close—when the doors opened. As if at one of those long-ago mess calls, the men formed a single line as they filed in.

Since he didn't know anyone here, Thorpe took a seat at random. He found himself across the table from Jed Ledbetter. The Alabamian grinned at him, displaying tobacco-stained false teeth. "Was I right, John, or what? Ain't this fine-lookin' grub?"

"That it is, Jed." Thorpe meant it—platters of ham and chicken alternated with bowls full of green salad, peas, and mashed potatoes and gravy. Along with the unofficial liquids lurking in hip flasks, there were milk and Coca-Cola and ice water. He filled his plate full. He was eating better here than he had lately down in Rocky Mount. Times were no less hard there than anywhere else in the country.

He heard so much talk of Pickett's Charge and what might have been at Gettysburg that he couldn't help himself. "Don't you forget Pettigrew's boys," he said at last. "We went up the hill on Pickett's left, and a whole great lot of us never came down again."

Maybe he'd touched glory then. He wasn't quite sure. He did remember being too excited to be afraid, even when the Federal guns on the flank tore great bleeding holes in the tight gray ranks.

Somebody said, "Reckon they call it Pickett's charge on account of his fellas got to the top o' the hill and in amongst the Yankees, and Pettigrew's didn't."

"One of the reasons they got to the top is that we shielded them most of the way with our bodies," Thorpe retorted hotly. Then he stopped, amazed at the anger he could still feel sixty-nine years after the fact. He managed a laugh. "It's water under the bridge now, that's for certain."

"So it is," the other veteran answered, "and bodies under the ground, too." The whole table fell silent for a moment then. That shot had landed too close for comfort. Almost all the bodies were under the ground by now, and the ones that weren't—those at this reunion, for instance—would be soon.

Though tired, Thorpe found he wasn't sleepy. Along with dozens of other veterans, he sat in the dining hall for hours after supper was done, drinking coffee (some of it spiked), smoking, and listening to and telling tales. As his regiment's historian, he knew a lot of them. The ordinary passing of day and night seemed far away.

"It's always like this at these things," a graybeard with a chestful of reunion badges said. "When you're with your own kind, you want to spend all the time you can on doin' and talkin'. Your bed'll always be there."

And you won't, Thorpe thought. Now that he was here, he wished he'd started coming to reunions long ago. Well, that was water under the bridge, too.

A few at a time, the old men slipped out of the hall and made for their cottages. A little past midnight, someone made a horrifying discovery in his program book. He clambered up onto a chair and, teetering dangerously, waved his arms and waited for quiet. When he got it, he said loudly, "There's gonna be a God-damned band playin' us God-damned reveille at seven o'clock in the God-damned mornin' tomorrow. They must think we're still in the God-damned army."

Assisted by two of his comrades, he descended from his perch. The dining hall emptied quickly after that. Thorpe's ears were not what they had been, but he didn't think he could sleep through a band's worth of reveille.

Sure enough, at seven sharp the music blared out. Along with the rest of the men in Cottage C, Thorpe dressed and returned to the dining hall. This time, he made a point of finding Jed Ledbetter. The Alabamian looked up, grinned his yellowed grin, then resumed his attack on a plate of bacon and eggs.

Thorpe had been reading his own program book. He said, "I don't mind getting up early today, because the morning's event is the United Confederate Veterans' business meeting."

Ledbetter grinned again, evilly. "An' you reckon you'll just doze right through it, you mean."

"It has to be easier than sleeping in a tree, don't you think?" Thorpe asked, deadpan.

"Remind me to watch out for you, John," Ledbetter said. "You may be a quiet one, but you got yourself a devil hidin' there inside."

The two veterans sat side by side on the bus that took them to the Mosque Auditorium at Sixth and Laurel. Confederate battle flags flew everywhere in Richmond. A forest of them waved in front of the Mosque; an enormous one was stretched behind the speaker's platform. The building's ceiling fans stirred the thick air but did little to cool it.

The introductions of aged UCV dignitaries by other aged UCV dignitaries went on and on. Some of them seemed hardly more lively than Stonewall Jackson's horse Old Sorrel, whose stuffed carcass was on display back at the Soldiers' Home. As he'd thought he might, Thorpe dozed through the speeches. Every so often his head would fall forward onto his chest and wake him; in those moments, he saw he was far from the only old soldier having trouble staying awake.

After lunch, the Confederate veterans filed onto the buses that took them across town for the dedication of the Richmond Battlefield Parks. They rolled east along the section of Franklin Street called Monument Avenue, past the memorials to Matthew Fontaine Maury, to Jackson, to Jefferson Davis, to Lee, and to Jeb Stuart. Thorpe hadn't been with the Army of Northern Virginia for the Seven Days Campaign, whose sites took up much of the Battlefield Parks, but he'd fought at Cold Harbor two years later, holding Grant's men away from the Confederate capital.

His bus was one of the first to arrive, so he got a spot near the speakers' stand. A solidly built, dark-haired U.S. Army colonel was leaning down and shaking hands with a good number of veterans. "Who's he?" Thorpe asked.

"Let's have us a look." Jed Ledbetter checked his program. Behind his thick reading glasses, his eyes widened. "God damn me if it ain't U.S. Grant III."

Thorpe waited to hear no more, but began trying to make his way through the crowd. It wasn't easy; too many other ex-Rebels had the same idea. But at last he got to clasp hands with the Federal commander's grandson and namesake. "Thank you for coming here, sir," he said.

"I'm pleased to do it," Colonel Grant answered. "I wasn't sure what kind of reception I'd get, seeing what my name is, but everyone's been very kind."

"Your grandfather was doing the job he thought right, sir; so were the men who fought for him," Thorpe answered. "We knew that then, and we know it now. Nothing could have shown it better than his kindness and theirs at Appomattox, when the Federals fed us and let us keep our horses and mules."

"He always felt you southern men were doing the same, and doing it bravely," Grant said. "We always were brothers, even when we fought."

"Yes," Thorpe said. By then, though, Colonel Grant had turned to another old soldier. Thorpe went back to his place without resentment. It was just the reverse: that a Grant would come here to pay tribute to his grandfather's former foes said all that needed saying about reconciliation between North and South.

Perhaps not quite all; Jed Ledbetter played the part of the unreconstructed Rebel. "*I* won't shake his hand," he said when Thorpe had returned from the bunting-draped platform. "I wouldn't have shook his grandpappy's hand, neither. General? Ha! He just kept throwin' bluecoats at us till he wore us to death, is all."

"They were brave men, too," Thorpe said. "When they came across the open country at us here at Cold Harbor, shooting them felt like murder." He paused a moment in surprise and realization. "I expect they felt the same about us the third day at Gettysburg."

"Didn't stop 'em," Ledbetter growled. Then he made a sour face. "All right, John, I see your point. God damn if I have to like it, though."

As the afternoon's speeches wore on, a couple of Confederate veterans passed out from the heat. But doctors and nurses were at the ready, and soon revived them. Thorpe noticed that Jed Ledbetter clapped as loud as anyone else after Colonel Grant spoke. In fact, the colonel got the loudest hand of the afternoon.

Ledbetter pulled out a pocket watch as the old soldiers reboarded the buses. "We better be back by six," he said. "Somebody'll pay hell if I miss 'Amos 'n' Andy' on the radio." He sounded much fiercer at that moment than he had when he was grumbling about General Grant. Several men echoed him, some profanely. But the organizing committee had taken into account the nearly universal passion for the show: no reunion events were scheduled while it was on.

Fortunately, the buses did return on time. Thorpe listened to "Amos 'n' Andy" along with everyone else in his cottage, then went to dinner, and then to the Mosque for a reception honoring the veterans. To his surprise, he actually got asked a sensible question there. A man in his middle thirties came up and said, "Sir, do you think what you went through was as hard as the fighting in France?"

"That's a hard question to answer, young fellow. You were Over There?" Thorpe asked. The man nodded. Thorpe watched his eyes go distant and watchful; yes, he'd seen the elephant. The Confederate veteran said, "We weren't up against the big cannon and the machine guns and the gas, as you boys were, but we didn't have your supply train or your doctors, either. War's hard any which way, I expect."

"True enough." The Great War soldier nodded again. "Thank you, General."

Thorpe stayed away from the next day's business meetings at the Mosque. Talking with the assembled veterans at the Soldiers' Home was more enjoyable. When he let out that he'd been a captain, a lot of them gave him a hard time; most, in those days, had been youths with no rank to their name.

At one point that afternoon he asked Jed Ledbetter to move so he could get past him and go to the bathroom. Ledbetter sprang to his feet with alarming spryness. "Yes, sir, Captain, sir!" he cried, coming to a brace surely stiffer than any he'd used back in his soldier days.

Thorpe looked around at the grinning veterans. "If it's all the same to you gents, I think I'd sooner be demoted back to General so I can be like everybody else," he said. Amid raucous laughter, the rest of the Confederate soldiers gave him his wish.

Around four, Ledbetter got up and left the talk of old battles won and old battles lost. "I'm gonna take me a nap," he announced when a couple of eyebrows went up. "I wanna be at my best fo' the ball tonight, do some fancy steppin' with the pretty young things."

Thorpe looked forward to the dance, too, but the talk was even better, with names that echoed across the decades like far-off musketry. Some he'd been through: Gettysburg and the Wilderness, Cold Harbor and Appomattox. Some were from before the days when the Forty-seventh North Carolina had joined Lee's army: Antietam, Fredericksburg, Chancellorsville. And some came from the west: Shiloh, Stone's Mountain, Vicksburg.

One white-haired Texan had fought at Palmito Ranch more than a month after the surrender at Appomattox. "Yeah, we

whupped the Yankees," he said, "but if we'd've knowed y'all
had done give up, we wouldn't've bothered."

Jed Ledbetter came back to the dining hall in time for supper.
He made a point of sitting by Thorpe for the trip to the ball at
the Grays' Armory. As the bus rattled down the street, they
exchanged addresses. "Sure I'll write to you, John," Ledbetter
said. "What the hell else I got to do all day?" He cackled with
laughter.

A flask came by. Thorpe sipped from it, passed it to his new
friend. He said, "We can put all we've got into the dance tonight, seeing as we'll be in cars for the grand parade tomorrow."

"I heard tell about that," Ledbetter said, nodding. "Don't
know as I like it much. I marched in plenty o' these down
through the years." He paused and loosed that cackle of his
again. " 'Course, I was younger then."

The ballroom swept Thorpe back to the days when he'd been
younger, much younger. Had the girls been in crinolines and
hoop skirts that swept the floor, had the gallants been without
gray beards and canes, the scene might have been one from his
first stay in Richmond all those years before.

The moment the music started, he even forgot his comrades'
age. Most of them forgot it, too, swinging their partners through
the Grand March as if they were going off to battle in the morning. Several of the young ladies exclaimed in pleasure; they
might not have expected the old soldiers to have so much vim
left.

No sooner had that idea crossed Thorpe's mind than a girl
behind him let out an indignant squeak and exclaimed, "Why,
General, you forget yourself!"

"No, miss—I remember, by God!" the veteran retorted.

Fiddlers played tunes that went back to the War Between the
States. Thorpe discovered his feet still knew how to jig. He was
out of breath and his heart pounded heavily in his chest when
the music stopped, but the applause from his partner, a very
pretty little strawberry blonde about the age of his oldest great-
granddaughter, resolved him to dance all night.

The American Legion band played square dance music.
Thorpe felt lighter on his feet than he had in thirty years, maybe
more. He knew he was cutting a sprightly figure. Some of the
veterans wilted as the evening went on and retired to the side-
lines, but he stayed out on the floor, just as he'd told himself he
would.

"General, shouldn't you take a rest?" asked the blond girl. (her name, he'd learned, was Marjorie).

He shook his head. "Miss, I haven't so many nights of dancing left in me that I can afford to waste even part of one."

Marjorie's laugh displayed small, even white teeth. "All right, General, since you put it that way, let's cut us a rug!"

Thorpe was one of the last veterans still dancing when the band played "Dixie." The armory echoed with shouts and cheers and old men's voices cracking as they tried to turn loose Rebel yells. Thorpe yelled with the best of them, pumping his fist in the air.

Marjorie stared, wide-eyed, not just at him but at all the old soldiers; maybe, just for a moment, she too saw them as they'd been so long ago. Emboldened by that thought, Thorpe leaned forward and pecked her on the cheek. She smiled and squeezed his hands between hers. "Thank you, General," she said. "I've enjoyed this evening much more than I thought I would."

"So have I, Miss Marjorie," he said. "Oh, I'm tired, I'll not deny, but I don't grudge a minute of it."

But when, a little past midnight, he got into a nightshirt and pulled back the covers on his steel cot, he felt a dull pain in the left side of his ribcage. He curled his lip in mild scorn at the weakness of his flesh. Though he hadn't done so much in years, he was sure he'd be fine come morning. He lay down, prayed briefly, and fell asleep.

He awoke in darkness, amid old men's snores. The pain was back, and suddenly seemed big as the world. He sat up, started to get out of bed . . .

Thorpe looked down at the cuff of his gray coat. It bore the double twist of braid that showed captain's rank. He looked at the hand protruding from the cuff. The flesh was smooth and unspotted, the tendons no longer upraised like old tree roots pushing through thin soil.

He had no time for surprise. He and the rest of the men in gray and butternut and occasional looted Yankee blue hurried through the cover afforded by a stand of old pine woods. The trees thinned ahead. He could see the line of the Weldon Railroad, the burned ruins of what had been Reams Station south of Petersburg, the low parapet the Federals had thrown up twenty or thirty yards east of the train tracks.

"Keep your ranks, boys," he called to the men of Company A. The troopers of the Chicora Guards just grinned and nodded. They'd been through enough fights to know what to do without being told.

The Federals held their fire, no doubt waiting for their foes to reach a point from which they would be unable to get away cheaply. Suddenly, from not far behind Thorpe, Brigadier General William McRae shouted, "Don't fire a gun now, but dash for the enemy."

The soldiers in gray traded grim looks. If McRae's ploy failed, they were the ones who would pay the butcher's bill. No choice, though, but to obey. Drawing his Army Colt, Thorpe cried "Forward!" and ran to the attack at the head of his company.

The Rebels burst out of the pine woods yelling like fiends. The Northern soldiers yelled, too, in surprise and alarm. Muzzle flashes stabbed outward from the parapet; thick clouds of black-powder smoke rose above it.

A Minié ball cracked past Thorpe's head. Confederate soldiers fell, screaming and writhing in pain. But the charge was across only a couple of hundred yards of ground. Since the Rebels did not pause to fire and reload their rifle muskets—always deadly dangerous out in the open—they drew near the parapet before too many of them fell.

Thorpe tripped on a cross-tie as he ran across the railroad track. He stumbled, almost fell, caught himself just in time. Then he was at the low Federal earthwork. A man in blue scrambled up to meet him, thrust with a bayoneted Springfield. Thorpe fired the Colt pistol at point-blank range. The Federal wailed and reeled backward, clutching his belly.

Other southern men were up on the Union works now, too, some fighting hand to hand, others shooting down into the trenches behind the parapet. Some bluecoats fired back, but more threw down their guns and threw up their hands in token of surrender.

The cheering Confederates swarmed forward. A ragged private seized a flag from a color bearer who seemed too stunned to stop him. A glum Federal who wore a major's shoulder straps on the plain blue blouse of a private turned to Thorpe and said, "Captain, your men fight well; that was a magnificent charge."

"Thank you, sir," Thorpe said, nodding to his courteous captive.

The Rebels began hustling more prisoners off to the rear. They must have bagged a couple of thousand Yankees, Thorpe thought proudly. But the cost was not light. Men of the Chicora Guards who'd seemed to have charmed lives all through the company's hard fighting were down now, dead or wounded. No doubt the story was the same all through the Forty-seventh North Carolina. The surgeons would be busy tonight.

Thorpe peered east. The Federals not hit or captured were abandoning their works and retreating in that direction. They wouldn't tear up any more of the Weldon Railroad here, not for a good while to come; Confederate cavalry—Wade Hampton's boys—galloped up from the south to speed the Yankees on their way.

The rattle of gunfire slowed to a lethargic *pop-pop-pop* and finally petered out. Thorpe glanced back over his shoulder. The sun was almost down. Hard to believe the fighting had lasted most of the day. In the middle of the action from the moment it began, he'd had no time to think . . . about what he was doing here at Reams Station, about how he'd returned to August 1864, to his youth, again.

"That's over," he said to no one in particular. "All over."

"So it is," agreed the Union major, who he somehow hadn't gone back with the rest of the prisoners. "So it is—in a way. Welcome, John. We've been waiting for you a long time; you're one of the last to join the ranks."

Under the orange light of the setting sun, dead and injured men of both sides, their wounds suddenly vanished, sprang to their feet and went around slapping one another on the back. "That was a good shot you nailed me with, Eb." "Just luck, Willie, just luck. Fact is, I was aiming for Joseph there next to you."

Proud, bullet-torn battle flags from North and South fluttered together in the evening breeze. Under them, the men of both sides gathered, all sound and well as they had been before the battle started. "I got me some good coffee here," a Yankee announced. "Who'll swap me some baccy for it?" A Rebel stepped forward, smiling, to make the trade.

Thorpe stared, not fully understanding, not yet. The northern major touched him on the forearm. "Did it not seem real, John?" he asked quietly. "Was it not as in the old days?"

Then Thorpe knew beyond any doubt. "Yes, by God, it was," he said.

He woke next morning in a shelter tent he shared with Benjamin Bunn and George Westray. The lieutenants were already up, and bent over a chessboard. They set the game aside to go out with him and take morning roll for the company. He smiled as he walked in front of the drawn-up men. So many faces he hadn't seen in so many years!

After the roll was taken, the Chicora Guards lined up for mess call, and then for drill. Before they could begin their evolutions, though, the drummer began the monotonous patter that summoned soldiers gray and blue to battle. "Dismissed to get your war gear!" Thorpe called. Cheering, the men trotted back to their tents and bedrolls, snatched up rifles and cartridge boxes.

Thorpe followed a little more slowly. He wondered which fight it would be today.

"Poor old John," Jed Ledbetter said as the hearse pulled away from the Soldiers' Home. He took off his hat and held it over his heart. "Poor old John. He went and missed the grand parade."

As I've said, I love baseball. If I were the athletic type, I would have tried to play. Since I'm not, I sometimes play beer league softball, which is not the same thing at all, at all. Those of you who have done likewise will recognize that a good deal of this story is drawn straight from life. I never met anyone like Michael, though. I wish I had.

DESIGNATED HITTER

YOU FIND ALL KINDS PLAYING BEER LEAGUE softball. I ought to know. They let me play, for instance.

I've been a baseball nut since I was a kid. Unfortunately, I'm also a klutz. I can hit, a little; I can't field at all. As soon as they saw me with the leather, the rest of the Gators—that's my team, in case you hadn't worked it out—took to calling me Dr. Strangeglove, after Dick Stuart, a notorious nonfielding first baseman with the Pirates and Red Sox back in the sixties. I have to say I earned the name.

So when we go out there, I'll catch some of the time. That's pretty safe for the team—there's no stealing in slow-pitch. If we're way ahead or way behind, I'll get in an inning or two at first. Mostly I'm a designated hitter. The leagues we play in—a lot of beer leagues, come to that—all fifteen guys on the team get to hit, even if only ten can be on the field at any one time.

I'm also our official scorer, statistician, what have you—damn sight better at that side of the game than playing, worse luck. And at beer and pizza, I'm a champ. That's as important as the game, just about.

Besides, my girl thinks I look good in the uniform.

Which is more than I can say for some of the Gators who are nine times the ballplayer I'll ever be. Joe Humphreys, our real first baseman, looks like an avocado with a beard in his dark green softball togs. And Stuart Boileau at short is skinny enough to be a lizard. He has this habit of licking his lips all the time, too, which doesn't hurt the image. Once at Shakey's we ordered him a pepperoni-and-bugs pizza. If they would've served it, he would've eaten it.

All of which brings me around by easy stages to the oddest-looking ball player I ever saw. This was at the start of last year's spring leagues, and my Gators were in deep Bandini. A couple of guys have been transferred out of state since last fall, and two or three more were working nights for a while. We were plain strapped for troops. A bare ten had shown up for our opener, and our archrivals, the Tomcats, trounced us, 14–5.

I didn't exactly cover myself with glory in that game, either. I was a fat 0 for 3, though I got on my last time up when their pitcher embarrassed himself by throwing my comebacker eight feet over the first baseman's head. I razzed him as I stood out there, and he gave it right back. "That's the only way you'll ever reach against me," he said, which was near enough true that I shut up.

After me came our leadoff hitter. Stuart did us proud with a sharp single to center. Like an idiot, I tried to go to third on it, even though the other guys had a fellow with a rocket for an arm out there. Gave it all I had—headfirst dive into the bag. Well, actually shoulderfirst—something went *crunch-pop* when I hit. "Ouch!" isn't what I yelled. I jammed it good. My right arm was in a sling for the next couple of weeks.

To add insult to injury, I was out.

Sling and all, I showed up at the park next Tuesday night. Even if I couldn't play, I liked hanging around with the guys— and I can drink left-handed.

It didn't look like there was going to be a game, though. Only nine of us were there, counting me, which you shouldn't. You're supposed to field ten in softball, but it's legal to go out there with nine. Eight or fewer and you forfeit. "Where's Roy?" I asked Wes Humphreys, Joe's little brother (he's only six-three) and our manager.

"Called me this afternoon—he's got the flu. Sounded like hell."

"Bad." Without Roy we didn't have a prayer of fielding a team. And with a forfeit, we'd be two games back of the Tomcats right off the bat. In a ten-game season, that's death.

Wes knew all this better than I did. He hates losing, and won't take it lying down. So now he called to this fellow sitting in the bleachers watching us loosen up: "Hey, man! You play this game?"

"Me?" The guy looked startled. "A little, maybe." He had an accent that wasn't Spanish. Not a good sign, if we were after a ballplayer.

Well, he had to be foreign, or else the melting pot had gone and melted down. I'd noticed him watching us the week before, too. I couldn't help it. He was a medium-dark, medium-heavy black guy, maybe thirty, but his hair—he cornrowed it, very neatly—was Irishman red, I mean flaming, and hung past his shoulders. He wore a mustache and goatee that were even brighter. I went to high school with a Japanese kid who spoke pure, hush-ma-mouf Arkansas—turned out his folks had been resettled there during the war, and stayed a while afterward. He jolted me every time he said something. Looking at this guy now was like that—his hair and his hide spectacularly didn't match.

Wes would have taken him if he was a giant panda covered with chocolate feathers. "Come on down!" he said, waving. "We've got open roster slots. You can join us for the season if you want, or sign up and then duck out after tonight—we'll have more people here next week. Whatever you want."

Wes is a good talker. He has to be. He sells glassware for a living. You could see the guy thinking it over. Finally he shrugged and ambled on over to us. He didn't have a uniform, of course, but his clothes were grubby enough to play in: faded Levi's, a Coors T-shirt, and beat-up running shoes. About what we wear to practice.

He said his name was Michael, with a bit of a guttural on the "ch." He shook hands with everybody (left-handed with me), then Wes dug our ancient spare glove out of the bottom of his duffel bag.

Michael hadn't been stretching when he said he played "a little." He lunged awkwardly for balls when he was playing catch, blocked grounders with his shins or his feet as often as he fielded them cleanly. He threw from the elbow, girl-style, not too straight. I could see Wes regretting things already, but Michael was a warm body, anyhow, and catching he wouldn't be all that much worse than I was.

When it was Michael's turn to hit in our warm-ups, Wes, who was pitching BP, waved him to the plate. He looked worse up there than he had in the field. He stood straight up and down, with his left foot so far in the bucket it wasn't ever pointing at third base: more like at our dugout off third. He held his bat at a funny angle, with his hands a couple of inches apart. Yeah, I know Ty Cobb did the same thing, but Ty Cobb's grandmother had to be a more stylish hitter than this Michael.

Wes gave him a nice, fat pitch to hit. He took a clumsy swing, missed. He muttered something under his breath and tossed the ball back. Next pitch, he hit a little ground ball that dribbled between Stuart at short and Pete Sadowski, our third baseman: a hit, sure enough. Not impressive, but it'd look like a line drive in the box score, as the saying goes.

"Attaboy!" Wes yelled.

Next pitch was another clean miss. Michael took the one after that, then hit a bloop just past first that Joe couldn't quite reach. In a game, that would have been a double. Then a grounder straight at Pete on third, except it hit a pebble and kicked away from him. Another miss. Then a pop fly over Stuart but too short for the outfielders. Then a big bouncer right at Stuart, but on the last hop it flattened out and went between his legs. Then another bloop that sent Joe puffing down the line. He couldn't catch that one, either.

This must have gone on for another five minutes. Every so often Michael would miss, and those incandescent cornrows would fly as he shook his head in annoyance. But when he hit, it would be one little bleeder or bloop or bad hop after another. Nothing like art, but nothing like outs, either. Finally our left fielder, Ted Canter, who was far and away the best athlete on the team, slid six feet on his belly to snag one of those pops maybe two inches off the ground.

"Good catch!" Michael shouted. He tossed the bat to somebody else.

Nobody said anything for a few seconds. We weren't quite sure what we'd seen, or what to make of it. Wes stood on the rubber, scratching his head. At last he said, "Remind me not to play poker with you, man. You'd probably draw four to a ten and end up with a royal flush."

"Yeah, Flush!" Pete yelled, so Michael got his nickname. He smiled, and looked a lot younger. He was pretty sober most of the time.

We let the other team have the field for their warm-ups. They were an outfit called Snafu. They played like their name a lot of the time, too. Still, they were pretty cocky, seeing us short a guy. We gathered around Wes while he made out the lineup sheet. He was still scratching, trying to figure out where to bat Michael. On form he deserved to hit last, but if all those hits were legit, he was a clear third hitter. Wes finally compromised and put him sixth.

It turned out to be a busy sort of game. Snafu got two runs in the first and another four in the second. Michael got knocked ass over teakettle in a play at the plate. The throw was high, and as he went up for it, the runner, a big Samoan built like a line-backer, cut the legs out from under him. He was safe; Michael never did get the ball. He found it and threw it back to Wes.

"Way to hang in there, Flush," Wes said, nodding. Michael just dusted himself off and went back into his crouch.

We were hitting, too, scoring as fast as Snafu. I was in a 1-0 slow-pitch game once, but most of them aren't like that. We finally won this one 13-11 when Snafu made back-to-back errors, the first one with the bases loaded, in the last inning.

Michael? Damned if he didn't go four for four: a soft liner over second, another one of those dinkers back of first—though he got thrown out trying to stretch that one—and a couple of ground balls with eyes. The second one started our big rally; he scored a couple of runs, in fact.

At Shakey's afterward, Pete got a pitcher of Bud and set it in front of Michael. "You got a choice, Flush," he said, as threatening as you can be with a big grin on your face. "Tell me you'll be back next week, and you can drink it. Otherwise I'll pour it over your stupid head.'

"When do we play?" Michael said. We all cheered. It got pretty drunk out. That's an advantage early games have—they give you more time to party afterward. I remember asking Michael what he did.

He thought about it. It took a few seconds; he had nothing against beer. Finally he said, "Some of this, some of that. I spend a lot of time looking."

I backed off in a hurry. "Say no more." I'd been unemployed not too long before that. A bad feeling.

By the next game, I had that miserable sling off, thank God—ever try to bathe in one? I'm glad I wear a beard. Shaving left-handed is something I'd sooner not think about. I was still combing my hair that way, though. The arm wasn't ready for anything serious. It twinged whenever I lifted it higher than my shoulder.

We had enough people there this time, and Wes made Michael a DH. He was awful shaky in the field. He knew it, too, and didn't say boo. But in warm-ups he put on another hitting show. He looked terrible up there, but he wasn't making any outs.

Wes threw his hands in the air. "All right, I'm convinced!" He batted Flush third. It worked, too. He was up three times, got three more cheap but effective hits, and we won again. Not only that, for once Snafu kept their act together for a whole game and knocked off the Tomcats, so we were tied with them again. Even the postgame pizza wasn't as greasy as usual. A fine week.

I was up for the next game. We had some momentum, we were going against another weak team—a gang called the Mother Truckers—and I was well enough to play. My arm still grumbled, but I could use it. To make sure I didn't hurt it again, I went through warm-ups doing just what I would have done anyway: throwing knuckleballs.

Typical of me to have my one baseball talent be absolutely useless. What good is someone who can throw a knuckler only with a slow-pitch ball? But I've got a mean one, if I say so myself. And a knuckleball is the easiest thing in the world on your arm. Look at Hoyt Wilhelm or Phil Niekro or Charlie Hough—big leaguers all, well into their forties.

A knuckleball comes up to the plate (or to whoever's trying to catch it) with about as much oomph as a marshmallow. But if you've thrown it right, you've killed almost all the spin on the thing, and every tiny little air current can have fun with it as if flies.

If you're a batter, it's like a drunken moth heading your way. It'll dance. It'll float. It'll shimmy. The best one I ever threw seemed to stub its toe halfway there, and hop on one leg the rest of the way. Marvelous fun. Hitters have no idea what it'll do next. That's fair; neither does the guy who threw it. Catchers hate it—they can't handle it, either.

Trouble is, sometimes it doesn't knuckle. Then it might as well be batting practice. Think of a hanging curve, only more so.

Tonight, though, playing catch with Pete, I had a good one. He caught it the first time I threw it, barely; it looked like a scoop of ice cream sitting right at the top of his glove. "Damn thing has the staggers," he said, and fired it back to me harder than I can throw even when my arm's fine. My mitt popped. My hand started burning.

But I had my revenge. Pete's a pretty fair ballplayer. He caught most of what I threw, lunging and stabbing and guessing which way the rabbit would hop. But he dropped a couple, missed one clean and had to chase it, and took one right in the leg. It's hard to hurt anybody with a knuckler, especially with a slow-pitch ball, but he did the Stanislavsky routine, yelling and bouncing up and down and generally making an ass of himself.

When he was done with that nonsense, he flipped the ball to

Michael, who was next to him loosening up with Ted. "Here, Flush," he said, "trade places with me. This bastard"—which was the nicest thing he'd called me since I plunked him—"throws like you hit."

One of Michael's gingery eyebrows went up. "Really?" he said, and threw me the ball. He was better than he'd been a couple of weeks before, starting to get his whole arm into it.

But with that funky old glove he was still using, he couldn't have hung on to the first knuckler I gave him if he were Johnny Bench. I was proud of it. It wobbled seven different ways, and the last one caught him right in the chest.

He picked up the ball and looked at it as if it'd taken a bite out of him. "Do that again," he said, like he didn't believe what he'd seen. He couldn't've picked a better way to flatter me. The next one wasn't as good. It only broke once, but down and away, and zigged under his glove and past him.

He ran after it hard and burned it back to me—mustard on it. If he ever learned to throw right, he'd have a good arm. "How do you do that?" he said.

It made me proud. "Mind over matter," I told him grandly, flexing what passes for my right bicep.

His eyes got big and round. They were a light, golden brown, an interesting color. "Let me have another one."

Hell, I'd throw that thing all night if somebody'd catch it for me. I give him credit: he fought it all the way, catching the ones that didn't knuckle too much, even a couple of good ones, getting his glove on most of them. But several got by him, and I'm afraid I nailed him a few more times, the last one in a tender spot. Knuckleball or not, he doubled over.

So did Pete, but he was laughing. "Ohh, that stings!" he sang out in falsetto.

Wes came rushing over. He wasn't mad at Pete. He was mad at me. "Don't you go racking Flush up, Dr. Strange," he growled, and he meant every word of it. "He's worth more to this team than you'll ever be, you goddamn clown."

"Do not blame him," Michael said when he could talk again. "That is a remarkable talent he has, and the ball eluded me time after time. Pete is right: I think he does pitch like I hit."

"Remarkable, my left one," Wes snorted. "You okay?"

"Yes, yes." Michael sounded impatient. It was about time to play; we started crowding into the dugout. Michael slapped me on the back. "Congratulations. I doubted your people could do such a thing."

"Huh?" I said, but just then Stuart flied out, and Michael had to go out on deck. When he came up, he singled between second and first—nobody'd got him out since he had joined us. He promptly scored when Wes' brother, Joe, boomed one past the center fielder. He tried to stretch it into a triple, slid hard into the Mother Truckers' third baseman, and they started wrestling. Joe's all right off the field, but he plays rough. He picked on somebody his own size; that third baseman had "Whale" lettered on the back of his shirt. Both benches emptied. We managed to pry 'em apart without any punches getting thrown.

In the fun and games, I forgot about Michael's peculiar remark. I didn't make anything much of it, anyway. He had the same right to life, liberty, and the pursuit of weirdness as any other Gator.

Sure enough, he ended up going 3 for 3, two rollers and a humpbacked liner nobody could reach. We won; I think it was 8–5.

At Shakey's afterward I remembered again. "Hey, Flush," I said, and looked around for him.

"He took off, man," Ted told me. "Gulped a beer and split. Probably afraid you were gonna clunk him some more."

"Smartass. Something I wanted to ask him. Oh well, if I think of it, I'll catch him with it next week."

But when next Tuesday rolled around, Michael didn't show. He hadn't called; he hadn't left word. He just wasn't there. Wes cussed me up one side and down the other. He had no more idea than I did whether it was my fault, but he took no chances. And when we lost—nobody hit a lick—he reamed me all over again. He plain hates to lose.

Michael didn't come back, either, and it took us a couple of games to get used to having him gone. We lost one of those, and then lost to the Tomcats again, and ended up tied for third with Snafu. Lord, Wes was furious.

We played in two summer leagues, then a fall one, then took a rest for winter—Sun Belt or not, it's too damn cold. Life went on. Joe got married (again); Wes got divorced (again); Ted's wife had twins; Pete got busted for drunk driving and spent a night in jail.

We were going to get together last week for our first spring practice, but it got canceled, of course—that was the day the aliens showed up. God knows how they did it from somewhere out around the orbit of Uranus, but they sent every country their message in its own number one language.

Naturally, you saw the one who was talking to us here in the States the same way I did. Humanoid, sure, but not from here, even if he did wear a pin-striped three-piece suit (to reassure the natives, I suppose): not with elephant-gray skin and bright blue hair. Those first few awful seconds, with everyone wondering whether they were going to blow us away, I was too freaked to notice that he cornrowed it.

Then I saw a couple of the others going back and forth behind him. They were a little out of focus, but brown skin and brick-red hair isn't a combination you forget in a hurry. "Ohmygod," I said, all one word.

The one in front started talking. His English had the same raspy accent as Michael's, but he knew how to handle himself in front of a camera. "I greet you in peace," he said, and you believed him. He had a presence Dan Rather would kill for.

"I greet you," he said again, "And congratulate you, and extend to you the invitation of the Confederacy of Sentient Beings to join our ranks. You have fulfilled the three criteria for membership. You have gained control of the atom. True, you use it in war, but your national struggles are over now. Yes, and this ship itself is armed. That is only proper: danger must be guarded against.

"You seek to explore space. A race without the curiosity to step outside its cradle is not worth knowing.

"And you have at last begun to master your own minds and use them directly, not merely through the clumsy mediation of the body." He glanced at something on the desk in front of him: whatever an alien uses for a paperweight, maybe. It lifted up about six inches and hung in the air. I didn't think it was special effects. What I thought was more like, *No wonder Michael was such a good place hitter.*

"Of the three," he went on, "this last is the key, for without control of the mind, no race can truly be said to be mature. We searched for it long in you, and began to fear you lacked it. Then one of our investigators"—remember how the picture cut away to a redheaded black man in a Gators cap? That's Flush, all right—"found a member of your folk using the talent in one of your games. Where it exists, it can be trained. We shall do this for you: it is the least we can do to welcome you among us. We will be landing soon, my friends. You are no longer alone."

The screen went blank after that, right? And you've seen the broadcasts since, everything we'll gain by joining this Confederacy of theirs: the trade, the ideas, far horizons when we'd almost forgotten what that meant. Everybody's going nuts celebrating the end of war, the end of poverty, the end of everything bad. I sure hope they're right.

But I'm a little worried. That "mature" thing Grayface was talking about. All I've been thinking of is that goddamn knuckleball and what it must have looked like to Michael, especially when he was used to shoving things around with his own mind and looking for evidence we could do it, too.

Well, "soon" is tomorrow now. But their ship is armed. They said so. I wonder what happens when they realize we *can't*.

Like I said, I'm a little worried.

What could be more important for any society than making its next generation better and smarter people than the current one? Yet to whom do we entrust so much of the task of raising our children? All too often, to day-care workers who can't find work much above the minimum wage and to teachers who majored in education because it was easy. We get what we pay for, though, here as anywhere else. The probability of "Gladly Wolde He Lerne" reflecting reality is effectively zero. Too bad.

GLADLY WOLDE HE LERNE

*ONLY THE COLD, GREEN-BLUE GLOW OF MER-*cury vapor lamps lit the campus lot when Ted Collins pulled in. He had to park a long way from the lecture hall. He hauled his attaché case off the front passenger seat and locked the car. Then, already weary from a full day's work, he trudged over the asphalt toward the hall.

It was more than half full when he came in. Even so, it was quiet; the rest of the educators there were as worn as he was. Some of the superintendents, administrators, program specialists, and supervisors looked fresh out of college. Others, like him, were a few years older, already experienced in managing school district affairs.

Whatever their backgrounds—Collins himself was an assistant superintendent for education planning and research—they all had one thing in common. They were all ambitious enough to go to night school to learn what they needed to know to advance in the educational bureaucracy.

Professor Vance walked in. She strode briskly to the podium and tapped at the microphone to make sure it worked. Collins took out his notebook and a pen. He'd heard from people who had been through this course that Vance didn't believe in wasting time.

She didn't. As soon as she found the mike was live, she plunged straight into her lecture: ''Anyone can be a success at the district level. Policies are blurred there, responsibilities vague; very often you never see the actual clients who depend

184

on you for educational services. If you hope to go farther in education, you'll have to lose that pervasive vagueness. You got by with it at the university, you can get by with it at district offices, but it's a fatal handicap in an actual school setting. Here's what I mean. . . .''

By the time that first lecture was done, Collins wondered what had possessed him to want to become a principal in the first place. He thought about dropping the class and staying comfortably in his present job. He shook his head. When he started something, he wasn't the sort to back away from it.

He ended up acing Vance's course. He took the others he needed, one or two a semester, always at night, as he could fit them into the rest of his life. He went through an internship program at an actual junior high school campus. He took the state-required examination for certification. Before long, he got an interview. The committee let him hang for two weeks before they let him know he'd been accepted. Kranz Elementary School had itself a new principal.

When Collins got the news, he threw the biggest party he'd ever given—and ended up with the biggest hangover he'd ever had. The hangover eventually went away. As for the size of the party—well, what the hell? With the raise he'd get from his promotion, he could afford it and then some.

He started his new job in the fall. It was as challenging as he'd hoped it would be. Budgeting for a single school was a much more complicated—and, as Professor Vance had warned so long ago, a much more precise—business than planning for districtwide programs, where you could always shuffle money between dozens of different accounts.

Human relations counted for more at the school-site level, too. Little by little, he learned how to build rapport with the faculty. As principal, he also came into contact with pupils, something he'd never done back in the district office. Dealing with them made the problem of handling a staff look simple. But again, he learned.

He got on with the rest of his life, too. He married a curriculum specialist from the district office where he'd worked before. He took up golf. After a while, he was shooting in the mideighties. He grew a mustache. After a while, it turned salt-and-pepper.

Satisfying as his principal's assignment had been, he slowly decided it didn't give him everything he needed. He hated the idea of being in a rut for the rest of his life. He talked things over with his wife. "Go for it," she said. "I know it'll be tough. Even if you don't make it—and so many people don't—you'll be better for the experience. But I think you will. I think you can do it."

"You're wonderful," he said, and kissed her. The very next day, he enrolled in night school again.

The moment he walked into his first class, he saw most of his fellow students were folks a lot like him: solid men and women who'd already built up solid careers but wanted something more. Oh, there were a couple of people in their early thirties, but only a couple. He knew they were the ones he'd have to watch out for, the whiz kids, the ones on the fast track to the top. He was no whiz kid. He was a grinder. That had always worked till now. He had to hope it would keep on working.

"Congratulations," Dr. de la Vega said as he walked to the front of the classroom and sat down on the table by the podium. "Congratulations just for being here, and for wanting to be the best." His mild smile turned savage. "Now we'll see how many of you I can run out of the program over the next twenty weeks."

He meant it, too. Nothing was watered down here, nothing simplified to let the slower people keep up. If you couldn't keep up, too bad. Grimly, Collins buckled down to do the work. He ended up with a high B in the course, and felt prouder of it than of most A's he'd earned.

Every course in the whole program turned out to be like that. Collins learned to live on coffee and four hours of sleep a night. At a physical, his doctor warned him all that coffee could bring on an ulcer. He kept drinking it. Without it, he would have had to quit, and he'd come too far to do that.

As time went on, he became ever more conscious of the responsibility that came with jobs at the top of the hierarchy. He had to look hard at himself to find out whether he truly wanted it. Without false modesty, he decided he did.

Before he was even allowed to take the exams at the end of the program, he had to convince an interview board he was worthy. The exams themselves made the ones he'd taken to qualify for principal look like a pop quiz. When he learned he'd passed, everybody at his school gave him a party. He got his picture in the local paper, along with half a dozen other tired-looking people.

More interviews—now he could pick and choose, because there were always more jobs than people qualified to fill them.

He finally settled on one not far from where he lived, in a top-notch school. "We're delighted to have you," the principal there said, shaking his hand.

Once his exams were over, Collins had cut way back on his caffeine intake. Even so, he hardly slept the night before his first day on the new job. "Am I really good enough?" he asked his wife as he picked at breakfast that morning.

"You bet you are," she said. "Now, go get 'em."

For all her encouragement, he needed a deep breath to still the fear inside him as he walked up to the enameled door with the tarnished brass 7 on it. He opened the door. He went inside.

"Good morning, class," he said, forcing his voice to steadiness.

"Good morning, teacher," the children chorused.

Teacher. He felt ready to burst with pride. After so long, after so much hard work, at last he'd reached the pinnacle of his profession.

Part of this one comes from driving over forty miles each way back and forth to work for seven years. Part of it comes from having an unusual last name myself. And part of it is just pure silliness. When I sit down to write, I usually have an ending firmly in mind. This time I just had an opening scene and let things roll from there. The results are intended to amuse; if any deep profundity lurks herein, I certainly haven't found it.

THE BARBECUE, THE MOVIE, AND OTHER UNFORTUNATELY NOT SO RELEVANT MATERIAL

T.G. KAHN LOOKED OUT THE WINDOW AT THE traffic going by on Imperial Highway. He wished he were under the warm Los Angeles summer sunshine, instead of sitting here cooped up in an office trying to put a newsletter together.

He sighed. He had gone through some impressive finagling just to get an office he could see out of. Until a few weeks ago, he had worked in an enormous interior room, the kind where you needed to leave a trail of bread crumbs to find your way through the maze of partitions. "Cubicle, sweet cubicle," one typist's sampler read, which perfectly summed up the place.

The newsletter he was writing bored even him. He sighed again. "It beats sleeping on a park bench, I suppose," he said out loud, and mounted another dispirited attack on his word processor.

The phone rang, its chime booming like Big Ben over the soft, incessant Muzak. Kahn's fingers jerked. A rash of consonants broke out on the screen. He stared at them reproachfully as he picked up the receiver. "T.G. Kahn."

"Someone here to see you, Mr. Kahn."

"Thank you, Doris." His secretary still worked across the corridor in the huge office from which he had recently escaped. "Send him in."

"Yes, sir," Doris said, and giggled. Kahn wondered if his ears were playing tricks on him. Doris hadn't even cracked a smile for the limerick about the crypt at St. Giles, whereupon he had given her up as a hopeless case.

The door to his office came open. So did his mouth. The door closed. His mouth stayed open.

The man who walked into his office was in his late twenties, a few years younger than Kahn, and looked vaguely Semitic. He had a thick Fu Manchu mustache and the strangest hairdo Kahn had ever seen—and, living in Los Angeles, Kahn had seen some lulus. The top of the man's head was shaved. So was a strip that ran from ear to ear through the bare spot on top, and an inch or so on the forehead. The rest grew long, in greasy braids.

The man wore a heavy fur coat over leather trousers and boots. He must have been dying out there in the heat, Kahn thought. Two scabbards hung at the fellow's belt, one holding a knife, the other a curved sword. He smelled of sweat and rancid butter. The worst thing was that Kahn recognized the costume, though not the person in it.

He rose from his chair, feeling hot blood rush to his face. He had not been in a fight since the sixth grade, but he wanted to punch this fellow's lights out. "If you're not a singing telegram, pal, you're in big trouble," he said between clenched teeth.

The man did not burst into song. Kahn, who tended to think too much for his own good, took another look at the cutlery the fellow was carrying and decided that trying to kill him might not be such a good idea after all.

He stood irresolutely, and the moment passed. His shoulders sagged. "Very goddamn funny," he said bitterly, hearing the weakness in his own voice and hating it. "I presume you know my father."

To his amazement, the man in front of him went down on his knees, then thumped his forehead on the cheap indoor-outdoor office carpet. The door clicked shut at the same time. That made the stale, greasy stench worse, but it also kept anybody walking down the hall from seeing what was going on inside.

Fat lot of good that would do, Kahn realized. He clapped a hand to his forehead in horrified dismay. Doris, damn her blabbing soul, would spread this all over the office, and so would everyone else who had spotted this kowtowing weirdo. How would he ever be able to look people in the face again?

He had to drag his attention back to the fellow, who, his face still against the nubby knit nylon, had started to talk. "No,

Excellency,'' he was saying in a voice Kahn seemed to hear between his ears rather than with them, ''never did I have the privilege of meeting that great hero Yesugei. I—''

''Say, you *are* good,'' Kahn said with grudging admiration. Not one in a million knew who Yesugei was or cared. He wished—oh, how he wished!—he didn't himself. ''What are you, one of dad's grad students? If you wanted to get hold of me, why didn't you just call?''

The man lifted his head from the rug, and looked at Kahn with as much perplexity as Kahn was giving him. ''I had not thought to find the phrase 'grad student' on your lips, mighty lord.''

Kahn's head was starting to spin. The most likely idea he'd had—and it wasn't very—was that the maniac who would not get off the rug was some Syrian or Egyptian studying with his dad who wanted a favor from him. That would explain the flowery speech, at least. Why the fellow had to get into costume for that, though, was beyond him.

''Look, tell me what you want and take off, okay?'' he said.

The stranger's head went thump on the carpet again. ''Merely the boon of observing you for a brief while, mighty lord.''

That was so far from anything Kahn had expected that he blurted, ''Who the devil do you think I am, anyway?''

''Surely your Excellency can be no one else but Temujin, Genghis Khan—''

''Yes, thanks to my old man, I *am* Temujin Genghis Kahn,'' Kahn said, wishing for the nine millionth time that his father had dug ditches for a living instead of being a professor of Mongol history. It had made him the only first-grader at Oakdale Elementary School ever to be called exclusively by his initials.

The fellow on the floor went on as if he had not spoken: ''—unifier of the Mongols, conqueror of north China, subduer of the Khwarizm Shah, ravager of Russia, builder of the hugest empire the world has ever seen—''

''—tech writer, in debt, divorced, driving an old Toyota,'' Kahn finished the litany. He looked down at the stranger groveling before him. ''You're carrying on as if I were the real one, or something.''

That hangdog, puzzled look was back on the man's face. ''Again you use strange terms, O Khan. Assure me, I pray, the pangloss properly renders my words into the Mongol speech.''

''Mongol?'' Kahn was too far out of his depth not to come back with the automatic truth. ''This is English.''

"English?" The stranger's eyebrows rose. "I've heard of it, I think. Then this is not the imperial yurt at Karakorum?"

"It's Los Angeles."

"Where?"

They stared at one another, each plainly convinced the other was crazy. At last the stranger said in a small voice, "Tell me the date, please."

"Huh? It's July 16th."

"The year?"

Now positive he was humoring a madman, Kahn gave it to him. The next question confused him for a moment: "In what era is that?"

He finally figured out the meaning. "Christian. A.D. *Anno domini.* The Common Era—c.e.—if you don't care for Christian dating of any flavor."

One of those terms must have been familiar to the stranger. He screwed up his face and began to swear in a style that was bizarre but effective just the same. Kahn filed a couple of the choicer epithets to use himself. "Lizard piss" could come in handy almost any time, but he decided to save "sucker at the tit of a syphilitic sow" for when he really needed it—say, when a Mercedes cut him off on the freeway.

When the stranger finally ran out of oaths, he turned a face full of storm clouds on Kahn. "You are certain this is not central Asia in what you would call—let me think—the early thirteenth century?"

"Not the last time I looked," Kahn said solemnly. He wished he could remember the security guard's extension.

But instead of turning violent, the man in the Mongol clothes burst into tears. Kahn watched, amazed, as he unashamedly wept until he had cried himself out.

At last the stranger pulled himself together. He smacked fist into palm in frustration. "Oh, to have come so close and still missed! What are seven hundred miserable little years against fifty or sixty thousand?"

Kahn's head was aching badly by now. He had had as much of this exchange as he could stand. "I'm so sorry," he said with exquisite, ironic politeness. "You must be a time traveler, sir, and all this time I took you for a nut."

The stranger waved it aside. "A natural error. However, if I were a nut, I would not be able to do this, for instance." Afterward, Kahn would have sworn the fellow only pointed his finger at the office window, the window he had schemed so long and hard to get. A ray of blue light shot from the stranger's fingernail. The next moment, the glass wasn't there any more.

July smog immediately started competing with the bland but breathable product the air conditioner turned out. Kahn coughed.

The stranger's eyes went ecstatic (they also began filling with tears that had nothing to do with emotions). "The scent of burning hydrocarbons!" he exclaimed, breathing deeply, at least until he choked. "Undoubtedly from buildings torched in the search for loot."

"No, from dinosaurs torched in the search for a parking space." Kahn's tongue led its own life, wild and free, while he tried to figure out whether he believed what he had just seen. He decided he did. His eyes might fool him, but he trusted his lungs. No way they could hurt so much unless the window glass really had disappeared.

"To have come so close!" the stranger said again. Now that he was no longer abasing himself, Kahn saw that the motions of his lips did not match the words the tech writer was hearing. The fellow shook his head in chagrin. "There goes my academic career, all because the scrofulous temporal phase link dropped me into the Late Middle First Primitive instead of the Mid-Middle." He started to cry again.

He seemed to be talking more to himself than to Kahn, but his—what had he called it?—his pangloss kept working. "I can't understand it. I was supposed to home on the mental vibrations of Temujin, Genghis Khan—"

He and Kahn realized at the same time what must have happened. Fury replaced the tears. Kahn waited for that finger to blast him to wherever the window had gone. The look on the fellow's face said that might not be good enough—the sword might come out instead.

Then the stranger tried to master himself. It was a visible process, and audible. "Because I observe savages," Kahn heard, "must I behave as one?"

His earlier wild mood swings made *yes* an all too likely answer to that. Kahn said quickly, "Can't you just go on to the Temujin you really wanted to see?"

"It doesn't work that way," the stranger answered bleakly. "Once I am out of the temporal flow, returning only snaps me back to my own time, and then what am I? A graduate student in ancientest history without fieldwork, without a dissertation—and a laughingstock for the entire collegium."

For the first time, he seemed a real person to Kahn, because the tech writer understood what he was feeling. His own education had ground to an ignominious halt a few months after he'd got his bachelor's degree, when he had to admit his brain simply was not up to graduate work in physics—that being a subject as remote from Mongol history as possible.

He said, "Maybe you could do your work on twentieth-century America instead of the Mongols."

"I don't know anything about the Late Middle First Primitive," the time traveler said petulantly—narrow specialization looked to be a universal constant.

"Maybe if you had a guide." Anything, Kahn thought, to get the fellow's mind off his anger, and off his ferocious finger. "I could do it, if you like. We've come a long way since the thirteenth century, you know."

"I doubt it."

Stung by the morose dismissal, Kahn snapped, "I'm going home in a few minutes. Come along if you want, or else don't."

"I'll come," the stranger said, sighing. "I may as well. It won't help, though. Nothing will help."

He was so woebegone that Kahn's sympathy revived. "It won't be so bad. You'll get to see just about all of Los Angeles during the ride." As far as he could remember, that was the first time he had ever had anything good to say about his daily commute. He lived in Reseda, in the western part of the San Fernando Valley, about forty-five miles northwest of where he worked. Some days it felt as if he spent more time in his car than on the job.

After saving the document he had been working on when the time traveler had arrived, Kahn undid his tie, slung his sport coat over his shoulder, and said, "Well, let's go, uh—what do I call you, anyhow?"

"My name is Lasoporp Rof. My friends would call me Rof. You call me Lasoporp."

So there, Kahn thought as they walked out of the building. The security guard gave Lasoporp Rof an odd look, but only a brief one. Clothes did not make the man, not in L.A.

The time traveler showed a small revival of interest in the parking lot. "This is your trusty Mongol steed, Temujin Genghis Kahn, able to travel long distances without tiring?"

"You can call me T.G.," Kahn said, pleased to get a little of his own back. "And this is my trusty Japanese Toyota, Lasoporp, able to travel long distances without running out of gas."

Lasoporp Rof grunted and got in. "How far must we fare to your yurt?" he asked when the tech writer had joined him.

"My condo," Kahn corrected absently. "How is it you know all this Mongol history without knowing anything else?"

"Some records of the Mongols survived the First Great Lacuna to be translated into Snoit."

"That's your language?"

"Gods and goddesses, no! But it was a liturgical language all through the First Intermediate and the Second Primitive, up to about nineteen thousand years before my time."

"Oh."

"How long will the journey to your yurt take, T.G.?" Lasoporp Rof asked as Kahn got on I-605 going north.

The tech writer ignored the slip; he was concentrating on his driving. "An hour if there were no traffic, an hour and a half on a regular sort of day, two hours if things jam up bad." Close to a dozen different combinations of freeways would get him home. None was much faster than any of the others.

The first choke point was on the Santa Ana Freeway, where it narrowed from four lanes to three a little south of the junction with the Long Beach Freeway. Traffic crawled along, but by moving from lane to lane Kahn was able to stay right at sixty. He blinked; he couldn't remember holes opening up so conveniently. He was not about to complain, though.

"We are passing cattle?" Lasoporp Rof asked.

"We're passing trucks," Kahn said. He glanced over at his passenger. "Don't you know the difference between animals and machines?"

"What is a machine?"

Defeated, Kahn gave his attention back to the road. The Santa Monica and Hollywood freeways branched off the Santa Ana a little east of downtown. He took the Hollywood. That was the shortest route, even if it always did knot up just north of the civic center.

And it was knotted, except that, as before, spaces kept appearing like magic for Kahn. Other drivers looked at him with envious disbelief as he slid from one to the next. He had never seen anything like it. The second time he had that thought, his head snapped around toward Lasoporp Rof. He'd never ridden with a time traveler before, either. "Do you have anything to do with this?" he demanded.

"With what?" Lasoporp Rof asked. "Oh, do you mean am I helping us get through the herd? I find this nomadic excursion grows boring after a while, so I'm exerting a slight probability distortion to help us along. I can take it off if you like."

"That's all right," Kahn said hastily. He did not even bother correcting Lasoporp Rof about the right name for the traffic jam; plenty of times he'd felt like one wandering sheep in a million. "I wish I could do it, that's all."

"Can't you?" Lasoporp Rof said, surprised yet again. "Here, let me induce you. It will help pass the time."

He put his hand on the back of Kahn's head. As the tech writer drove, he began to have a feel for where a hole in traffic might be, could be, would be, *was*. Guiding the car into that hole was as easy as breathing. They were nearly at the junction of the Hollywood and Ventura freeways when Lasoporp Rof said, "Now you're doing it all yourself."

"Am I? By God, I am!" Maneuvering the Toyota as if it were a halfback dodging clumsy tacklers, Kahn felt grateful enough to do anything this side of human sacrifice for Lasoporp Rof. He even thought about putting the time traveler on a plane to North Carolina to meet his father. To him, though, anything to do with his dad was not this side of human sacrifice.

He had an idea. Instead of staying on the westbound Ventura, he went north on the San Diego Freeway several miles to Devonshire, got off, went up to Chatsworth Boulevard, then headed west. He was whistling when he pulled into the parking lot.

"This is your yurt? No, your condo, you called it?" Lasoporp Rof asked.

"No, this is a Mongolian barbecue place, a restaurant that serves Mongolian-style food," Kahn said. When Lasoporp Rof looked blank, Kahn went on. "When you go back to whenever your own time is, won't you want to be able to tell everyone about the authentic"—well, sort of authentic, he amended mentally—"Mongol feast you had back in the First Primitive? You wouldn't even be lying."

For the first time since Lasoporp Rof had discovered Kahn was not a world conqueror and mass murderer, the time traveler actually looked happy. "Thank you, T.G.; perhaps I may yet bring some valuable knowledge with me, after all. Yes, let us go in."

A bored Oriental woman seated them and handed them menus. "She does not even recognize my costume," Lasoporp Rof said plaintively. "How can she be a real Mongol?"

"She probably isn't. Mongolia and the United States—this country—aren't friendly with each other."

"Ah, still you live in fear of the savage Mongol horsemen!"

"Not quite," Kahn said, and was saved from disappointing Lasoporp Rof with further explanations when the waitress came back. He ordered tea for both of them and steamed rice, then pointed to the trays of meats and vegetables lined up in front of the barbecue, saying, "We'll build our own." That was what most people did; she nodded and left.

Kahn led Lasoporp Rof up to the food. After they had taken bowls, the tech writer said, "There's lamb, beef, pork, and turkey. Help yourself." He wielded the set of aluminum tongs in each tray.

Imitating him, Lasoporp Rof said, "These are sliced thin so as to cook quickly?"

"That's right." Kahn grinned; it was the first question the time traveler had asked that actually made sense. Kahn added sliced onions, bean sprouts, celery, and cilantro to his bowl, then splashed hot barbecue sauce and curry sauce over the contents. "Spicy," he warned, but Lasoporp Rof again followed suit.

Then Kahn handed his full bowl to the cook behind the round barbecue griddle that was the most nearly genuine part of the whole operation. The cook grinned, displaying gold teeth. He upended the bowl. Meat and vegetables snarled as they hit the hot iron. The cook stirred them with a long-handled wooden spoon, chivvied them three-fourths of the way around the griddle, and deftly put them back in the bowl. Kahn returned to his seat while the cook barbecued Lasoporp Rof's dinner. The time traveler watched, fascinated.

When he rejoined Kahn, the tech writer had to show him how to use a fork; he held it as if it were a dagger. His eyes watered at the first mouthful, but he bravely emptied his bowl, exclaiming, "I feel as if I'm tasting history!"

Having no atmosphere, the place was not expensive. Kahn peeled off a ten, a five, and a couple of singles and left them on the table as he and Lasoporp Rof walked out. The time traveler said, "Though you are enemies of the Mongols, I see your people has adopted their custom of paper money."

"Uh, yes."

Lasoporp Rof looked around as they were getting back into Kahn's car. The landscape was typical Valley urban sprawl: a couple of gas stations, a 7-Eleven, a donut shop, streetlights, and cars, cars, cars. The time traveler sighed. "This is not the steppe, I suppose?"

"Does it look like the steppe?" Kahn asked. He had meant it as a rhetorical question, but realized it wasn't: how would Lasoporp Rof know what the steppe looked like?

"I really wish I could see the steppe." Lasoporp Rof sounded so sad that Kahn wished he had kept some of the books his father had pushed on him instead of unloading them because they reminded him of his godawful name. They would have given the time traveler some picture of Mongol life.

"Picture!" The force of his inspiration made Kahn want to hug himself with glee. He fired up the Toyota. "Come on, Lasoporp, I'll show you the steppe, by God."

"It is close by?" the time traveler asked eagerly.

Kahn drove through several lights that probably should have turned red but stayed green. (He was learning.) He pulled into a small shopping center. "Wait for me here. I won't be long—amuse yourself quietly till I come back." He hurried into the record store across the way.

When he got back with his package, he gasped and thanked his lucky stars he hadn't parked by the big display window. "Close your coat!" he shouted.

"You told me to amuse myself."

"I said 'amuse,' not 'abuse.' " Sweating, Kahn shook his head in relief that no one had happened by. "Never mind; not your fault. It's not our custom to do that kind of thing in public, that's all."

Lasoporp Rof let out an audible sniff.

The drive back to Kahn's condominium went faster than it had any right to. Lasoporp Rof was sulkily silent until they were actually inside and Kahn flicked on a light. "That is not fire. I've seen fire. It flickers."

"It's done with electrically heated wire." When Kahn saw that meant nothing to the time traveler, he asked, "Well, what do your people use for artificial light?"

"Sun pills, of course," was what he heard through Lasoporp Rof's pangloss. It made no more sense to him than his explanation had to Lasoporp Rof.

He gave up. Waving the time traveler to his couch, he said, "Sit down, make yourself at home. Can I get you a beer—a cold, mildly alcoholic drink?" Kahn laughed at himself. He was starting to give definitions without even thinking about it.

"Yes, thank you."

When the tech writer came back with two cans of Coors, he found Lasoporp Rof examining the Israeli-made menorah that decorated his coffee table. "What a strange coincidence," the time traveler said, picking it up. "If you had one of these in my own time, I would think you were Jewish."

"Very strange," Kahn mumbled. With some reluctance, he let it go at that: it was either let go or spend the next three weeks asking questions.

He turned on the television. Lasoporp Rof watched curiously as the screen lit up in bright colors and music came out of the speaker. It was a denture-adhesive commercial. Feeling his cheeks grow hot, Kahn was glad to get rid of it and turn on his VCR. The warning about unauthorized duplication at the front of the tape meant nothing to Lasoporp Rof, and this time the tech writer did not bother to explain.

Then the movie came on: a 1964 epic starring James Mason, Omar Sharif, Robert Morley, and a Telly Savalas who still had hair. Kahn realized the time traveler could not read the credits rolling across the screen. "It's called *Genghis Khan*," he said helpfully.

Lasoporp Rof almost jumped out of his furs and leathers. "This is a real record of his life?"

"No, a drama based on it. How could it be a real record, Lasoporp? We can't travel in time."

"First Primitive," Lasoporp Rof said, as if reminding himself. That did not keep him from being a spellbound audience for the Far Eastern horse opera. Kahn had only seen parts of it on late-night TV. The knowledge of Mongol history his father had crammed down his unwilling throat made him wince at the inaccuracies, but Lasoporp Rof was plainly eating it up, battles, overwritten love scenes, and all.

When it was done, the time traveler said, "Let me see it again, so I am sure I have the sense impressions fixed in my memory. Together with the meal, it should give me enough material to keep my professors happy."

Kahn blanched. Watching this two-hour turkey once had been bad; going through it twice came too close to cruel and unusual punishment. As he watched, he felt a twinge of guilt at what he was doing to far future historiography. He stifled it, but it made him wonder how much of what his father called historical fact was based on similarly trashy sources. A good bit, probably. He smiled, liking the idea.

At last the ordeal was over. Lasoporp Rof leaned over and kissed Kahn on both cheeks, then square on the mouth. "Thank you, T.G., thank you, thank you," he said, and then he was gone, vanishing suddenly and silently as a popped soap bubble.

Kahn blinked and shook himself like a man emerging from a dream. He wondered if the evening had been just that, or an out-and-out hallucination. But his living room still reeked of rancid butter, there were beer cans on both ends of the coffee table, and never in his wildest nightmares would he have rented *Genghis Khan*. Besides, tomorrow morning the janitor would be asking him where his office window had gone.

And there was that probability distortion stunt—

He looked at his watch and saw to his surprise that it was only a little past ten. Thanks to Lasoporp Rof's trick, he really *had* made good time on the road. He got out his address book, picked up the phone, and punched buttons.

"Hello?"

"Jennifer? Hi, this is T.G. Feel like dinner and a movie Saturday?" He held his breath with the effort of bending the odds, then let it out in a disappointed gust as she said she was going to a party that night. That made the third time she'd told him no.

"—but I'd love to, the weekend after," she finished. Kahn made the arrangements and hung up, feeling a bit like a world conqueror, after all.

In the course of research for an upcoming novel set in 1942, I read Albert Speer's memoirs, and also some of those left behind by the Jews of the Warsaw ghetto. Combining Speer's—and Hitler's—grandiose vision of the Berlin that would rise after Germany won the war with the desperate reality of Jewish life under Nazi rule led to this story. Thank God it's fiction.

IN THE PRESENCE OF MINE ENEMIES

HEINRICH GIMPEL GLANCED AT THE REPORT on his desk to see again how many *Reichsmarks* the United States was being assessed for the *Wehrmacht* bases at New York, Chicago, and St. Louis. As he'd thought, the figures were up from those of 2009. Well, the Americans would pay—and in hard currency, too; none of their inflated dollars—or the panzer divisions would move out of those bases and collect what was owed the Germanic Empire. And if they collected some blood along with their pound of flesh, the prostrate United States was hardly in a position to complain.

Gimpel typed the new numbers into his computer, then saved the study on which he'd been working for the last couple of days. The Zeiss disk drive purred smoothly as it swallowed the data. He turned off the machine, then got up and put on his uniform greatcoat: in Berlin's early March, winter still outblustered spring.

"Let's call it a day, Heinrich," Willi Dorsch said. Willi shared the office with Gimpel. He shook his head as he donned his greatcoat. "How long have you been here at *Oberkommando der Wehrmacht* now?"

"Going on twelve years," Gimpel answered, buttoning buttons. "Why?"

His friend cheerfully sank the barb: "All that time at the high command, and a fancy uniform, and you still don't look like a soldier."

"I can't help it," Gimpel said; he knew too well that Willi

was right. A tall, thin, balding man in his early forties, he had a tendency to shamble instead of parading, and wore his greatcoat as if it were cut from the English tweeds some professors still affected. He tried to set his high-crowned cap at a rakish angle, raised an eyebrow to get Dorsch's reaction. Willi shook his head. Gimpel shrugged, spread his hands.

"I suppose I'll just have to be martial for both of us," Dorsch said. *His* cap gave him a fine dashing air. "Doing anything for dinner tonight?" The two men lived not far from each other.

"As a matter of fact, we are. I'm sorry. Lise invited a couple of friends over," Gimpel said. "Let's get together soon, though."

"We'd better," Dorsch said. "Erika's saying she misses you again. Me, I'm getting jealous."

"Oh, *quatsch*," Gimpel said, using the pungent Berliner word for rubbish. "Maybe she needs her spectacles checked." Willi was blond and ruddy and muscular, none of which desirable adjectives applied to Gimpel. "Or maybe it's just my bridge game."

Dorsch winced. "You know how to hurt a man, don't you? Come on, let's go."

The wind outside the military headquarters had a bite to it. Gimpel shivered inside his overcoat. He pointed off to the left, toward the Great Hall. "The old-timers say the bulk of that thing has messed up our weather."

"Old-timers always complain," his friend answered. "That's what makes them old-timers." But Willi's gaze followed Gimpel's finger. He saw the Great Hall every day, but seldom really looked at it. "It's big, all right, but is it big enough for that? I doubt it." His voice, though, was doubtful, too.

"You ask me, it's big enough for damn near anything," Gimpel said. The Great Hall, built sixty years earlier in the great flush of triumph after Britain and Russia had gone down before the guns and tanks of the Third Reich, boasted a dome that reached over two hundred twenty meters into the sky and was more than two hundred fifty meters across: sixteen St. Peter's cathedrals might have fit within the enormous monument to the grandeur of the Aryan race. The wealth of a conquered continent had brought it into being.

The dome itself, sheathed in weathered copper, caught the fading light like a great green hill. Atop it, in place of a cross, stood a gilded Germanic eagle with a swastika in its claws. Atop the eagle, a red light blinked on and off to warn away low-flying planes.

Willi Dorsch's shiver had only a little to do with the chilly weather. "It makes me feel tiny."

"It's a temple to the *Reich* and the *Volk*. It's supposed to make you feel tiny," Gimpel answered. "Set against the needs of the German race or the state, any one man is tiny."

"We serve them, not they us," Willi agreed. He pointed across the Adolf Hitler Platz toward the *Führer*'s palace on the far side of the immense square. "When Speer ran that one up, he was worried the size of the building would dwarf even our Leader himself." And indeed, the balcony above the tall entranceway looked like an architectural afterthought.

Gimpel's short laugh came out as a puff of steam. "Not even Speer could look ahead to see what technology might do for him."

"Better not let the security police hear you talk that way about one of the *Reichsvaters*." Dorsch tried to laugh, too, but his chuckle rang hollow. The security police had to be taken seriously.

Still, Gimpel was right. When the *Führer*'s palace was erected, another huge Germanic eagle had surmounted the balcony from which the Germanic Empire's leader might address his citizens. The eagle had been moved to its present position on the roof when Gimpel was a boy. In its place went an enormous televisor screen. Adolf Hitler Platz had been built to hold a million people. Now when the führer spoke, every one of them could get a proper view.

A bus purred up to the *Oberkommando der Wehrmacht* building. Gimpel and Dorsch filed aboard with the rest of the officials who greased the operation of the mightiest military machine the world had known. One by one the commuters stuck their account cards into the fare slot. The bus's computer debited each rider eighty-five *pfennigs*.

The bus rolled down the broad avenue toward South Station. Berlin's myriad bureaucrats made up the majority of the passengers but not all. A fair number were tourists, come from all over the world to view the most wonderful and terrible boulevard that world boasted. Blasé as any native, Gimpel normally paid but scant attention to the marvels of his home town. Today, though, the oohs and ahhs of those seeing them for the first time made him notice them also.

Sentries from the *Grossdeutschland* division in ceremonial

uniform goose-stepped outside their barracks. Tourists on the sidewalk took photos of the *Führer*'s guards. Inside the barracks hall, where tourists would not see them, were other troops in businesslike camouflage smocks, assault rifles in place of the ceremonial force's obsolete *Gewehr 98s*, and enough armored fighting vehicles to blast Berlin to rubble. Visitors from afar were not encouraged to think about them. Neither were most Berliners. But Gimpel reckoned up *Grossdeutschland*'s budget every spring. He knew exactly what the barracks held.

Neon lights came on in front of theaters and restaurants as darkness deepened. Dark or light, people swarmed in and out of the huge Roman-style building that held a heated indoor pool the size of a young lake. It was open at all hours of the day and night for those who wished to exercise, to relax, or simply to ogle attractive members of the opposite sex. Its Berlin nickname was the *Heiratbad*, the marriage baths, sometimes amended by the cynical to the *Heiratbett*, the marriage bed.

Past the pool, the Soldiers' Hall and the Air and Space Ministry faced each other across the street. The Soldiers' Hall was a monument to the triumph of German arms. Among the exhibits it so lovingly preserved were the railroad car in which Germany had yielded to France in 1918 and France to Germany in 1940; the first Panzer IV to enter the Kremlin compound; one of the gliders that had landed paratroops in southern England; and, behind thick leaded glass, the twisted remains of the Liberty Bell, excavated by expendable prisoners from the ruins of Philadelphia.

Old people in Berlin still called the Air and Space Ministry the *Reichsmarschall*'s Office, in memory of Hermann Göring, the only man ever to hold that exalted rank. Willi Dorsch used its more common name when he nudged Gimpel and said, "I wonder what's happening in the Jungle these days."

"Could be anything," Gimpel answered. They both laughed. The roof of the ministry had been covered with four meters of earth, partly as a protection against aerial bombardment, and then planted, partly to please Göring's fancy (his private apartment was on the top floor). The old *Reichsmarschall* was almost half a century dead, but the orgies he'd put on amid the greenery remained a Berlin legend.

Willi said, "We aren't the men our grandfathers were. In those days they thought big and weren't ashamed to be flamboyant." He sighed the sigh of a man denied great deeds by the time in which he chanced to live.

"Poor us, doomed to get by on matter-of-fact competence," Gimpel said. "The skills we need to run our empire are different from those Hitler's generation used to conquer it."

"I suppose so." Dorsch clicked his tongue between his teeth. "I envy you your contentment here and now, Heinrich. I almost joined the *Wehrmacht* when I was just out of the *Hitler Jugend*. Sometimes I still think I should have. There's a difference between this uniform"—he ran a hand down his double-breasted greatcoat—"and the one real soldiers wear."

"Is that your heart talking, or did you just all of a sudden remember you're not eighteen years old any more?" Gimpel said. His friend winced, acknowledging the hit. He went on, "Me, I'd fight if the Fatherland needed me, but I'm just as glad not to be carrying a gun."

"We're all probably safer because you don't," Dorsch said.

"This is also true." Gimpel took off his thick, gold-framed glasses. In an instant, the street outside, the interior of the bus, even Willi beside him, grew blurry and indistinct. He blinked a couple of times, returned the glasses to the bridge of his nose. The world regained its sharp edges.

The neon brilliance of the street outside dimmed as the bus passed by the theaters and shops and started picking up passengers from the ministries of the Interior, Transportation, Economics, and Food. *More uniforms that don't have soldiers in them,* Gimpel thought. The buildings from which the new riders came were shutting down for the day.

Two of those ministries, though, like the *Oberkommando der Wehrmacht,* never slept. A new shift went into the Justice Ministry to replace the workers who left for home. German justice could not close its eyes, and woe betide the criminal or racial mongrel upon whom their omniscient gaze lighted. Himself a thoroughly law-abiding man, Gimpel still shivered a little every time he passed that marble-fronted hall.

The Colonial Ministry was similarly active. Much of the world, these days, fell under its purview: the agricultural towns of the Ukraine, the mining colonies in central Africa, the Indian tea plantations, the cattle herders on the plains of North America. As if picking that last thought from Gimpel's mind, Willi Dorsch said, "How many Americans does it take to screw in a light bulb?"

"The Americans have always been in the dark," Gimpel answered. He clucked sadly. "Your father was telling that one, Willi."

"If he was, he sounded more relieved than I do. The Yankees might have been tough."

"Might-have-beens don't count, fortunately." Isolation and neutrality had kept the United States from paying heed as potential allies in Europe went down one after another. It faced the Germanic Empire and Japan alone a generation later—and its oceans were not wide enough to shield it from robot bombs.

Just ahead lay another monument to German victory: Hitler's Arch of Triumph. Gimpel had been to Paris on holiday and seen the Arc de Triomphe at the end of the Champs Elysées. It served as a model for Berlin's arch and was a model in scale as well. The Arc de Triomphe was only about fifty meters tall, less than half the height of its enormous successor. The Berlin arch was almost a one hundred seventy meters wide and also a one hundred seventeen meters deep, so that the bus spent a good long while under it, as if traversing a tunnel through a hillside.

When at last it emerged, South Station lay not far ahead. The station building made an interesting contrast to the monumental stone piles that filled the rest of the avenue. Its exterior was copper sheeting and glass, giving the traveler a glimpse of the steel ribs that formed its skeleton.

The bus stopped at the edge of the station plaza. Along with everyone else, Gimpel and Dorsch filed off and hurried across the plaza toward the waiting banks of elevators and escalators. They walked between more displays of weapons that had belonged to Germany's fallen foes: the wreckage of a British fighter, carefully preserved inside a Lucite cube; a formidable-looking Russian tank; the conning tower of an American submarine.

"Into the bowels of the earth," Dorsch murmured as he reached out to grab the escalator handrail. The train to Stahnsdorf boarded on the lowest of the station's four levels.

Signs and arrows and endless announcements over the loudspeaker system should have made it impossible for anyone to get lose in the railway station. Gimpel and Dorsch found their way to their commuter train almost without conscious thought. So did most Berliners. The swarms of tourists, however, were grit in the smooth machine. Uniformed youths and maids from the *Hitler Jugend* helped those for whom even the clearest instructions were not clear enough.

Even so, the natives grumbled when foreigners got in their way. Dodging around an excited Italian who had dropped his cheap suitcase so he could use both hands to gesture at a Hitler

Youth in brown shirt, swastika armband, and *lederhosen*, Dorsch growled, "People like that deserved to be sent to the shower."

"Oh, come on, Willi, let him live," Gimpel answered mildly.

"You're too soft, Heinrich," his friend said. But then they rounded the last corner and came to their waiting area. Dorsch looked at the schedule board on the wall, then at his watch. "Five minutes till the next one. Not bad."

"No," Gimpel said. The train pulled into the station within thirty seconds of its appointed time. Gimpel thought nothing of it as he followed Dorsch into a car; he noticed only the very rare instances when it was late. As the two men had in the bus, they put their account cards into the fare slot and then took their seats. As soon as the computer's count of fares matched the car's capacity, the doors hissed shut. Three more cars filled behind them. Acceleration pressed Gimpel back against the synthetic fabric of his chair as the train began to move.

Twenty minutes later the engineer's voice came over the roof-mounted speakers: "Stahnsdorf! All out for Stahnsdorf!"

Gimpel and Dorsch were standing in front of the doors when they hissed open again. The two commuters hopped off and hurried through the little suburban station to the bus stop outside. Another five minutes and Dorsch got up from the local bus. "See you tomorrow, Heinrich."

"Say hello to Erika for me."

"I'm not sure I ought to," Willi said. Both men laughed. Dorsch got off the bus and trotted toward his house, which was three doors down from the corner.

Gimpel rode for another few stops, then descended himself. His own house lay at the end of a cul-de-sac, so he had to walk for a whole block. *It's healthy for me,* he told himself, a consolation easier to enjoy in spring and summer than in winter.

The *snick* of his key going into the lock brought shouts of "Daddy!" from inside the house. He smiled, opened the door, and picked up each of his three girls in turn for a hug and a kiss: they ranged down in age from ten by two-year steps.

Then he lifted his wife as well. Lise Gimpel squawked; that was not part of the evening ritual. The girls giggled. "Put me down!" Lise said indignantly.

"Not till I get my kiss."

She made as if to bite his nose instead, but then let him kiss her. He set her feet back on the carpet, held her a little longer before he let her go. She was a pleasant armful, a green-eyed brunette several years younger than he who had kept her figure very well. When he released her, she hurried back toward the kitchen. "I want to finish cooking before everyone gets here."

"All right," he said, smiling as he watched her retreat. While he hung up his greatcoat and took off his tie, his daughters regaled him with tales out of school. He listened to three simultaneous stories as best he could. Lise came out again long enough to hand him a goblet of liebfraumilch, then started away.

The chimes rang before she got out of the front room. She whirled and stared indignantly at the door. "I am going to boot Susanna right into the net," she declared.

Gimpel looked at his watch. "She's only ten minutes early this time. And you know she's always early, so you should have been ready."

"Hmp," Lise said while he went to let in their friend. Meanwhile, the girls started chorusing, "Susanna is a football! Aunt Susanna is a football!"

"Heinrich, why are they calling me a football?" Susanna Weiss demanded. She craned her neck to look up at him. "I'm short, yes, and I'm not emaciated like you, but I'm not round, either." She shrugged out of a mink jacket and thrust it into his hands. "Here, see to this."

Chuckling, he clicked his heels. *"Jawohl, meine Dame."*

She accepted the deference as no less than her due. *"Fräulein Doktor Professor* will suffice, thank you." She taught medieval English literature at Humboldt University. Suddenly she abandoned her imperial manner and started to laugh, too. "Now that you've hung that up, how about a hug?"

"Lise's not watching. I suppose I can get away with that." He put his arms around her. She barely reached his shoulder, but her vitality more than made up for her lack of size. When he let go, he said, "Why don't you go into the kitchen? You can pretend to help Lise while you soak up our Glenfiddich."

"Scotch almost justifies the existence of Scotland," she said. "It's a cold, gloomy, rocky place, so they had to make something nice to keep themselves warm."

"If that's why people drink it, your boyfriend is lucky he didn't set himself on fire here a couple of years ago."

"My *former* boyfriend, *danken Gott dafür,*" Susanna said. All the same, she blushed to the roots of her hair; her skin was very fine and fair, which let him watch the blush advance from her throat. "I didn't know he was a drunk, Heinrich."

"I know," he said gently. If he teased her too far, she'd lose her temper, and nothing and nobody was safe if that happened. "Go on; Lise's trying that recipe you sent her."

The girls waylaid Susanna before she made it to the kitchen. Though she'd never been married, she made an excellent ersatz aunt; she took children seriously, listened to what they had to say, and treated them like small adults. Gimpel smiled. Come to that, she was a small adult herself. He knew better than to say so out loud.

Walther and Esther Stutzman arrived a few minutes later, along with their son Gottlieb and daughter Anna. Anna promptly went off with the Gimpel girls; she was a year older than Alicia, the eldest of the three. Heinrich Gimpel stared at Gottlieb. "Good heavens, is that a mustache?"

The younger male Stutzman touched a finger to the space between his upper lip and his nose. "It's going to be one, I hope." At the moment, the growth was hard to see. For one thing, he had only just turned sixteen. For another, his hair was even fairer than his father's. And for a third, he'd chosen to keep untrimmed only a toothbrush mustache; the first *Führer*'s style was newly popular again.

Walther Stutzman differed from his son in appearance only by the presence of twenty-odd years and the absence of any vestiges of a mustache. As he handed Gimpel his topcoat, he asked quietly, "Tonight?"

"Yes, I think Alicia's ready," Gimpel answered as quietly. "I told her she could stay up late. How has Anna done the past year?"

"Well enough," her father said.

"We're still here, after all," Esther Stutzman put in. A slim woman with light brown hair, she peered at Gimpel through glasses thicker than his own. Somehow, in spite of everything, her laugh managed to hold real mirth. "And if she hadn't done well, we assuredly wouldn't be."

"Wouldn't be what, Aunt Esther?" Alicia Gimpel asked, a doll under one arm.

"Wouldn't be standing out here in the hall talking if we expected the curly-haired *Gestapo* to be listening in," Esther said. Her grin took all sting from the words.

Imitating her father, Alicia said, "Oh, *quatsch*!" Anna Stutzman tried to sneak up behind her, but she whirled before she got tickled. Both girls squealed. They ran off together, Alicia's brown curls bobbing beside Anna's blond ones. They were very much of a height; though Anna was a year older, Alicia was tall for her age.

"Dinner!" Lise called from the kitchen. Everyone went into the dining room. Heinrich Gimpel and Anna's brother Gottlieb dropped the leaves on the table to accommodate the unusual crowd. Walther, meanwhile, fetched a couple of extra chairs, while Susanna Weiss arranged them around the table.

They all paused to admire the fragrantly steaming pork roast before Gimpel attacked it with fork and carving knife. With onions, potatoes, and boiled parsnips, it made a feast to fight the chill outside and leave everyone happily replete. Most of the talk that punctuated the music of knife and fork was praise for Lise's cooking.

Smooth wheat beer mixed with raspberry syrup accompanied the meal. The two younger Gimpel girls, who usually were allowed only small glasses, got grownup-sized mugs. They proudly drained them dry, and were nodding by the time their mother brought out dessert. They munched their way through the little cakes stuffed with prunes or apricots or mildly sweet chocolate, but the filling sweets only made them sleepier. The food slowed Alicia down, too, but she was buoyed by the prospect of sitting up and talking with the adults.

Seeing her daughter's excitement, Lise Gimpel said, "She doesn't know yet how boring we can be, with our chatter of children and taxes and work and who's going to bed with whom."

"Who *is* going to bed with whom?" Esther asked. "It's more interesting than taxes and work, that's for certain."

Susanna parodied a Hitler Jugend song: "In the fields and on the heath, we lose strength through joy." Gottlieb Stutzman blushed almost as red as she had before. Teasing him, she said, "Why, Gottlieb, don't you hope to meet a friendly maiden when you go to work your year in the fields?"

"It is not practical, not for me," he answered stiffly, rubbing a finger over his peach-fuzz mustache.

"It is not practical for any of us, as Susanna knows." Walther Stutzman gave her a severe look. "It is also not practical for us to sing that song anywhere but among ourselves. If the Security Police hear it—"

"It's wiser not to draw the attention of the Security Police in any case," Lise Gimpel said with her usual solid good sense. "Even children know that." She looked at her own two younger

children, who were valiantly trying not to yawn. "After I get
the table cleared away, time for the little ones to go to bed."

Heinrich Gimpel nodded to Walther and Gottlieb Stutzman.
"Nice to have some other men in the house for a change," he
said.

"You are outnumbered, aren't you?" Walther said. "Me, I
kept the numbers even. But then, that's what they pay me for."
He had a moderately important post with the computer design
team at Zeiss.

Everyone, even the men, pitched in to help Lise cart dirty
dishes and leftovers (not that there were many of those) back to
the kitchen. The two younger Gimpel girls took off their party
dresses and put on long cotton nightgowns. They collected kisses
from the grown-ups, then went off to their bedroom, not without
a couple of sleepily envious glances at Alicia, who got to stay
up.

Alicia herself looked curious and excited. She sat on the edge
of the couch, her eyes now on her parents, now on Susanna or
Esther or Walther or Gottlieb. As Lise Gimpel had said, her
eldest daughter didn't know what the grownups talked about
after she went to sleep, and could hardly wait to learn.

Her gaze swung to her friend Anna. "You've found out what
the secret is," she said accusingly.

"Yes, I have." Anna sounded so serious that Heinrich Gimpel's heart went out to her. Alicia, though, put on what he thought
of as her angry face. Anna also saw that. Quickly, she added,
"After tonight, you'll know, too."

"All right," Alicia said, part way mollified. Then she said,
"Why are all of you staring at me like that? I don't like it." She
twisted around to bury her face against a sofa pillow.

"It's an important secret, dear," her mother answered.
"Come out, please. It's such an important secret, you can't even
tell it to your sisters."

That got through to Alicia. Heinrich saw her eyes go wide.
He said, "You can't tell it to anybody at all. We waited until
you were old enough so we could tell you, because we wanted
to be sure"—*as sure as we could be*, he glossed mentally—"you
wouldn't give us away by telling someone you shouldn't."

"I've known for a year now," Anna said to Alicia, "and I
didn't even tell *you*. See how important it is?" Hearing the pride
in her voice, Gimpel glanced over to Esther and Walther. They
looked proud, too—proud and frightened. The fear never went
away, though showing it anywhere in public was also dangerous.

"What is it, then?" Alicia said. "You're right, Anna; I never knew you had a secret, and I'm your best friend." She sounded hurt, but only a little: her time to learn had come. She repeated, "What is it?"

Heinrich and Lise did not answer, not right away. Now that the moment was here, all the gentle introductions they had planned seemed worthless. Yet coming right out and saying what had to be said—that, Gimpel feared, was likelier to horrify Alicia than to enlighten her. While they hesitated, Susanna Weiss did the job with one blunt sentence: "You are a Jew, Alicia."

The girl stared, then shook her head, as if at a joke. "Don't be silly, Aunt Susanna. There are no more Jews, not anywhere. They're *kaput*—finished." She spoke with the assurance of one reciting a lesson well learned in school.

Heinrich Gimpel shook his head, too, to contradict her. "You *are* a Jew, Alicia. Your sisters are Jews, too. So is Susanna. So are Esther and Walther and Gottlieb and Anna. And so are your mother and I."

The color slowly drained from Alicia's cheeks as she realized her father meant what he said. "But—but," she faltered, and then rallied: "But Jews were filthy and wicked and diseased and racially impure." All the textbook lessons; Heinrich remembered how he had learned them, too. Perhaps trying to convince herself, Alicia went on. "That's why the wise *Reich* got rid of them. That's what my teacher says."

"One of the hardest lessons anyone learns is that not everything your teacher tells you is true," Walther Stutzman said. "For us, it's doubly hard."

"Is Anna filthy?" Lise Gimpel asked.

"Of course not," Alicia said indignantly. She looked to her friend as if wanting Anna to tell her this was all just a game. But Anna looked back with impressively adult solemnity; she knew what rode on holding this secret close.

"Are your father and I wicked?" Lise persisted. "Is Susanna diseased?"

"I can get to feel that way, the morning after too much Scotch," Susanna said.

"Hush, Susanna," Lise said.

"But—what happens if anyone else finds out I'm—I'm a Jew?" Alicia said. She pronounced the name with difficulty; it was too strong a curse to find in the mouth of a well-brought-up ten-year-old. "If my friends at school know, they won't like me any more."

"It will be worse than that, dear, if your friends at school find out," Heinrich Gimpel said. "If anyone learns you're a Jew, the *Einsatzkommandos* will come for you, and for your sisters, and for your mother and me, and for the Stutzmans, and for Susanna." He made his voice hard and implacable, impressing on his daughter that he meant exactly what he said.

Lise tried to soothe Alicia. "No one has to find out, my little one. No one will unless you give yourself away, and us with you. We are well hidden these days, those few of us who are left." Even her sunny spirit was not proof against the memory of the millions who had died, first in Europe and then, a generation later, in the *Vernichtungslagers* outside New York and Los Angeles. Shaking her head, she repeated, "We are well hidden."

"My father helped there," Walther said. "He altered the *Reich*'s genealogical data base to show us all to be of pure Aryan blood. No one looks for us any more, not here in the heart of the Germanic Empire. No one thinks there is any reason to look. We are safe enough unless we give ourselves away. One day, maybe, not in our time but when your sons or grandsons have grown up, Alicia, it may be safe for us to live openly as what we are once more. Till then, we go on."

Alicia tossed her head wildly back and forth; her eyes were wide and staring, like those of a trapped animal. "It will never be safe! Never! The *Reich* will last for a thousand years, and how can there be room in it for Jews?"

"Maybe the *Reich* will last a thousand years, as Hitler promised," Heinrich said. "No one can know that until it happens, if it does. But there have been Jews, Alicia, for close to three thousand years already. Even if the Germanic Empire lives out its whole time, it will still be a baby beside us. One way or another, as Uncle Walther said, we go on. It's hard to pretend not to be what we really are—"

"I hate it," Susanna Weiss broke in.

"We all hate it," Gimpel continued. "But when times are dangerous for Jews, as they are now, what other choice do we have?"

"This isn't the first time Jews have had to be what they are only in secret," Esther Stutzman said. "In Spain a long time ago, we pretended to be good Catholics. Now we have to pretend to be good National Socialists. But underneath, we still are what we are."

"I don't want to be a Jew!" Alicia shouted, so loud that

Heinrich looked nervously toward the windows. If one of the neighbors heard, the Security Police were only a phone call away.

He took a deep breath. "You have a way out, Alicia." She stared at him, tears and questions in her eyes. He said, "You can just pretend this night never happened. You know we will never betray you, no matter what you decide. If you choose not to tell your husband one day, if he is not one of us, and if you choose not to tell your children, they will never know you—and they—are Jewish. They'll be just like everyone else in the Germanic Empire. But one more piece of something old and precious will have gone out of the world forever."

"I don't know what to do," Alicia said, the most adult sentence that had ever crossed her lips.

"It's not so bad, Alicia," Anna Stutzman said. "I cried, too, when I found out."

"So did I," Gottlieb added, which made Alicia's eyes widen; he was so much older than she that she thought of him as practically a grownup.

Anna went on. "But it's special in a way, like being part of a club that won't take just anybody. And it's not like what we are is written on our foreheads or anything like that, even though it does feel that way at first. But if we keep the secret, no one will find out what we are. We even have our own special holidays—today is one."

"What's today?" Alicia asked.

"Today is the festival of Purim," her father answered. "The Germans and the Spaniards Aunt Esther was talking about were not the first people to want to get rid of the Jews. We've always stood out a little because we're different from the other people in a country. And a long time ago, in the Persian Empire—"

He got out the Bible to help tell Alicia the story. It had both Old and New Testaments, of course; keeping one that didn't would have been suicidally dangerous. Having a Bible at all entailed a certain small risk, although the National Socialists, having won their wars, were more inclined to tolerate quiet Christianity these days.

"And so," Heinrich finished, "King Ahasuerus hanged Haman on the very gallows he had built for Mordecai, and Mordecai and Queen Esther lived long, happy, rich lives afterward." Alicia, caught up in spite of herself by the ancient tale, laughed and clapped her hands.

Very softly, Susanna Weiss said, "I wish someone had built

a gallows for Hitler and Himmler. So many of our people gone.''
She stared down into her snifter of Scotch. Sometimes Gimpel
thought she felt guilty for living on where millions had died.

"I wish I could tell my sisters,'' Alicia said.

Walther Stutzman grinned at Heinrich, who smiled back. The
year before, Anna had said, *I wish I could tell Alicia*. Gimpel
knew more than a little relief that his daughter was beginning
to adjust to the new and shocking knowledge; he remembered
his own confusion when he'd learned of his heritage.

But what Alicia had just said was also dangerous. He told her,
"You can't tell them yet—they're too little. They'll learn when
their time comes, just as you have now. But if the secret reaches
the wrong ears, we're all dead. Just because there aren't many
Jews left doesn't mean people have stopped hunting us. We're
still fair game.''

"Are we—the people in this room—are we all the Jews who
are left?'' Alicia asked.

"No,'' her father said. "There are others, all through Greater
Germany and the rest of the empire. In time you'll meet more,
and some may startle you. But for now, the fewer Jews you
know, the fewer you can give away if—if the worst happens.''

Alicia's eyes went far away. Gimpel knew what she was doing: thinking about family friends and wondering which were
of her own sort. He'd done the same thing himself. Finding out
about Walther Stutzman had been his biggest surprise. The
Stutzmans looked like perfect Aryans, and, a generation before,
much more had been made of Jews' allegedly grotesque features.

Lise said, "Even though we have our own holidays, Alicia,
we can only celebrate them among ourselves. The little three-
cornered cakes we had tonight are special for Purim—they're
call *Hamantaschen*, Haman's hats.''

"I like that,'' Alicia said. "Serves him right.''

"Yes,'' Lise said, "but that's why you won't be carrying any
of them to school for lunch. People who aren't Jewish might
recognize them for what they are. We can't afford to take any
chances at all, do you see?''

"Not even with anything as little as cakes?'' Alicia exclaimed.

"Not even,'' Lise said. "Not with anything, not ever.''

"All right, Mama.'' The warning about *Hamantaschen*
seemed to have impressed Alicia about the depth of the precautions she'd have to take to survive. Gimpel was glad something

had. His own father had shown him photographs smuggled out of the *Ostlands* to warn him how necessary silence was. He still had nightmares about those pictures after more than thirty years. But he still had the photos, too, hidden in a file cabinet. If he thought he had to, he'd show them to Alicia. He hoped the need would not arise, for her sake and his own.

"*Is* it all right, Alicia?" he asked her. "I know this is a lot to put on a little girl, but we have to, you see, or there won't be any Jews at all any more."

"It's all right, Father, it really is," she answered. "It— surprised me. I don't really know if I like it yet, but it's all right." She nodded in a slow, hesitant way that said she thought she meant it but wasn't quite sure.

That sufficed for Heinrich Gimpel. Finding out you were a Jew in the heart of the National Socialist Germanic Empire was not something anyone, child or adult, could fully take in at a moment's notice. A beginning of acceptance was as much as he could hope for. Alicia had given him that.

His daughter and Anna Stutzman yawned together, then giggled at each other. Susanna Weiss got up, grabbed her handbag, walked over to Alicia, and kissed her on the cheek. "Welcome to your bigger family, dear. We're glad to have you." She turned to Heinrich. "I'd better get home. I have an early class tomorrow morning."

"We ought to go, too," Esther Stutzman said. "Either that or we'll wait till Anna falls asleep—which shouldn't be more than about another thirty seconds—and bundle her into the broom closet." Her daughter let out an indignant sniff.

Lise and Heinrich passed out coats. The friends stood gossiping on the front porch for a last couple of minutes. As they chattered, a brightly lit police van rolled by. Alicia gasped in horror and tried to bolt inside. Her father held her arm until the van turned a corner and disappeared. "Everything's fine, little one," he said. "They know of us only if we give ourselves away. Do you understand?"

"I—think so, Father."

"Good."

The Stutzmans and Susanna walked off toward the bus stop. The Gimpels went back inside. Lise went with Alicia to get her ready for bed. Heinrich rinsed off the dishes and started loading them into the washer. He was still busy when Alicia came out for a good night kiss. Usually that was just part of the nighttime routine; tonight it felt special.

He said, "You don't have to be frightened every second, darling. If you show you're afraid, people will start to wonder what you have to be afraid of. Keep on being your own sweet self and no one will ever suspect a thing."

"I'll try, Papa." When she hugged him, she clung for a few extra seconds. He squeezed her, then ran his hand through her hair. "Good night," she said, and hurried away.

Lise walked into the kitchen a couple of minutes later. She dragged in a chair from the dining room, sat down, and waited till the sink was empty and the washer full. Then, as the machine started to churn, she got up and gave him a long, slow hug. "And so the tale gets told once more," she said.

As he had with his daughter, Heinrich held on to his wife. "And so we try to go on for another generation," he said. "We've outlasted so much. God willing, we'll outlast the Nazis, too."

"And of course, now that the tale is told, the risk we'll get caught also goes up," Lise said. "You did well there, keeping her from running from the police van."

"Couldn't have that," Gimpel agreed. "But she'll be nervous for a while now, and she's so young." He shook his head. "Strange how our greatest danger lies in making sure our kind goes on. No one would ever suspect you or me."

"Why else buy pork?"

"I know." Gimpel took off his glasses, wiped his forehead with his sleeve, set the spectacles back on his nose. "Why else do all the other things we do to seem like perfect Germans? I can quote *Mein Kampf* more easily than Scripture. But it's not so easy for a child. And we have two more yet to go." He let out a long, worn sigh, hugged Lise again. "I'm so tired."

"I know," she said. "It's easier for me, staying home with the *Kinder* like a proper *Hausfrau*. But you have to wear the mask every day at your office."

"It's either pretend to others I'm not a Jew or pack it in and pretend the same thing to myself. I'm not ready for that. I remember too well." He thought again of the hidden yellowing photographs from the east. "We *will* go on, in spite of everything."

Lise yawned. "Right now, I think I'm going on to bed."

"I'm right behind you. Oh—speaking of the office, on the way home today Willi said he admired how content I was here and now."

"Good," Lise said at once. "If you must wear the mask, wear it well."

"I suppose so. He also asked if we were busy tonight. I told him yes, since we were, but we'll be going over there one evening soon."

"I'll arrange for my sister to stay with the girls," Lise said. "Let's give Alicia a little more time to get used to things before we take her out."

"Sensible. You generally are, though."

"Ha!" Lise said darkly. "I'd better be. So had you."

"I know." He chuckled. "Besides, with the girls at home we'll be able to play more bridge."

"That's true." Lise also laughed. Both of them, by now, were long used to the strangeness of having good friends who, if they knew the truth, might well want to send them to an extermination camp. Heinrich *was* looking forward to getting together with Willi and Erika Dorsch for an evening of talk and bridge. Within the limits of his upbringing, Willi was a good fellow.

Gimpel pondered the limits of his own upbringing, which were a good deal narrower than Willi Dorsch's. In one way, telling Alicia of her heritage was transcending those limits. In another, it was forcing them on her as well. In still another— He gave up the regress before he got lost in it. "Didn't you say something about bed?"

"You're the one who's been standing here talking," Lise said. "Let's go."

Although I'm Jewish, I'm not particularly observant: I eat pork, for instance. One morning, after a breakfast of bacon and eggs, I thought, That's so good, I wish it were kosher. "The R Strain" followed shortly thereafter. Curiously, after Stan Schmidt bought it but before it saw print, there was a story in *Science News* about the babirusa, a Southeast Asian pig that actually does more or less chew its cud. One of the scientists who was working on the babirusa saw the story in *Analog* and thought her work had given me the idea. It didn't, but who knows? It might have.

THE R STRAIN

*EVEN IN LOS ANGELES, IT IS OUT OF THE OR-*dinary for the star of a press conference to be a small pink pig. Peter Delahanty had been anxious about how Lionel would react to the SV lights, but the shoat was doing just what he'd hoped: ignoring them. He was happily feeding his face from a plastic washtub full of potatoes and carrots. Delahanty beamed at him like a proud father, which, as he headed Genetic Enterprises, in a way he was.

Still cameras flashed and stereovision cameras whirred, but there were, after all, only so many pictures to be taken of a pig. After a while, Delahanty took the tub away from Lionel and put it on a table by the lectern.

Following it with his eyes, Lionel let out a grunt of piggy indignation. "Sorry, pal," Delahanty told him. "Maybe later." As if he understood, Lionel settled back—he really was a good-natured beast. His throat and jaws began to work.

More flashes went off. "That's what you came to see, ladies and gentlemen," Delahanty said. "Lionel's one of Genetic Enterprises' new R strain of pigs—R for ruminant, of course. In other words, unlike ordinary, unimproved swine, he chews his cud."

"Just why is that an improvement?" asked a lady reporter in the second row.

"It makes him and his brothers and sisters more efficient food processors. Ruminant animals—cattle, sheep, goats, deer, an-

218

telope are some of the ones occurring in nature—partially digest food, then store and and regurgitate it for rechewing and more complete digestion. They get more out of a given amount of food than nonruminants. Lionel will gain weight on less feed or lower-quality feed than an unimproved pig.''

"Which means lower cost to the farmer?" someone asked.

"Exactly."

"But of course buying your R strain is going to be more expensive for the farmer. What's the net savings?''

Delahanty turned to a chart behind him. "Here you have costs for the R strain compared to those for ordinary swine. As you can see, the break-even point is at three and a half months if the farmer buys piglets; it's even sooner if he chooses to have fertilized ova implanted in his own sows. And the extra expense is all in the first generation; the R strain breeds true.''

"Will they interbreed with unmodified pigs?" a man with a gray mustache wondered.

"No," Delahanty said. "There may be matings, but no offspring from them. The genetic changes are too great for interfertility.''

Another woman had a question: "How hardy are your new pigs? Can they survive the poor treatment they may get, say, in a Third World country?''

"At least as well as any other pigs," Delahanty said firmly. "Probably better, since they'll thrive on less food. One of the reasons Genetic Enterprises developed the R strain was to provide more protein for overpopulated developing nations.''

He fielded more queries about costs, and several on the genetic engineering techniques that had gone into Lionel and his ilk. After half an hour or so, the reporters' ingenuity flagged. Finally, though, someone asked the question Delahanty had been hoping for: "What do these beasts of yours taste like?''

He smiled. "I'll let you all be the judges of that. The chops and hams on the buffet to my left here come from the R strain. If there aren't any more questions—''

The surge forward was so sudden and urgent that Lionel snorted in alarm. But somebody was still waving a hand—not a reporter but a cameraman, a fellow with curly brown hair and a big nose. "Yes? You want to ask me something?" Delahanty called.

"Yeah, if I could," the man said. "My name's Stan Jacoby. Here's what I want to know . . .''

Delahanty had been ready for every question the reporters

had thrown at him, and a good many they hadn't. Now, though, he felt his jaw drop. "Mr. Jacoby," he said in the most spontaneous answer of the press conference, "I'll be goddamned if I know."

The phone rang three times before Ruth picked it up. "It's for you, dear," she shouted.

Rabbi Aaron Kaplan muttered something unrabbinic that his wet beard mercifully swallowed. "Unless it's an emergency, get a number and say I'll call back," he called over the hiss of the shower. He expected to be dragged out dripping—when did anyone calling a rabbi *not* think it was an emergency?—but he got to finish bathing in peace.

Somewhat mollified, he surveyed himself in the steamy bathroom mirror as he dried off. There were gray threads in the beard and a bald spot at his crown, but his stocky frame had not changed too badly since his days as a high school linebacker twenty-five years before.

Ruth came in with a scrap of paper. He smiled at her, thinking how lucky he was; if she had not been a rabbi's daughter, she would have been a *rebbitzin* decorative enough to make half his congregation nervous.

At the moment, she was giggling. "What's so funny?" he asked. She gave him the paper. He recognized Peter Delahanty's name; they had worked together on a couple of fund-raising committees. Underneath were a phone number and a one-sentence message: "Wants to know if pigs can be kosher."

He laughed. "A practical joke?"

"I don't think so. He seemed very sincere."

"Well, all right, I'll call him. He's got *chutzpah*, if nothing else." Kaplan went into the bedroom, put on a T-shirt and pair of shorts. Not for the first time, he was glad he hadn't added video to his phone system.

He punched the number. "Genetic Enterprises, Dr. Delahanty's office," a woman said. He asked to speak to Dr. Delahanty. "May I ask who's calling?" the secretary said. When he gave his name, she answered, "One moment. I'll connect you."

"Oh, Rabbi Kaplan. Thanks for returning my call." Delahanty sounded young and earnest. If he was a practical joker, he was first-rate.

Kaplan said, "My wife tells me you were inquiring about the

possibility of, uh, pork being acceptable under Jewish dietary law.''

"Yes, that's right. You see—"

Kaplan cut him off. "I'm afraid it's out of the question. Leviticus 11:3 and 11:7 are the relevant passages. Here, let me give you the exact wording." He reached for the Bible on the nightstand. " 'Whatsoever parteth the hoof, and is cloven-footed, and cheweth the cud, among the beasts, that shall ye eat.' And again, 'And the swine, because he parteth the hoof, and is cloven-footed, but cheweth not the cud, he is unclean to you.' The fourteenth chapter of Deuteronomy repeats the same prohibitions. So I really don't see how—"

It was Delahanty's turn to interrupt. "Forgive me, Rabbi Kaplan, but I do know that under normal circumstances Jews are not supposed to eat pork. Let me tell you about Lionel, though.''

"Lionel?" Kaplan echoed, confused.

"Yes. This would have been easier if you'd caught the news last night. Lionel is a pig who chews his cud . . . Are you there, Rabbi Kaplan?''

"I'm here," Kaplan said after a long pause. "I think you'd better tell me more." He felt a headache coming on.

"The easiest thing to do would have been to say that pigs is pigs, whether they chew their cuds or not. That would have been that," Ruth said when he finally got off the phone with Delahanty and, still wearing a bemused look, explained the dilemma to her.

"Simplest, yes, but would it have been right?" Kaplan said, shaking his head. "It goes against everything I've been brought up with to say 'kosher' and 'pig' in the same sentence. But if a pig has a cloven hoof and chews its cud, doesn't it meet the criteria the Bible sets for permitted beasts?''

"It meets the criteria for trouble,'' his wife said practically. "If you start saying pork is kosher, you'd best thank God there's no Jewish Inquisition, because if there were, it would burn you at the stake.''

"At the chop, actually,'' said Kaplan, who had a weakness for bad puns.

Ruth did not groan, as he had hoped she would. She set her hands on her hips, saying, "I'm serious, Aaron. Do you want to make yourself a laughingstock for the congregation, to say nothing of other rabbis?''

"Of course not." Just the same, he winced as he imagined the headlines: "Only in Los Angeles." "Rabbi Kaplan's Favorite Ham Recipes." A caption under a picture of a pig: "Funny, he doesn't *look* Jewish." Oh, he was opening a can of worms, and no mistake.

But it was such a *pretty* problem. Kaplan had been a rabbi going on twenty years now: a teacher, a counselor, a preacher, a social worker, sometimes even a scholar. Not since his student days, though, had he had a chance to be a theologian.

His wife recognized his faraway stare, and it alarmed her. She chose a question close to the issue at hand: "Aaron, have you ever tasted pork?"

As she had intended, that snapped him out of his reverie. He looked at her in surprise. He was Conservative, not Orthodox; he did not pretend to observe all the minutiae of dietary law. Pork, however, was something else. It was like asking if he had ever been unfaithful—exactly like that, he thought uncomfortably.

"Once," he admitted. "I was eighteen, in my senior year in high school, and out to do anything my father didn't want me to do. And so, one morning I stopped for breakfast with some friends, and I ordered bacon and eggs."

"Was it good?"

"You know, I really don't remember." He supposed that was like a lot of infidelity, too—he had been too nervous to enjoy it. "What's all this about?"

"If you decide this meat could somehow be kosher, I was just wondering how you were going to react when people said you did it because you liked pork yourself and wanted an excuse to eat it."

"That's ridi—" he began, and then stopped. It was not ridiculous, even in the twenty-first century. It might very well be one of the kinder things Orthodox rabbis would say. They would, he thought with a curiously mixed metaphor, crucify him if he had anything at all good to say about pigs. The only thing they could not do was excommunicate him; Judaism didn't work that way. It was something of a relief, but not much.

Ruth was still watching him. "You're going ahead with this."

"You know me too well." He sighed. "I'm going to investigate it, anyhow."

"I wish you wouldn't."

"I sort of have to," he said, but he was talking to her back. Sighing again, he went into his study. His books would not argue with him. He went first, as would anyone unraveling a problem of Jewish law, to the *Shulkhan Arukh*, the *Ready Table* of Joseph Karo. Published in 1564, it was still basic almost five centuries later, and its commentators reached to modern times.

Chapter 46 sounded promising: "Laws Concerning Forbidden Food." He turned to it in some hope. It had nothing to do with pork, but dealt with meat and milk dishes; with eating food prepared by Gentiles or from utensils used by Gentiles; with wormy fruit, vegetables, and fish. Karo, reasonably enough, had never entertained the prospect of a pig that chewed its cud, nor had the rabbis who came after him.

Kaplan did find a reference to swine in Chapter 5, "Laws Regarding the Cleanliness of the Place for Holy Purposes." There Karo remarked, "The mouth of a swine is considered like a chamber pot, for the reason that it pecks at excrement."

The rabbi frowned. In modern times, pigs were no more filthy than any other domestic animals. Perplexed, he got down the *Guide for the Perplexed*, Maimonides' great twelfth-century effort to reconcile religion and science. He found the reference to pork in Chapter 48 of Part III:

"I maintain that the food which is forbidden by the Law is unwholesome. There is nothing among the forbidden kinds of food whose injurious character is doubted, except pork, and fat. But also in these cases the doubt is not justified. For pork contains more moisture than necessary, and too much of superfluous matter. The principal reason why the Law forbids swine's flesh is to be found in the circumstance that its habits and its food are very dirty and loathsome. It has already been pointed out how emphatically the Law enjoins the removal of the sight of loathsome objects, even in the field and in the camp; how much more objectionable is such sight in towns. But if it were allowed to eat swine's flesh, the streets and houses would be more dirty than any cesspool, as may be seen at present in the country of the Franks. The saying of our Sages is well known: 'The mouth of a swine is as dirty as dung itself.' "

Again, the medical argument that swine's flesh was inherently dirty: a physician himself, Maimonides would naturally reason thus. And again, it did not necessarily apply now, or indeed even in Maimonides' day; chickens hardly had cleanlier habits than pigs. The quotation from the Talmud was in the same vein, if of even weightier authority than Maimonides.

Who else had spoken of the pig? He thought of one source, and pulled a well-thumbed book from a shelf apart from the religious tomes. As usual, Ambrose Bierce had a word for it: "Hog, *n*. A bird remarkable for the catholicity of its appetite and serving to illustrate that of ours. Among the Mahometans and Jews, the hog is not in favor as an article of diet, but is respected for the delicacy of its habits, the beauty of its plumage and the melody of its voice. . . ."

Smiling, he put the *Devil's Dictionary* away. Bierce's mordant wit helped put things in perspective. He was certain his predicament would have amused the old cynic immensely, and perhaps inspired a fresh verse or two from that worthy bard, Father Gassalasca Jape, S.J.

At that, the mythical Father Jape might have sympathized with Kaplan. In Bierce's time, Catholics refrained from eating meat on Fridays. Somehow the Catholic Church had survived when the prohibition was lifted.

But the ban against pork was centuries older than Christianity itself. And Judaism, unlike Christianity these last seventeen centuries, was mostly a minority religion, all too often a persecuted one. Jewish dietary laws expressed and emphasized the separateness of the Jews of the Diaspora from the peoples among whom they lived. Because they helped Jews maintain their cohesion, they became emotionally ingrained in believers; that was why even the thought of modifying them brought such a wrench with it.

And yet, he thought, Judaism always retained a certain flexibility other faiths lacked. In the Middle Ages, Jewish thought never accepted Aristotelian science as part and parcel of the tenets of the faith as the Church had—and therefore never had to go through a painful repudiation when Renaissance scientists showed that Aristotle did not, after all, know everything.

Adaptation to a changing world had been going on ever since. Among the observant in both Israel and the United States, a common item was a switch that could be set in advance to turn electrical appliances on and off on the sabbath, when kindling a light was forbidden.

So—there was the question: was eating one of Delahanty's R strain an accommodation to be gratefully accepted, or was it abomination? Whichever way he decided, he was going to be in trouble. He wondered if he ought to call another rabbi, someone older and maybe wiser. He thought it over, decided not to; it felt too much like passing the buck. The problem had been dumped in *his* lap, and he had to deal with it now. The time for others to judge would be later.

Ruth knew better than to disturb him in his study, but she pounced when he emerged. "Well?"

He spread his hands. "I don't have any answer yet, I'm afraid."

"Wonderful."

He did his best not to notice the sarcasm. "The trouble is, the authorities so automatically think of pigs and pork as being beyond the pale that they don't even discuss conditions under which it might be permissible."

"Shouldn't that tell you something?" Ruth asked pointedly.

"The rabbis of the Talmud didn't have modern technology to complicate their lives. All they had to worry about was famine, insurrection, and Roman legions—they didn't know when they were well off."

"Now what?"

"I think I'll call Delahanty back. Maybe he can tell me something that would make this all make sense."

"I can tell you something that would make this all make sense: forget it."

But Kaplan was already hitting the phone buttons. The chief of Genetic Enterprises came on the line at once. He seemed so bright and eager, Kaplan thought, and almost as intrigued as the rabbi over mutual problem. It had to be honest intellectual curiosity; even if every Jew in the country started eating the new product, it wouldn't bump consumption up more than a couple of percent.

"Damn, too bad," Delahanty said when Kaplan told him of the unpromising turn of the research. Without being asked, he went on, "How about this, then? Suppose I shoot you all the information about the R strain. That might help."

"So it might." Kaplan paused and continued. "I want you to understand, Dr. Delahanty, no matter how intriguing the possibilities are here, there's no guarantee I can find these beasts of yours acceptable."

"Well, of course." Delahanty sounded surprised. "You have to do what you think is right, Rabbi. I'm just glad you didn't laugh at me and hang up."

"You're lucky you didn't talk with my wife."

Delahanty laughed. "Am I? Do you have your floppy ready?"

"Just a second." The rabbi loaded a disk into the base of the phone unit. "All right, go ahead." There was a faint whir from the drive as the floppy recorded the data Delahanty was sending. When it was done, Kaplan said, "Thanks. I'll get back to you."

"I ought to be thanking you."

"Nonsense. I haven't had this much fun in a long time." After they said their good-byes, Kaplan took the floppy over to the computer and played it back.

Most of it, he discovered, consisted of Genetic Enterprises advertising videos. If half of what they said about the R strain was true, as soon as the first little porker turned thirty-five, it was going to get elected President. Rhapsodies over how nutritious the meat was, however, did not matter to Kaplan. Ordinary pork was perfectly edible. The problem lay elsewhere.

The rabbi learned that the R strain's digestive tract was modeled after that of cows, sheep, and goats, but was not created from their genetic material. From the tone of the video, he gathered others had tried that approach and failed.

He was glad Genetic Enterprises had done something new; it was a minor point in favor of the R strain. Leviticus 19:19 said, "Thou shalt not let the cattle gender with a diverse kind." In the *Shulkhan Arukh*, Karo extended that to working with a team of different animals, such as a horse and an ox, and said that two mules working together should be examined to ensure that both were the get either of a stallion and jenny or of a jack and mare: otherwise they were animals of diverse kind. Some authorities, in fact, noted Karo, reckoned one mule an animal of diverse kind and forbade its use. If the R strain had some of the genes, say, of a sheep, that argument could have been raised against it.

Kaplan waded through a series of charts and graphs extolling the R strain's ability to put on flesh quickly. Again, that was beside the point. Moreover, while it was important to farmers, the rabbi found it mind-numbing after a while. He hit the fast-forward button.

He jabbed the stop control. There stood Peter Delahanty. He hadn't changed in the year or so since Kaplan had seen him last: he was fair, just past thirty, good-looking in an abstracted way, and very sincere. This had to be the press conference he had mentioned. Maybe, Kaplan thought hopefully, it would give a tidy summary of all the data with which he had been bombarded. Lionel was certainly cuter than a pie chart.

The questions Delahanty had gotten were interesting, and his answers did help clarify matters, but only from a dollars-and-cents standpoint. Kaplan listened for fifteen minutes or so. He was about to give up and turn off the disk when a reporter with a bushy gray mustache stood up and asked, "Will they inter-breed with unmodified pigs?"

When Delahanty said no, Kaplan felt like Archimedes in his bath. For that matter, a naked, dripping man running through the streets shouting "Eureka!" would attract no more attention in Los Angeles than back in ancient Syracuse, unless the police decided he was on angel dust and shot him.

He called Genetic Enterprises again; by now he did not have to look up the number. "I have the determination," he said when Delahanty came on the line.

"And?"

"In my opinion, Jews may eat animals of the R strain, as they may any other beasts that have divided hooves and chew a cud."

"Do you really think so? Do you mind if I ask you why you say so?"

"I was hoping you would," Kaplan said truthfully; he had enough ego to want his reasoning appreciated. "The key is that properly speaking, these R strain beasts are not pigs at all."

"No? What would you call 'em, then? They look like pigs, they oink like pigs, they taste like pigs—though I don't suppose you'd know about that. You told me you weren't going to find the R strain kosher just to be doing it; it seems to me that's what you've done. I don't want that, Rabbi Kaplan."

Kaplan almost burst out laughing. Of all the ridiculous situations in the world, for him to be explaining to an Irishman why a pig wasn't a pig had to fall into the top ten.

He said, "I was going to say no until I heard you tell the press that the R strain and ordinary swine weren't fertile with each other."

"No, they're not," Delahanty agreed. He sounded doubtful, then suddenly excited. "Oh, I follow you, I think. One scientific justification for calling two populations distinct species is that they can't breed together. Is that it? Wouldn't it just make the R strain a different kind of pig, though?"

Admiring his quick wits, Kaplan quoted Leviticus 19:19: " 'Thou shalt not let thy cattle gender with a diverse kind.' The clear implication there, of course, is with a diverse kind of cattle. But the R strain can't gender at all with pigs. And if they can't gender with pigs, how can they be pigs, no matter what they look like?"

After a minute Delahanty said, "You'd make a good Jesuit, Rabbi."

Kaplan grunted. Being a good Jew struck him as quite hard

enough, without the added burden of lifelong chastity. Despite all his other strictures, Karo did not enjoin anything of that sort: In Chapter 150, he recommended cohabitation nightly for married men of strong constitution, twice a week for laborers working in the town where they lived, and once a week for those working in a different town. His injunctions included scholars, although Rabbi Eleazar said that "he used to have cohabitation with such awe and fear that it appeared to him as if a demon was forcing him to do it."

While he was musing on Karo's prescriptions, Delahanty said something he missed. "I'm sorry?" he said, embarrassed.

"I asked how serious you were about all this. Giving an opinion is easy, but do you mean it?"

"Of course I do," Kaplan said indignantly.

"Then—" Delahanty hesitated, went on. "Look, if you think I'm out of line, tell me and I'll shut up, and I certainly won't think any less of you. But I would like to ask . . . having said what you've said, would you eat meat from the R strain yourself?"

He should have guessed the question was coming, but it took him by surprise just the same. Suddenly and bitterly, he understood how Ruth felt. Intellectually, he had convinced himself that the R strain was acceptable. Emotionally, Lionel, pink and plump and curly-tailed, was a pig, no two ways about it.

"Rabbi?" Delahanty said when he did not reply at once.

Having given the response he had, Kaplan saw he had no choice now. "I would eat it," he said. "I will eat it. By your phone code, Genetic Enterprises is in Westwood or somewhere close by. Give me your address; I can be there in a half hour. I don't care to make commercials for you, though, if you don't mind."

"I put you on the spot," Delahanty said. "I apologize; that was nasty of me. Don't let me make you do anything you wouldn't want to."

"You're not. Tell me that address now, please."

"Are you sure?"

"I'm sure," Kaplan said firmly. He wrote down the street number Delahanty gave him, exchanged another minute or so of small talk, and hung up.

He threw on a battered corduroy jacket and was on his way down the hall when Ruth called "Where are you going?" from the den.

Sheepishly (under the circumstances, he thought, that was

not quite the right word), he explained. He stayed right where he was; at that moment he didn't feel much like facing her.

"You told him his pigs were kosher," she said in a voice so flat he could make nothing of it.

"Yes, and this is what it got me." He heard her get up. "What are you doing?" he asked in some alarm.

"Getting a hat."

"What for?"

"So I can come with you, of course."

He was still gaping when he stepped into the hall. He finally found his tongue. "What are you coming with me for? You were the one who told me to say the R strain was *trafe* and have done with it. You can't want to go eat pork with me."

"But it's not pork, or that's what you told Delahanty."

"But to you it is."

"Who's the rabbi in this house?" she said, and laughed at his thunderstruck expression. "Besides," she added softly, "it'll be easier if you're not alone."

"Thank you," he said. That wasn't nearly strong enough. He went over and hugged her. "Have I told you any time lately I think you're wonderful?"

"Yes, but I never mind hearing it again. Come on; let's get this over with."

Traffic on the Santa Monica Freeway never moved fast. Old gasoline-fueled cars, alcohol-burners, and electrics crawled along together. Kaplan had just about decided to make his next car, somewhere in the indefinite future, an electric. With more and more fusion plants coming on line, they were definitely the coming thing. Smog was down, too; not out, but down.

They drove past billboards in Spanish, English, Korean, Japanese, and Hindi. Every decade, it seemed, some new group of immigrants settled in southern California in droves. Kaplan's neighborhood supermarket stocked nine different chutneys and seventeen curries.

With their superior climate, Westwood and Santa Monica had long dominated the L.A. area, leaving the old downtown to stagnation again after its rebirth in the 1970s. Skyscrapers flung long afternoon shadows across the San Diego Freeway as Kaplan and his wife swung north.

The parking garage in the building that housed the headquarters of Genetic Enterprises went down eleven levels underground. The elevator's surge was like a rocket lifting off, but it was not the only reason the rabbi's stomach had for lurching.

Genetic Enterprises kept its labs elsewhere in the city, where rents were lower. This was where the executives worked. When Kaplan opened the door to the receptionist's office, a delicious smell rolled over him like a wave. It was not really unfamiliar; one could not live in Los Angeles without coming across it now and then. But it had never had anything to do with him before.

Delahanty came out almost at once to shake his hand. "Good to see you again," he said, politely adding, "A pleasure to meet you," when Kaplan introduced him to Ruth.

"Shall we get on with it?" she said harshly.

"Of course," Delahanty said. "Thank you for coming, both of you. I understand how difficult this must be for you."

You don't begin to, Kaplan thought, but he and his wife followed Delahanty back into his office. On the desk lay a meat-filled platter. "Blade-cut por—uh, chops," Delahanty said. "Here, let me heat them up for you." He popped them into a microwave oven, which obviously had been brought in for the occasion.

As the microwave hummed, Kaplan sighed inaudibly to himself. Perhaps even without meaning to, Delahanty had eliminated a possible last-ditch excuse to chicken out—another inappropriate phrase, the rabbi thought ruefully. He might have begged off by saying that the beast now reheating had not been slaughtered by a *shokhet*—any ritual butcher would have laughed himself silly at the notion of practicing his skill on a pig. But Kaplan did not insist that his beef and mutton come from the *shokhet*'s knife; he bought them at the supermarket. And so he could not honestly apply a standard to the R strain different from the one by which he judged other acceptable meat.

But he did avoid cuts from the hindquarters of the carcass. The section of meat through which the sciatic nerve passed was not kosher, in memory of the laming blow the angel of the Lord had inflicted on Jacob when they wrestled through the night. Blade-cut chops, though, came from far forward on the beast.

The reverie was done long before the microwave turned itself off. When it chimed, Delahanty took out the platter and produced some plastic cutlery from a desk drawer. "Would you like me to step out for a few minutes?" he asked.

"No, that's all right," Kaplan began, but Ruth broke in, "Yes, please."

"Of course," Delahanty said quietly, and shut the door behind him as he left.

The fantasy that flitted through Kaplan's mind this time was frankly paranoid: he wondered if this was all an elaborate practical joke to get him to eat forbidden food.

He and Ruth looked at the gently steaming chops and at each other. Gathering his pride, the rabbi said, "Me first," and picked up knife and fork. The meat was tougher, grainier than veal, which to his eye it most closely resembled. He speared it with his fork and brought it toward his mouth.

Chapter 92 of the *Shulkhan Arukh* dealt with laws concerning one dangerously ill and one forced to transgress a precept. Karo wrote, "If one who is dangerously ill requires meat, and only forbidden meat is obtainable, an animal should be slaughtered for his sake in order not to feed him with forbidden meat, as it is apprehended lest he will become aware of having been fed on forbidden meat and he will become nauseated thereby."

Kaplan had come across that passage before. Now he had no doubt it described something real. When a couple of hours of theoretical knowledge came up against forty years of ingrained practice, distress was inevitable.

He clamped his jaw shut to hold down his gorge, then realized he could not eat that way. He took a deep breath, chewed, swallowed, then set his jaw again.

"Well?" Ruth demanded. "How is it?"

He laughed shakily. "You know, it's just like the time I ate bacon and eggs when I was a kid. I have no idea what it tasted like."

"Well, let's find out, shall we?" Ruth cut a large piece and chewed with deliberation. "Not bad," she said reflectively. "Nothing to write home about, but not bad."

The second bite, Kaplan found, came much easier than the first. This time he too, was able to consider the flavor of the— of the R strain, he told himself firmly. "Different," he agreed.

They ate a chop apiece, not with any great speed or relish, but steadily. Looking at the meat still on the platter, Kaplan asked, "Still hungry?"

"Not especially."

"Neither am I. Even honestly believing that was acceptable food, it was harder than I ever thought it would be."

Ruth nodded. "You did very well."

"Thanks. So did you, and thanks for that, too." He hugged

her again. "Shall we give Delahanty his office back and show him the dreadful deed is done?"

"Just a second." She took a tissue from her pocket and brushed at his beard. "Now."

"Okay."

Not surprisingly, the head of Genetic Enterprises had been hovering just outside in the hallway. He hurried in, saw the bones on the platter. "Rabbi, Mrs. Kaplan, thank you very much," he said, shaking hands with them both.

"It's all right," Kaplan said. "You've given me one of the more, ah, interesting afternoons of my life, that I can tell you."

"I really didn't mean to pressure you," Delahanty said. But, like any scientist, he was curious by nature and could not help asking. "How did you like it?"

"We got through it," Kaplan said.

Later, driving home, he wondered if he had been short with the man. Then he thought of twenty-five hundred years of history, of conquest and captivity under Babylon; persecution by the Greeks; savage and futile war against Rome; European ghettos and Christian mobs; Dreyfus; the Holocaust, still too appalling for any sane mind to take in; round after round of war in the Middle East, and no end in sight. No end to Jews in sight either, though.

Without much thought, he had managed to sum up the history of a people in four words. That wasn't bad.

He changed lanes.

This one is in large measure my wife Laura's fault. She gave me the ending. Of course, I'm partly to blame, too, because I'm the one who went and wrote a story around it.

LURE

*MIOCENE ITALY. TO BE PRECISE, A SWAMP IN MI-*ocene Italy, in what would be Tuscany ten million years from now, give or take a few thousand. It certainly *smelled* like a swamp, Harvey Cutter thought as he squelched through the mud to check his latest trap.

The smells of mud, stale water, and rotting vegetation never changed much, the hunter thought as he scraped his hip boots one after the other on a branch. Or was that *never would change*? Despite a hundred years of commercial time travel, English tenses remained ill-adapted to the phenomenon.

The branch on which he'd cleaned his boots was part of a myrtle shrub. Maybe an uptime botanist could tell the difference between it and its modern equivalent, but Cutter couldn't. The mosquitoes, he thought resentfully as one bit him on the arm, also hadn't changed much.

But he wasn't hunting plants and he wasn't hunting mosquitoes, even if they were hunting him. He was hunting primates for the San Diego Cenozoic Zoo, and he wasn't having a whole lot of luck.

Things had been easier on his last run, when he'd brought back a dozen *Notharctus*—plenty to start a breeding colony—from Eocene North America. *Notharctus* looked like a lemur and wasn't much smarter than a squirrel. He could have caught a hundred if he'd wanted them.

Now he was after larger—and smarter—game. Hominoids, even offbeat Miocene hominoids like the ones he was after now, were nobody's fools. That wasn't surprising; people and the great apes were the survivors of the hominoid clan.

Something squealed in pain and terror out on the firmer ground farther east. Cutter's head whipped around. A *Dicerath-*

erium was down and kicking, with several wolfish *Cynodesmus* scrambling over its bulky body and already beginning to feed.

Cutter was glad *Cynodesmus* preferred dry ground. They would have attacked him just as cheerfully as they had the big, rhinolike *Diceratherium*. They had no fear of man. In the Miocene, primates—any primates—were prey, not predators.

Calling *Cynodesmus* wolfish and *Diceratherium* rhinolike did not really do the beasts justice, Cutter knew. Unlike the plants and the bugs, Miocene mammals resembled their modern equivalents about as much as would clay models made by a talented ten-year-old with a little more imagination than he really needed.

As if to prove the point, a small herd of *Syndyoceras* daintily picked their way around the gorging pack of *Cynodesmus*. They looked something like deer and something like antelopes, with their striped hides resembling those of zebras, but they had two horns above their eyes and two more halfway down their noses, which made them different from anything that had gotten past the Pleistocene.

Cutter squelched on. He could see the stand of willow where he'd set this new trap. He could see the net too, undeployed and empty. He said something rude under his breath. He got up to the trap and saw footprints by the fat juicy red apple he'd set out as bait. They were the right kind of footprints. He said something rude out loud, loud enough, in fact, to scare a flock of Miocene more-or-less sparrows off their perches. They flew away, chirping angrily.

"Hell with it," he said out loud. He looked around for a reasonably dry patch of ground, took out a ration pack, and ate lunch. He scattered paper and cellophane over the landscape with reckless abandon. All the wrappers were aggressively biodegradable; none of them would show up in the seam of lignite that would memorialize this landscape in the distant present.

Temper somewhat restored, he examined the footprints round the snare again. They were the prints of his quarry, all right: marks about half as big as his own bare feet would have made, and of the same general shape. The imprints of the beast's opposable great toes, though, were slightly set off from those of the others, and not quite in line with them. Only men and their immediate ancestors had feet fully adapted to walking erect.

The hunter started off toward the next stand of willows, a couple of miles away. That one was bigger than this little outpost, and held his camp and three traps. None of them had caught anything, either, though one had been robbed the day before yesterday.

Several sluggish streams ran between the two copses. Cutter forded them with care. The other day, he had watched a crocodile drag a young ancestral hippo off a stream bank and into the water. He corrected himself: the little hippo hadn't lived long enough to be ancestral to anything.

He got to the base camp without being bitten by anything more ferocious than more mosquitoes. Then he checked his traps in this strap of trees. They were all unsprung, though two of them had fresh prints nearby. No wonder the Italian hominoid had a reputation for being hard to catch, Cutter thought.

He found droppings under a big, shaggy willow and set another trap there. When he suddenly looked up in the middle of the job, he saw brown eyes watching him through the leaves. A moment later, they were gone.

He walked back to his camp. That was really too dignified a name for it, he thought. It was just a clearing where he'd pitched a light tent to keep the rain off his sleeping bag. The sun was still in the sky, but he decided to eat anyway.

He got out another ration pack. But for the degradable packaging, he knew, the packs were adapted from old military food: P-rations, T-rations, something like that. He didn't remember the letter. If they'd made soldiers eat stuff like this all the time, he thought disparagingly, no wonder nobody'd fought a war in a long time.

He threw away the cup of what, for a lack of a suitably noxious word, was called stew. *What dessert comes with this pack?* he wondered, feeling rather like Little Jack Horner. Instead of a plum, however, he pulled out a cellophane package with four cookies in it.

Sighing resignedly, he started to eat one, then stopped and gave it a long look. "Be damned," he said, and started to laugh. He glanced back toward where his traps were set, then looked at the cookie again. "Why the hell not? How could it make things go worse?"

Harvey Cutter's nostrils twitched as he walked toward the new exhibit. "Be damned," he said. "It even stinks like Miocene mud. Good job."

Lucy Durr beamed at him. She was second assistant curator in the primates section of the zoo, and had designed the enclosure. "Glad you approve," she said. "The photos you gave us helped a lot in putting it together."

"Good. I hoped they would."

Lucy put her hands on the rail and leaned on it as she peered across the moat at the pair of brown-furred creatures on the far side. "They're interesting beasts, Miocene hominoids that aren't part of the dryopithecid group that led to the great apes or the ramapithecids humans are descended from. They're just—by themselves. I'm glad we have them. Hardly any zoos do."

"I believe that. They're bloody hell to catch. From the fossils, they're supposed to have been common around there. You couldn't prove it by me. I saw one in a tree for half a second, and I finally managed to catch these two. Other than that, forget it."

Cutter reached into his pocket, pulled out some cream-filled chocolate sandwich cookies, and threw them across the moat to the animals he'd captured. The beasts were nimble enough on the ground. On all fours, they hurried over to the cookies. They grabbed them with hands not much different from Cutter's and greedily gobbled them up.

Lucy clucked the horrified cluck of any zookeeper who catches a visitor feeding the animals. Then she glanced over at the hunter. "How do they know those are good to eat? They haven't had any here, I know that, and they certainly never had any back in the Miocene."

"Oh, but they did," Cutter said. Now Lucy was frankly staring at him. He went on. "I wasn't having any luck with fruit for bait, and so—"

"You tried something else. Sure. But why cookies?"

He grinned at her. "Well, what would you use if you were going after *Oreopithecus*?"

I haven't the slightest idea whether this story is fantasy or science fiction. I think it might have fit well in the old *Unknown*, which often walked the fine pixilated line between the two genres.

SECRET NAMES

*MADYU WAS BOILING UP A BATCH OF WILLOW-*bark tea when Jorj, the tribe's chief hunter, poked his head into the shaman's tent. "What do you want?" Madyu asked crossly, not caring to be interrupted in the middle of his spells. He was convinced they added to the pain-relieving value of the tea.

"We will be setting out shortly, wizardly sir," Jorj answered. He was a big, broad-shouldered man of about forty, with strong features and a brown beard just beginning to go gray. His skill with a bow had made him rich; he wore a silver quarter from the Old Time in each ear and owned a necklace strung with many more. He did not have it on now, for fear of a mistimed jingle spooking the prey. He went on, "Some magic to bring the beasts to us would be welcome."

"Oh." The spells on the willow-bark tea would have to wait: it was no cure for the ache of an empty belly. Madyu said, "I'll set to work at once, Jorj Rainbowstar."

The shaman kept his voice low, but Jorj's head whipped around in alarm all the same. No one in the tribe save Madyu and perhaps a favorite woman had any business knowing the hunter's secret name; should an enemy somehow come into possession of it, he might use it to wreak all sorts of baneful sorcery.

Jorj said, "I hope the gods are more in the mood to listen to you than they were last moon-quarter. We came back almost empty-handed."

Madyu knew the chief hunter was obliquely criticizing him for having used his secret name. He dipped his head to acknowledge the rebuke. "I shall do my best, I promise you. Magic is chancy and imperfect, as you no doubt know."

"Oh, aye. If it weren't, we'd all be fatter than we are, and that's a fact." Jorj laughed a big, booming manly laugh that finished the job of putting the shaman in his place. Madyu, who

237

was scrawny, clumsy, and nearsighted to boot, felt his ears turn hot. Laughing still, Jorj left the tent and started shouting to the rest of the hunting band.

With a last mournful look at the bronze tea kettle, Madyu decked himself in the raiment required for hunting magic. He, too, had a coin necklace. His, unlike Jorj's, was made of quarters silvery on the outside but with a copper center. Most shamans preferred those to silver. For one thing, they had to have been made by sorcery; no modern smith could turn out anything like them. For another, the numbers they bore were consistently bigger than those on silver coins. Each shaman had his own explanation for why that was so, but all agreed it had to have some sort of magical import.

Madyu bowed to north and south, east and west. He patted the ground to show his reverence for the earth powers, waved his hands through the air to draw the attention of the sky gods. Then he began the first prayer of the ritual, the one to make keen the noses of the hunting hounds.

He was a conscientious craftsman and did his best to ensure the hounds' success. Not only did he call the beasts *dawgs* after the fashion of his own tribe and those closest to it, he also named them *sheeyas*, as did the KayJun clans to the east, and *perros*, as did the Makykanoes to the west and south. He did not know or presume to guess which language the gods spoke, but preferred to cover as many bets as he could.

He went on to bless the hunters' boots to ensure that they slipped through plain and woods without making a sound. He also blessed their bows and arrows to make the shafts fly straight and true. Again he used all three local languages, and a couple more besides. When tribes met to swap pots and horses and women and metal, shamans generally went off by themselves and traded names. Things were, after all, merely things, and manifested themselves only in this world. But their names, now, their names held power, for names echoed through the spirit world as well.

At any rate, true names, secret names, created those echoes. Madyu remembered the war he'd headed off by ascertaining the secret name of a rival tribe's chieftain and threatening to do dreadful things to the man's ghost unless he called off his warriors.

While never easy, that sort of coup was at least possible with human beings, who acquired their secret names from one another. But who could be sure what the secret name of a dog was, or a willow, or a shoe? That was why shamans swapped names back and forth: in the hope of hitting the one true one among the many.

Having done his utmost with the hunters' animals and gear, Madyu cast the best spells he knew on the beasts they hunted. As he incanted, he thought that any visiting shaman would have admired his technique: He had the cup made from the tip of a wild bull's horn, the turkey feather, the white-haired deer tail, the rabbit's foot, and the squirrel skin all ready where he could reach them without interrupting his ritual. He summoned the prey by every name he knew, no matter how exotic. As he did whenever he said the word, he wondered what tribe called a simple, ordinary squirrel a *bepka*.

He was hot and tired and covered with sweat by the time he finished the hunting magic. Heat and sweat had to be lived with in Eestexas. Legend said that in the Old Time people could make the air around themselves cool whenever they wanted. Madyu, a thoroughgoing realist, did not believe the legend for a minute: if people had ever enjoyed such a useful skill, they wouldn't have been stupid enough to lose it.

When he went outside, he squinted against the glare. The sun beat down with almost physical force. The tribal encampment was nearly deserted, with most of the men at the hunt and the women out in the fields. Children ran between tents, raising hell. One of them stopped to grin at Madyu. "Look, look, look!" he squealed, pointing proudly. His grin had a gap in it.

"I see, Hozay," Madyu answered gravely. "What did the tooth fairy leave you?" As he spoke, his hand twisted in the gesture that kept the fairy from stealing teeth that weren't ready to leave their owner's head.

Hozay reached into his belt pouch and took out two good iron arrowheads. "Look, look, look!" he said again.

"Very nice indeed." Madyu fought down a stab of jealousy. The tooth fairy hadn't left him anything so fine when he was a boy. But then, Hozay's parents were close kin to Ralf, the chief, and the tooth fairy seemed to favor people who were well off. *Those that have, get, even from fairies,* the shaman thought resentfully.

He couldn't stay mad at Hozay, though. For one thing, he looked almost irresistibly cute with his missing tooth. And for another, he didn't stick around as a focus for Madyu's pique—he dashed off yelling after his friends.

The shaman walked over to the creek, stripped off his linen

shirt and buckskin leggings, and dove in. He came up snorting and blowing and at least a little relieved. Then he went down again, swam underwater over to a rock on which a red-ear turtle was sunning itself. The turtle stared in disbelieving reptilian horror when he splashed up in front of its pointy nose. It leapt off the rock and into the creek, frantically churned away. In the water, it was more graceful than Madyu.

He swam a while longer, then went back to reclaim his clothes. He discovered they were not there to be reclaimed. None of the small boys was in sight, either, which gave him more than a little reason to suspect the clothes had not ambled off by themselves. The shaman said a couple of choice things under his breath, added a couple of choicer ones out loud. The shirt and leggings failed to reappear. Swearing and dripping, Madyu went back to his tent without them.

A few of the women had come back to the encampment for a midday meal. They giggled when they saw Madyu. Ralf's tribe had no strong nudity taboo, nor did its neighbors; given the Eestexas climate, nudity was often more comfortable than clothes. But a wet, angry, naked shaman had obviously just fallen victim to a prank, and so became fair game.

Among the gigglers was Hozay's older sister, Neena. That only made Madyu more furious. Some shamans eschewed marriage, believing a celibate life made their magic stronger. Of those who did take a woman or two, most chose from outside their own tribe. That was not a law, but it was fairly strong custom: knowing as he did the secret names of his tribesfolk, a shaman might be tempted to try using sorcery to win a girl's heart.

Madyu would never have stooped to such a thing, however pleasant he found the picture of auburn-haired, softly curved Neena sharing his tent. He resolved to go courting at the trade fair a couple of moons hence. But despite that resolution (which he had made, and broken, before), he did not care to have Neena laughing at him. Even a scrawny, clumsy, nearsighted man has his pride.

As the shaman had expected, his missing garments lay close by the tent. The imps who'd absconded with them—and if Hozay wasn't one of them, Madyu would go out and eat grass for supper—knew how far they could go in provoking him. Had leggings and shirt vanished for good, some small backsides would have had an encounter with the switch. Madyu sighed as he got dressed: this one was a clean win for the boys.

Toward evening, a commotion announced the return of the hunting band. Madyu put away the Old Time book he'd been trying to decipher ever since he'd traded another shaman a six-tool pocket knife for it. The man was a cheat; if Madyu ever learned his secret name, he'd regret the day he was born. The book's faded cover proclaimed that it had to do with medicine, but instead of talking about how to fix a broken leg or what to do about measles or lockjaw, it went on and on about genes and enzymes and other such incomprehensibilities. Madyu was sometimes tempted to use its pages for kindling, but keeping it around and looking through it every now and then reminded him not to be too eager in a deal.

With some trepidation, he came out of the tent. If this hunt proved as bad as the last one had been, Jorj was liable to clout him into the middle of next week. But the chief hunter wore a grin as wide as a longhorn's span. When he saw Madyu, he clouted him, all right, but it was a happy clout, not an angry one. The shaman staggered just the same.

Jorj caught him, steadied him, and patted him on the back. "Look at the fine wizard we have here!" he shouted to anyone who would listen—and he hadn't even been into the blackberry wine. "Look at all the ducks we brought back, thanks to his spells."

"Ducks?" Madyu quacked, but his startled voice was drowned by a chorus of cheers from the rest of the hunters and from the women of the tribe. Madyu looked from one smiling hunter to the next. Sure enough, they were carrying two or three or even four fat ducks apiece, with some of the shining feathers now dark with blood.

"Hardly ever seen such a big flock before," Jorj boomed. "They were tipping up in that pond—you know, the one near what's left of the Old Time road—and they were so busy eating, they barely noticed us shooting at 'em till they were dead. Wonderful spells, Madyu! I wish they'd work that well all the time."

"So do I," Madyu said in a hollow voice. He'd magicked rabbits and squirrels, turkey and cattle and deer—he hadn't said word one to the gods about ducks. But here they were, dozens of them. The tribe would feast for a week.

He saw Neena looking right at him and cheering as loud as anybody. When he smiled at her in a tentative way, she smiled back, not tentatively in the least. All at once, the world seemed a brighter place. Maybe he hadn't asked the gods for ducks, but if they sent ducks his way, he'd take credit for them.

He puffed his chest out as far as it would go (standing there beside Jorj, he still looked like nothing much). "I tried something new this time," he declared. "It had to do with genes and enzymes."

"Never knew ducks wore jeans," Jorj said. Joke as he would, though, the meaningless and therefore necessarily magical words impressed him. "Whatever those en-things are, use 'em some more. They were something else."

"I'm glad," Madyu said, bemused still.

By then the women of the tribe were busily plucking the ducks, putting aside feathers for ornament and for fletching arrows, and the soft underdown for pillows, quilts, and jackets. As casually as he could, the shaman strolled over to Neena and asked her for one of the metallic green feathers from a male mallard's head. Their fingers brushed for a moment when she gave it to him. He felt a spark, and from her friendly expression, she might have, too.

Before long, the savory odor of roast duck drove even lustful thoughts from his mind. Some of the women took out crocks of currant jelly to accompany the feast. Crisp skin crackled under Madyu's teeth as he bit into a juicy thigh; rich hot fat filled his mouth. He ate until he could hold no more, then licked every finger clean.

The rest of the tribe stuffed themselves. Dogs yapped and snarled over gnawed bones thrown in the dirt. A little girl hit her baby brother over the head with a drumstick. He toddled off, crying. Their mother paddled her. She ran after him, crying even louder.

"Here, wizardly sir." Jorj passed Madyu a skin of wine. "Always goes good."

Madyu took a pull, then another one. He smiled, nodded his thanks, and belched enormously. Not to be outdone in politeness, Jorj belched back.

Then the chief hunter said, "Oh, what with all the ducks and everything, I almost forgot."

"Forgot what?" Madyu asked absently. He was watching Neena again. Even if she had been his woman, he was too gorged to imagine anything but watching at the moment. Yet watching was a pleasure, too, albeit a small one.

Jorj's answer brought back his full attention: "We came across an Old Time building nobody's ever seen before, far as I know."

"*Did* you?" The descendants of the handful of people who had survived the Big Oops (a term that had as many interpretations as there were shamans), had been picking their ancestors' bones for the past two hundred years. There were a lot of bones to pick, though. Every so often, somebody came across one with meat still on it. Madyu glanced at the dogs, which were still quarreling over remnants of roast duck. He wondered if the godlike men of Old Time would look at his scavenging tribesfolk the same way. No matter. "Where is it? How do I get to it?"

"It's on a patch of fairly high ground that overlooks the pond where we took all those ducks, thanks to your magic." Jorj thumped Madyu on the back and almost knocked him over even though he was sitting on the ground. "It's surrounded by oaks and creepers. I suppose that's why nobody noticed it before."

"Oh." Madyu's spirts plummeted. So many Old Time buildings were nothing more than tumbledown ruins, hardly worth going through. By the way Jorj had spoken, he'd hoped for something better from this one.

The chief hunter was better at noting animals' vagaries than those of his fellow men, but he saw how disappointed Madyu looked. "Cheer up, shaman. I didn't mean there are oaks and creepers growing up through the building. They're just around it. One must have blown down in the last storm, to let us see the walls through the new gap. The building is in halfway decent shape, maybe better. Part of the roof still looks to be on."

At that, Madyu did feel better. If it was true—let the gods make it true! He bent his head, muttered a quick prayer. Then he said, "Will you take me to it tomorrow?"

"Me?" Jorj frowned but finally nodded. "I suppose I owe you that much after you brought us all those lovely ducks."

"What I find in there might make me a better wizard yet," Madyu declared. The ducks hadn't been his doing, but if Jorj insisted on giving him credit for them, he wasn't too proud to take it.

After a breakfast of duck soup and porridge, Madyu followed Jorj into the woods. The chief hunter moved as confidently as if he were walking down the Old Time road not far from camp. Toting a spear he wasn't used to, Madyu blundered along behind him, peering this way and that at every noise. He didn't know why he bothered; he never could see what made them. He thanked the gods he didn't have to go out hunting all the time; he would have been the laughingstock of the tribe.

Because he didn't hunt all the time, he was soft. He'd been

puffing and panting for quite a while when Jorj stopped and pointed. "There it is. Do you see?"

"No." Madyu had to walk a fair way in the direction Jorj's finger gave before he could make out a smear of lighter color against the greens and browns of the woods.

"I'll come along, if you like," Jorj said, but he didn't sound as if he meant it. The magic that often lingered in Old Time buildings was dangerous even to shamans. The chief hunter wanted nothing to do with it.

"You don't need to," Madyu told him. If anything worth having did rest inside the building, he wanted it all to himself. But after a moment he added, "Could you stay within earshot in case there are snakes instead of demons in there?"

"Fair enough," the chief hunter agreed. He reached into the pack he wore on his back. "Figured you'd say that, so I brought along a songbird net. The ducks won't last forever, however much we wish they would. Pigeons and starlings aren't bad eating, either."

While Jorj looked for a likely spot to string up his net, Madyu scrambled over the moss-covered trunk of the fallen oak. When he made it to the other side, he let out a soft whistle. Jorj had been right: the newly revealed building wasn't badly overgrown at all. After a moment, he saw why: it was surrounded by a stretch of the same hard black tarry stuff the men of Old Time had used to make their roads.

He'd seen other buildings protected that way. They never failed to puzzle him. For a road, the black, hard stuff was almost ideal; even if it was too hard for horses' hooves, it kept the roadway from being overgrown. But why offend the earth powers by slapping it over what could have made a perfectly good vegetable plot? It made no sense that he could see.

For the moment, though, whys did not matter. The black stuff had cracked here and there, allowing some bushes to push up through it, but enough remained to hold the worst of the woods at bay. Windows bare of glass stared blankly out at Madyu like dead men's eyes. Hefting his spear, he advanced on the building.

He tried the door once. When it didn't open, he went over to one of those windows; Old Time locks were tougher by far than any made these days. Had he not known for a fact that the men of Old Time enjoyed both godlike power and godlike goodness, that might have made him wonder about their integrity.

Before he scrambled in through the window opening, he paused to sniff. His nose caught none of the rank order of cat piss, so no cougar—otherwise known as puma, catamount, or, though Eestexas had no mountains, mountain lion—had denned in there any time recently. Just to stay on the safe side, the shaman thrust in his spear and poked around as far as he could reach. Nothing screeched or hissed or writhed under the point, so he scrambled in himself.

His boots scrunched on drifted leaves. He stood still for a couple of minutes, letting his eyes adjust to the gloom. Then he looked around to see what sort of building this was.

A few feet ahead stood a closed door, the frosted glass panel inset into its upper half still miraculously intact. When Madyu saw that door, hope that he'd come upon a real find began to flower in him. If this place had been looted before, the door would have been ajar, the glass broken, or, more likely both.

Gilded letters marched across the glass. Some had peeled away, but the shaman could still read the words they made: VETERINARIAN'S OFFICE. All at once his breath came quick and short, as if he and Neena lay joined together on his pallet. In the Old Time, veterinarians had been shamans specially charged with healing animals. An unplundered veterinarian's office might yield—

"Anything," he said aloud, in soft, wondering tones. "Anything at all."

He went up to the door and twisted the knob. He let out a whoop when it refused to turn—would a looter have locked a door behind him when he was through? It seemed anything but probable. He smashed the glass with the butt of his spear. After the rest of his searching was done, he would gather up the sharp shards to use in cutting blades and as arrow points. Nothing from the Old Time went to waste.

He reached into the opening he'd made and opened the door from the inside. The chamber thus revealed was better lit than he'd expected. A quick look showed why: part of the roof had fallen in, baring the office to the sky—and the rain.

"Oh, a pestilence," Madyu groaned. Everything that had lain anywhere near floor level was long years ruined. Cobwebs lay thick upon every shelf. They covered countless jars of pills. Madyu would have fought shy of those no matter what. Old Time medicines, whether meant for animals or men, were likelier to kill than cure when given by someone who did not thoroughly understand them, which, in the days since the Big Oops, meant everybody.

The shaman went over to a low cabinet with a great many

drawers. He pulled one open, tearing more cobwebs. He felt like shouting—in fact, he did shout—when he discovered it was full of little sharp knives of several sizes and shapes. They were as bright and unrusted as if they'd been forged the day before. He scooped them out of their neat pigeonholes, stuffed them into the stout leather sack he'd brought for booty, then tried another drawer.

This one held hollow needles attached to glass cylinders. No one these days knew why the men of Old Time had chosen to imitate rattlesnake fangs, but they had. The shaman took a few of the bigger ones; sometimes women in the tribe used them to stick sauces deep inside a joint of meat. Other than that, so far as he knew, they had no use.

Other drawers were full of things that had no use whatsoever that he knew about. A lot of them, however, were made of metal and glass, so they were valuable even if not useful in and of themselves.

But next to the cabinet stood a real prize, a metal bookcase full of books. Or, rather, almost full of books: those on the bottom two shelves had at some time in the unknown past been chewed up and turned into rats' nests. The bookcase, though, was sheltered from the elements, and had kept its smooth coat of paint. Rodents hadn't been able to get at the volumes on the upper shelves.

Madyu pulled one out, dusted it off, held it close to his nose to read the title on the spine: *Collected Numbers of the Journal of American Veterinary Medicine*. That looked as if it might be interesting. But when he opened the volume, the collected numbers flaked to pieces under even the gentlest touch.

"Pox-ridden paper!" Madyu growled. So many books from Old Time were like girls who teased but wouldn't deliver; instead of giving up the precious information they contained, they crumbled away to nothingness.

Scowling at yet another such betrayal, the shaman pulled out another volume, this one also labeled *Collected Numbers*. He opened it even more cautiously than he had the first. All at once, he grinned in startled pleasure. The numbers collected here were not what the title claimed. Bound inside the spine were half a dozen copies of an Old Time magazine with which he was already familiar, one whose pictures displayed not only incomprehensible ancient artifacts like cameras, CD players, and Toyotas, but also a good many perfectly comprehensible ancient pretty girls in various interesting states of undress.

He closed this volume with the same care he'd used to open it, then stowed it in his leather sack. He had more than a little hope that he would be able to get it safely back to the encampment. Unlike the real *Journal of American Veterinary Medicine*, the magazines that had hidden behind the lying binding were made from a shiny, coated paper that was better at withstanding the ravages of time than was the more common kind.

The shaman plucked out more books, searching for others printed on the coated paper. He found a couple and put them into the sack. Several others, made from the ordinary variety, disintegrated as soon as he opened them. He murmured a prayer of regret at having destroyed so much irreplaceable wisdom, but did not know what else he could have done.

He picked up the heavy sack, closed the office door behind him, and left the ruin by the window through which he'd entered. He was surprised to note how far the sun had crawled across the sky; he hadn't paid attention to the shadows as he ransacked the Old Time office.

He hallooed for Jorj, and felt a good deal of relief when the chief hunter hallooed back a moment later. Jorj had the knack for moving quietly through the undergrowth; in a couple of minutes, he simply seemed to appear in front of Madyu out of thin air. He pointed to the bulging leather sack. "Ha! No demons, eh?"

"None that I saw, anyhow," Madyu answered. He'd only meant to be strictly accurate, but saw he'd also succeeded in frightening Jorj. Well, that wasn't such a bad thing. Hiding a smile, he went on, "No snakes, either."

"Good, good. What do you have in there, anyway?"

"Some little knives of good steel, some hollowed needles, glass and metal junk, and some books."

"Books," Jorj's voice informed the word with scorn. "Why bother bringing out books, shaman? What good are they?" Like almost everyone else in the tribe, the chief hunter was illiterate.

"You'll like some of them. Pictures from Old Time." Madyu's hands shaped curves in the air. As they did so, he thought again of Neena.

Jorj's eyes lit up. "You'll trade some?"

"Why not?" Madyu said. "I see you've also done pretty well for yourself."

More than a dozen dead songbirds, their little yellow legs bound together with twine, hung head down from Jorj's belt, along with a possum and a couple of chipmunks. "Could be worse,'' the chief hunter allowed. "I just wish there was more meat to each one. But as long as I do even this well, we won't be down to eating grubs and grasshoppers the way we had to a couple of years ago.''

"The gods be praised for that,'' Madyu said, and meant every word of it. Grasshopper stew was vile; no matter how long the insects cooked, they crunched horridly between the teeth. And Chief Ralf had been about to run him out of the tribe for weak magic before the famine finally broke. Madyu never had figured out why the gods got so angry at him, or why they finally decided to relent.

Shaman and chief hunter walked back to the encampment in companionable silence, each well enough pleased with his day's work. Thanks to his tasty burden, Jorj got the big half of the wishbone's worth of greetings, but Madyu created some enthusiasm among the men when he told them about the pictures of Old Time girls he'd found.

Neena happened to be standing close by just then, and let out a sniff loud enough to make him regret for a moment having come across the volume with pictures. Soon enough, though, thoughts of profit ousted regret. It wasn't, worse luck, as if Neena were his woman.

After supper but before sunset made reading impractical, Madyu settled down with the other two books he'd brought back from the ruin. One of them, its title page proclaimed, was about the diseases of cats. He read three or four pages, then put the book down with a grunt of disgust. It was as imcomprehensible as the one with which the other shaman had cheated him.

He wondered if he was the problem, but shook his head. He read pretty fluently, and the Old Time language wasn't that far removed from the English his tribe spoke (he never had figured out why the language bore that name; he didn't know of a place called Eng anywhere within shouting distance of Eestexas). But this book was crammed full of words he not only didn't know but couldn't define from context: What did *distal* mean, for instance, or *pancreatic function*?

He thought about trading the book to a Maykano; maybe the peculiar words were Spanyol, not English at all. If they were, someone from a southern tribe might get more out of the volume then he could. And if not, well, it wouldn't be the first time he'd diddled someone in a trade.

He picked up the other volume with a certain amount of resignation, convinced from the outset that it would be even worse than the one he'd just set aside. Even its title looked like a nonsense word: *Taxonomy*. "Tax-on-uh-me?" he said, sounding it out. He had some idea what taxes were—tribute that you paid to your chief, or that a weak tribe paid to a strong one next door. He couldn't see why anyone would want to write a book about that, or why a veterinarian would need it once it was written. He also doubted Old Time folk had had to worry about anything so mundane as taxes.

But, being a stubborn sort, he decided he would keep going in the book until he found out what its name meant—names, after all, were powerful. He turned to the preface and found, to his surprise, that not only did it tell him what he wanted to know, it did so in a fashion he had little trouble understanding.

Taxonomy, he gathered, was a way of organizing living creatures by how they were related to one another, something like the genealogical charts some shamans drew for their tribes. He whistled softly to himself. The Old Time folk thought big if they aimed to keep track of how everything was related to everything else. He admired their presumption without wishing to emulate it. Just to begin with, how did they propose to keep track of all the different names every living thing had?

Two paragraphs further on, the preface told him: binomial nomenclature. That formidable pair of words almost made him put down the book then and there. But the preface went on to explain what it meant: two names, one generic, to tell what sort of creature an animal was, and the other specific, to tell exactly what sort it was.

That had the shaman scratching his head again. But this *Taxonomy* book, despite its intimidating title, did a much better job of explaining things than did the volume on the diseases of cats. It gave the example of the dog—which, for no reason Madyu could see, it called *Canis familiaris*—and the wolf—which it styled *Canis lupus*. The generic name they shared said they were closely related to each other, while their different specific names said they weren't the same.

"Makes sense of a sort," Madyu admitted. It made enough sense, at any rate, for him to keep reading. His eye lit on a sentence in the next paragraph and would not go away: *The so-called scientific name attached to any organism remains constant throughout the world, enabling researchers to communicate effectively and accurately regardless of their native languages.*

He stared at those words until darkness made them illegible.

If they meant what he thought they did, he'd just stumbled across the biggest Old Time treasure ever, bigger than gold, bigger than jewels, bigger even than the usable firearms and ammunition that still turned up every once in a while. If the whole world had once recognized a single (or rather, double) true appellation for every animal and plant, was he not holding a book full of secret names?

He wanted to run screaming through the encampment, shouting, "I've got it! I've got it!" He wanted to get drunk. He wanted to get laid. He wanted to beat Chief Ralf at checkers and then laugh in his face. He wanted to do all those things at once. But none of them, or even all of them at once, would have given him a tenth part of the exaltation he felt sitting there quietly in the dark.

He did his best to keep a sense of detachment. For one thing, he might have been wrong, though he didn't think he was. For another, even if he was right, he didn't know which secret name went with each animal.

That night, he slept with the book beside him on his pallet. When he woke up, the first thing he did was make sure it was still there. When he saw it was, he couldn't have been happier even if it had been Neena there, looking back at him with her big green eyes full of love. He weighed that thought, was a little surprised to find it true, and stroked the book's faded cover as tenderly as if it had been Neena's soft, smooth skin.

Without bothering to break his fast, he opened *Taxonomy*. He felt like cheering when he discovered that many of the scientific names contained therein had more familiar ones alongside them, though the latter were written in brackets and in smaller letters, as if to show they really weren't quite as good or as scientific—a word to conjure with, he thought, and smiled to himself inside his tent—as the impressive products of binomial nomenclature.

Navigating through classes, orders, families, and genera took some doing, but before too long he found that the white-tailed deer's scientific name, its secret name, was *Odocoileus virginianus*. He said it several times. It filled the mouth in a way that *white-tailed deer* never could. Saliva filled his mouth, too, at the thought of venison roasted with bacon and wild onions.

He left *Mammalia* and went over to *Aves*. He ran his finger down each column of names until he found what he was looking for. "*Meleagris gallopavo*," he intoned reverently, and then again: "*Meleagris gallopavo*." Not only were the secret names true, they were also beautiful. He knew he'd never be content just to say *turkey* again.

At this point hunger, excitement, and a bursting bladder drove him outside. After imagining the rich savor of *Odocoileus virginianus* and *Meleagris gallopavo*, duck hash made from rather stale duck proved a disappointment. He was even more disappointed to see Jorj sitting around fletching arrows. "You're not going out today?" he asked in tones of despair.

"Hadn't planned to, no," the chief hunter said. His big, blunt fingers picked with surprising delicacy through a pile of feathers. He found one that suited him and began trimming it to fit the groove in an ashwood arrow.

"But if you do—if you give me time to make a proper magic, a *scientific* magic first—if you do, you'll bring back deer and turkey both," Madyu said. Jorj stared at him; he'd never made that definite a prediction before. "I promise," he added, thinking he'd already said enough to ruin himself if by some disastrous mischance he was wrong.

"How can you promise what we'll catch?" Jorj demanded. "You don't know what we'll stumble on out there in the woods. You don't know the first thing about what hunting is like; you're only good for stumbling over yourself."

"But I know what I'm talking about when it comes to magic, I truly do," Madyu said. The hunter shook his head and started to go back to feathering his arrow. Desperately, Madyu added, "Did I help you bring in all those ducks?" He knew the real answer to that was *no*, but since Jorj didn't know it, he played the card without compunction.

Jorj looked at the bright blue duck feather he held in his hand, then back up at Madyu. Slowly, deliberately, he set aside the feather and put away his tiny fletching tools. When he got to his feet, he towered over the shaman. "All right," he said. "We'll hunt. But if you're wrong—if you're wrong, wizardly sir, you'll not have the chance to make many more such mistakes. Do you understand me, Madyu?"

"I understand you—Jorj." The tiny pause there should have reminded the chief hunter that Madyu knew and might have used his secret name. It was not as good a threat as Jorj's big, hard, bunched fist, however. Even with a secret name, magic had a way of going wrong (Madyu suddenly wished he hadn't remembered that just before the most important conjuration of his life). Brute force was inelegant but always worked.

Still shaking his head, Jorj went off to gather the hunting

band. Madyu hurried back to his tent. He began to incant as he'd never incanted before; whatever his doubts and worries, they washed away in ritual chants and passes, dances and prayers.

Again and again he intoned the majestic secret names he'd learned. When he held the white-furred deer tail, his cry was, *"Odocoileus virginianus!"* When he pranced with a turkey plume, *"Meleagris gallopavo!"* rolled trippingly off his tongue. As an added touch, he tried to pronounce the secret name as if he were a turkey himself. *"Gallopavo!"* he gobbled. *"Gallopavo!"*

Being a meticulous man, he did not forget some magical encouragement for the pack of *Canis familiaris* that coursed with the hunters. The dogs had as much to do with a hunt's success as the men, sometimes more. They were more susceptible to magic, too, as they lacked the wit that sometimes blunted it when it was turned against people.

At last he had done all he could do. He stayed in his tent regardless, not caring for the loss of dignity that would come from the women of the tribe watching him pace nervously back and forth while he waited for the hunters to return.

Staying inside didn't end up helping his dignity, either. Hozay and some of the other boys started chanting, "Madyu don't dare show his face, show his face, show his face . . . !" With the insane persistence small boys would sooner show in mischief than in honest work, they kept chanting it for a good part of the afternoon.

Madyu looked through the *Taxonomy* book again. If the secret name for *pest* or *infernal nuisance* appeared therein, however, he could not find it.

After much too long, Hozay got tired of singing his old song. If he'd kept quiet because of that, Madyu might possibly have found it in his heart to forgive him. Instead, though, he came up with a new one, which he proceeded to bellow out in a boy's falsetto that hurt like a sore tooth: "Neena says Madyu's too skinny! Neena says Madyu's too skinny! Neena says—"

The shaman's temper went up in flames like a dead, dry pine struck by lightning. He burst out of the tent, aiming at nothing less than Hozayicide. Neena's little brother ran like a rabbit, dodging Madyu's every effort to lay a hand on him. And as he ran, he kept singing his new and infuriating one-line ditty.

Finally, puffing and defeated, Madyu drew to a halt. At almost the same time, Hozay decided to shut up. The one had nothing to do with the other. Hozay had heard—as Madyu did, too, a moment later—the hunting band coming back from the woods. Little boys know instinctively that adults do not take kindly to their mocking other adults. This does not stop little boys, but it will sometimes make them cautious.

Adults, however, commonly do not care in the least about punishing mockery when they are the ones dishing it out. Madyu stood alone in the middle of the encampment, waiting for the hunters' scorn to land on him—and to obliterate him. The way the rest of the day had gone, he knew his sorcery had to have failed.

Jorj came into the clearing, spotted the shaman. Pointing at Madyu, he looked back over his shoulder and yelled, "Here he is!" His bass bellow made Madyu cringe—by the sound of it, the hunters would not be content with mere insults. They'd want his blood. Had he thought running would do any good, he would have run.

Shouting, the rest of the hunting band followed Jorj into the open space around the encampment. They roared down on Madyu. He needed a few seconds to realize they were cheering him, not cursing.

The ones who came out of the woods first were carrying turkeys, some more than one bird. The ones who came later had tied gutted deer carcasses to spearshafts that they bore on their shoulders, two men to a spear. All in all, they were bringing back three or four times as much meat as they usually did even on a good day.

Jorj, who as chief hunter did not have to haul prey, hurried into his tent. He came out with his necklace of silver quarters, which he proceeded to throw around Madyu's neck. "Best magic since Old Time!" he shouted, loud enough to be heard in the next encampment. "The turkeys waddled right up to us, the deer just stood there waiting to be killed, just the way our great shaman said they would."

Madyu hadn't quite said anything like that. He hadn't really expected to achieve anything like that; he thought he knew what magic could and couldn't do. *But I never made hunting magic with* real *secret names before*, he thought dizzily. He let a big grin stretch itself over his face and did not bother setting the record straight.

"Well, wizardly sir, what do you have to say for yourself?" Jorj boomed.

The shaman blurted the first thing that came into his head: "Let's eat!"

The hunters cheered again, louder than ever. Boys and girls came running to gape at the enormous catch. Among them was Hozay. Madyu was so full of triumph that gazing at his tormentor only made him wonder how much the tooth fairy would bring if he knocked all the little monster's teeth down his throat.

The racket the hunters and children made brought the women in from the fields early. They stared at the young mountain of meat, too, and then sent up their own screams of joy. Jorj yelled, "We're rich, do you know that, rich! We have more food than we know what to do with. We have so much, we can smoke some and sell it to tribes that aren't lucky enough to have a shaman as clever and—what was that fancy word you used, Madyu?—as scientific, that's it, as ours. We can—"

Madyu stopped listening about then, because Neena threw herself into his arms, kissed him, and exclaimed "Oh, Madyu, you're wonderful!"

The shaman came up for air stunned and gasping, but his hands knew what to do. They grabbed Neena here and there. An instant later his idiot mind yammered that she would surely pull away—after all, hadn't she said he was too skinny? But she didn't. In fact, she snuggled closer. Off to one side, Hozay looked as if he were about to be sick. That felt almost as good to Madyu as Neena's warm and yielding softness. By way of experiment—he *was* a scientific man—*he* kissed *her* this time. Not only did she return the kiss, but, he noticed dimly, Hozay looked even sicker. Since the experiment was successful, he repeated it.

Emboldened further still by the results of the second trial, he whispered, "Will you come to my tent tonight?"

"Of course I will," she whispered back, her breath moist in his ear. Then she went on, "Why didn't you ask me a long time ago?"

He stared at her. "I—I didn't think—"

"Why ever not?"

"Well—well—" The more he pondered that, the more he wondered himself. He found only one answer that made any sense whatever: "After all, Neena, I know your secret name."

"So what?" She tossed her head so her shining hair flipped back over her shoulder. Then she pointed to one of the gutted deer carcasses. "Did you use it in a spell on me, the way you did with those?"

"Of course not," he said, indignant at the very suggestion. "I'd never do such a thing."

"Well, then," she said, as if that settled everything. By the way she was looking at him, maybe it did. Her premise wasn't even slightly scientific; Madyu knew that. But however scientific he thought he was, he was a shaman first, and also knew logic sometimes didn't matter. This felt like one of those times.

His arms tightened around Neena again. She sighed against his cheek. He nodded happily, pleased at the logical confirmation of his illogic. Sure enough, this *was* one of those times.

When I wrote this story in early 1984, I used as my guide to the names of the features on Mimas the map in the back of the NASA publication *Voyages to Saturn*. These names, however, had not yet been formally approved by the International Astronomical Union. Mimas' biggest crater ended up being named for the moon's discoverer rather than being based on the Arthurian theme that dominates the rest of its nomenclature. "Les Mortes d'Herschel," however, doesn't make much of a title, so I've decided to leave well enough alone.

LES MORTES D'ARTHUR

THE SLOPE THE SPACESUITED RUNNER WAS climbing would have been impossibly steep, even on Luna. The tracking camera relayed her image to the studio a few kilometers away. "Lovely, isn't she?" murmured Rannveig Aasen.

"She certainly is," Bill Bennett agreed. "Moving with grace on a very low gravity world is a skill few people have occasion to acquire."

As if to prove his point, the runner made a slight misstep. Instead of gliding smoothly forward, she bounced a good five meters up off the ground. She had the presence of mind to hold her pose for the eleven seconds it took for her to return.

"That could happen to anyone," Bennett said sympathetically. "Mimas' surface gravity is only .008*g*. To put that in perspective for you folks back home, Luna pulls more than twenty times as strongly." The transmitter flung his words and picture across one and a third billion kilometers toward Earth. At light speed, they would reach perhaps that many sets an hour and a half later with the slightly misleading legend "Live—from Saturn" superimposed.

The girl reached the summit without further mishap. She paused for a moment before the large bronze bowl there, then reached up and thrust the rod she carried in her right hand over the edge of the caldron. A great sheet of yellow-orange flame, twice as tall as a man, sprang into being.

"It's a hologram, of course," Rannveig said, "the same principle that makes stereovision possible. Mimas is almost nothing but ice, and has no atmosphere at all. But it still makes me want to reach out and warm my hands over it.''

"Me, too," Bennett said. "We'll return to our coverage of the sixty-sixth Winter Olympic Games in a moment, but first these words." Bennett disappeared from the monitor screen, to be replaced by the Interplanetary Broadcasting Company's keynote symbol for this part of the games: an ancient black-and-white *Voyager* image of Mimas, with the great crater Arthur dramatically shadowed near the terminator.

When the commercial break was done, the camera cut away from the broadcasters to the icy plain at the foot of Arthur's central peak for the opening parade of athletes. Bright blue eyes twinkling, Rannveig Aasen undid the belt that held her in her chair, pushed off, and caromed around the studio like an insane billiard ball with a cometary tail of long blond hair.

The director howled curses into her earphone, but she always managed to keep an eye on the monitor and did not miss a beat in her commentary. "The two men and two women at the head of the procession, the ones in the light blue and white spacesuits, are the Greek contingent," she explained for her distant audience. "Greece has been part of United Europe for more than a hundred fifty years now, but still fields an independent team at every Olympic Games, in keeping with its place of honor as the homeland of the Olympic ideal."

Bennett listened to her with nothing but admiration, a word also describing his feelings as he watched: the female form does not sag at all in .008g.

The terrestrial portion of the Winter Games was being held at Klagenfurt in United Europe that year, so the athletes crossed the ice in their national groups in French alphabetical order. That put the United States—or rather, États-Unis—near the front, just after the Chinese Empire, instead of toward the end.

"This is the first time in four Olympiads that the Americans have sent a team—if I can call one man and one woman a team—to Mimas," Bennett remarked. "They haven't had much low-g training and aren't expected to contend for medals, but it's good to see them competing here again. Private contributions raised enough money for two berths aboard the Arab World ship *Nasser*."

Several larger groupings passed—Eastern Europe, the Anzac Federation, Japan, Luna. The team from the Arab World looked smart in spacesuits of green, white, and black. "Security is tight here," Bennett said, "thanks to threats from Israeli, Turkish, and Armenian nationalists."

Moscow had fielded a strong group. So had Siberia. There were a couple of Swiss athletes in red suits with white crosses. They had traveled with the United Europeans in the same way the Americans had with the Arabs. United Europe, as the host nation, came last, just behind the contingent from Zaire.

Rannveig was finally back in her seat. "Personally," she said, "I think the United European uniforms are busy."

"So do I." Bennett nodded. "But then, they almost have to be, since they're blending so many sets of former national colors. Some of the rivalries that went with those old colors aren't dead yet, either, and the newer one between United Europe and Eastern Europe is also no laughing matter, I'm afraid. You Europeans are a contentious lot," he said to Rannveig, who came from Oslo.

"No, we're not," she replied in mock anger.

"You certainly are."

They pythoned it back and forth for another minute or two before Rannveig started the wrap-up of opening-day coverage, remarking, "Our viewers may be wondering why only a relative handful of teams are represented here, as compared with Klagenfurt."

"Cost is the villain," Bennett said. "Fares from Earth to the Saturn system still run over fifteen hundred ounces of gold. That's one of the major reasons we've seen so little from the United States in recent years, for example. If spaceflight were cheaper, we'd see many more nations participating."

"Something to look forward to, perhaps, in games to come." Rannveig closed out: "Thanks for joining us for the opening ceremonies from the Mimas Winter Olympic venue. Tomorrow we'll be bringing you first-round coverage of the most spectacular of all Olympic events, the five-kilometer ski jump. Program your sets to 'Olympics' now, so you won't miss a moment of the action. See you then."

The old *Voyager* picture of Mimas reappeared on the monitor. This time, though, a bright red line superimposed on the image showed the ski-jump track descending from the summit of Arthur's central peak—the largest athletic arena in the solar system. Ten kilometers away, a red oval showed the landing area.

"That went off very well," the director said, adding, "all things considered," with a pointed glower Rannveig's way. She paid no attention, leaning back in her chair to let a makeup man scrub her face clean.

Bennett did the same, enjoying the damp sponge on his forehead, cheeks, and chin. He was very little changed when the ministrations were over: an open-faced, light brown man in his early thirties; burnsides, popular after a lapse of fifty years, looked good on him.

So did his engaging smile, even if it was a touch smug at the moment. He had a right to feel self-satisfied. IBC did not hire many Americans; most were too parochial to do well outside their own small bailiwick, and few spoke anything but English or Spanish. But his French, once again the dominant international tongue, was fluent as any native speaker's; to his own way of thinking, at least, he had a better accent than Rannveig did.

"Care for a drink?" he asked, and she gave an eager nod.

They swung hand over hand from the rings set in the hallway ceiling toward the bar. Brachiating was the easiest way to get around on Mimas; the gravity was really too weak for walking, especially indoors, but just enough to make free-fall-style gliding impractical, too. "I wonder why we ever came out of the trees," Rannveig said, darting ahead.

The studio was part of the same complex that housed the Olympic athletes. The two broadcasters sped past pressure doors and spacesuits in niches: like any structure exposed to vacuum, the Olympic village was divided into hundreds of gastight segments. The front door to every suite was a bulkhead in its own right.

Once she had hooked her feet under the brass rail, Rannveig ordered aquavit with a beer chaser. Bennett chose rum and Coke; since the rediscovery of the original formula in the ruins of Atlanta, Coca-Cola was all the rage again.

The drinks came in squeeze bulbs with nipples, as they would have in free-fall. An incautious lift would have sent the contents of glasses flying.

The monorail shuttle returned to the Olympic complex from the parade ground. Athletes and coaches began drifting into the bar. Most of the competitors, knowing they would have to be at their best tomorrow, were moderate. Their mentors had fewer compunctions. The Muscovite coach, in a red and gold sweater, and his Siberian counterpart, who wore his team's snowy white, challenged each other to a duel of vodka. Empty squeeze bulbs accumulated in epic numbers around them.

The two of them argued more or less amiably as they drank.

The Muscovite spit Slavic consonants at his opposite number. The Siberian replied in French, letting Bennett follow his half of the conversation. For a czarist nobleman, Russian was fit only for talking with servants, infants, and pets.

"It seems hardly fair for peasant upstarts to have better accommodations than we do," he said.

The Muscovite coach answered. The Siberian rolled his eyes. " 'All quarters are equal,' indeed. *Merde*—why has the Olympic committee placed us where we cannot even see the competition area?"

No one could see the competition area; the window in the bar was the only one in the Olympic village. The Muscovite must have pointed that out, because the Siberian said, "It is the principle of the thing, though principle, I suppose, is something a Marxist cannot be expected to understand."

The Muscovite's only comment to that was a belch. He fell asleep a few minutes later. His counterpart's triumphant smile also quickly dissolved in snores.

Except for one Jew, the members of the Arab World's team were teetotalers. They sipped fruit juice and passed a pipe back and forth.

A ski jumper was turning cartwheels in midair. Rannveig touched Bennett's hand. "Look at the loonie showing off."

"You can hardly blame her. This is the only place where she can compete against Earth people on even terms—Mimas makes everyone strong." He finished his drink. "Do you mind if I drift around a bit?"

"Heavens, no. Have a good time. I certainly intend to." She looked at him archly. "Don't do anything I wouldn't enjoy."

He grinned. "That doesn't leave much out." They had ended up in bed a couple of times during the trip to Mimas, more out of boredom and simple propinquity than anything else. It had been fun, but nothing on which to build a grand passion.

The ski jumper from Luna landed on her head, laughing. "Was that half a turn too many or too few?" Bennett asked her.

"I sort of lost track up there," she said. She looked at him curiously, trying to place him. Most of the athletes were still in the tight pullovers and hose they had worn under their spacesuits, which made his conservative green velvet doublet, tunic, and Paisley neck scarf stand out by comparison. "I know!" she exclaimed after a moment. "You're from IBC!"

He admitted it. She insisted on buying him a drink. Not much happened in the controlled environment of Luna, so stereovision was even more popular there than it was on Earth. "I'm just a media addict," she said.

"Nonsense," he said gallantly. "How could you get into that kind of shape sitting in front of a set all the time?" He bought the next round himself, and the one after that; he was sure his expense account was stretchier than hers.

He glanced over and saw Rannveig deep in conversation with a big man as blond as she was. *Another Scandinavian*, was his first thought, but then he noticed the fellow was wearing the eye-searing blue, red, and green of Eastern Europe. They did not seem to be having any problems getting along, though.

Nor was he, with the girl he had met. *A promising evening all the way around*, he thought.

"And now," Rannveig said, "I'd like to introduce our expert analyst, Angus Cavendish, bronze medalist for United Europe in the five-kilometer ski jump in the 2192 Winter Games."

"I thank ye very much," Cavendish said. He was a small, dapper man in his early forties, just beginning to gray at the temples and on his cheeks. The Scots burr with which he flavored his French should have given his voice an air of impressive deliberation. It probably would have, too, if he spoke a little slower, but he was too excitable for that. He always reminded Bennett of a tape recorded at eight centimeters a second and played back at sixteen.

"Tell us, Angus, what's the most difficult thing about this event?" Bennett asked. He had the slightly too good feeling hangover pills always brought.

"The training for it," Cavendish said at once. "For where d'ye find the like conditions in the inner solar system? It's only the rich countries can afford to ship their skiers out here for the sake o' the exercise: the Arab World, Luna, Japan, Siberia."

"Then how do you account for your own medal?" Rannveig asked.

"Me, lass? I was assistant engineer on a supply ship to the Mimas Saturn station and borrowed my skis from a computer tech there. You look down the rosters of the teams and you'll find a great lot of spacers among 'em. We're the ones who come to Mimas on our own business and learn a bit while we're here."

Following the script they had roughed out, Bennett said, "Why don't athletes from nations that can't afford to send them here train on the moons of Mars? Those have an even lower surface gravity than Mimas."

"So they do, but they don't have Arthur; they're too puny. Look here, now." The screen behind the broadcasters displayed the trademark image of Mimas. Cavendish used a pointer. "The crater is a hundred thirty kilometers across and ten deep, with the central peak six kilometers high. The body that struck Mimas to make it must have been ten kilometers across (almost the size of Deimos, mind); if it had been any bigger, it would've cracked the moon apart."

"From what you've told us, then, I take it the technique for jumping on Mimas is quite different from the one skiers use back on Earth," Rannveig said.

The screen showed the ninety-meter jump at Klagenfurt. A skier appeared at the top of the slope, pushed off, and went into her tuck. "There's the first difference already!" Cavendish cried. "You can't simply tuck and run here or you're done for in the jump. At $.008g$, you see, you don't build up the velocity even in five kilometers that you do in the ninety meters on Earth. You have to use poles all the way down."

"But there are risks in that too, aren't there?" Bennett asked.

"That there are. In the low gravity, each push sends you off the slope. The more you bounce about, y'see, the less time there is to be pushing. You have to dig in at just the right angle to come down again quick as you can. If you've done it right, you spring off at the end with about the same speed as off the ninety-meter hill back home—near a hundred kilometers an hour."

As if on cue, the jumper in the monitor screen launched herself into space. "With the local gravity so low, you'd think you'd almost be able to jump clean off Mimas," Rannveig said.

" 'Tisn't so," Cavendish snorted. "The escape velocity's over a hundred seventy meters a second; you scarcely reach the sixth part of that. Nay, with the ramp angled up at forty-five degrees, you take about four minutes to sail up two and a half kilometers—three and a half over the floor of Arthur. Then it's down again. Overall, you're flying between nine and ten minutes."

"It must be a marvelous view," Bennett said.

"That it is." The line was planned, but Cavendish's eyes went genuinely misty. "You think you can see forever; in fact, it's about thirty-five kilometers."

The screen behind the Scotsman showed the jumbled vista of the crater floor. Small pits and mounds of ice began lazily flowing out of the picture at the edges; what remained grew larger and larger. "Of course, eventually you have to think about landing," Bennett said.

"So you do," Cavendish said dryly. "There's the rub. You hit the slope at more than a hundred and ten kilometers an hour, and you don't dare tumble. They have subsurface pipes to heat—if that's the word I want—the landing zone a hundred degrees or so, up to -30° centigrade, same as the runway. Still, rip your suit and you're gone. Almost every games, it seems, they add a name or two to the memorial plaque at the peak of Arthur."

"Is it worth it, then?" Bennett asked. That line was in the script, too, but he meant it. Risking one's life unnecessarily struck him as insane.

Cavendish's reply caught him by surprise. It came from the man, not the commentator: "Lad, for the feeling you get when you're up there, why, dying'd be a small price to pay."

There was a moment of dead air before Rannveig took up the slack, saying quietly, "All the athletes here today would agree with you, Angus."

The broadcast going back to Earth cut away from the studio to the pressurized lodge at the top of the runway. Like the Olympic village complex below, it rested on pylons sunk in the ice. The camera focused on the airlock door, which opened to let out the first contestant.

She wore the deep blue of the Anzac Federation; her clear faceplate showed intense concentration on her features. "This is Marge Olbert," Rannveig said. "She's twenty-six, from Canberra, a junior ecology officer aboard the *Wirraway*, one of the Anzac Line's asteroid-belt freighters."

"Ah, then she'll have some work at very low gravity," Cavendish said. "A plus for her."

The starting light went from red to green. Marge Olbert dug her poles into the ice. "A good push-off!" Cavendish cried. "See, she's still low enough to take a second shove. That's the way to do it—keep the polework as near parallel to the runway as you can!"

The ski jumper landed, pushed, flew; landed, pushed, flew. Each thrust of the ski poles added to her velocity; so, little by little, did Mimas' weak pull. "Oh, excellent form—she'll be close to that hundred-kilometer-an-hour mark," Cavendish said.

Marge Olbert was rocketing down the slope now. "A shame we're in vacuum," Bennett said. "The wind shrieking by Ms. Olbert would give the audience an added sense of her speed."

Cavendish chuckled. "They can tell she's going fast, never fear."

She used her poles powerfully on the short upslope at the end of the run, gave a last great spring, and launched herself into the void. Red numbers appeared on the monitor: 97.43.

"A splendid takeoff velocity," Cavendish said. He unobtrusively checked a chart he was holding in his lap. "She'll be out past ten and a quarter kilometers. The women's record only 10.6. Could well be the longest women's jump of the first day. She'll give the other lassies something to think on."

The flick of a switch brought the transmission from Olbert's suit radio into the studio. "Oh, my," she was saying again and again. "Oh, my." A reminiscent grin spread over Cavendish's face.

Marge Olbert was soaring up toward her maximum altitude when coverage cut back to the slope, where another jumper had already begun his run. "They'll be going about every five minutes," Bennett explained, "so one will be landing, another just past high point, and a third jumping at about the same time."

"That's right, Bill," Rannveig said. "On the runway now is Jozef Jablonski of Eastern Europe." Bennett wondered at the sudden warmth in her voice until a close-up showed the face of the man she had been with the night before. She went on, "He's twenty-nine, an air force captain from Gdynia; his hobbies include basketball, chess, and wargaming."

Not all of that was on Jablonski's personal data sheet. Bennett smiled a little.

"He's a strong-looking brute," Cavendish said. Rannveig jerked her head, whether in agreement or indignation Bennett could not tell. The Scotsman carried the narration: "Good form into the upslope—aye, a mighty push there, and now the leap . . . 101.74 kilometers an hour! A fine first jump; it'll go well past eleven kilometers."

A tight telephoto showed the expression of almost religious awe that Jablonski was wearing as he sailed high over the frozen surface of Mimas. "With a shot like that, you don't need words," Cavendish murmured.

The monitor split into thirds, simultaneously tracking Marge Olbert hurtling down toward her landing, Jablonski nearing apogee, and the next contestant on the runway, a Siberian woman who crossed herself before she began her descent.

Dream-smooth, the girl from the Anzac Federation touched down, steadying herself with her ski poles. "Here's her distance, now," Cavendish said. "It's 10,290 meters—a splendid opening jump." As Marge Olbert killed her momentum on the reverse slope beyond the landing zone, a crawler came out to pick her up and take her back to the Olympic village. Her raised fist said she knew what she had done.

Then Jozef Jablonski was landing, not as gracefully as his predecessor but safe enough. Red numbers superimposed on his image gave the length of his jump: 11,149 meters. "Astonishing that only a four-kilometer-an-hour difference in takeoff velocity will produce so much extra distance," Rannveig said. She did not sound astonished; she sounded proud.

"It's enough to send Jablonski over two hundred meters higher than Marge Olbert, and keep him over the ice twenty seconds longer," Bennett said, echoing the quick calculations one of the technical people was feeding into his earphone.

One after another, the jumpers flew through their parabolas. With sixty-eight competitors in all, the first round was scheduled to last nearly six hours. As Cavendish had guessed, Marge Olbert's distance kept holding up, though the girl from the United States, making her first jump off Earth, startled everyone by coming within seventeen meters of it. On the men's side, Jozef Jablonski stayed in solid contention, if not among the very leaders.

They were down to the last half dozen competitors when Bennett remarked, "So far we've had one of the safest first days ever for the Mimas venue—only a couple of minor spills and no serious injuries. What do you think accounts for our good fortune, Angus?"

"Nothing but luck, so far," Cavendish said. "If we're as well off after all three days of jumping are done, then we'll have something to brag about."

The dismissal irritated Bennett, but at that moment another jumper soared off the ramp. His annoyance instantly turned to excitement. "Look at that!" he exclaimed. "We'll have a new leader if Shukri al-Kuwatly lands safely!"

"He was a favorite, aye," Cavendish said, "but who would've thought he'd have a takeoff velocity of 103.81 kilometers an hour? That comes to a jump of over 11,580 meters, enough to put him in front by more than 40 meters. Watching his form, I own I didn't think he'd be off so strong."

Back at the top of the runway, a Muscovite in red and gold waited for the starting light. Rannveig said, "It has to be disheartening for Dmitri Shepilov to stand up there knowing what his predecessor has just done."

"I suspect he's been through worse," Bennett commented, reading from Shepilov's data sheet. "He comes from a guards regiment of Muscovite ski troops, and he saw combat against the Siberians in the Ural skirmishes a couple of years ago. After that, a ski jump should be small potatoes."

"I wonder," Angus Cavendish said with a grin. "Then it was only the eye of his sergeant on him, not the whole of Earth and Luna."

Shepilov's speed down the ramp was slower than al-Kuwatly's at every checkpoint, but still respectable. He launched himself at just over a hundred kilometers an hour, a jump that projected out close to an even eleven kilometers.

Coverage of the next athlete, a man from United Europe, was brief; attention switched away to al-Kuwatly, who was heading down toward his landing. "I don't look for any trouble from him," Cavendish said. "He's still half a kilometer up, almost two minutes away from putting his skis to the ice, but already he's in good position, as he should be. Nothing'll go wrong here."

The slow-motion shots of what happened next would be replayed endlessly. Seeing everything live, Bennett was chiefly conscious of how fast sportcasting banality turned to horror. He had actually been laughing at Cavendish, for no sooner were the Scotsman's words out of his mouth than they were all watching al-Kuwatly's hands open and his ski poles drift away.

Everyone in the studio stared in consternation at the sudden misty globe around al-Kuwatly's head, the rime forming on his faceplate and the sides of his helmet. "His suit's failed!" Rannveig cried, a split second ahead of Bennett and Cavendish.

They could do nothing but watch. Had it been he up there, Bennett knew he would have been thrashing wildly, clawing at his helmet to try somehow to maintain the pressure. But the jumper from the Arab World held the posture he had been in at the moment of disaster. Only very slowly did his bent arms begin to straighten and slump to his sides.

As a veteran spacer, Cavendish was the first to recognize what that meant. "Murder!" he shouted. "That's a killed man up there, else he'd be making shift to save himself." He might have been reading Bennett's mind, but he generalized where the younger broadcaster had not.

Al-Kuwatly's flight path did not, could not change. Trailing vapor, he plunged toward the landing slope. He hit the ice like a thrown cloth doll, then bounced and tumbled bonelessly. If he had not been dead already, the impact would have killed him.

Sickened, Bennett turned away from the big monitor screen behind the broadcasters. As a result, he was the only one of them looking at the bank of screens to one side that showed what all the active cameras were picking up. He saw Dmitri Shepilov raise his right arm; it looked as if the Muscovite was starting to point. Then vapor spouted from his helmet, too. "Shepilov's hit!" he cried.

No one had paid any attention to Louis-Philippe Guizot, the jumper who came after the Muscovite. Perhaps because he was from United Europe, Bennett's yell made Rannveig check another of the side screens for his safety. Guizot was only a few hundred meters from the takeoff ramp when his image was also shrouded by fog. "On, no!" Rannveig cried, and covered her face with her hands.

Bennett learned to hate Mimas' low gravity. Shepilov had been near the apex of his jump when he was hit; he flew on, a corpse, for five dreadful minutes before crashing on the landing slope as al-Kuwatly had before him. It was even worse with Louis-Philippe Guizot. Propelled by the leap he had taken before the assassin struck, he soared above Mimas as if still alive, then spun down in a hideously lazy descent.

"This is madness!" Bennett said. "Who but a madman could think to mar the Olympic Games with violence? Even in wartorn ancient Greece, the Olympic truce held good; the modern games have been the victim of attack only twice, and the last time was more than a hundred years ago."

The director spoke in his ear. His voice went hard as he relayed the news to his distant audience: "We have just received a radio transmission claiming responsibility for the atrocity that has taken place here today. Here is a recording of that transmission."

The tape was scratchy; the transmitter must have been a tiny one, and Saturn's radio emission chopped up the signal. But it was perfectly understandable. "As it is the Olympic language this year, I shall speak French," a man's voice said. It had a faint guttural accent and was full of irony and a good humor that chilled Bennett. "Shukri al-Kuwatly was but the beginning. We of the Second Irgun vow to continue our war against Arab tyranny until the Star of David once more flies above Israel. We regret the need to harm others, but those who share pleasures with oppressors must also share their fate. A very good day to you all.''

The voice cut off, leaving behind only the impersonal hisses and pops of background noise.

The director cued Bennett through the earphone: ''Three, two, one—all right, you're on.'' The light above the camera lens turned red.

''Welcome once again to the Mimas venue of the sixty-sixth Winter Games,'' he said. ''Competition, of course, has been suspended after yesterday's tragic events. When and if it will resume remains unknown; that largely depends on whether the cold-blooded killer who so callously took the lives of three athletes can be detected and apprehended. For any of you who may not have been with us yesterday, here is Rannveig Aasen with a review of what took place.''

''Thank you, Bill,'' she said gravely. She summarized the previous day's jumps. Behind her, the big monitor screen reran in quick succession the deaths of al-Kuwatly, Shepilov, and Guizot. Rannveig said, ''Examination of the bodies has shown that each of the three athletes was murdered by a burst from a high-powered laser weapon. They were killed instantly; none, of course, had any chance to defend himself.''

''How could such a thing happen?'' Bennett said. ''As we noted before, security is supposed to have been tight. With us now is Major Katayama Hitoshi, head of Mimas security. Come join us, Major Katayama.''

Moving smoothly in the low gravity, the security chief came over and sat down by the two broadcasters, then strapped himself in. ''Thank you for being with us at this difficult time. Tell, me, if you will, where did your precautions break down?''

Katayama grimaced, not caring for the blunt question. He was a stout, hard-faced man with iron-gray hair. After a moment's thought, he said, ''I am afraid this will seem self-serving, but much of the failure took place on Earth, when a killer was allowed to board a ship for Mimas. Once that happened, his or her success was probably inevitable.''

''How can you say that?'' Rannveig challenged. ''Surely you searched everyone's baggage for arms of all sorts. I know mine was opened, and Bill's, too.''

''Yes, that is so,'' Katayama said. He spoke slowly; he was very tired but was still picking his words with care. ''Explosive guns and missile weapons are easy to detect. With lasers, sadly, the same is not the case. Laser tubes are too ubiquitous. They are at the heart of your stereovision equipment, of still-picture holocameras, of computers' scanning devices, and in dozens of other everyday tools. Skilled terrorists find it all too simple to improvise deadly weapons. It is an unfortunate fact of life.''

"Even so," Rannveig persisted, "why didn't your force of guards keep the assassin from reaching cover, or track him down after he did his work?"

"Let me point something out, Ms. Aasen," Katayama said coolly. Rannveig bridled, but he went on before she could interrupt: "I have twenty men here. As your colleague Mr. Angus Cavendish pointed out on an earlier broadcast, at the peak of a jump an athlete can see for thirty-five kilometers, which means he can be seen and shot at from that distance. The area of a circle with a radius of 35 kilometers is more than 3,800 square kilometers, or about 190 square kilometers per guard. I hope you see my difficulty."

Off-camera, Bennett winced. Katayama was not an easy man to shake. The broadcaster had no intention of giving up without a fight, though. He asked, "Have you had any luck with photos from the observation satellite in synchronous orbit above Arthur?"

"A very intelligent question, sir." The security chief nodded. "Unfortunately, the answer is no. We were in dark phase at the time of the attack, with the only light outside the area of competition coming from Saturn's other moons. They are either small or distant or both, and in any case received only a bit more than one percent of the sunlight per unit area than Luna does. And exactly because it is in synchronous orbit, the satellite is over six hundred kilometers above us. Perhaps computer processing of its images will show more. That is our best hope, I think."

Bennett gave up. Katayama seemed to have all the answers, and a depressing lot they were. Rannveig, however, was still smarting from the rebuff she had taken. She said, "Forgive me for one last question. Why didn't any of your guards spot the flash of the laser when it was fired?"

The security chief's smile was like a shark's. "In vacuum, of course, there is no flash," he said, as if to a foolish child. "We only see beams of light because they shine through dust and vapor floating in air. I wish it were otherwise, but it is not."

"Thank you, Major Katayama," Bennett said quickly. "We'll be back with more after these messages."

As the commercials began, Katayama departed, looking pleased with himself. Rannveig shook her head in disgust. "Well, he put me away, didn't he? That's what I get for forgetting my homework."

Bennett touched her hand. "Don't worry about it. It's the same question almost everybody on Earth would have been asking himself."

"Do you think so?" she said doubtfully, but she looked a little happier.

When they returned to the air, they replayed the tape claiming responsibility for the attack. "For the reaction of the Second Irgun, IBC correspondent Jorge Martinez visited the group's headquarters in Buenos Aires," Bennett said. "Here is his report."

The tape filled the monitor screen. Along with a flock of other reporters, Martinez was standing in front of a gray stone building in a run-down part of the city. Out came a slight, curly-haired man with a mustache too big for his face and fierce, ever-watchful eyes. "The Second Irgun's spokesman is known only as 'Menachem,' " Martinez said quietly.

They watched "Menachem" begin to read from a card he pulled out of his hip pocket: "We applaud the blow against the Arabs who have stolen our homeland from us, but we did not strike it. That is all we have to say."

"What proof do you have for your denial?" one of the reporters shouted.

"Menachem" fixed him with an icy glare. "I have said that is all we have to say." Then, with the air of a man making a great concession, he went on, "Had it been us, we would have chosen Itzhak Zalman, the *apikoros* who loves his masters better than his people and joined the Arab team. His time may yet come, if not on Mimas, then when he returns." He went back into the headquarters building, slamming the door behind him.

"Not the most convincing denial on record," Rannveig commented.

"Hardly," Bennett said. "The only thing to say in its behalf is that the Second Irgun is not in the habit of ducking the blame for its terrorist acts. The notorious Baghdad bombings of a few years ago are a case in point."

"If not the Second Irgun, though, who benefits from the killings? Savage as they were, they have succeeded in embarrassing the Arab World, thanks to the disclosure of Shukri al-Kuwatly's illegal suit."

"There you're right, Rannveig," Bennett said. "Cheating is almost as old as the Olympics, I'm afraid; drug use and such things as electronically rigged fencing foils go back to the twentieth century. Al-Kuwatly's suit is just the latest in a long line, and one of the more ingenious. It was discovered to have a gas vent opening in the small of his back—in effect, a small reaction motor to add to his speed down the runway. With a surface gravity as low as Mimas', even a few extra centimeters per second could have been decisive."

"Yes; al-Kuwatly would have been the leader at the end of the first day of competition," Rannveig said.

"In the rash of speculation surrounding him, however, we shouldn't lose sight of the other two athletes who were slain. Our sincerest condolences go to the families and friends of Dmitri Shepilov and Louis-Philippe Guizot, who also fell victim in this savage attack."

"As happens all too often in acts of terrorism, it is the innocent who suffer," Rannveig agreed. "That's true not only of the men who died yesterday but also, in a lesser way, of all the athletes who came to Mimas in hopes of victory and instead find themselves encompassed by tragedy. For the competitors' reaction to yesterday's events, let's go to Angus Cavendish."

"Thank you, Rannveig." The Scotsman was sitting at the Olympic village bar. "With me here is Itzhak Zalman, the Arab World jumper who, as you heard, has been threatened by the Second Irgun." Also with them, unmentioned but plainly visible, was one of Major Katayama's security guards, a sidearm on her hip. Cavendish said, "Tell me, Itzhak, what are your thoughts on the menacing statement read by Menachem?"

Zalman, ironically, looked rather like a younger version of the terrorist leader, but his face was more open, calmer. He spread his hands. "I'd sooner accept the present as it is than live in the dead past. I've been threatened before. You can't let it worry you or it'll affect your performance."

"Spoken like a true competitor," Cavendish said. "Let me ask this, then: how do you feel about what your teammate al-Kuwatly had done to his suit?"

"He was a fool," Zalman said flatly. "I knew nothing about that, and I can still hardly believe it. My own jumping suit conforms to every standard. What good is a medal you've cheated to win?"

"Aye, that's a poser, though there's some who don't care, I'm sorry to say. Am I right in thinking you're doing your best to stay in condition during the delay in the jumping?"

"Oh, of course. I can't go out on the ramp, naturally, but I'm doing both stretching and weight work. The weight rooms have been packed."

"What's the atmosphere there?"

"About what you'd expect—nervous. After all, none of us knows whether the person working out beside him is a killer." Zalman thought for a moment, amended his last statement: "No—*one* of us does."

"You've put your finger on the true calamity of these games," Cavendish said. "Olympics may have been disrupted before this, but never by people connected with them. Thanks for joining us, Itzhak, and best of luck when the competition resumes."

Zalman nodded soberly. "I will take all the luck I can find, thank you. Being who I am, I need it." He bounced away.

Cavendish said, "We'd hoped to have a member of the team from Moscow with us, but they've all declined to speak on camera. Joining us instead is Nikolai Yezhov of Siberia. Welcome, and thank you for being with us today."

"My pleasure." Yezhov's French had less of an accent than Cavendish's. Short, stocky, and solid, he looked formidable in his spotless white tunic with the cross of Saint George on an embroidered patch on his left shoulder.

"Did ye know Shepilov well?" Cavendish asked.

"Not very, I'm afraid." Aristocratic contempt showed briefly in the Siberian eyes. "The Muscovites always stick close to themselves. Not cultured."

"Er, yes." Cavendish changed the subject in a hurry; from a Russian-speaker, "not cultured" was the kind of insult that started fights. The Scotsman said, "What reaction have ye noticed among the athletes to word of al-Kuwatly's suit?"

Yezhov's smile seemed genuinely amused. "The only sin is to be found out, is it not?"

Every question Cavendish asked was getting him into trouble. Gamely, he tried again after a glance at Yezhov's fact sheet. "This is your first time off Earth, nay?"

"Oh, certainly. I was a simple stereovision installer in Kolyma, by the Sea of Okhotsk, a weekend skier, I think the saying is, when the Little Father honored me by including me on this year's team."

"Aye, just as ye say, 'a weekend skier.'" Cavendish finally let himself smile. The czar's recruiting and training methods were notoriously effective, and started at about age six. "A coincidence, then, that you took the Siberian downhill championship four years ago and have held it ever since?"

Yezhov's expression was bland. "Yes, as a matter of fact, or at least my first win. The favored skier broke his leg in a fall, opening the door for me."

"How lucky for you." Cavendish sighed. Despite his best efforts, Yezhov remained opaque. He might claim greater sophistication than his Muscovite counterparts, but he was no more forthcoming. Cavendish thanked him again for appearing, then passed the show back to the studio with obvious relief.

Rannveig handled the sign-off. "We'll be returning you to your regular programming now," she said. "Stay tuned to this station for developments as they break. When and if competition resumes, of course, you'll see all of it here." The monitor cut to a commercial.

Glancing at it, Bennett said, "Meanwhile, our advertisers are out slitting throats because they just lost five hours of guaranteed high ratings."

"I wish Katayama had said more," Rannveig said, adding with a curl of her lip, "He was so busy pointing out how none of this was his fault that I think he hardly cares whether he ever catches up with the killer."

"If his precious satellite didn't show him anything, he's got damn-all to go on," Bennett said. "No wonder he's asked for copies of our tapes." He paused. "I wonder . . . think back to Shepilov. Didn't it seem to you that he'd spotted something in that split second before the laser got him?"

"What if he did? Our job is to report, not to investigate."

"There's still a bit of a different tradition left in the United States. I've never had much of a chance to go ferreting things out, but I think it would be interesting to try."

She shrugged. "If your idea of fun is trying to do the same thing the professionals are doing, don't let me stop you. But I expect I'll have a better time with Jozef than you will staring at tapes."

"You're probably right," Bennett admitted. Rannveig's expression said she was sure she was right. She detached her seat belt and bounded out of the studio. Faintly envious of her carefree attitude, Bennett made a copy of yesterday's event and fed it into a stereovision set.

In a way, watching death for the second, third, or twentieth time was harder than seeing it when it actually happened. There was always the dreadful, futile impulse to cry "Look out!"

Bennett sped through the murder of al-Kuwatly at fast forward; the athlete from the Arab World had never known he was in danger. Shepilov, though . . . Bennett got up, holding tight to the arm of his chair to keep from drifting to the ceiling. He studied the hologram from several angles, and became more convinced than ever that the Muscovite's arm motion had been deliberate.

And if it was—Bennett interfaced the stereovision set with the big IBC computer. It took several false starts before he got the machine to do what he wanted: to give him a printout showing what section of Mimas' surface Shepilov had been trying to point at.

The circle that came out shaded in the printout was north of the jumpers' flight path, much closer to the landing area than to the runway. Depressingly, it was also about two kilometers across. But Bennett did not stay depressed for long. Major Katayama had been grousing about trying to cover 3,800 square kilometers; Bennett only planned to examine a bit more than three.

He checked his spacesuit's systems with the caution of a neophyte, then cycled through an air lock and bounded down onto the surface of the moon. Looking about, he could almost have thought himself on Luna. Dirty ice looked very much like rock, and one set of jumbled craters much like another.

Yet there were differences, after all. Aside from the very low gravity, the sun, while still too bright to look at, was hardly more than an incandescent point in the sky. And one could never see several moons at once from Luna—not natural ones. Enceladus, Dione, Rhea, and orange Titan all showed visible disks, though none could compete with even the attenuated sun as a light source.

Remembering Angus Cavendish's comments on the jumpers' form on the runway, Bennett tried to stay as low to the ground as he could while he loped along. Even so, his motion was swift and almost dreamlike. He began to understand, however dimly, the feeling the athletes had as they soared into space.

The reporter steered by the inertial compass in his helmet. To his surprise, he saw people with lights moving about in the area he had decided to search. One of them saw him, too, and came bounding his way. A challenge rang in his earphones:

"Who the devil are you, and what are you doing snooping around here?"

"Bill Bennett, IBC," he replied, and added pointedly, "I might ask you the same question." But the words were hardly spoken when he saw that all the people he was approaching wore the robin's-egg blue spacesuits of Security.

"Bennett, eh?" The guard was close enough to peer through his faceplate. "So you are," she admitted, lowering her side arm. "I think you'd better come talk to Major Katayama."

The security chief greeted Bennett with a smile as chilly as Mimas' ice. "How did you find out where we were searching?" he demanded. "If one of my people has been blabbing, I'll send him out here without a suit."

Bennett explained his method. He saw Katayama relax slightly. The broadcaster tried to retake the offensive: "Suppose you tell me why you decided to look here."

"I don't have to tell you a damn thing," Katayama said. Bennett was aware of how true that was; it had been a good many years since what had once been called freedom of the press got more than lip service from officials. Public relations, though, still mattered. Katayama relented.

"Basically, we used a more sophisticated version of what you did," he said. "Once we had autopsy data, we could plot the trajectories of the beams that killed the three jumpers. This is where the lines came together. All the same, we still have a couple of square kilometers to go over."

Bennett hid his smile. The security chief's technique hadn't narrowed the area down much better than had his own. "Any luck so far?"

"We're still busy."

No, Bennett translated. "Do you mind if I join you?" he asked.

After a brief hesitation, the Security chief shook his head. "Suit yourself. You might be lucky; who knows?"

Katayama's people were working in pairs. One would leap twenty or thirty meters off the surface, shining a spotlight down onto the ice to light a large area for the other team member to examine. The spots were brighter than the feeble sun, and illuminated inky shadows that might otherwise have made perfect hiding places. The security personnel also carried metal detectors.

Without any such special gear, Bennett had to do the best he could using his helmet lamp and his eyes. He quickly learned not to look straight down; being mostly ice, Mimas reflected seventy percent of the light that struck it, more than enough to dazzle.

There were enough minerals in the ice to give the terrain some color beyond pure, cold blue-white. Some chunks—was that the word, Bennett wondered, or would "rocks" be better?—were grayish, others brown. The broadcaster nearly shouted for Katayama when he saw a rusty streak. But it had nothing to do with blood. It was only a tiny inclusion of iron ore, trapped for ages in the surrounding ice.

Bennett squatted to peer into a cave. He spied the edge of something green, hidden almost out of sight. He did not let excitement run away with him. Green beryllium compounds—emeralds, if you like—were a fairly common part of the stew of light elements from which Mimas had been made.

But if it was a crystal, it was very large and regular. Excitement shot through Bennett as he looked more closely—no crystal ever had writing on it!

He scrambled into the cave and reached down for it. The cold bit at his gauntlets, which were not as well insulated as his boots. He did not mind, though, not when he was holding an expended heavy-duty charge cube in his hands.

Then he keyed his suit radio, and Security personnel converged as if drawn by a magnet. They scoured the cave from one end to the other, and discovered two more of the plastic cubes, both better concealed than the one Bennett had found.

Katayama held out his hand for that one. Reluctantly, Bennett surrendered it. "It's one of the standard sizes," he said, "but not a type I know." He was looking at what were presumably instructions on the side of the cube. They were written in the Roman alphabet, but in no tongue he recognized. Whatever the language was, it went in for wild combinations of consonants.

"Made in Praha," the security chief said. He seemed more willing to be informative now that Bennett had done something useful for him. Seeing that the name meant nothing to the broadcaster, he actually unbent far enough to explain: "Prague, you would call it, I think."

"An Eastern European brand, then."

"Yes." Katayama fairly purred. "We have some interesting new questions to ask, wouldn't you say?"

"You certainly do. Shepilov must have seen the light leakage here when the killer fired at al-Kuwatly. Pity the cave roof kept the observation satellite from picking it up."

"Yes. Still, we make progress." Katayama put his people back on the search to see if there was anything else to be found. Bennett helped for a while, but lightning did not strike twice. He headed back toward the Olympic complex.

One disadvantage of spacesuits was the difficulty of getting out of earshot. Katayama's voice rang in his helmet as if the security chief were still standing beside him: "Don't use this until you get clearance from me. Do you understand?" When Bennett tried to ignore the order, Katayama snapped, "Acknowledge!"

"Acknowledged," the broadcaster said sulkily, but most of his pique had evaporated by the time he returned to the Olympic village. Katayama had not said anything about poking around on his own.

When he got back to the studio, he checked a list he already knew pretty well. It confirmed what his memory told him. Most of the Eastern European jumpers had had their turns toward the middle or end of the first day's run. They would not have had a lot of time to make any murderous preparations, and there would have been enough people about so that they could hardly have counted on not being noticed when they went to use an air lock.

He frowned. The conspicuous exception was Jozef Jablonski. Rannveig was not going to like hearing that. Unfortunately, she was probably going to, if not from Bennett, then from Katayama. If the broadcaster could follow his nose this far, so could the security chief.

As it happened, he got a chance to broach the subject when Rannveig came over to share a table with him at dinner. She bristled, just as he had known she would. He spread his hands placatingly. "I'm not telling you what I think, only what I found," he said, and wondered whether he was lying. "But we can both guess what Major Katayama will make of it. In his shoes, I'd do the same. Who else would use an obscure brand of charge cubes made in Prague but an Eastern European?"

"Someone trying to put the blame on one." Bennett made shushing motions; she had spoken so loudly that heads had turned.

He said, "Security men won't look at it like that; they shave with Occam's razor. Do you know what your, ah, friend did after he jumped? Does it leave him in the clear?"

"No," she said, her voice low now, and troubled. "He told me he went back to his room and fell asleep. He was laughing at me; he said I'd kept him awake too long the night before."

"Not good."

"No," Rannveig said again. Bennett could see her wondering. She had, after all, met Jablonski only the other day. But then she shook her head, as if coming to a decision. "I can't believe it. He's just too—open—to kill from ambush. And what about the tape from the Second Irgun?"

"They denied it," he reminded her. "That's not like them; usually they're only too happy to take credit for their outrages."

"But why would Jozef want to kill any of the men who were shot?" she demanded. "What's the point? What would it gain him?"

"What would it gain anyone?" he asked. Neither of them could find a answer.

Bennett did not tell anyone but Rannveig about the find north of the jumpers' flight path, and he had no reason to think she had noised it about. Nevertheless, rumors of all sorts raced through the Olympic village overnight. At breakfast Bennett heard claims that three different people had been arrested; one of them was drinking a bulb of coffee not three meters from him at the time.

He also heard that Jozef Jablonski was a secret Jew, which probably would have infuriated the skier from Gdynia; that the assassin was a renegade *ronin* from Japan (now there was a delightful prospect, he thought); that Moscow was about to declare war on Siberia or the Arab World or Eastern Europe or the Chinese Empire—which it did not border. But then, Moscow was always about to declare war on someone.

Brachiating back to the studio, Bennett almost ran into Itzhak Zalman. As they both slowed to avoid the collision, the jumper winked and said, "So tell me, have I been elected Pope in there yet?"

"Twice," Bennett said solemnly. As the athlete burst out laughing, he added, "Some of them also have you as a member of the Second Irgun, with Menachem's threat part of your masquerade." He thought he saw Zalman's amusement slip for a moment, then told himself he was letting his suspicions run away with him. Pretty soon he wouldn't be able to look in a mirror and trust the face he saw.

How much the rumors about arrests were worth was proved when the second round of jumping was canceled again. The program that went back to Earth was correspondingly short. Because Bennett had been muzzled, there was next to nothing to say beyond repeating as many variants on "The investigation continues" as a skilled team of scriptwriters could concoct.

"Well, there's the easiest day of work I've had in a while," Angus Cavendish said when the shortened broadcast was over. "I think I'll check out a suit and do a bit of walking about. I haven't had the chance to play sleuth like you, Bill."

"Where did you hear about that?"

The Scotsman laid a finger by the side of his nose. "A wee birdie told me."

"A birdie in a Security suit?" That was Rannveig.

"However you please." Cavendish grinned. "Come with me, if you care to, and share the glory when we find the kern to blame for all this."

"Thank you, but no. Whatever Bill may fancy himself as, I'm no detective."

Cavendish turned to Bennett. "Are you game, Sherlock?"

"Why not? I'm at loose ends."

"Good. Nothing like a few brisk laps around the village to get the blood going."

Bennett tried to swallow a groan. That meant Angus was going to run the legs off him. The Scotsman was older, but he was also in better shape, more used to spacesuits, and had his bronze medal to prove himself a master at effective motion on Mimas. Rannveig, curse her, was giggling as she left the studio. The only exercise she was likely to get was more fun than anything you could do in a suit.

"Twenty-five laps suit ye?" Cavendish asked when they were outside. When they were by themselves, they spoke English, but his burr was still strong.

"Whatever you say," Bennett answered.

"Shall we be off, then?" The Scotsman bounded away. Bennett followed. Cavendish held back to let him stay close. "Don't forget to kick up your oxygen flow," he warned. "Remember, you're working hard."

"I know," Bennett said. His breath was loud in his helmet; he would be panting soon. Cavendish's breathing sounded perfectly even in his earphones. He gritted his teeth and tried to keep up, but he kept bounding too high off Mimas and metaphorically spinning his wheels while he waited to descend.

The view on the far side of the Olympic village showed the moon as it had been for billions of years before men had come to it: a giant lump of ice, much bombarded by cosmic debris in its early days. The far side of the village looked much like the near, although it had nothing to match the big view window in the bar and although most of the air locks led out toward the competition site. Bennett hardly glanced at the enormous, boxy structure as he puffed along behind Cavendish.

The Scotsman had gone around a good many times himself before he grunted. "What a queer thing that is," and did his best to come to a quick stop—not easy with the velocity he had to shed. Still, he did better than his companion, who stumbled to a halt a quarter of a kilometer beyond him.

"What's the matter, pull a muscle?" Bennett asked. That would be funny, to have Cavendish's athletic body let him down.

But the Scotsman answered, "Nay, lad, nay," and pointed at the side of the building. Following his finger, Bennett saw a ring of frost high on the wall.

He wondered if it indicated a problem, but laughed at himself for the thought. "It's probably been there since the village was built," he said.

"No," Cavendish said at once, "because I didn't see it when I was here as a jumper. I made the laps then, same as we're doing now."

"That's crazy. Nothing ever changes in vacuum. Are you sure you haven't just forgotten?"

"I am." Cavendish sounded so positive, Bennett had to believe him. "Bloody odd, I call it." With a shrug, he resumed his interrupted exercise. He shook his head the next several times the two of them bounded by the curious patch.

By the time they went back in to clean up, though, he seemed to have stopped worrying about it. Bennett, on the other had, was still chewing on it as he stepped out of the shower cubicle in his quarters. That was a piece of plumbing that had required less adaptation to Mimas' conditions than he would have expected, though a stream of warm air, not gravity, kept the water moving.

Naturally, the phone chimed while he was drying himself. In his annoyance, he forgot to cancel the video feed. Rannveig nodded appreciatively. "As good as I remembered."

More pleased than embarrassed, he draped himself in his towel. "What's going on?" he asked, adding, "I thought you'd be with Jablonski."

"He's being questioned," she said bleakly.

"Oh. I'm sorry."

"So am I. I still think he's innocent, but there's evidence that points at him and none leading anywhere else, so what choice does Katayama have? I don't blame you for finding the charge cubes, or anything childish like that. And that reminds me—you really are turning into a first-class troublemaker, aren't you?''

"Am I? How?"

"Itzhak Zalman's asked for political asylum."

"He has? My God, with whom? Why?"

"With the Chinese, of all people; I think the Chinese coach must have been the first person he saw after he decided his cover was no good any more.''

"His cover?" Bennett floundered.

Rannveig gave him an incredulous look. "You mean you don't even know? He panicked when you told him there was a rumor about him being a member of the Second Irgun—because it happens he *is* a member of the Second Irgun."

"I will be damned," Bennett said. That had never occurred to him. "I suppose Katayama's grilling him, too."

"He'd like to, but the Chinese coach hasn't let Zalman out of her suite; she's up on her hind legs over diplomatic immunity."

"That won't last, not in the face of murder," Bennett predicted. He could understand the Chinese coach's worry, though; no quarter was given on either side in the clandestine war between the Arab World and the exiled Israeli nationalists.

Bennett dressed, then called Katayama. The security chief came on the line after a delay of a few minutes. His face was impassive, but there was something like warmth in his voice, and the fact that he was talking to Bennett in person showed how the broadcaster's stock had risen. "Well, Mr. Bennett, you've helped me twice now. What can I do for you?"

"What's the story with Itzhak Zalman?"

Katayama's smile touched only his lips. "News travels quickly, I see. We have a recording in which he states he planned no violence, only a loss of face for the Arab World upon the disclosure of its slipshod security procedures. The value of this statement, of course, remains problematical. We would like to interrogate him in greater detail, but, ah—"

"I've heard." Bennett nodded. "What about Jablonski?"

"About what you would expect. He denies any knowledge of the killings, says he was alone, asleep, and that if he were guilty he would have a better alibi." A slight lift of one eyebrow showed how often Katayama had run into that sort of infinitely regressing logic.

Bennett thanked him and let him go; no point in using up his store of goodwill by keeping the Security chief away from his job for half an hour. There had been something else the broad-caster had been thinking of doing when Rannveig's call drove it out of his head. He snapped his fingers in annoyance, trying to remember.

He was on the point of giving up when it came back to him. He punched the chief maintenance engineer's number.

He did not get the head of the engineering department; that worthy had no reason to drop what she was doing on account of his call. The assistant he talked to was a blond young man whose Anzac-flavored English was amusingly different from Cavendish's. He described the frost he and the Scotsman had seen.

"We'll check it out, mate, never fear. Don't get browned off," the engineer said cheerily.

"What was that?" Bennett snapped, sensitive to anything that sounded like a racial slur. Then he recognized the idiom. "Never mind," he said lamely. "Would you call me back when you find out what it was?"

"Will do, mate. G'day to you." The screen went dead.

Having done everything he could think of, Bennett settled down to wait for the return call. He checked the computer for a listing of entertainment programs and found on one of the stereovision channels a docudrama he hadn't seen.

The show was based on the works of a great twentieth-century author, and harrowingly realistic. Characters got killed off one after another; even the hero ended up in a cancer ward. The blizzards made Bennett feel colder than anything on Mimas had.

He jumped at the chime of the phone. Switching off the stereovision was something of a relief. The Anzac engineer looked out of the screen at him. "Thanks for the call, mate. Bloody funny thing, that," he said, unconsciously echoing Cavendish.

"Is it dangerous?" Bennett asked. "That's what I was worried about."

"Shouldn't be. Can't cipher out how the hell it got there, though—it would've taken enough outgassing to suck all the air from a set of rooms, but we've had no exploding guests, for which I'm bloody grateful, I can tell you."

"Whose rooms would it have been?"

"I'll have to check, mate. Let me feed the outside wall coordinates into the computer . . ." He turned away and fiddled with a keyboard for a minute or two. "Here we go," he said, and gave Bennett the name.

"Thanks," said the broadcaster; he had to stop himself from adding the Anzac's infectious "mate." He broke the connection and went back to the stereovision docudrama with the nagging feeling he was missing something, maybe something important.

"There!" He could have kissed the ugly, unshaven *zek* on the stereovision screen. He broke a fingernail punching Katayama's phone code. The woman he talked to had been one of the Security people closest to him when he found the expended charge cube; she smiled and went to fetch her chief without any argument.

This time Katayama took longer to come to the phone. When he finally did, he growled, "No matter what you think, Mr. Bennett, I am not at your beck and call. I am trying to do an important job, and your interference does not help. Now, and quickly, what is it?"

"I beg your pardon," Bennett said sincerely, "but I wonder if you might answer me one question."

The Security chief heard him out. "Yes, of course that's still true," he said, as if surprised anyone needed to ask. "I suspect it will be true two hundred fifty years from now, too; some things don't change. Now, I wonder if you'd tell me what possible importance there is to that." He framed the last sentence as a request, but it came out a command.

Bennett explained. As he did, he half expected his jerry-built structure of logic and wild guesses to come crashing down on his head and leave him looking like an idiot. Katayama listened in silence, not showing what he was thinking.

When Bennett had finished, the security chief ran a hand through his hair. "I take it you write thriller plots?" he said at last.

"No." Below the camera's angle of vision, Bennett clenched his fists. This was what he had set himself up for, trying to help . . .

But Katayama was saying, "I can find out quickly whether or not you are right—no small virtue, in my line of work."

"Will you call me back?" the broadcaster asked tensely. He knew he had had to do as he did, but he hated the idea of being excluded as soon as things came to a head. He still had too much of the old American reporter's itch to be in on the action instead of just talking about it.

Katayama, on the other hand, had no use for reporters unless they served his own purposes. "I make no promises, Mr. Bennett," he said, and hung up.

In .008g it was impossible to pace, but bouncing off the walls, floor, and ceiling, as Rannveig had in the studio, was not the worst way to get rid of tension. Bennett had worked up a good sweat by the time the phone chimed again. "Hello?" he panted.

His disheveled appearance managed to wring a blink out of Katayama. "What have you been doing?" the Security chief asked, then said at once, "Never mind; I am not interested in knowing. I have called to tell you what you are going to do. Listen carefully."

Bennett and Rannveig took their places in the IBC studio. When the red light on the camera flashed on, Bennett began, "A very pleasant good day to you out there, wherever you may be. There have been a number of important developments since we spoke with you last."

"That's right, Bill," Rannveig said. "We expect this to be the last day of shortened coverage of the games. The jumping should resume tomorrow."

"The arrest of Jozef Jablonski has lifted a great burden of fear from everyone's shoulders," Bennett agreed. Rannveig nodded, a little glumly; Bennett went on, "The evidence against Jablonski is overwhelming. The site from which the killer fired from ambush has been discovered, and the discarded charge cubes found there were manufactured in Eastern Europe. It is most unlikely that anyone from another country would have had such an obscure brand in his or her possession."

"Moreover, Jablonski cannot account for his whereabouts at the time of the murders," Rannveig said. "He is currently being subjected to intensive interrogation, and his confession is expected shortly by Major Katayama."

Bennett said, "As you can imagine, ladies and gentlemen, the people most relieved are the athletes themselves. For some of their reaction, let's go to Angus Cavendish."

"Thank you, Bill," the Scotsman said. As before, he was sitting at the bar—*getting to be quite a fixture there*, Bennett thought. Almost everybody there was watching the stereovision set in a corner of the room, and thus at the moment watching themselves watching themselves. For any news more reliable than rumor, they depended on the IBC broadcasts as much as Earth did.

Cavendish alluded to that point: "I'd think almost all the athletes on Mimas are tuned to us now. Along with the set here, there's another in the weight room, and of course in all the suites."

"Who's that with you, Angus?" Rannveig said.

"Marge Olbert, the first-round women's leader. Tell me, Mademoiselle Olbert, what are your feelings now that an arrest has been made?"

"I am, how does one say it, full of relief," she replied in halting French.

"Eager to jump again, are you?"

"But yes, naturally, and I hope to do well, it could be to win a medal." Her sudden and unexpected smile transformed a rather plain face into a pretty one. "And if I do, at the least they will know what flag to fly for me when I am on the platform of the winners. For Monsieur Zalman this is not true, is it not so?"

"An interesting point you bring up, lass." Cavendish had the minutiae at his fingertips. "As a matter of fact, there is a precedent. In the Summer Games of 2104 a woman from the United States defected to Indonesia after the first two events of the modern pentathlon. She won a silver, and took it under Indonesian colors."

"Ah." Marge Olbert hesitated, then went on. "I only hope they have arrested the right man. This Second Irgun, it is supposed to be very bad, no? If somehow there is a mistake, that would not be good."

"There's confidence Itzhak Zalman had naught to do with the killings," Cavendish said. "Even if there weren't, he's been too closely guarded for his own protection to let him go off doing mischief."

"I hope you are right," the Anzac jumper replied. She left, and Cavendish interviewed several other athletes. They were all of them polite, but none said a great deal.

"That's one of the abiding problems of sports journalism," Rannveig said when the show came back to the IBC studio. "The clichés were invented in the twentieth century, and they've been repeated ever since."

"Perhaps we can get a fresher perspective from a competitor with a different background," Bennett said. He made the call he had set up the night before. "Thank you for joining us again, Monsieur Yezhov."

The Siberian dipped his head in a courtly gesture of acknowledgment. "Not at all," he said, his French excellent as usual.

"Would you care to give us your reaction to the arrest of Jozef Jablonski?"

"I was, to be frank, surprised: he seemed a very decent fellow, though I did not know him well." Yezhov paused, considering his next words. "But if he is truly the one who perpetrated these abominable deeds, then I am glad to see him in custody. I look forward to the recommencement of the games.''

Bennett's heart was pounding in the effort to stay natural. ''Are you—'' he began, then broke off at the sound of a knock on the outer door of Yezhov's suite.

''I shall ignore that,'' the Siberian said politely.

''No need,'' Bennett assured him. ''We don't want to inconvenience you when you are kind enough to talk with us; we'll cut away and then come back to you when you're finished. If your visitor's business isn't too personal, though, perhaps you might leave the vision link open with us while you turn down the sound so we can tell when you're coming back.''

''A capital idea. I shall do as you suggest.''

Yezhov reached out for the volume toggle, then turned his back on the phone camera and glided toward the door. Instead of going to a commercial or a taped segment, though, the director kept the Siberian's image in the big screen behind Bennett and Rannveig.

''Welcome to those watching all over Earth,'' Rannveig said quickly. ''We apologize for starting our coverage late, but—''

At that moment, the Siberian touched the door control switch. The door slid open. A security guard thrust a pistol in Yezhov's face. Half a dozen more, including Major Katayama, rocketed past him into his suite. One doubled back to wrench the Siberian's hands behind him and clap manacles on him; the rest began tearing the place apart. Somehow the impact of everything was greater because on the screen it all took place in silence.

''—at this moment you are watching the capture of Nikolai Semyonovich Yezhov, the assassin whose crime has marred these Winter Games.'' Rannveig went on, ''I'm proud to say that my colleague here at the IBC sports desk, Bill Bennett, played a key role in Yezhov's arrest. How did that happen, Bill?''

''Let's wait a moment before going on with the details, Rannveig,'' he said. Modesty was not what held him back; far from it. He felt full to bursting with triumph. But the story came first. ''Here's our camera crew arriving at Yezhov's door. Let's watch as the security patrol searches the suite.''

The picture on the screen behind the broadcaster shifted from the view out of Yezhov's phone to one from the IBC crew. One of the Security women tore down a rug on the far wall of the suite to reveal a circular scar, two meters wide, cut in the metal and ceramic and inelegantly patched.

''There you see how the killer avoided being spotted or per-

haps even being captured at an airlock when he returned to the
Olympic village after he had committed his three murders. He
did not use the locks either to leave or enter the village complex. Instead, he cut his way out of the building with a laser
torch, undoubtedly the same one he used to kill Shukri al-
Kuwatly, Dmitri Shepilov, and Louis-Philippe Guizot. Once he
had the opening cut out, he simply jumped to the ice below and
went to his ambush point.''

"Of course.'' Rannveig nodded. "A fall of forty meters here
is nothing, the same as less than a half a meter on Earth.''

"That's right, and the return jump is the same—easy for anyone in Yezhov's excellent condition. To go without being noticed, all he had to do was close the door to his suite; like all
doors here, it's gastight, so there would have been no pressure
drop outside his rooms to give him away. Afterward, sealing
compound let him repair the damage he'd done, as we can see
now.''

"Where did he go wrong, then?''

"Over something he had no way to hide. Some of the water
vapor and CO_2 that escaped from his suite condensed against
the side of the building. The slab he'd cut out was free of the
crystals—once replaced, it looked like a bull's-eye. But it was
on the side of the village away from the jumping, where hardly
anyone ever goes. And even it they did, they'd think the deposit
of ice had been there forever. Angus Cavendish knew better,
though.''

"I suppose he was also aided by Siberia's national colors,''
Rannveig said, thinking fast on her feet. "His white spacesuit
would have made him hard to spot both on the ground and from
the observation satellite.''

"Yes.''

While they talked in the studio, the Security team was examining the case of the stereovision set in Yezhov's room. The
IBC camera crew caught a technician's exclamation: "There's
tampering here, no doubt about it.''

"Take it to the lab,'' someone else said. "If there's more
inside, we'll have nailed down where he got his laser tube.''

"Yezhov said he installed stereovisions in, where was it, Kolyma,'' Rannveig remembered.

"Unh-hunh,'' Bennett said. "That was something else that
should have made us take a hard look at him, but didn't.''

"Why should it have?'' Rannveig asked. The question was
not just for the audience but for herself. Bennett simply had not

had time to explain everything to her, although she was coming through like a trouper.

He said, "Kolyma was one of the biggest slave-labor camps in the days of the old Soviet Union. From what I've been able to learn, that's still true in czarist Siberia—and slaves need guards." Both Siberia and Moscow, he felt sure, would censor this part of the broadcast, but the rest of the world needed to know. He would never have found out himself if he had not seen the show about Aleksandr Solzhenitsyn the day before.

On the screen behind the broadcasters, Nikolai Yezhov directed an ironic bow toward Major Katayama, his head being the only part of him still free to move. "My compliments," he said with as much aplomb as if they had met at a banquet rather than as killer and captor. "I take it the announcement of Jablonski's arrest was for my benefit and not sent on to Earth?"

Katayama nodded brusquely. "You admit this, then?"

"My dear sir, at this stage of affairs, what good would it do me to deny it?"

The security chief grunted. "Not much. Do you have anything to say before we deal with you?"

"May I request a lawyer?" Both Yezhov and Katayama smiled at that; the world was a harder place than it had been a couple of hundred years before. Having been caught, the Siberian could not expect to live long.

"Get on with it," Katayama told him.

"Yes. How should I put it? Perhaps that I chose to strike a blow for Holy Mother Russia against the godless Marxists who still disgrace us all by holding Moscow. We in Siberia have cast them down; even China and Eastern Europe overthrew their ilk years ago. I do not care if peace was sworn; between us and them there can be no peace."

That led inevitably to Katayama's next question: "If your fight was with Moscow, why did you also kill the other two, and why cover your tracks?"

Now Yezhov looked at the Security chief as at any fool. "To avoid embarrassing my country, of course. Too many people in the world would not understand how honor compelled me to act as I did."

At last something angered Katayama. When he answered, Bennett could hear in his words the revived tradition of *bushido* that had gone with Japan's emergence as a military as well as an economic power in the late twenty-first century. "There is no honor in shooting men from ambush," he said implacably.

He turned to the Security people who held the Siberian, snapping, "Get him out of here."

The camera crew followed them down the corridor and almost ran into the coach of the Siberian team, who came swinging from one ceiling handhold to the next like a desperate ape. When he spotted the camera, he almost threw himself in front of it. He started speaking in Russian, a true measure of how upset he was.

He checked himself after half a sentence and began again in French: "I must say, on behalf of Siberia and the czar, that what Nikolai Yezhov has done is the act of a solitary madman. I condemn him as strongly as any man alive; my heart goes out to the dear ones of the men—*all* the men—whose deaths he caused. Our Russian brothers of the People's Republic of Moscow must know the firmness of the treaty of Sverdlovsk—"

He went on for some time. After a while he began repeating himself, but the director did not cut him off. The chance that his apology might be heading off a war was too real to disregard, and the urgency behind that apology made for incomparably dramatic stereovision.

The Siberian coach finally finished and departed to give his condolences to his Muscovite opposite number, his head still hanging in shame. The director's finger stabbed toward Rannveig; the camera in the studio swung her way.

She said, "Once again the specter of nationalism has wounded the Olympic Games, the games that should be the chief symbol of cooperation between nations. Nation-states have existed for more than six hundred years now. If they haven't yet learned to live together in that time, will they ever?"

"I think that may be too dim a view, Rannveig," Bennett said. "Your own United Europe is a case in point, and Eastern Europe, and the Arab World. Step by step, we make progress."

"But will it be enough?"

He shrugged. "The only answer is that we're here. We haven't managed to blow ourselves up, quite. And tomorrow, in spite of everything, the Games begin again. That's worth remembering, you know."

"Cut," the director said.

This one is a thought experiment. If you put people or animals in an environment where cold can kill them, they'll adapt by becoming short and stocky, with small appendages less vulnerable to frostbite. Look at arctic foxes and Eskimos, for instance. If you put people or animals in an environment where heat can kill them, they'll also adapt, becoming long and lanky, sometimes with large appendages to help radiate heat. Look at big-eared fennec foxes and the Tutsi people, for instance. What I wondered was, what happens if you put people—it has to be people this time—in an environment where stupidity can kill them?

LAST FAVOR

JEROME CARVER GLANCED AT THE ENRICO *Dandolo*'s west-facing view panel. It seemed awash with flame. "Spectacular sunset," the big black man remarked.

"What else is new?" Patrice Boileau was the only other person in the tradeship's control room. She did not bother looking up from the screen where she was checking a computer subroutine.

"You're spoiled," Carver said in mild reproof.

Patrice shrugged. "There'll be another one along tomorrow. Maybe I won't be busy then."

She was likely right, Carver thought. With an oranger sun and thicker air than Earth's, the whole world of Ephar ran to glorious nightfalls and early mornings. The towers and spires of the city of Shkenaz, silhouetted blackly against the glowing sky, added a touch almost of Arabian Nights fantasy to the scene.

As the trader watched, Ephar's sun slid below the horizon. Full darkness, though, was still some time away. Carver had no trouble spying the figure dashing from Shkenaz's walls toward the greenskin town outside or the mob at the fugitive's heels. He groaned. "Oh, God, they've caught a late one."

This time Patrice did join him in front of the view panel. Of themselves, her hands knotted into fists. "Maybe he'll make it," she said. "If he gets back to his own kind before they catch

290

him, they'll let him go—it's not the gods' will that he die this time.''

''If,'' Carver said grimly. Greenskin towns, by law, had to be more than three *gibyat*s from the walls of a city. Say, a kilometer and a half, the trader thought. He wondered what misfortune had stranded the luckless runner inside Shkenaz so late. He must have known the risk he was taking.

Patrice stepped up the gain on the panel. The distance between the fleeing green centauroid and his blue-skinned pursuers seemed to swell, but that was only electronic illusion. ''Run, damn you, run,'' Carver muttered.

It was no good. A thrown stone made the greenskin stagger. That was all the fastest members of the mob needed to catch him and drag him down. Bodies thrashed, one of them not for long. After a while, realizing there was no sport left to be had, the troop began walking back to Shkenaz. Every so often a blue would spring into the air, in sheer high spirits.

Carver swung the west-facing camera to look at the greenskin village. Sure enough, two or three males stood near the boundary stone. They must have seen everything. They made no move to retrieve what little was left of their fellow, though. They would not till morning. If a blue patrol caught them coming out at night, the whole village might die to expiate their sin.

With a wordless sound, half fury and half frustration, Carver stabbed a finger at a button under the view panel. The panel went dark. ''Three thousand years,'' the trader said.

Patrice had never been on Ephar before. ''Three thousand years of what?''

''That.'' Carver waved to the blank view panel. ''Maybe even longer, but three thousand years the locals have records for. The separate villages, the night ban . . . the murders.'' In the six months since the *Enrico Dandolo* had landed, he had seen three now. That accorded fairly well with the data other ships visiting the Araite Empire had gathered.

''I don't—want to believe that,'' Patrice said.

''Believe it,'' he told her. ''The best part is, under the Code we can't do a damn thing about it, either.''

Now she stared at him. ''What? Why not?''

''No complainants.'' Traders rarely meddled in the affairs of worlds without spaceflight. When they did, they needed ironclad documentation that a local group not only seemed oppressed but felt itself to be. Judging from a purely offplanet perspective was, sensibly in most cases, against the rules.

"I don't believe it!" Patrice exclaimed.

Carver shook his head helplessly. "Believe it. It's true. Never one, in the two hundred years since tradeships have been coming here. Not the blues, of course—why should they complain? But not the greenskins, either. They just shrug and say they are all guilty by inheritance and deserve whatever the blues hand out to them. They believe it. As long as they believe it, officially there's nothing we can do."

"Officially," Patrice said. There was precedent for bending the Code when it needed bending. On Ephar, it looked to need more than bending.

"I understand you." Carver ran a hand down his dark forearm, reminding her of his race. "Don't you think I, of all people, want to see the greenskins free? The night ban is just the worst of a whole set of restrictive laws. Greenskins can't hold land, they can't intermarry with the blues, they can't—oh, a raft of things. Basically, they live by their wits, because that's all they're allowed to own. And—" He slammed the flat of his hand down on the console in complete frustration. "—they won't do a damned thing about it."

"You've tried?"

"My last trip in. I'm not the only one, either. It's never done a bean's worth of good. They won't take weapons, they won't learn civil disobedience, they aren't interested in our trying to change attitudes among the blues. They're—content. And it drives me crazy."

"I don't blame you a bit," Patrice said. "What are you going to do now?"

"Keep trying. What else?"

Carver tramped toward Shkenaz. A few puffy clouds floated in the green-blue sky. The breeze was at the trader's back, and full of strange sweetnesses. Had it been blowing the other way, it would have brought him the stink of the city.

Only a long trampled swath of foliage, abruptly ending, showed what had happened the evening before. As soon as the sun was up, the greenskins had taken away their dead fellow.

Carver felt his eyes keep sliding back to the mute evidence of violence. Walking along beside him, Lloyd Michaels noticed—Carver's fellow trader did not miss much. "Nothing we can do about it," he said.

"I know," Carver ground out. He stopped to adjust his pack;

the straps were digging into his shoulders. "Heaven knows we've tried. It galls me, though, to watch a lynching and then deal the next day with the lord who condoned it."

"I daresay we do that on a lot of primitive worlds, and on a good many that aren't." Michaels's face looked too round and pink and innocent for him to be as cynical as Carver knew he was, a fact he used to shameless advantage on every planet where the locals were sophisticated enough to try to read human expressions.

"They don't usually get their victims to agree they should have been lynched," the black man retorted.

"There is that," Michaels agreed mildly. "If we knew how they did it, we could make a fortune selling the secret offworld."

Carver glared at him, a little less than half sure he was joking. "I'm going to talk to Nadab today," he said at last.

"Old Baasa's pet greenskin? Sure, go ahead. I expect he'll be there." Michaels cocked an eyebrow at his companion. "It won't do you one damn bit of good."

"I'll do it anyhow," Carver said. He walked on, looking neither to the left nor to the right, plainly ready to ignore anything more Lloyd Michaels might say. Michaels kept his mouth shut, the most annoying thing he could do.

The walls of Shkenaz drew near. The gates were open. The guards—blues, of course—leaned back, their weight supported by hind legs and stiff, thick tails. They were bored, Carver thought.

Some—not all—of that boredom fell away as the traders drew near. Even though humans had been going in and out of Shkenaz since the *Enrico Dandolo* landed, they were still strange enough to be interesting. The guards came forward and down onto all four running legs, held spears across the entranceway to block the traders' path. "With whom have you business in the city?" one of them demanded sternly.

Carver studied the male as if seeing him for the first time. Centauroid was only a vague description of the locals' body plan; the guard's hindquarters were not much like a horse's, and his upthrust torso even less like a man's. His face was most alien of all, with a wide toothless beak of a mouth, twin nostril slits, and insectile compound eyes.

The trader wondered how strange he looked in those eyes.

Michaels said, "We meet today with the mighty lord Baasa, representative in Shkenaz of the Araite Emperor, may his reign be long and prosperous.'' The guttural local language was made for sounding arrogant.

The guard swung up his spear. "Pass, then, into Shkenaz, and may our governor's graciousness shine upon you.''

Change the style of architecture and the shape of the inhabitants, Carver thought, and Shkenaz was much like any other primitive town on a preindustrial world. Intelligent beings needed places to live, to trade, to worship, and arranged those places in fairly standard patterns.

Differences, though, counted, too. Because of the way the locals were made, Shkenaz seemed spacious to a biped like Carver, although the townsfolk probably would have disagreed. Few animals shared the streets with the natives, who were strong enough to do their own hauling.

On a street corner, a greenskin scribe wrote a letter for a blue; another blue waited his turn. Carver pointed. "They're polite enough now, but I wonder how many wolf packs they've run in after dark.''

"As many as they could, I have no doubt,'' Michaels said.

By now, most of the locals were used to seeing humans in town, and gave them no more than casual glances. The trumpet-shaped ears of a farmer in town with a piece of scrap iron on his back, though, rose in surprise and his head whipped around to follow the traders as they walked toward the main market square. The junk shop owner with whom he was dickering, a greenskin, took advantage of his surprise to close the deal on the spot.

Carver, who was in earshot when he did, felt like cheering. "We got that fellow some extra silver there,'' he said.

"So we did,'' Michaels agreed. "We also may have got him in trouble some time down the line for cheating a poor honest yokel who had come into Shkenaz to cheat him. When you're a blue here, you can afford a long, selective memory for such slights.''

Black skin, as Carver had discovered, had its uses. He felt his cheeks go hot, but his companion could not see him flush.

Shkenaz's central agora had the air of barely controlled chaos usual to marketplaces. Sellers loudly sang the virtues of six-legged meat animals, knives, perfumes, fruits, grains, pots of clay, and brass. Would-be buyers just as loudly named them liars and thieves. Business got done all the same.

A bookseller waved a three-fingered hand to draw the humans' attention. When he had it, he held up a leather-bound codex. "Illuminated by that painter from the eastern provinces whose work you like," he called cajolingly.

"Do you want to stop?" Carver asked.

"Not with Baasa expecting us. Keep the powers that be happy first." Michaels turned to the waiting greenskin. "Another time, Harhas. We go now to an audience with the august governor of your great city."

Harhas dipped his head. "May it be prosperous for you."

Temples and Shkenaz's town hall fronted one side of the agora. Before the town hall, as before public buildings in every town of the Araite Empire, stood a statue of Peleg. Peleg was the ancient king of a city-state somehow (Carver was not sure how; no human was) connected with the rise of the empire. More than three thousand years before, a greenskin had assassinated him. Greenskins had been paying for it ever since.

A servant was waiting outside the hall. "I am to take you to his Excellency."

The humans followed him up the ramp. A mosaic that ran the whole length of the wall showed in gruesome, imaginative detail what had happened to Peleg's murderer. Golden tesserae gave the work its title: *Justice*.

An artisan was replacing a few tiles that had fallen out of a particularly lurid scene. The artisan was a greenskin. "Nice to be reminded of where you stand in the public's esteem, isn't it?" Michaels murmured. Carver grunted, too mortified for the greenskin's sake to say a word. Baasa's servant glanced back at them. They did not translate for him.

Locals, most of them blues, bustled by, too intent on their own affairs even to notice the craftsman at work. To Carver, somehow that was the worst part of the whole business.

The servant ducked into a chamber and emerged a moment later. "His Excellency will see you now."

"Good day, good day," Baasa rumbled from behind his desk as the humans came in. An icon of the reigning emperor hung on the wall behind him, a reminder of the power that sprawled halfway across this continent. Baasa needed no more than such a symbolic reminder to administer Shkenaz. He was shrewd and fairly able . . . . and if that did not suffice, Carver thought, he had Nadab.

The greenskin stood at a table to one side of his master's desk. Like most of his kind, he had eyes a little larger than those of blues, and ears of not quite the same shape. Still, even taking skin color into account, the visible differences between Nadab and Baasa were less than those between Michaels and Carver.

"Shall we begin?" Carver said.

"Yes, let us," Baasa answered. Nadab merely dipped his head a couple of centimeters to show he was ready.

The humans unslung their packs. As with long-distance caravans on ancient Earth, trade goods worth hauling across light-years had to combine low bulk and high value. Michaels went first. He was a jeweler, and offplanet baubles had grown popular on Ephar over the years. Pearls sold especially well, as they had no local equivalent.

While Michaels and Baasa haggled, Carver made small talk with the governor's aide. At last, seeing Baasa deeply involved in a hot dicker, Carver dared say, "I am sorry one of your people perished last night, Nadab."

"It has happened before," the greenskin said with a fatalism that never failed to chill Carver. "It will happen again. In the end, we are the better for it."

As near as the trader could remember, Nadab had used exactly those words the last time a greenskin had died from missing the sunset curfew. Now, though, he seemed on the point of going on when Baasa interrupted to ask, "How much of the *kohath* spice did we set as value for a shimmerstone"—the name the locals gave to pearls—"of this size?"

"Sir, let me see it." Nadab walked over to Michaels, who held out the gem. The greenskin examined it. "Seven measures," he said at once (literally, it came out "one-one"; the locals used six as their counting base).

"Oh, you thief!" Baasa and Michaels said together. They pointed fingers at each other and laughed. One had been claiming five, the other ten. Neither, though, cared to argue with Nadab.

The greenskin returned to his place. When Carver tried to pick up the conversation where the two of them had left off, he deftly changed the subject. A few minutes later, another disputed point cropped up. Nadab settled it with the same quiet competence he had shown before.

At last Michaels said, "That's about it for me, your Excellency. Why not let Jerome take his turn?"

"Very well." Baasa swung his unwinking gaze on Carver. "What have you to offer me today?"

"Knowledge itself," Carver replied in what he hoped was an impressive voice. "What could be more valuable to you and to the empire than knowledge? It is by knowing many things, after all, that we humans learned the art of flying from star to star.''

Baasa's ears quivered and came to attention. "You would sell the secret of your flying ship?" he demanded. Reading tone into an alien's words was always risky, but Carver thought he heard disbelief warring with greed.

Before he could say anything, Nadab broke in: "My lord, if he makes that claim, he seeks only to befool you. We lack too many of the mechanic arts known to his people to hope to duplicate what they can do.''

The Araite Empire's technology was about on a par with that of Rome in earthly history. Like the Romans also, the locals were more sophisticated intellectually than they were with their hands. Knowing there were things one could not do was a realization many societies never reached.

Carver dipped his head to Nadab and turned back to Baasa. "Your esteemed counselor is right, of course, your Excellency.''

The governor gestured impatiently. "I pay the greenskin to be right. What good is he to me if he is wrong? So you cannot tell me how to fly, eh? What knowledge do you sell, then?''

"Knowledge that will put you on the road to learning such things for yourself and that will show you the direction that road takes.''

"Riddles," Baasa muttered. Local "science," again like Rome's, was of two sorts: collections of random facts with little theory unifying them—what passed for chemistry was like that—and, more common, huge forests of speculation springing from an acorn's worth of knowledge. Medicine and physics were both tarred with that brush.

"Not so," Carver said. "Here, for instance." He drew from his pack translations of Galileo, Bacon's *Novum Organum*, and his prize, an edition of *On the Origin of Species* with its concepts intact but examples drawn from Ephar's biology. None of the three was so far beyond local thought as to be incomprehensible; taken together, they ought to stir things up a good deal.

That was what Carver had in mind. The best way to help the greenskins, he had decided, was to change the society of which they were a part. It was slower than more open forms of aid, but in the long run much more certain.

Baasa was working through the summaries printed on the flyleaves of the books. "See what you think, Nadab," he said, passing them on to his aide. He turned back to Carver. "Give me a price. The ideas may be interesting, though the style is rather flat.''

Carver winced. He hoped that was a ploy to knock down the price, but suspected that it was not. Some good linguists and computer people had put his translations together, but it took more than competence to be elegant in a language not one's own. It took inspired genius, and Joseph Conrads did not come along every day, or every century, either.

Nadab read faster than Baasa. He set the books on the table in front of him. "Quite abstract," he said. "Still, if they are affordable, perhaps you might seek to acquire them as curiosities.''

"Yes, perhaps so," the governor agreed. "Curiosities they certainly are. Well, trader, what do you say to five measures of *bulun* powder apiece for them?''

"Your Excellency, who is esteemed throughout the empire for his generosity, is pleased to joke with me." Carver was appalled for a couple of reasons. The first was the paltry offer. The translations had not come cheap; fifteen measures of *bulun* powder would not begin to pay off what they had cost him.

Even Lloyd Michaels, who had kept out of his fellow trader's dicker till then, was moved to protest, "Surely savants throughout the empire should have the chance to learn of these ideas for themselves.''

"And you, your Excellency," Carver said to Baasa, "and your assistant deserve the credit you will gain for being the first to pass this new knowledge on to your people.''

Baasa swung his head Nadab's way. Nadab said quickly, "I deserve no credit. I am but a greenskin. All that I have I owe to my lord the governor. Without him I am as nothing, nor do I seek any acclaim for aiding him, in any way I can.''

The hell of it was, Carver thought, that he sounded as if he meant it. He would have been much easier to deal with were he only mouthing polite phrases.

Nadab's self-effacement out of the way, Baasa proved a little more interested in dealing. He upped his offer to eight measures of *bulun* powder a book, then to ten, which was about half what Carver needed to break even. When at last he got up above ten measures, the haggling turned serious.

Baasa said, "Twelve measures, then, and four parts, and three parts of parts.''

"Twelve and three-quarters, by your reckoning," Nadab said to Carver while the trader was still wrestling with the fraction that needed converting. He ruefully shook his head and stuck his calculator in his hip pocket. If Nadab felt like showing off, that was fine with Carver.

In the middle of the dicker, a servant poked his head into the chamber and said to Baasa, "Your pardon, Excellency, but the delegation from Asnah has arrived."

"Oh, a pestilence! I did not expect them until tomorrow. I suppose I must formally greet them, as protocol requires." The governor started to walk out, then turned back to warn Carver, "Think not that I shall forget where we stand: seventeen and three parts per volume, and I doubt you will squeeze another measure from me."

"And a half, that is," Nadab supplied as Baasa hurried away.

"Yes, of course," Carver said abstractedly. He had Baasa gauged now, and did not think he would end up losing money. Nadab, though, was harder to figure. "May I ask a question without fear of giving offense?" he said to the greenskin.

"How can seeking to learn give offense?"

Carver could have named twenty different ways from twenty different worlds, but forbore. He said only, "I hoped you might see the advantage to your people of helping to spread enlightenment in the empire. That you do not surprises and disappoints me. If you have some reason I cannot see, I would be grateful for your telling me what it is."

The greenskin was some time silent; the trader could make nothing of the steady gaze that met his. At last Nadab said, "You tread on overgrown ground, outlander. Be careful lest you stumble."

Carver waited.

Something like a sigh hissed through Nadab's nostril slits. He picked up the adaptation of *On the Origin of Species* and turned it over and over in his hands. Again he was a long time finding words. When he did speak, he sounded as if he was choosing them carefully: "I did not know, outlander, that this notion of change over time was familiar to your people."

Carver's eyes slid to Michaels. His comrade was staring back at him. Of all the things he had thought he might hear, this was the last. He said, "I did not know the folk of the empire had come across it, either."

He started to go on, then stopped. Anything he said might be wrong. But no one in the couple of centuries of fitful contact between Ephar and the universe outside had had any clue that the locals were within light-years of developing the concept of evolution.

"Ah, yes, the folk," Nadab murmured. Carver thought he heard irony in the local's voice, and warned himself not to let his sympathies—or his imagination—run away with him. Then, abruptly, he was sure he had not. In the language of the empire, "folk" and "blue" sprang from the same root.

Excitement flowered in him. He had brushed against something more important than *bulun* powder here; he was sure of it. "Tell me," he said, "have you greenskins writings of your own? Ones the folk of the empire"—he used the term with deliberate emphasis—"know nothing about?"

If Nadab said yes to that . . . But he did not. He only asked, "Outlander, how could it possibly matter to you?"

"If for no other reason, then as trade items," Carver said.

Before the words were out of his mouth, he knew he had made a mistake. Nadab's eyes might be unreadable, but there was no mistaking the finality with which he said, "I see little point to discussing what are, in any event, shadows."

The trader cast about for a way to put things right. Nadab stonily rebuffed his efforts. Baasa came back, assuring that the subject would stay closed. Distracted, Carver ended the dicker too soon. The city governor fairly glowed with self-satisfaction; he did not often get the better of a bargain with humans.

"If I may suggest something, Excellency," Nadab said.

"Yes? Go on. Say what you mean." Baasa was in a magnanimous mood.

"You have been gracious enough to speak kindly of my prose style, inadequate though it is. Perhaps, before you release these works to learned males all over the empire, I might do my poor best to make them conform to the rhetorical standards such publication requires."

"A capital suggestion," Baasa exclaimed. "See you to it, Nadab. Only make sure you proceed with it. I would not want the works long delayed."

"Certainly not, Excellency."

It was all perfectly smooth, perfectly respectful, and, from the locals' point of view, perfectly sensible. Somehow, though, Carver was sure that whatever sprang from Nadab's pen would be flawed: not obviously flawed, maybe, or no one would look at the books at all, but with enough errors to keep them from having the influence for which he'd hoped.

He could not say that out loud, not with no proof, not with

the greenskin enjoying his overlord's deserved confidence. But for whatever reasons, Nadab was plainly unenthusiastic about letting real science come to the attention of the empire as a whole. If Carver had been frustrated before about the way greenskins acted, now he was bewildered as well, and more than a little annoyed.

He did what he could, saying, "If you have any trouble with the concepts in the books, Nadab, please feel free to call on us humans for help."

"That is generous of you," the greenskin said. "If I encounter difficulties, be sure I shall consult you. I believe, however, that my grasp of what is, after all, my own language should prove adequate to the task."

"What task do you have in mind?" Carver said, but in Trade English, so that only Michaels understood.

"Well, of course we haven't had a great deal to do with the greenskins," Captain Chen remarked that evening over tea and cakes. She was a tiny, very competent woman whose size belied her strength of will. She went on, "They aren't rich enough to trade with the likes of us."

"Some of them must be," Michaels said. "Nadab has been Baasa's right-hand man for years. Are you telling me he hasn't spent some time lining the pockets he doesn't wear?"

"I would doubt that myself," the captain said dryly.

"So would I," Carver agreed. "But even if he has, he doesn't dare show it. What do you suppose happens if somebody in a greenskin village starts looking too prosperous?"

"The blues come out and burn his house down around his ears," Michaels supplied, "and probably his neighbors' houses, too, just on the off chance that they're thinking wicked thoughts about living above subsistence level."

"You've got it," Carver said. "We have tapes to prove it. It doesn't happen very often, though. The greenskins have been pariahs for a long time now; they know how to lay low."

" 'Pariah' isn't quite the right word," Captain Chen said, precise as usual. "The greenskins play an important part in local society: shopkeepers, scholars, artisans, merchants. They aren't menials by any means."

"So long as the sun is in the sky," Carver said. "They aren't menials after dark, either—they're fair game. Still, I take your point. It's just because of the role they play that I wondered if they have a literature of their own."

"From the way Nadab clammed up about it, you'd have thought Jerome asked him how many blue children he'd eaten lately," Michaels added.

The captain pursed her lips. "Interesting," she said judiciously, "but I'm not sure how important it is."

"*Something* odd is going on there," Carver insisted. "Nadab knows about evolution, and none of the natural philosophers among the blues does. I'd lay money on that."

"The other thing," Michaels said, "is that he didn't want them knowing about it, either."

Carver gave him a grateful look. "So you saw that, too?"

"Interesting," Captain Chen said again. "The more enlightened, the more scientifically oriented a society is, the less the inclination it usually has for harassing its minorities, at least openly. You'd think Nadab would grasp that."

"I think perhaps he does," Carver said slowly.

Michaels parted company with him there. "That's crazy, Jerome. Nobody wants to be persecuted forever."

"Till my first trip to Ephar, I would have said the same thing." Carver scratched his head. "But if the greenskins don't, they certainly hide it well. And I don't just mean Nadab. None of them seems interested in changing the way things are."

"They *are* a small minority," the captain said, "and very vulnerable because of that. They must know it."

"That's true enough," Carver admitted. "I've never seen a greenskin I'd call a fool."

"Hardly," Michaels agreed. "A greenskin who was a fool wouldn't live long."

"But still—" Carver said.

"Yes, but still," Captain Chen said. "Yes, it is a puzzle. If it can be arranged so as not to disturb the imperial authorities in Shkenaz, you might pay a visit to the greenskin village."

"There's no profit in it," Michaels said.

"Money and profit are not always the same thing," the captain said.

The locals' faces did not show many emotions a human could read, but the set of the blue guards' ears and the way they only stood aside at the last moment for Carver to pass told the trader plenty about what they thought of his having anything to do with greenskins.

Nadab came out past the village boundary stone to meet Carver. It was safe enough; local noon had only just passed.

The greenskin waved a hand. "Welcome, outlander. Shall we stroll?"

"Whatever you wish, of course," the trader said, falling in beside Nadab. After a little while he asked casually, "How are you coming with your, ah, editing of the volumes Baasa acquired?"

Nadab did not miss a beat. "Well enough." Carver shook his head in rueful admiration: the greenskin was as polite as he was uninformative.

They went into the village. Carver had walked past it many times, and seen it from the *Enrico Dandolo*'s view panels, but he had hoped actually being in it would give him some new perspective on the way greenskins lived their lives. He found himself disappointed. The houses were as he'd already known they were: old, not especially prosperous, but on the clean side by local standards.

Some elderly males stood in the village square. They crowded around to get a good look at Carver. Females and children peered from doorways. Most of the adult males in their prime were working in Shkenaz.

Also in the square was something Carver did not remember noticing: a statue of Peleg. Maybe, he thought, he had not wanted to see it before. He pointed at it. "Why do you have this here?"

"To remind us of our shame." It was a chorus from all the greenskins in earshot, even the youngsters. Carver realized he must have asked a ritual question. The humiliation drilled into each succeeding generation chilled him. Was this, he wondered, why the greenskins never questioned their oppression?

He doubted it. Surely some rebels would arise to challenge the way things were. Or would they? He was thinking in human terms. The strange smells on the breeze, the proportions of the buildings around him, even the ruddy quality of the light reminded him that those did not apply here. In all his dealing with the locals, he had never felt them so alien as they seemed in this quiet little square.

Lost in his thoughts, he missed something Nadab had said. "Your pardon, I pray."

"I said, also to remind us of our separation."

Baasa's aide, Carver knew, was the most prominent greenskin attached to—not *in*—Shkenaz. That did not keep several of the old males from hissing at him in anger—or was it alarm? The trader frowned. Nadab had told him something important. The only trouble was, he was not sure what.

He found no easy way to ask straight out. Maybe changing the subject would let him come back later. He said to Nadab, "I must tell you how much I admire the wisdom you and your people display."

This time, the murmurs from the old males were gratified. "You are most kind," Nadab said. He pointed toward the *Enrico Dandolo*. "Our ignorance is all too manifest when set beside such achievements as that."

"We are not the proper comparison, though, are we?" Carver asked. "I was thinking of how much more you know than, say, the most learned blue savants of the empire."

The shot was blind, but it hit. Silence slammed down in the square. From far off, Carver heard a flying hunter screech as it swooped down on something in the not-quite-grass. The old males waited for Nadab's lead. Nadab did not seem inclined to do much leading.

At last the greenskin said, "Come wander with me. We will, I suppose we must, discuss this further." One of the old males spoke in harsh protest, almost too fast for Carver to follow. Nadab said, "Be still, Ithamar. The need is here. This has been spoken of among us, as you know."

"The time is not yet ripe," Ithamar insisted.

"And I say it is. Who has the broader perspective, you or I?"

Ithamar lowered his head and bent his forelegs in respect. "May you be right," he said. He still did not sound as though he thought Nadab was. The rest of the old males left the square.

The building nearest the statue of Peleg was larger than the rest in the greenskin village, and did not look like a home. Carver guessed it might have the same sort of importance in the village that the local governor's hall did in Shkenaz. Pointing at it, he asked, "Is that where your people keep the books you do not show the blues?"

"I have never said there are such books," Nadab said. The trader felt his shoulders sag. Whatever Nadab was contemplating, it was not simply opening up to him. Too bad.

"Will you show me what is in there?" Carver persisted.

"Presently, presently." Was that amusement in Nadab's voice? Greenskins seldom seemed amused; they seldom, Carver thought, had much to be amused about. Nadab went on. "Now, as I said, we will wander."

Having no choice, the trader wandered. The village did indeed remind him of a moderately poor chunk of Shkenaz, set outside the city walls. It seemed quieter than such a chunk, but that, the trader thought, could just have been because Shkenaz's big central marketplace went a long way toward making the whole town raucous.

"You see," Nadab said, "that we are no threat to outbid Baasa for your goods."

"You might well be, could you compete fairly with his kind."

"What is fair?" Nadab said, sounding surprisingly like a six-limbed Pilate. Unlike the Roman procurator, he undertook to answer the question, at least metaphorically: "Fair is that all advantages have corresponding disadvantages to make up for them."

"The reverse also has to be true," Carver said harshly. "Your disadvantages are all around me. Where are the offsetting advantages? Those I do not see."

"Well, we are still just walking about," Nadab said. He dipped his head to a male coming by. "Good day to you, Kohath. How does it fare in the city?"

"Much as always, Nadab. Compound interest is such a painful mystery to those caught in its toils." Kohath turned the corner; Carver heard him open a door. On few worlds, the trader thought, would a banker live so modestly. He wondered if that was one of the mysterious advantages of which Nadab had spoken. He doubted it. No one on Ephar made a virtue of abstaining from worldly goods.

More males were coming back from Shkenaz now. Carver glanced at the sky. The sun had slid a long way down toward the west. The trader was surprised when Nadab led him out past the boundary stone and into the fields again. By the look of things, so were the blues who made up the guard squad. They muttered among themselves as the greenskin and Carver walked by.

"Is this safe?" Carver asked. He wished he had his stunner. He hadn't thought he'd need it. Michaels, he knew, would have something sharp to say about showing that kind of confidence on an alien world.

But Nadab seemed unconcerned. "Safe enough, so long as I am back within the village by sunset. Being busy so much, either here or within the walls of Shkenaz, I have too few chances simply to amble this way. When one comes, I make the most of it."

Traveling as he often did for weeks at a time cooped up inside a metal shell, Carver understood that sentiment down to the ground. He said quietly, "Thank you for sharing the moment with me."

"Not to do so would be unjust to the one who made it possible," Nadab said. He looked from Carver to the *Enrico Dandolo* a few hundred meters away. "And, of course, would be inappropriate, as your people have posed the problem now facing me on behalf of mine."

The trader grew alert. *Now we come down to it*, he thought. He said, "We have never intended anything but good for greenskins, Nadab. We want to end your oppression, if we can."

"That is why, then, you offered Baasa the volumes you did?"

"Certainly. Why else?"

"Who could say, judging beings so strange?" *A nice way to remind me*, Carver thought, *that I'm as alien to Nadab as he is to me, and a point worth getting across*. Nadab went on, "I thought perhaps your purpose was to destroy my entire people."

Carver stared. There are times when, no matter how well one speaks a language not his own, he will hear something, understand it perfectly, and still doubt his ears. This was one of those times. The trader spread his hands in a gesture of confusion. "We wish your folk nothing but good, Nadab. We think it wrong for you to be forced into separation on account of the color of your skin. My own race"—he touched the dark brown skin of his arm— "has too much of that in its own past. Save for your being green and Baasa blue, we know your kind and his are no different."

It was Nadab's turn to look sharply at the human. "You know that, do you?" He astonished Carver by throwing back his head and letting out the strangled snorts that served the locals for laughter.

"What's funny?" the trader demanded, a bit angrily.

"Only that I came close to confusing skill with wisdom, a mistake I thought myself too wise for." The oblique reply did little to soothe Carver's temper. Nadab said, "Never mind. I see you bear me and mine no malice. Ignorance we shall cope with: we have before, often enough."

The calm confidence with which the greenskin spoke only nettled Carver further. Somehow Nadab had put the shoe on the other foot, and the trader did not care for it. He was unused to being forced into the role of ignorant outsider, with the local as sophisticate.

"I think we can return now," Nadab said. He still sounded,

Carver thought, quite full of his own importance. And then, as he turned, that note vanished from his voice. "Or perhaps not."

Carver looked back toward the greenskin village. The blue guards had spread into a line between him, Nadab, and the buildings. "What are they doing?" the trader asked. But even as he spoke, he knew. His glance went to the sun. Not much daylight was left.

Nadab's head swung in the same direction, then back to Carver. "Yes, outlander, it is exactly what you think. If I am not on the other side of the boundary stone by sunset—"

"But that's murder!" Carver burst out. Immediately afterwards, he felt like a fool. Hunting down any greenskin outside his village when the sun went down was murder. He had seen that in gruesome telephoto from the safety of the *Enrico Dandolo*. Somehow, though, it had not occurred to him that even that violence might be perverted further by deliberately keeping a greenskin from reaching sanctuary.

Nadab, with three thousand years of tradition to guide him, had no such naïveté. He said, "It happens. From time to time, it happens. Now all that remains to be seen is whether they are out for their own amusement, or have something more in mind."

He walked slowly toward the blue guards. They held their line, positioning themselves so he had no chance of breaking past them back into the village. Carver stood where he was, feeling extraordinarily helpless. He wished he were carrying a Kalashnikov to mow down the blues, who were waving clubs and spears and yelling threats at Nadab.

The greenskin said loudly, "Let me by. Baasa will not be pleased to learn I have come to harm at your hands."

Strangled snorts came from the blues. "We'll take our chances on that!" one shouted. "That's what you think," said another.

Carver saw Nadab's shoulders sag. Such was what passed for a greenskin's power in Shkenaz: if Nadab's patron tired of him, he was as much at the mercy of the blues as was the lowliest greenskin tinsmith.

A small crowd of greenskins had gathered just on the safe side of the boundary stone. They watched and waited, making no move to help Nadab. Carver was sure they would not. The whole village stood hostage to the blues of Shkenaz. Everyone knew it, greenskins and blues alike. The ritual of death would be played out with no interference.

The lower edge of the local sun's red, swollen disk touched the western horizon. The blues sidled forward. In a couple of minutes, Nadab was theirs in perfect legality. He drew back a few paces toward Carver, not that running would do him any good.

Or would it? That retreat, that pathetic reflex of life trying to prolong itself even to no purpose, broke the trader's horrified paralysis. "Nadab!" he shouted. The greenskin kept his eyes on the blues, but his ears twisted toward Carver. The trader yelled, "Run for our tradeship!"

Nadab stood motionless for another long moment. He had, Carver thought, been so sure of his imminent death that he needed time to realize he might live yet. Then he whirled and dashed toward the *Enrico Dandolo*. Carver, slower on two legs than the greenskin was on four but also closer to the ship, began to run, too.

The blues shouted in outrage. They were bound in the same web of custom as Nadab, though, and hesitated before giving chase: a sliver of sun still glowed above the horizon. Then it was gone, and they came pelting after Nadab and Carver. The trader heard their three-toed feet pounding behind him.

His chest felt on fire. He was not very young and not very light and not at all used to sprinting cross-country. He did not want to think about what would happen if he stepped in a hole or tripped over a bush. The blue guards might keep right on after Nadab. On the other hand, they might—or some of them might, which would be just as bad—decide to stop and kill him. He hoped that would stay just a thought experiment; he had no desire to test it empirically.

He also hoped people on the *Enrico Dandolo* were alert. The ground-level hatch was closed. If it didn't open in the next few seconds—he was less than a hundred meters from the ship now, only a few meters behind Nadab and not nearly far enough ahead of his pursuers—things would get embarrassing. They'd get a great deal worse than that for the greenskin.

The hatch slid upward. Relief sobbed through Carver's throat. "Go on!" he yelled or, rather, croaked, to Nadab. The greenskin's toes clicked on metal. A moment later, Carver's boots clattered inside the cargo bay.

The hatch came down much faster than it had risen. None too soon—one of the blues was close enough to the *Enrico Dandolo* to hurl his bludgeon after Nadab. It belled off the descending door. Then the guards were pounding on the hatch with clubs and fists. The din was tremendous.

Carver stood with hands on knees, his head lowered, trying

to catch his breath. Nadab was panting, too, but looked around the cargo bay with lively interest. The fluorescent strips in the ceiling proved particularly intriguing. "Not fire, yet they give light," he said. "Have you, then, imprisoned glowfliers behind that glass? No, surely not," he corrected himself: "too bright for that."

"They work by the same power as our calculators," Carver told him.

If the trader had expected a surprised outburst, he did not get one. "Ah. Interesting," was all Nadab said. Carver had no chance to take things further. The inner door to the compartment came open. People burst in, shouting questions—mostly variations on "What the hell is going on?"

Carver explained. The crewfolk shouted in anger. The way the empire treated greenskins was abominable enough without cheating them besides. Patrice Boileau burst out, "We should up ship now and have nothing more to do with these savages."

"That would not solve the problem," Nadab said. Abrupt silence fell in the cargo bay, punctuated only by the banging from the blues outside. It was not so much for what Nadab said as for how he said it. Given the limits of his lipless beak, his Trade English was as fluent as anyone else's in the compartment.

Captain Chen, as befitted her station, recovered her wits first. "We did not know you spoke our language," she said, adding a moment later, "We did not know anyone on Ephar did."

"I doubt any blues do," Nadab said, again in Trade English.

The humans looked at one another. Lloyd Michaels said to Carver, "Seems we were on to something there back in Shkenaz a few days ago,"

"So it does," the black man said.

"So you were," Nadab agreed.

Captain Chen drove for the heart of the issue, asking, "Why do you choose to reveal this to us now?"

"Because at last I am convinced you do mean well for my people." Nadab sounded as if the question had surprised him. "Jerome Carver here would not have risked himself to save me were it otherwise."

"But—" That strangled protest came from everyone in the compartment at the same time. Carver managed to articulate it: "Ever since we came to Ephar, Nadab, we humans have been working to better the lot of you greenskins and help you take your full, rightful place in the empire."

"What makes you think those two things are one and the

same?'' Nadab asked. The only flaw in his speech, Carver thought, was that he sounded pedantic. He thought about that, then reconsidered: another flaw was that the greenskin made no sense at all.

Patrice might have been reading his mind. "How could you not want to be free from persecution?" she demanded of Nadab. "How many of you have died for the sake of hatred?"

"Many, very many," Nadab said, answering the second question first. "We believe, though, that they let us atone for a murder by one of ours long ago, a murder that was surely the stupidest thing a greenskin ever did, and so they are not in vain."

"I don't follow that," Patrice said. Carver nodded; he found it tragic that such a clever being as Nadab should be trapped like a fly in superstition's cobweb.

"In any case," Michaels said, "a cargo bay is hardly the place for this kind of talk. What say we go up to the control room."

"Good," Captain Chen said briskly. "From there we can also tell the blues outside to go away, and that Nadab is under our protection."

"That is very generous," the greenskin said, "but what makes you believe they will listen to you?"

"They'll listen," the captain said, her voice grim. "Come along." She led them up the spiral stair to the control room.

"You half-built beings have an easier time of this than I," Nadab complained. He had to twist his body awkwardly all the way up the stairs, and slowed Patrice and Carver, who were behind him.

Captain Chen stalked over to the intercom, flipped a switch to channel it through the outside speakers. "Get away from our ship!" she roared to the blues below. The volume control was all the way to the right; she must have sounded like an angry god. She went on, "Nadab is under our protection. We do not allow you to harm him."

One of the blues ran, hurrying back toward Shkenaz. The rest stayed where they were, though for upwards of a minute they simply stood in place, giving up their pounding on the cargo hatch. Carver thought the noise had stunned them. More attuned to the subtleties of his people's body language, Nadab said, "They do not believe their ears."

When the blues did regain their tongues, he was quickly proved right. "But the greenskin has violated his parole," a guard shouted, and even the humans could hear his incredulity. "He is now ours, to do with as we wish."

"He is not," Captain Chen declared, still at the top of her electronic lungs. "You forced him to stay outside his village past sunset. Otherwise he would not have."

"What has that to do with it?" the blue yelled back. "The act is all. Had the gods wished him to live, they would not have let us detain him."

"Oh, shut up," Captain Chen snarled, but in Trade English. She clicked off the intercom and the outside mike. "Let them scream their fool heads off out there. Eventually they'll get tired and go away."

"No, they will not," Nadab said.

"Well, then, let them have their fit. They can't hurt the ship, and now—" The captain pointed at the switched-off intercom— "they can't bother us any more, either." She folded her arms across her chest, glowered at the greenskin. "Now, perhaps, you will start making sense of yourself."

"I am more curious about what you intend doing with me," Nadab said.

"How you answer our questions will make a difference in what we decide, you know," Carver told him.

The greenskin considered. "Yes, that has some truth to it. Very well; ask what you will."

Despite the invitation, the control room stayed silent a moment. Patrice spoke first; working as she did with computers, she was used to breaking down questions into the smallest possible pieces. She said, "Why did you say bettering your people's lot was not the same thing as taking an equal part with the blues in the life of the empire?"

"Because we better ourselves precisely by not taking an equal part," Nadab replied at once.

"Riddles," Michaels said. Carver just suppressed an urge to kick him in the shin.

"Riddles have answers," Captain Chen said sharply. She glared at Michaels, who looked away; even the boldest man thought twice about risking her anger. She turned back to Nadab. "Go on."

"I would think the matter obvious," the greenskin said. "As Carver showed me, you people grasp the concept of life's changing over time, depending on the circumstances brought to bear upon it."

"Evolution," Carver supplied.

"If that is your word; I have not met it before. We have been aware of it for something close to two thousand years ourselves."

The humans stirred. "Longer than we have," Michaels muttered. This time, no one shushed him. He went on. "Our arts were at a much higher level when we first thought of the notion of evolution than yours are now, to say nothing of what yours must have been so long ago. If what you say is true, how did you learn of it so quickly?"

"And what does it have to do with the greenskins' plight?" Captain Chen asked.

Nadab opened and closed his hands several times. "Are you all blind?" he said, in the local language this time. He returned to Trade English. "Think: what restrictions have applied to us greenskins since the one we never name slew Peleg and fled under cover of darkness?"

"*That's* why they don't let you out at night!" Carver said.

"Yes, of course," Nadab said impatiently. "Can you not answer a question without being diverted down a double hand— no, excuse me, you would say half a dozen—sidetracks?"

Carver threw the greenskin a curious look. He saw he was not the only one doing so. Always before, on Ephar, he had felt himself more able, more sophisticated than the locals. Now, though, Nadab seemed in control of things, not any human. Taking turns, Carver and his companions spelled out the prohibitions greenskins had to endure: no intermarriage, no owning land, all the rest.

"Enough," Nadab said at last—yes, he was in control. "What sort of lives do we lead, then, as a result of all this?"

"Narrow ones," Carver told him. "Forgive me, but that is the truth as we humans see it. You are restricted to a tiny handful of trades among the many in the empire, and insecure in your hold on those because you are so vulnerable to the blues." The rest of the people in the control room nodded. Carver pointedly added, "As the events of the day have shown."

"All true, but all, I fear, superficial," Nadab said. "The key is in the sort of—"

The chime of the phone from the weapons turret interrupted the greenskin. Like all weapons officers, Anastas Shumilov always stood his watch there rather than in the control room so he could aim the guns by hand if the electronics were damaged. Shumilov said, "Captain, forgive me for interrupting, but a fair-sized mob is coming this way."

No one had been paying attention to the view panels. "Oh, dear me," Michaels said, or words to that effect.

"I guess that blue guard wasn't just running away," Patrice added. Her comment, though less colorful than Michaels's, was as inadequate.

Blues with torches, blues with clubs, blues with spears were streaming out of Shkenaz toward the *Enrico Dandolo*. Carver started to worry when he saw locals in bronze helmets: if soldiers were part of the crowd, it all too likely had official sanction. His concern doubled when he saw blues hauling stout timbers of the sort they would think able to batter down the outer cargo bay door, and doubled again when he spotted Baasa near the rear of the mob—official sanction, indeed.

Nadab said, "If you thwart them over me, they will surely turn on my people's village." Carver was sure bitter experience informed the greenskin's words.

"No, they won't," Captain Chen ground out. She spoke to Shumilov: "Wait until the front-runners are within fifty meters of the ship, then hit 'em with the searchlight."

"Aye, aye." The weapons officer wasted few words. A minute later, the view panels lit up bright as day. Suddenly the blue's torches seemed feeble and insignificant, not the frightening harbingers of fury they had been, blazing in the darkness. The locals came to a ragged halt.

Captain Chen clicked on the outside speakers. "Go back to your city," her amplified voice roared. "The greenskin Nadab is under our protection. We will not let him be harmed."

That blunt announcement set the blues screaming again. They started to surge forward. The captain said, "Do you need to be reminded of what our weapons can do?" The surge collapsed.

Tradeships had used their guns a couple of times on Ephar. The most recent occasion had been seventy-five years before. After that, imperial authorities forbade attacks on offworlders. They were too expensive to be worthwhile.

But the locals were still anything but happy. "Give us the greenskin!" they shouted. "Let us finish him!" Searchlight or no, weapons or no, the blues hauling the makeshift ram began moving forward.

Captain Chen's jaw tightened. Carver understood her dilemma. Opening fire on the mob not only would ruin the *Enrico Dandolo*'s trading mission, it also would cause endless red tape when the ship got back to civilization. Not opening fire, though, would be seen as weakness . . . and there was always the horrible off chance the locals really could break in. Not every ship got back to civilization to worry about red tape.

While the humans watched the head of the mob, Nadab spotted several blues slipping away from the rear. "As I thought," he said. "They will avenge me upon my village."

"What? No, they won't." Relieved at finding an action she could take, Captain Chen snapped an order to Shumilov: "Give me a few rounds of tracers. Shoot to miss, but show them they can't have the greenskins."

"Tracers, aye." Machine guns hammered. They made an ideal weapons system on pretechnological worlds, being both raucous and spectacularly lethal. Lines of glowing red reached across the night. The locals abruptly lost interest in going any closer to the greenskin village. The blues with the ram looked to be having second thoughts, too.

Baasa's retinue pushed through the mob so the local governor could confront the *Enrico Dandolo*. He seemed dubious about the honor of that, but spoke up as boldly as he could: "Send Nadab the greenskin out to us and we will go home. Having broken our strongest law, he must face justice."

"No," was all Captain Chen said.

Carver gestured for the mike. The captain gave it to him. He said. "The toughs outside the village deliberately kept Nadab from returning in good time. What's more, I'd guess they did so at your orders. Now you say he has broken the law. How do you have the crust to call that justice?"

"It is our ancient way, by which we and the greenskins have always lived. The excuse is nothing, the act all. If Nadab was out of his village, he must atone for his guilt."

"As I predicted he would say," Nadab told Carver.

Rage ripped through the black man. He spoke into the microphone again: "It is not our ancient way, and we do not accept it. Go back into Shkenaz; leave us—and Nadab—at peace. You have seen we own the power to enforce our demands. Go back to your homes, all of you. There is nothing for you here." Carver switched off the mike.

Captain Chen eyed the view panel. Hardly any of the blues outside were going home, but they were not advancing on the *Enrico Dandolo*, and they were not heading for the greenskin village: the tracers had effectively discouraged that. "Good enough," the captain said. For Shumilov she added, "Use the guns to keep them where they are, but don't fire into the mob itself without my order."

"Aye, aye," the weapons officer said, and fell silent again. He talked as if he were afraid his pay would be docked for every surplus word he used.

The blues kept milling about without doing anything much except beginning to argue among themselves. "Stalemate," Captain Chen said, sounding pleased with herself. "Eventually they'll get bored and leave us alone." She turned to Nadab. "Where were we when that mess started?"

"They will not get bored. They will not go away," the green-skin said, in much the same tone, Carver thought, as he would have said, *The sun will come up tomorrow*. Nadab went on. "As for where we were, I was remarking that the key to our problem lies in the sort of occupations in which we are permitted by law to engage."

Carver admired the way Nadab instantly repaired the broken thread of conversation. The trader started to tick off greenskin jobs on his fingers: "Scribe, banker, jeweler, shopkeeper—"

"You need not go through the entire catalog," Nadab said with a sting in his voice that Lloyd Michaels might have envied. "Far simpler to notice what they have in common."

Again Carver—and, he saw, his companions—danced to the greenskin's tune. Carver rubbed his chin as he thought. Before anything occurred to him, Patrice said, "We were talking about this a while ago, Jerome, remember? More than any other lo-cals, the greenskins live by their wits."

"Exactly!" For the first time, Nadab seemed satisfied with the humans he was facing. He spread his hands in an expansive gesture, then let them drop again when no one picked up what was plainly a cue. "Surely you can extrapolate from what you know."

"We know many things," Captain Chen said shortly. She was losing patience. Her wave encompassed the control room, which anyone on Ephar was centuries from matching. "What in particular applies to you?"

"When I learned you knew of evolution, I did not think I would have to be so elementary," Nadab said. So there, Carver thought. The greenskin resumed. "If you are raising livestock and desire a larger beast, what do you do?"

"Breed the largest ones you have to each other." Michaels gave the obvious answer, sounding as if he were humoring the greenskin. "Then breed the largest of the next generation to each other, and . . ." His voice trailed away. Carver felt a tingle of something between awe and dread as he saw where Nadab was leading the humans. Michaels was more serious than Carver had ever heard him: "You're saying this applies to you."

"How could it not?" Nadab said. Though nothing about him had changed, he suddenly looked vastly different to Carver. The trader would rather have gone on seeing Nadab as a representative of a tormented minority than as the result of an age-long experiment in controlled breeding. Things would have been much more comfortable that way.

"You claim you greenskins have been breeding for brains for all this time?" Captain Chen sounding rattled was as unnerving as Lloyd Michaels being serious.

"Say rather we have been bred for them," Nadab said. "After the crime of the one we do not name, the restrictions you know were forced upon us. They acted as they had to act, whether we knew of it at the time or not. Those of us who were clever enough to make their way in the face of such difficulties survived and bred; those who were not starved or were killed on account of their stupidity, either by offending the blues or from being caught out after sunset . . . as I was. Do you doubt now that I am something different from any blue you have known—and from yourselves?"

Before any of the humans could answer, the machine guns' harsh chatter made them all jump. Tracers stabbed into the night, warning the blues away from the greenskin village again. "I do thank you," Nadab said, "but how long will you keep that up? All night? A day or two? As long as you are here? Do you think the blues will have forgotten by that time? They have not forgotten us in three thousand years."

An ancient joke floated into Carver's mind: *If you're so smart, why aren't you rich?* It rang eerily apt here. The trader said, "If you were what you say you are, Nadab, I'd expect your kind, not the blues, to be masters within the empire."

Nadab cocked his head; had he had eyebrows, Carver thought, he would have lifted one. "Baasa listened to my advice. After I am gone, he will have another greenskin by his side: we reckon better, we remember better, we pull things together better than any other aides he is likely to find. Do you think him the only city governor who has discovered our usefulness? Do you think the emperors themselves have not?"

"He's right," Patrice said softly. "Check the records. Every blue official traders have dealt with has always had a greenskin at his elbow." From the way she stared at Nadab, she too was seeing him with new eyes.

"Of course," the greenskin went on, "we also have the advantage of being disposable at need." Was that bitterness? Somehow Carver doubted it. Nadab sounded altogether matter-of-fact. *Alien*, the trader thought.

"Let's say you do rule behind the scenes." Captain Chen had recovered her briskness, to Carver's relief. She reached a hand toward Nadab as if to pull the answer to her next question from him. "Why, then, haven't you people used your position of power to better your lot and get rid of the burdens you suffer under?"

Nadab drew back a pace; his tail switched up and down, a gesture of dismay. "Because we do not wish to, and we must not. We have been atoning for the nameless one's crime all these years by making ourselves into a people that will not act so stupidly as he did. If there were no longer pressure to force wisdom upon us, we would fall back into sloth and ease, and cease to improve ourselves."

"That's the craziest—" Lloyd Michaels began, but stopped before he finished the sentence. Carver understood: from the greenskins' point of view, what Nadab was saying was perfectly logical. And intelligence was not always what set basic premises; it only worked from them.

Carver understood something else as well. "That's why you were going to butcher the science books Baasa bought from me. If the blues catch on to evolution, they may realize what you've become."

"What we are becoming," Nadab corrected gravely. "But yes, you are in essence correct. I doubt they would approve." Even in Trade English, the greenskin had a gift for understatement.

"How can you presume to speak for all your people?" Captain Chen demanded. "What of those who do not care to be persecuted for the sake of an ancient crime? Don't they want us to do whatever we can to lighten their load?"

"You humans have been coming to the empire for two hundred years now, your reckoning. In that time, how many greenskins have sought such aid from you?"

"None." The captain did not sound happy about admitting it. Nadab let the silence grow behind that solitary word.

The tracers punctuated it. The humans jumped again. Nadab repeated quietly, "How long will you keep that up?"

"What would you have us do?" Captain Chen's voice was no louder.

"Open a door and let me out."

"No!" Patrice and Michaels spoke at the same time, while Carver said, "They'll kill you out there." Captain Chen said only, "You know what the consequences will be if we do that. Why do you want us to?"

"The consequences for me will be bad in any case. My life is forfeit now all through the empire, and I do not care to live outside it. Would you take me to your world with you? Being a curiosity there, the only one of my kind, has no appeal. So I count myself doomed, come what may. I do not wish my village, and perhaps greenskin villages all through the empire, to be injured on my account."

The captain spoke to the air. "Shumilov, are you listening to this?"

"Aye." The weapons officer's voice was machine-flat.

"Comments?"

A moment's pause, then Shumilov said. "He's right."

Captain Chen made a sour face. She turned back to Nadab and repeated, "You know what will happen to you out there."

"Yes: the same as would have happened had I let the blue guards have their sport with me at sunset."

"You don't *want* to live," Carver said harshly.

"Of course I do. Who does not? Why would I have run for your ship here when you cried out if I did not want to live? I thought you were giving me a new option, one none of my people ever had before. But"—the greenskin waved at the view panel that showed the mob of blues— "I see that is not so. I was wrong."

He sounded so downcast at the admission that Michaels asked, "Do you want to go out there and die just to punish yourself for making a mistake?" At first Carver thought his fellow trader was letting his sardonic imagination run away with him; then, looking at Nadab, he wondered if Michaels hadn't hit it dead center.

All Nadab said, though, was, "My people are more important than I am. I have my duty to them. You outlanders have a word for the concept; do you not recognize it?"

Carver winced. So did Captain Chen. She said, "I have another duty also: not to send anyone out to certain death."

"You do not send me. You merely let me go. And if you do not, you condemn the greenskins in my village and others you have never seen to a fate worse than mine."

Anastas Shumilov fired off another burst, the longest one yet. "They're getting harder to convince," he remarked.

"You may also end up slaughtering a good many blues who have done you no harm," Nadab said.

"How can you sympathize with *them*?" Carver said. "After all they've done to your people—"

"They are the instruments of our improvement," the greenskin said mildly. "Does the raw clay hate the kiln that burns it to make it into a vase?" Nadab swung his unwinking eyes to Captain Chen. "Now will you let me do as I must do?"

"Damn you." The captain turned on the control board as if it were an enemy and stabbed a button with wholly unnecessary violence. The door to the stairwell that led down to the cargo bay slid open.

Captain Chen said nothing more. If Nadab's so smart, Carver thought, let him figure that out for himself. He was; he did. Without hesitation, he started down the stairs. His voice floated up after him: "My people are in your debt."

"Oh, shut up," the captain muttered. She watched Nadab's progress on the ship's internal monitor. He went straight to the cargo bay's outer door. Captain Chen made him wait several minutes. At last, still shaking her head, she let the door rise.

The outside mikes picked up the roar the blues let out when they saw Nadab. It sent atavistic chills racing up Carver's spine; though he had never seen one, his glands scream *lion*. The instant Nadab was outside the ship, Captain Chen sent the cargo bay door slamming shut.

Like the tide rolling in, the blues surged forward. Nadab did not die tamely. He sprinted for the greenskin village like an antelope trying to break through a hundred prides of big cats. He still had that one chance in ten billion of winning freedom.

He never got fifty meters from the *Enrico Dandolo*. The blues dragged him down and took their vengeance on him—and then on his corpse—for his presumption. Carver made himself watch it all, even when the flames sprang up. His only consolation by then was that Nadab could not possibly be feeling what was going on any more.

Once they were done amusing themselves with Nadab—or once there was nothing left to amuse themselves with—some blues started for the greenskin village. Quite without orders (in itself unheard of before) Shumilov fired a burst to warn them back. To his credit—not that any human was ready to give him much—Baasa had the Shkenaz garrison keep the mob away. At last the blues began drifting back toward the city.

"Poor bastards," Michaels grunted. "Some of 'em'll be all tired tomorrow from working so late tonight."

Carver threw himself into a chair buried his face in his hands. Patrice touched his shoulder. "You did everything you could, Jerome," she said gently. "You cannot blame yourselves that things here are different from what we thought. What can you do for people who have their own reasons, ones they find good, for not wanting their lot to change?"

He sat and thought about that for a long time. He knew that Patrice meant the answer to her question to be *nothing*, and that she had spoken mostly to lift him from his gloom. He was grateful to her for that. But her words sparked something in him that perhaps had not occurred to her.

He got up and went to his cabin. When he came back, he was carrying a large, fat codex. "What do you have there?" Captain Chen asked.

"An astronomy text based on Kepler and Newton. I intended to use it as a follow-up to the Galileo; it has the math to carry the blues forward from there."

"Intended?" Not for the first time, Carver remembered that Lloyd Michaels was too good a trader to let much get past him. "What will you do with it now?"

Carver threw the book down the disposal chute. "Call it a last favor for Nadab," he said. He walked out of the control room again.

Sooner or later just about everybody tries his hand at writing a bar story. This one's mine. It may also be of interest because it introduces the Foitani, who play such a prominent role in *Earthgrip* (Del Rey: New York, 1991). They aren't an entirely pleasant people, but given their history, they could hardly be expected to be.

NASTY, BRUTISH, AND . . .

ONLY HUMANS, AND NOT MANY OF THEM, KNOW why my favorite bar is called Hobbes'. That doesn't mean humans are the only people who go in, though, not by a long shot. Humans are spread this out here, a couple of thousand light-years from home. The night I'm thinking of, I was the only one in the place.

"What'll it be, Walt?" Raoul L'évesque's number-two bartender asked me when I came in. (No, Hobbes' isn't named for the owner, obviously.)

"Something nasty, brutish, and short," I told him. (*That's* why it's called Hobbes', and knowing it's worth a free drink.)

"Tequila and *mor*-fruit?" Joe suggested. He knows me. He reached for the tequila with one hand, the *mor*-fruit (it's called that, I suppose, because it's *mor* or less like lime) with another, and the saltshaker with another. That left one free to wave at somebody who'd come in behind me. (I told you I was the only human in the place.)

While I was licking the salt off the web of my thumb, I looked around to see who—or what—was in Hobbes' this time. There were three or four tables full of Joe's people: not surprising, since Rapti, the planet under this space station, was Joe's homeworld. It was early yet, but a couple of them looked about ready to slide under their tables. (That's what they get for being four-fisted drinkers.)

An Atheter was already swinging from the chandelier. She was good at it. Atheters live in trees when they're at home, and they have prehensile tails. This one waved an empty glass at Joe and screeched for a refill.

A couple of Egnants put their credit cards in the music machine, one after the other. Raucous noise started blaring, loud enough to drown out even the Atheter.

I walked over to the machine, saw how much they'd paid, and used my own plastic to outbid them for quiet. They let their lips skin back from their teeth, but cheered up again when I bought them drinks. Egnants aren't hard to deal with unless you try to talk about religion.

I sneezed when I sat back down at the bar. Joe's ears twitched in surprise. "What kind of noise is that?" he asked.

"I've got the edge of a cold—a small sickness humans get," I said, disgusted at the way the worlds worked. They keep saying they'll have a cure for colds Real Soon Now. I'll believe it when I see it; they've been saying that since before humans got off Terra. Greenbelly fever is dead as smallpox now, because it killed people and they threw research money at it till it went away. Colds are just nuisances. It's hard to get excited enough about a nuisance to get rid of it.

I ordered a beer to chase the tequila, took a sip, looked around some more. What would have been the second sip stopped halfway to my mouth. Off in a corner by him/her/itself sat a person whose species I didn't recognize, and I've seen a lot of them.

"Where's that one from?" I asked Joe. (Bartenders know everything. It's part of their job. If you don't believe me, just ask one.)

"Who?"

"The big blue one back there over my right shoulder." I didn't point at the person. You never can tell what gesture will offend somebody.

"Oh, him? He's a Foitan."

"No kidding!" Now I really had to work to keep from staring. "I thought they were extinct."

A lot of worlds in this part of space, Rapti among them, had Foitani artifacts; they were on the edges of what had been a really big Foitani empire maybe thirty, fifty thousand years ago. Then the really big empire fought a *really* big civil war. There are a lot of dead worlds in this part of space, too, and the Foitani killed most of them.

"So did we, until maybe fifty years ago," Joe said. "Then they started showing up every so often, traders mostly, but archaeologists, too. They only have a few planets now, and they're interested in their glory days."

I shivered a little. "Where's their homeworld? Do you know?"

"About as far from here toward galactic center as yours is away from it."

I shivered again, not a little this time. If the Foitani Empire had reached across thousands of light-years, how big *had* that war been? How many more dead worlds lay inside that sphere? More than I wanted to think about, I was certain. Not even humans were stupid on that scale.

I found myself walking back toward the Foitan. Tequila always makes me reckless. "Excuse me," I said. "May I buy you another of whatever you are drinking?"

The Foitan had a bug by its ear. It looked like a Rapti bug, which meant it ought to handle Spanglish. It did. The Foitan said something in a language I didn't recognize, but my own bug did. I heard, "Thank you, if I may do the same for you."

I waved to Joe, pointed at my beer and the bottle in front of the Foitan, held up a finger. Joe waved back; he'd seen me. "May I join you?" I asked the Foitan, nodding toward a chair across from him.

By the way of answer, he pushed the chair out with his foot so I could sit. My legs wouldn't have been long enough for that, but then, what I could see of the Foitan was a lot bigger than I was. He looked more or less humanoid, but only the biggest battleball players would have seemed like anything but children next to him. His face reminded me of what people might have looked like if they'd come from bears—blue bears—instead of apes: nasty, brutish, and tall, you might say. Actually, that's not fair. He was pretty impressive.

"My name is Naplak Naplak Kap," he said. "I have not seen your kind before. Is it polite to ask what you are called?"

"I'm Walter Harbron," I answered. "Walt will do."

"Walt," Naplak Naplak Kap said gravely. Just then Joe came over with our drinks. I took a pull at my beer; the Foitan half-emptied his new bottle. "Walt," he said again. He studied me. His eyes were large. They didn't seem to blink. "May I ask about your species? I do so only from curiosity and mean no offense."

"Yes, go ahead. May I ask about yours as well? I've never met any Foitani before; I'd like to learn more about you."

Naplak Naplak Kap's shrug was massive. "I came to this world to learn more myself. I am by profession a recoverer of the past, and we Foitani have much past to recover. What does your race call itself, and why are you here?''

"We're humans. As for me—'' I shrugged. ''I travel from star to star. I buy things, I sell things: sometimes material things, sometimes information. I haven't starved yet.''

"Ah. Profit.'' The bug's flat translation didn't give me any feel for how Naplak Naplak Kap felt about profit. Then he rumbled, ''Humans. Yes, I've heard of you people. You're widespread these days, aren't you?''

"We've done well for ourselves.'' I shrugged again. I didn't want to tell him that humans ranged as widely now as his folks had at their peak. Sure, we're just one species among many, but I still didn't want him to take it the wrong way. He was too big to risk riling.

"*Humans*,'' he repeated, this time, I thought, more to himself than to me. Suddenly he seemed to remember I was there. ''Excuse me. I seem to recall something about your species in a data base from our ancient days that the Raptics showed me. My computer did a better job of reading it than the locals could. May I check?''

"Go ahead,'' I told him. (What was I going to say?)

His computer looked like a computer—not like what we build, but it couldn't have been anything else. He talked with it in a language my bug couldn't handle. I suppose it was his own. He finished his bottle, almost absentmindedly. ''Yes, here we are,'' he said at last.

He spent long enough reading that, had he been a human, he would have been a rude one. Every so often he'd grunt. I didn't know whether he was surprised or angry or curious or what. Finally I got bored waiting. I said, ''May I ask what your records show?''

Once more, it was as if he had to remind himself I was sitting with him. ''Oh, yes, of course. I apologize.'' He put the computer back out of sight; by the way he fumbled about, my guess was that he wore it in a belt pouch. Then his eyes found mine again. ''According to this data base, your species should not exist.''

"We've tried to do that to ourselves a few times,'' I said, laughing. ''Hasn't worked yet.'' I drank some more beer. It was good. I could feel the chair pressing against my behind. ''I'm real enough. We're all real.''

"But you should not be,'' Naplak Naplak Kap said. He didn't

have much in the way of a sense of humor. Whether that goes for Foitani in general I couldn't tell you. "Let me explain."

"Go ahead." I nodded. (One more time: what was I going to say?)

"You know we once ruled in this part of space, yes?" (I nodded again.) "We explored farther yet, and once we touched on what I think must be your world." He dug out the computer again, did some quick figuring. "In the coordinates the Raptics use, the location of the planet's star was—"

I pulled my own computer out of my pocket, turned Raptic numbers into my kind . . . and felt my jaw drop. Those numbers worked out to just over a light-year from Sol. I rubbed my nose, which was starting to get numb. I said, "I guess that has to be my star, but the location's not quite right."

"You forget," Naplak Naplak Kap said, "these records are 28,000 of my years old."

I felt like an idiot (not for the first time). Stars didn't move fast, not compared to light, but they did move, and in umpty-ump thousand years Sol had gone a good ways. "Yes, I did forget," I said humbly. "Tell me about my savage ancestors."

"They were," Naplak Naplak Kap said. "They were vicious, too, and clever. One tribe managed to kill a Foitan despite his armor and weaponry, and was in the process of roasting him when my people took vengeance—from the air, at long range. We had learned."

"And so?" I asked. (What I wanted to do was cheer for those poor doomed cavemen.)

"And so we decided that even savage humans were danger-ous, and that they should not be allowed to live to develop tech-nology: we decided to destroy them." The bug in my ear put no expression into the words, which made them doubly chilling. Naplak Naplak Kap went on, "My species, it appears, did this often enough to have developed a protocol for it. We knew what we were about, I assure you."

"Go on," I ground out. Humans weren't innocent of such things, not while we were still on Terra and, sadly, not always after we got off, either. But having someone calmly talk about strangling us in our cradle—

"We prepared a respiratory virus genetically tailored to en-sure that your species would not become immune to it, then disseminated it widely throughout your planet's atmosphere. In a few generations, you should have disappeared, and your world would have been there for the taking. But our own Suicide Wars started soon after, so we never went back.''

"And we never died out." I felt like crowing.

"So you didn't." Guessing aliens' expressions is a fool's game, but Naplak Naplak Kap's seemed to say he thought it was my fault. "So far as I know, yours is the only species of which that is true."

In the middle of my triumphant chuckle, I sneezed three times in a row.

"My bug does not translate that noise," Naplak Naplak Kap said.

"It's nothing," I said. "Just a cold . . ."

I looked at Naplak Naplak Kap. He looked at me. Than I waved to Joe and bought him another drink. (What was I supposed to do?)

About the Author

Harry Turtledove is that rarity, a lifelong southern Californian. He is married and has three young daughters. After flunking out of Cal Tech, he earned a doctorate in Byzantine history and has taught at UCLA, Cal State Fullerton, and Cal State Los Angeles. Academic jobs being few and precarious, however, his primary work since leaving school has been as a writer. He has had fantasy and science fiction published in *Isaac Asimov's*, *Amazing*, *Playboy*, and *Fantasy Book*. His hobbies include baseball, chess, and beer.

And watch for *The Guns Of The South*, Harry Turtledove's extraordinary novel of the Civil War—coming in paperback in October 1993 . . .

Mr. President:
I have delayed replying to your letter of the 4th until the time
arrived for the execution of the attempt on New Berne. I regret
very much that the boats on the Neuse & Roanoke are not
completed. With their aid I think success would be certain.
Without them, though the place may be captured, the fruits
of the expedition will be lessened and our maintenance of the
command of the waters in North Carolina uncertain.

Robert E. Lee paused to dip his pen once more in the inkwell.
Despite flannel shirt, uniform coat, and heavy winter boots, he
shivered a little. The headquarters tent was cold. The winter had
been harsh, and showed no signs of growing any milder. *New
England weather*, he thought, and wondered why God had chosen to visit it upon his Virginia.

With a small sigh, he bent over the folding table once more
to detail for President Davis the arrangements he had made to
send General Hoke's brigade down into North Carolina for the
attack on New Berne. He had but small hope the attack would
succeed, but the President had ordered it, and his duty was to
carry out his orders as best he could. Even without the boats,
the plan he had devised was not actually a bad one, and President Davis reckoned the matter urgent . . .

*In view of the opinion expressed in your letter, I would go to
North Carolina myself. But I consider my presence here always necessary, especially now when there is such a struggle
to keep the army fed & clothed.*

He shook his head. Keeping the Army of Northern Virginia
fed and clothed was a never-ending struggle. His men were

making their own shoes now, when they could get leather, which was not often. The ration was down to three-quarters of a pound of meat a day, along with a little salt, sugar, coffee—or rather, chicory and burnt grain—and lard. Bread, rice, corn . . . they trickled up the Virginia Central and the Orange and Alexandria Railroad every so often, but not nearly often enough. He would have to cut the daily allowance again, if more did not arrive soon.

President Davis, however, was as aware of all that as Lee could make him. To hash it over once more would only seem like carping. Lee resumed: *Genl Early is still in the—*

A gun cracked, quite close to the tent. Soldier's instinct pulled Lee's head up. Then he smiled and laughed at himself. One of his staff officers, most likely, shooting at a possum or a squirrel. He hoped the young man scored a hit.

But no sooner had the smile appeared than it vanished. The report of the gun sounded—odd. It had been an abrupt bark, not a pistol shot or the deeper boom of an Enfield rifle musket. Maybe it was a captured Federal weapon.

The gun cracked again and again and again. Each report came closer to the one before than two heartbeats were to each other. *A Federal weapon indeed,* Lee thought: *one of those fancy repeaters their calvary like so well.* The fusillade went on and on. He frowned at the waste of precious cartridges—no Southern armory could easily duplicate them.

He frowned once more, this time in puzzlement, when silence fell. He had automatically kept count of the number of rounds fired. No Northern rifle he knew was a thirty-shooter.

He turned his mind back to the letter to President Davis. *—Valley*, he wrote. Then gunfire rang out again, an unbelievably rapid stutter of shots, altogether too quick to count and altogether unlike anything he had ever heard. He took off his glasses and set down the pen. Then he put on a hat and got up to see what was going on.

At the tent fly, Lee almost collided with one of his aides-de-camp, who was hurrying in as he tried to leave. The younger man came to attention. "I beg your pardon, sir."

"Quite all right, Major Taylor. Will this by any chance have something to do with the, ah, unusual gun I heard fired just now?"

"Yes, sir." Walter Taylor seemed to be holding on to military discipline with both hands. He was, Lee reminded himself, only twenty-five or so, the youngest of all the staff officers. Now he drew out a sheet of paper, which he handed to Lee. "Sir, before you actually see the gun in action, as I just have, here is a communication from Colonel Gorgas in Richmond concerning it."

"In matters concerning ordnance of any sort, no view could be more pertinent than that of Colonel Gorgas," Lee agreed. He drew out his reading glasses once more, set them on the bridge of his nose.

> *Bureau of Ordnance, Richmond*
> *January 17, 1864*
>
> *General Lee:*
> *I have the honor to present to you with this letter Mr. Andries Rhoodie of Rivington, North Carolina, who has demonstrated in my presence a new rifle, which I believe may prove to be of the most significant benefit conceivable to our soldiers. As he expressed the desire of making your acquaintance & as the Army of Northern Virginia will again, it is likely, face hard fighting in the months ahead, I send him on to you that you may judge both him & his remarkable weapon for yourself. I remain,*
>
> > *Your most ob't servant,*
> > *Josiah Gorgas,*
> > *Colonel*

Lee folded the letter, handed it back to Taylor. As he returned his glasses to their pocket, he said. "Very well, Major. I was curious before; now I find my curiosity doubled. Take me to Mr.—Rhoodie, was it?"

"Yes, sir. He's around behind the tents here. If you will come with me—"

Breath smoking in the chilly air, Lee followed his aide-de-camp. He was not surprised to see the flaps from the other three tents that made up his headquarters were open; anyone who had heard that gunfire would want to learn what had made it. Sure enough, the rest of his officers were gathered round a big man who did not wear Confederate gray.

The big man did not wear the yellow-brown that was the true color of most home-dyed uniforms, either, nor the black of the general run of civilian clothes. Lee had never seen an outfit like the one he had on. His coat and trousers were of mottled green and brown, so that he almost seemed to disappear against dirt and brush and bare-branched trees. A similarly mottled cap had flaps to keep his ears warm.

Seeing Lee approach, the staff officers saluted. He returned the courtesy. Major Taylor stepped ahead. "General Lee, gentlemen, this is Mr. Andries Rhoodie. Mr. Rhoodie, here is General Lee, whom you may well recognize, as well as my colleagues, Majors Venable and Marshall."

"I am pleased to meet all you gentlemen, especially the famous General Lee," Rhoodie said.

"You are much too kind, sir," Lee murmured politely.

"By no means," Rhoodie said. "I would be proud to shake your hand." He held out his own.

As they shook, Lee tried to take the stranger's measure. He spoke like an educated man, but not like a Carolinian. His accent sounded more British, though it also held a faint guttural undertone.

His odd clothes aside, Rhoodie did not look like a Carolinian, either. His face was too square, his features too heavy. That heaviness made him seem almost indecently well fleshed to Lee, who was used to the lean, hungry men of the Army of Northern Virginia.

But Rhoodie's bearing was erect and manly, his handclasp firm and strong. His gray eyes met Lee's without wavering. Somewhere in his past, Lee was suddenly convinced, he had been a soldier: those were marksman's eyes. By the wrinkles at their corners and by the white hairs that showed in his bushy reddish mustache, Rhoodie had to be nearing forty, but the years had only toughened him.

Lee said, "Colonel Gorgas gives you an excellent character, sir, you and your rifle both. Will you show it to me?"

"In a moment, if I may," Rhoodie answered, which surprised Lee. In his experience, most inventors were wildly eager to show off their brainchildren. Rhoodie went on, "First, sir, I would like to ask you a question, which I hope you will be kind enough to answer frankly."

"Sir, you are presumptuous." Charles Marshall said. The wan winter sun glinted from the lenses of his spectacles and turned his normally animated face into something stern and a little inhuman.

Lee held up a hand. "Let him ask what he would, Major. You need not forejudge his intentions." He glanced toward Rhoodie, nodded for him to continue. He had to look up to meet

334

the stranger's eye, which was unusual, for he was nearly six feet tall himself. But Rhoodie overtopped him by three or four inches.

"I thank you for your patience with me." he said now in that not-quite-British accent. "Tell me this, then: what do you make of the Confederacy's chances for the coming year's campaign and for the war as a whole?"

"To be or not to be, that is the question." Marshall murmured.

"I hope our prospects are somewhat better than poor Hamlet's, Major," Lee said. His staff officers smiled. Rhoodie, though, simply waited. Lee paused to marshal this thoughts. "Sir, since I have but so briefly had the honor of your acquaintance, I hope you will forgive me for clinging to what may be plainly seen by any man with some knowledge and some wit: that is, our enemies are superior to us in numbers, resources, and the means and appliances for carrying on the war. If those people"—his common euphemism for the Federals—"use their advantages vigorously, we can but counterpoise to them the courage of our soldiers and our confidence in Heaven's judgment of the justice of our cause. Those have sufficed thus far. God willing, they shall continue to do so."

"Who said God is for the big battalions?" Rhoodie asked.

"Voltaire, wasn't it?" Charles Venable said. He had been a professor of mathematics before the war, and was widely read.

"A freethinker if ever there was one," Marshall added disapprovingly.

"Oh, indeed," Rhoodie said, "but far from a fool. When you are weaker than your foes, should you not take the best advantage of what you do have?"

"That is but plain sense," Lee said. "No one could disagree."

Now Rhoodie smiled, or his mouth did; the expression stopped just short of his eyes. "Thank you, General Lee. You have just given much of my sales talk for me."

"Have I?"

"Yes, sir, you have. You see, my rifle will let you conserve your most precious resource of all—your men."

Walter Taylor, who had seen the gun in action, sucked in a long, deep breath. "It could be so," he said quietly.

"I await the demonstration, Mr. Rhoodie." Lee said.

"You will have it." Rhoodie unslung the weapon. Lee had already noted it was of carbine length, stubby next to an infantry musket. Because it was so short, its socket bayonet seemed the longer. Rhoodie reached over his shoulder into his haversack. That was made of mottled cloth like his trousers and coat, and looked to be of finer manufacture than even a Union man carried. Most of Lee's soldiers made do with a rolled-up blanket.

The tall stranger produced a curved metal object, perhaps eight inches long and a inch and a half to two inches wide. He clicked it into place in front of the carbine's trigger. "This is the magazine," he said. "When it's full, it holds thirty rounds."

"In fine, the rifle now has bullets in it," Taylor said. "As all of you will no doubt have noticed, it is a breechloader." The other aides nodded. Lee kept his own counsel.

With a rasping sound followed by a sharp, metallic click, Rhoodie drew back a shiny steel lever on the right side of the rifle. "The first round from each magazine must be chambered manually." he said.

"What about the others?" Venable whispered to Taylor.

"You'll see," Taylor whispered back.

Rhoodie reached into the haversack again. This time he drew out some folded papers. He unfolded one of them. It proved to be a target, a cutout roughly approximating the shape of a man's head and body. He turned to Lee's aides. "Will you gentleman please put these up at different ranges out to, say, four or five hundred yards?"

"With pleasure," Taylor said promptly. "I've seen how fast your rifle can shoot; I'd like to learn how accurate it is." He took some of the targets; Rhoodie handed the rest to the other aides. They stuck low-hanging branches through some, leaned others against bushes, both in the upright position and sideways.

"Shall I have them straighten those, sir?" Lee asked, pointing. "They will make your shooting more difficult."

"Never mind," Rhoodie answered. "Soldiers don't always stand up, either." Lee nodded. The stranger did not lack for confidence.

When the aides were through, a ragged column of thirty targets straggled southeast toward Orange Court House a couple of miles off. The knot of tents that was Lee's headquarters lay on a steep hillside, well away from encamped troops or any other human habitations. The young men laughed and joked as they came back to Rhoodie and Lee. "There's General McClellan!" Charles Marshall said, stabbing a thumb in the direction of the nearest target. "Give him what he deserves!"

The others took up the cry: "There's General Burnside!" "General Hooker!" "General Meade!" "Hancock!" "War-

336

ren!'' "Stoneman!'' "Howard!'' "There's Honest Abe! Give *him* his deserts, by God!''

Lee turned to Rhoodie. "At your convenience, sir.'' The aides fell silent at once.

"One of your men might want to look at a watch,'' Rhoodie said.

"I will sir,'' Charles Venable drew one from his waistcoat pocket. "Shall I give you a mark at which to begin?'' Rhoodie nodded. Venable held the watch close to his face so he could see the second hand crawling around its tiny separate dial. "Now!''

The rifle leaped to the big stranger's shoulder. He squeezed the trigger. *Craack!* A brass cartridge case flipped up into the air. It glittered in the sun as it fell. *Craack!* Another cartridge case. *Craack!* Another. This was the same sort of quick firing as that which had interrupted Lee's letter to President Davis.

Rhoodie paused once for a moment. "Adjusting the sights,'' he explained. He was shooting again as soon as the last word left his mouth. Finally the rifle clicked harmlessly instead of blasting out another round.

Charles Venable looked up. "Thirty aimed shots. Thirty-two seconds. Most impressive.'' He looked from the rifle to Rhoodie, back again. "Thirty shots.'' he repeated, half to himself. "Where is the smoke from thirty shots?''

"By God!'' Walter Taylor sounded astonished, both at the lack of smoke and at himself. "Why didn't I notice that before?''

Lee had also failed to notice it. Thirty closely spaced shots should have left this Andries Rhoodie in the middle of a young fogbank. Instead, only a few hazy wisps of smoke floated from the breech and muzzle of his rifle. "How do you achieve this, sir?'' he asked.

"The charge in my cartridges is not your ordinary black powder,'' Rhoodie said, which told Lee nothing not already obvious. The big man went on, "If your officers will bring in the targets, we can see how I did.''

Taylor, Venable, and Marshall went out to retrieve the paper men. They laid them on the ground, walked along the row looking for bullet holes. Lee walked with them, quiet and thoughtful. When he had examined all the targets, he turned back to Rhoodie. "Twenty-eight out of thirty, I make it to be,'' he said. "This appears to be a fine weapon, sir, and without a doubt very fine shooting.''

"Thirty-two seconds," Venable said. He whistled softly.

"May I show you one thing more?" Rhoodie said. Without waiting for a reply, he loosened the catch that held the magazine in place below the rifle, stuck the curved metal container into a coat pocket. Then he pulled another one out of his haversack and clicked it into position. The operation took only a moment to complete.

"Another thirty shots?" Lee asked.

"Another thirty shots," Rhoodie agreed. He drew back the shiny handle with the *snick* Lee had heard before. "Now I am ready to fire again. But what if the Americans—"

"*We* are Americans, sir," Lee broke in.

"Sorry. The Yankees, I mean. What if the Yankees are too close for aimed fire?" Below the handle was a small metal lever. Rhoodie clicked it down so that, instead of being parallel to the handle's track, its front end pointed more nearly toward the ground. He turned away from Lee and his staff officers. "This is what."

The rifle roared. Flame spurted from its muzzle. Cartridges flew out of it in a glittering stream. The silence that followed the shooting came hard and abrupt as a blow. Into it, Lee asked, "Major Venable, did you time that?"

"Uh, no, sir," Venable said. "I'm sorry, sir."

"Never mind. It was quite rapid enough."

Rhoodie said, "Except at close range or into big crowds, full automatic fire isn't nearly as effective or accurate as single shots. The weapon pulls up and to the right."

"Full automatic fire." Lee tasted the words. "How does this repeater operate, if I may ask, sir? I have seen, for example, the Spencer repeating carbines the enemy cavalrymen employ, with a lever action to advance each successive bullet. But you worked no lever, save to chamber your first round. The rifle simply fired, again and again."

"When the charge in a round explodes, it makes a gas that rapidly expands and pushes the bullet out of the muzzle. Do you follow me?"

"Certainly, sir. If I may remind you, I was an engineer." Lee felt irked at being asked so elementary a question.

"That's right. So you were." Rhoodie spoke as if reminding himself. He went on, "My weapon taps some of the gas and uses it to move the bolt back so the magazine spring can lift another round into the chamber. Then the cycle repeats itself until the magazine has no more ammunition left in it."

"Most ingenious." Lee plucked at his beard, not wanting to go on. Southern inventors had come up with a great many clever ideas during the war, only to have them prove stillborn because of the Confederacy's feeble manufacturing capacity. Nevertheless, the question had to be asked: "With how many of these repeaters could you supply me?"

Rhoodie smiled broadly. "How many would you like?"

"I would *like* as many as you can furnish," Lee said. "The use to which I might put them, however, would depend on the number available. If you can provide me with, say, a hundred, I might furnish them to horse artillery batteries, so they might protect themselves against attacks by the enemy infantry. If, on the other hand, you are fortunate enough to possess five hundred or so—and the requisite ammunition—I would consider outfitting a cavalry regiment with them. It would be pleasant to have our horsemen able to match the firepower those people are able to bring to bear, rather than opposing them with pistols and shotguns."

Andries Rhoodie's smile grew wider still, yet it was not the smile of someone sharing something pleasant with friends. Lee was reminded instead of the professional grimace of a stage magician about to produce two doves from inside his hat. Rhoodie said, "And suppose, General Lee, suppose I am able to get you a hundred thousand of these rifles, with their ammunition? How would you—how would the Confederacy—use them?"

"A hundred thousand?" Lee kept his voice low and steady, but only with a distinct effort. Rather than pulling two doves out of his hat, the big stranger had turned loose a whole flock. "Sir, that is not a piker's offer."

"Nor a likely one, if you will forgive me saying so," Charles Marshall said. "That is nearly as many weapons as we have been able to realize from all of Europe in three years of war. I suppose you will deliver the first shipment by the next northbound train?" Irony flavored every word.

Rhoodie took no notice of it. "Close enough," he said coolly. "My comrades and I have spent some time getting ready for this day. General Lee, you will be sending General Hoke's brigade down to North Carolina over the next couple of nights—am I right?"

"Yes, that is so," Lee said without much thought. Then all at once he swung the full weight of his attention to Rhoodie. "But how do you know of it, sir? I wrote those orders just today, and was in the process of informing President Davis of them when interrupted by you and your repeater. So how can you have learned of my plans for General Hoke's movements?''

"My comrades and I are well informed in any area we choose,'' Rhoodie answered. He was easy, even amused. Lee abstractly admired that; he knew his own presence overawed most men. The stranger went on. "We do not aim to harm you or your army or the Confederacy in any way, General. Please believe me when I say that. No less than you, we aim to see the South free and independent.''

"That all sounds very fine, but you did not answer the general's question,'' Marshall said. He ran a hand through his slick, dark blond hair as he took a step toward Rhoodie. "How did you learn of General Hoke's movements?''

"I knew. That's enough.'' The stranger did not back down. "If you order the northbound train's engineer to stop at Rivington, General Lee, we'll put aboard the first shipment of rifles and ammunition. That would be, hmm, about twenty-five hundred weapons, with several magazines' worth of rounds for each. We can supply as many again the night after that, until your army is fully equipped with new pieces.''

"A hundred thousand rifles would oversupply the Army of Northern Virginia,'' Lee said.

"The Confederacy has more armies than yours. Don't you think General Johnston will be able to use some when General Sherman brings the whole Military Division of the Mississippi down against him come spring?''

"General Grant commands the Military Division of the Mississippi,'' Walter Taylor said: "all the Federal troops between the Alleghenies and the river.''

"Oh, yes, that's right, so he does, for now. My mistake,'' Rhoodie said. He turned back to Lee, this time with a hunter's intent expression on his face. "And don't you think, General, that Nathan Bedford Forrest's troopers would enjoy being able to outshoot the Federals as well as outride and outfight them?''

"What I think, sir, is that you are building mighty castles in the air on the strength of a single rifle,'' Lee answered. He did not care for the way Andries Rhoodie looked at him, did not care for the arrogant way the man spoke, did not care for anything about him . . . except for his rifle. If one Southern man could deliver the fire of five to ten Unionists, the odds against which Confederate armies had to fight in every engagement might all at once be set at naught.

340

Rhoodie still studied him. Lee felt his cheeks go hot, even on this icy winter's day, for he knew the stranger could see he was tempted. The book of Matthew came into his mind: *Again the devil taketh him up into an exceeding high mountain, and sheweth him all the kingdoms of the world, and the glory of them: And saith unto him, All these things will I give thee, if thou wilt fall down and worship me.*

But Rhoodie did not ask for worship, and he was no devil, only a big, tough man, who was not too tough to wear a cap with flaps to keep his ears warm. For all that Lee had not taken to him, he spoke like a reasonable man, and now said, reasonably, "General, I will stay here and guarantee with my person that what I say is true. Give me the order for the train to stop and pick up the rifles and ammunition. If they do not come as I say they will, why, you can do whatever you please with me. Where is your risk in that?"

Lee searched for one. Try as he would, he could not find it. To no one in particular, Charles Venable said, "The fellow doesn't lack for brass, that's certain."

"No, he doesn't," Lee agreed. The major's remark helped decide him. "Very well, Mr. Rhoodie, I will give that order, and we shall see what arrives on that northbound train. If you make good on your claims, the first rifles will go to General Stuart's cavalry. After that, well, the divisions of General Anderson and Henry Heth are quartered closest to us here. Those men can have first call on the rifles among the infantry."

"*If* he makes good," Charles Marshall said heavily. "What if he fails?"

"What would you recommend, Major?" Lee asked, genuinely curious.

"A good horsewhipping, to teach him to brag no more."

"How say you to that, Mr Rhoodie?" Lee inquired.

"I'll take the chance," the stranger answered. Despite himself, Lee was impressed—whether the fellow could do as he said remained to be seen, but he thought he could. Rhoodie went on, "With your permission, General, some of my comrades will ride north with the rifles. You'll need instructors to teach your men to use them properly."

"They may come," Lee said. Afterwards, he thought that moment was the one when he first truly began to believe Andries Rhoodie, began to believe a trainload of fancy repeaters and ammunition could arrive from North Carolina. Rhoodie was just too sure of himself to doubt.

Walter Taylor asked, "Mr. Rhoodie, what do you call this rifle of yours. Is it a Rhoodie, too? Most inventors name their products for themselves, do they not?"

"No, it's not a Rhoodie." The big stranger unslung the rifle, held it in both hands as gently as if it were a baby. "Give it its proper name, Major. It's an AK-47."